Hilary Norman is the author of nine internationally bestselling novels written under her own name and translated into sixteen languages, including *The Pact* and *Susanna*, and of *If I Should Die*, a thriller published under the pseudonym Alexandra Henry. She lives with her husband in London.

Praise for *Too Close*

'This genuinely scary story of obsessive love is fast-paced with touches of sheer horror – and a real page-turner'
Daily Telegraph

'. . . a goose-pimply, page-turning read right to the end. Brr . . .'
Company, Book of the Month

'The devious plot chases up snakes and down ladders at a terrific pace gripping the reader's attention right to the last line.'
Jewish Chronicle

'A gripping psychological thriller of obsessive love.'
Publishing News

Also by Hilary Norman

Too Close

Hilary Norman

PIATKUS

Copyright © 1998 by Hilary Norman

First published in Great Britain in 1998 by
Judy Piatkus (Publishers) Ltd of
5 Windmill Street, London W1

This edition published 1998

**The moral right of the author
has been asserted**

*A catalogue record for this book is available
from the British Library*

ISBN 0–7499–3056–X

Set in Times by
Phoenix Photosetting, Chatham, Kent

Printed and bound in Great Britain by
Mackays of Chatham PLC, Chatham, Kent

She's dreaming the dream again.

Same every night.

She tries to fight sleep to evade it, but it always gets her in the end.

Every night.

He is drowning.

Same as he does every time.

He's done what he always does: jumped into the forbidden water to save her from the pondweed that's tangling around her ankles, pulling her under, choking her, making her panic, making her scream. But Eric is there – she knows he's going to be there for her. Her big brother's always there for her, ready to get her out of trouble, ready to save her.

Only this time, *he's* the one getting into trouble. Because she's pulling him down, she's still panicking, and he's all there is – all she has – to hold on to. And she can't breathe, she *has* to get her head clear, out into the air, and he's bigger and stronger than she is – he can hold on for longer than she can. Can't he?

Can't he?

Her face is clear of the water now and suddenly she can breathe again – oh, it feels so *good* to breathe. Her hands get a grip on the bank, her fingers claw crazily into the dirt, her arms – the muscles shrieking with pain – lever her up out of the water and onto the cool grass.

She flops down for a moment, getting her breath back, then she sits up and turns around.

3

Eric, I'm okay.
Eric, you can come up now.

In the dream, he always comes up, one last time.

Looking at her with his gentle, brown eyes.

Not accusing, at all. Just sad and kind and patient.

Tell them it was my fault, Holly, the way we always do.

He's speaking to her real breathless and fast, as if he knows these are going to be his final words to her.

Let me be good old Eric-the-fall-guy one last time, the way you always want me to be, the way you love it. Tell them I jumped in first and you told me not to and I wouldn't listen and you came in after me and tried to help me. It'll be easier for you that way. You know I've always tried to make things easier for you, Holly.

And then he goes under again. First his face, then the top of his head, disappearing beneath the surface.

Eric, you can come up now.
Eric, don't leave me.
Eric, I need you!

And she hears the sounds again.

The bubbles of air that come out of his mouth while he's struggling to breathe. The sound the water makes when it closes over his head that final time.

The first clump of earth hitting his coffin.

Her father weeping.

Her mother screaming.

And then the silence.

———————

1976

FEBRUARY

1996

For every waking minute of the eight months after her big brother Eric was drowned in the pond in the woods behind Leyland Avenue, seven-year-old Holly Bourne was in the dark. In the silence.

She went on with her daily life in Bethesda, Maryland, was compliant with her parents and her schoolteachers, but even on the hottest, most brilliant days that summer, neither the sunlight nor the cheerful outdoor sounds of other children playing ever seemed to penetrate Holly's heart.

She knew what was going on. She noticed things. The way her daddy fretted about her, the way he looked at her, his grey eyes (so exactly like her own, everyone always said) watching her anxiously. The way he glanced sidelong at her mother, as if he were hoping that she, too, was feeling for their little girl. But Holly knew that her mother no longer felt anything much for her daughter, except perhaps hate. In front of other people – Holly's teachers, other parents, their friends – her mother often said that she was proud of Holly, but Holly knew she didn't really mean it. Mother never talked about Eric's death, had never actually come right out and said that she *blamed* Holly for what had happened, but Holly knew that she did. Which was okay, as much as anything was okay now, because though she'd done what Eric had told her to in her dream – though she'd explained that it had all been his fault – Holly knew the real truth.

Everything important and good had been buried with Eric. All the laughter and the joy. All the scrapes they'd got into together. Big

7

brother and little sister. Eric had always been so kind to her, so patient and giving – everything that a young girl could dream of in an older brother. Always stepping in to get her out of whichever jam she'd managed to get herself into. Like the time she'd thrown a stone through old Mrs Herbert-down-the-street's bedroom window, and Eric had taken the blame. Or the time she'd slipped a packet of M&Ms into his coat pocket inside Van Zandt's Drugstore, and Eric had accepted the tongue-lashing and the threats of prosecution, and had not given her away. Or the time Holly had slit holes into Mary Kennedy's bicycle wheels with a penknife, and when Mary had accused her, Eric had sworn that she'd been someplace with him.

Or the time she'd stolen a five-dollar bill from their mother's wallet. Eric had really been mad at her that time, had sat her down and given her a real talking-to, had sworn that if he ever caught her stealing again he'd make sure *she* took the consequences. But then, after she'd pleaded with him a little, he had covered for her as always, had told their mother that he'd borrowed the cash to pay for a new pencil box because he'd lost his, and he was going to pay her back as soon as he could make up the money from extra chores. And their mother had believed him and had hardly punished him at all, because Eric was her favourite, and Holly didn't blame her for that because she figured that Eric would be anyone's favourite in any family.

It was all over now. Eric was dead and so Holly was being good, because there was simply no point in being bad any more. There was no fun, no thrill to be had from breaking rules or taking risks without Eric there to share it with or to shock. Without Eric there to prove to Holly, over and over again, how much he loved her, by getting her out of trouble. So Holly was being good. Which, she thought, was probably much the same as being dead.

Nobody talked about Eric any more. Nobody even mentioned his name if it could be avoided, but inside Holly's head it rolled around and around like a hot, smooth marble. For a long time it hurt, a heavy, burning ache, but then she got used to the pain, and at least it stopped her from thinking too much, stopped her from caring as much, which was welcome. Holly didn't care about anything much any more. She didn't seem to *feel* anything much at all either –

except the time she got her finger trapped in the window in her bedroom, and that hurt pretty badly for a while. But then that got easier, too, and before long there was nothing left of the pain, and her finger grew as numb as her mind.

Until September 22nd. It was a Wednesday, and it was afternoon. Three-twenty, to be exact. Holly remembered the time, because the instant she saw *him*, she realized it was a red-letter moment, and turned her head to look at the clock on her wall.

She was sitting on the window seat in her bedroom looking out of the window (the same window that had slammed down on her finger and made her see stars for a while) when the State-to-State removal truck came to a halt outside the house next door. The dark blue Chevrolet with two grown-ups in the front slid up smoothly behind the truck, and the boy got out from the back.

He was tall and slim and his brown hair was tousled, and from her vantage point Holly could see his face as he gazed at the house that was about to become his home, and there was such a look of excitement in his expression that she could almost feel it herself. And it seemed to her the first thing – apart from her finger – that she had truly, actually *felt*, in a long, long time.

Suddenly the boy looked up and saw her at the window up on the second floor of her house, and Holly didn't know what she looked like to him, wasn't even sure if she smiled down at him or not. But his mouth curved upwards at both ends, and his brown eyes seemed to spark at her, and no one had smiled at her that way since Eric had disappeared for the last time under the murky waters of the pond.

That was the precise moment when the darkness went away, and when Holly realized that this boy had been sent to Bethesda, to that house, by a higher power.

Had been sent to her – *for* her – to replace Eric.

His name was Nick Miller, she would learn later that day, and he was just looking: at his new house and at the little girl at the window who he supposed was going to be his next-door-neighbour. But for Holly Bourne, not yet eight years old and dragged out of the dark-

9

ness with all the suddenness and power of a Metroliner emerging from a black tunnel, everything was sealed for ever at that first moment.

Nick Miller had come to change Holly's life.

He belonged to her.

———————

1

'I heard from Eleanor Bourne the other week,' – Kate Miller said to her son, Nick, seizing a moment alone with him in the kitchen of his and his wife Nina's San Francisco house – 'that Holly's doing so well at her law firm in New York, they're pretty sure she's going to be offered a partnership.'

'Good for Holly.' Nick's brown eyes flickered, but his hands, carving a pineapple on a stone-topped counter, stayed completely steady. 'Even better for me.'

'Why say that?' Kate asked.

'Because success for Holly in New York means she's more likely to stay thousands of miles away from me.'

'Oh, honey, come on.' Kate laughed at him. 'It's been years.'

'I know it has.' Nick carved the final slice, set it with the mangos, strawberries and cherries on the big pottery fruit platter, and went to rinse his hands under the cold tap.

'You shouldn't hold grudges,' Kate said.

'Why not?' He felt his jaw clench, told himself to relax, reminded himself that having his and Nina's family under their roof was meant to be a joy in itself – particularly as they had all travelled to be with them today to celebrate the much greater joy of the end of the first trimester of Nina's first pregnancy.

'It's unhealthy,' Kate said.

'Not as unhealthy as living in the same town as Holly Bourne.'

'What's the matter with Holly Bourne?'

Nina Ford Miller, Nick's British-born wife, entered the kitchen carrying a tray of empty glasses, followed by Phoebe, her sister, and their father, William Ford. Kate's colour heightened a touch.

15

'Nothing much,' Nick answered lightly. 'My mother was just telling me how well Holly's doing in New York, and I said that was good because I like knowing Holly's as far away as possible.'

Ethan Miller came slowly in from the living room, looking at a folded copy of the *San Francisco Chronicle*. 'What about Holly?' he asked absently.

'Just what Eleanor told us last week,' Kate said.

'Oh, that,' Ethan said, sitting down at the big Mexican pine table and going on with his reading.

'Ice cream, everyone?' Nina asked, slipping an arm around Nick's waist. 'We have at least eight flavours and cheesecake.'

'One of the bonuses of pregnancy.' Nick said.

He kissed his wife's hair and felt his tension melting away. Nina's hair was long and honey-coloured and she thought it her best feature, though Nick thought her eyes, legs and nose came close.

'Whatever Nina craves,' he explained, 'I get to share.'

'Lucky for you it's ice cream, not coal,' Phoebe commented. 'What did Eleanor tell you last week, Kate?'

'It wasn't important,' Kate said.

'No, it wasn't,' Nick agreed, opening the freezer and taking out an armful of Häagen Dazs tubs.

'Who is this Holly Bourne?' William Ford asked, a touch irritably.

'Just a woman Nick used to know,' Phoebe said.

'Is it absolutely necessary for us to be talking about Nick's old girlfriends when we're here to celebrate Nina's pregnancy?' Ford's English voice, which still sometimes snapped of his years in the RAF, was only a few degrees warmer than the Cookies 'n Cream.

'Holly Bourne is not an old girlfriend,' Nick said quietly.

'More of a *bête noire* from what I've heard,' Phoebe said. She grinned, reached up and ruffled what was left of her father's reddish hair, so close to her own shade. 'Don't be so stuffy, Dad.'

'Your father's quite right,' Kate said. 'It was my fault for mentioning her.'

'Oh, pooh, Kate,' Phoebe said. 'Nina doesn't mind, do you?'

'Not in the least,' Nina said, meaning it. Nick had told her all about Holly Bourne, all about the childhood girl-next-door who had turned into a grade-A troublemaker.

'Let's go eat dessert.' Nick got out bowls and spoons. 'Someone bring the fruit?'

16

'I've got it.' Nina picked up the platter.

'Isn't that dish too heavy for you, Nina?' Ford shot Nick a look, but his son-in-law was already halfway through the door.

'It's not heavy at all, Dad. Stop fussing.' Nina went after Nick, Kate following with a jug of cream.

Ethan Miller put down the *Chronicle* and looked up at Ford. 'Something worrying you, William?'

'Only my daughter's health and happiness,' Ford answered.

'Dad, why are you making such a big deal about nothing?' Phoebe was mildly exasperated.

'I regard your sister's health and happiness as a very big deal.'

'As we all do,' Ethan told him easily, and left the kitchen, seeking a lighter atmosphere. Ethan hated tension.

'You have to stop this, Dad,' Phoebe told her father quietly.

'Stop what exactly?'

'You know perfectly well what. Trying to find fault with Nick when we both know that Nina hasn't been this happy in years.'

'All the more reason to want to protect her, in my book.' Ford was only fifty-two, but his face had grown craggy with years, and his green eyes, whenever he was angry or suspicious, came close to disappearing between furrows of creasing skin. 'Considering what she's been through.'

'What she's been through is exactly why you shouldn't spoil today. They've both longed for this, Dad – Nick just as much as Nina.'

'It's not Nick's longings I care about,' Ford said harshly.

Phoebe's nose wrinkled with frustration. 'You can be so unreasonable.'

Ford glanced towards the door. 'Nick Miller has a past, Phoebe.'

'Nina has a past, too, Dad,' Phoebe pointed out. 'You don't catch Ethan and Kate making nasty remarks about her.'

'I'd like to see them try.'

'They wouldn't,' Phoebe said, still keeping her voice low. 'They love Nina. We all love Nina. Especially Nick.'

'So why did he say he wants this Holly person as far away as possible?' William Ford returned to that subject like a dog to a smell. 'Man feels like that about a woman, she has to mean something to him.'

'From what I've heard,' Phoebe said, 'all Holly Bourne ever meant

17

to Nick was aggravation.' She linked her left arm through her father's, and pushed him towards the door. 'Now come on, Dad, I want to go and celebrate my niece-nephew-to-be.'

'My younger daughter's telling me to mind my own business,' Ford announced loudly as they entered the living room.

'It might be about time, Dad.' Phoebe grinned.

'Both my daughters are my business, Phoebe Ford,' William said, clearly. 'And you and everyone else had better remember that.'

Nina, sitting on the linen-covered sofa beside Nick and licking chocolate ice cream off the end of a spoon, turned to her husband and saw her own strain mirrored in his eyes.

'Take no notice, baby,' she said, softly, intimately, blocking out the rest of the family. It was a small gift they shared, a quiet, easy ability to soothe one another, to tune out of external disunity and tune in to each other instead. 'Dad's just being Dad.'

'It's okay,' Nick said.

'No, it's not.' She lowered her voice even further. 'It's very wrong of him, but we're okay, and that's what matters to me.'

Nick looked back into her eyes, loving her more than ever.

'Me, too,' he said.

Across the room, Phoebe took a cherry from the fruit platter and smiled at them both.

William Ford frowned.

2

I feel such guilt sometimes when I look into my wife's eyes.

If only, I wish, more often than I can count, I had told her everything about Holly and me. If only.

Nina trusts me. She believes she knows all there is to know about me. She told me everything about herself, every fragment of joy and all the many boulders of pain that might so easily have crushed her.

I told myself that because she had already been through so much, it would be unfair to burden her with my own troubles. I told her what I *wanted* her to know. But maybe if I had shared the whole story, the whole truth, I wouldn't have my bad dreams now. Maybe I wouldn't wake up in Nina's arms and feel so afraid.

I have so much more now than I ever imagined I could have. I have my wife and our child on the way. I have Phoebe, her sister. I have our splendid Edwardian house in Pacific Heights, with its pale primrose-and-white painted clapboard walls and its generous light-bringing windows and high ceilings. Room to breathe, room to paint. I paint the portraits I always have – and these days I make decent money out of doing so – and more remarkable still, thanks to Nina and Phoebe, I even have my whole new fantasy career, complete with Hollywood movie contract.

Most of all, I am free of Holly Bourne.

So why am I still so afraid, in the midst of all this new-found happiness? I guess because I'm just so scared of losing it. Not the career part, nor the home. I'm scared of losing Nina, or the baby.

Didn't some Greek writer say something about the fear of pain being worse than pain itself? I don't agree with him. Nothing could ever be worse than losing Nina.

I often grow impatient with myself. It's been six years. It's over. That part of my life – the Holly part – is finished. Gone. There's no sense in dwelling on it, no reason to share the darkness with Nina.

Yet I still feel shame when I see the trust in her eyes.

And I still feel afraid.

MARCH

3

Holly Bourne sits on the banquette beside her lunch date in Le Cirque on East Sixty-fifth Street in New York City, looks into his eyes and smiles at him. Her warmest, sweetest smile. Holly has rich brown hair which she wears tied back or pinned sleekly up when she is at the office or in court. Today is a Thursday, but she has taken the afternoon off and her hair, this lunchtime, cut sharp and blunt, hangs one inch above her shoulders.

Jack Taylor, successful, thirty-eight-year-old LA lawyer – more than accustomed to dealing with gorgeous women in his everyday life – is feeling the onslaught of another of those composure melt-downs he's been experiencing regularly since meeting Charlotte Bourne last fall on another trip to New York.

'You've shaken me, Charlotte,' he tells her now. 'I hardly know what to say.'

'Say yes.'

Though the first name on her birth certificate and passport is Charlotte, until she graduated from law school, passed the New York State bar exam and went to work for Nussbaum, Koch, Morgan on Wall Street, everyone in her world always called her Holly. Her parents named her Charlotte after her maternal grandmother, but almost from the moment of her Christmas Day birth onward, Holly – her middle name – was what they called her, what seemed to suit her, what stuck. She always liked the name well enough – Lord knew she *thought* of herself as Holly – but on the day of her first interview with Nussbaum, Koch, Morgan, she made the decision that Holly wasn't the right name for a sharp, ambitious lawyer heading for the top. Charlotte was more sober, more appropriate; a name to be trusted, relied on.

Jack Taylor agrees. Jack Taylor – whom Holly knows to be the farthest thing imaginable from a pushover in his professional life – has agreed with most things she has said since their first meeting six months ago.

'I may hate myself for asking you this question,' Jack says, 'but have you really thought this through?'

'Of course I have,' she answers in her lowest, calmest voice. 'I think everything through, Jack, always. As I'm sure you do.'

'I guess I just find it hard to believe my luck,' Jack says candidly. 'I mean, here you are, this stunning, brilliant, warm, sexy lawyer with a great job and hot prospects right here in Manhattan, and you tell me you're willing to give it all up to move to LA for me.'

'That's right,' Holly confirms. 'I am.'

'But how can you be sure? We've had so little time to be together.'

'I've had months to think about it,' Holly says simply. 'And I'm sure that I'm in love with you.' She frowns – just a tiny furrowing of her fine, arched, dark brows. 'That certainly can't be such a hard concept for you to take in. You must be used to women falling in love with you.'

'Not especially.'

'You should be. You're a very attractive man.'

Something gloriously like joy is stirring inside Jack's heart. She is such a galvanizingly, touchingly driven young woman, and the fact is that one look from her grey, cool eyes drives him almost as crazy as her wondrous mouth and her gifted, instinctively skilful fingers.

'You must know you are,' Holly says.

She reaches for his hand, places it, for just a moment, on her warm thigh, then moves it back onto the banquette and looks him over appraisingly. Jack Taylor may not be George Clooney, but he is a very nice-looking man, with beautifully kempt wavy fair hair, blue eyes, a straight, clean nose and a good mouth. He looks like many of the successful, polished attorneys in New York City, except that Jack, hailing from California, has a suntan. Holly has not yet made up her mind whether she is going to establish a tan when she moves to Los Angeles. It isn't the thing any more, of course, with all the melanoma awareness, but Holly likes herself with a touch of colour. Jack has already told her that he loves her pallor. She'll make her

24

own decision when she gets there. The really important decisions, after all, have already been made, so for as she is concerned.

'I find you extraordinarily sexy.' She returns to ego-stroking, keeping her voice soft, because the tables at Le Cirque are placed close enough for effortless eavesdropping, and this is private.

'And you,' Jack says, his heart in his words, 'are far and away the very finest thing ever to happen to me.' He shifts a little closer to her on the banquette, then smiles at the waiter pouring more wine into their glasses.

'I've already told you' – Holly lowers her voice still further – 'how long it's been since I felt this way about any man.'

She can see from his eyes, their pupils dilated, that he has a hard-on. She debates, for an instant, checking it out under cover of a napkin, but decides against. *He* knows he has an erection, knows that just talking to her can get him hard. That's what counts.

'I don't want to lie to you, Jack,' she goes on, softly. 'Your success – your standing as a lawyer – is very attractive to me, too.'

'You're an honest woman.' Jack squeezes her hand. 'That's one of the things I love most about you, Charlotte.'

'I've never seen much point being anything but honest. It's such a waste of time.'

Surreptitiously, she checks his pupils again. Maybe he doesn't have a hard-on, after all. Or maybe he really does love her even more than he wants her. That knowledge excites her. It bodes well.

Jack shifts again.

'What about the partnership offer?' He forces himself back to practicalities. Christ knows the last thing he wants is to talk Charlotte out of leaving New York, but he screwed up with his wife less than five years ago, and that was more than enough heartache to last him the rest of his life. 'NKM is a fine firm – and if you stay in New York, you won't have to worry about sitting for the California State Bar.'

'I've already taken the bar exam.'

Jack is startled. 'When? Why?'

'I sat it in February, because I knew there was a chance I might want to relocate someday. I should know by the end of May if I've passed.'

Jack looks at her for a long moment. 'You'll pass.'

'I hope so.'

25

'You never even mentioned you were studying for the exam.'

'No,' Holly agrees, steadily.

'You're full of surprises, aren't you?'

'I like to think so.'

'Have you found a job in Los Angeles?'

'Not yet.'

He takes another moment, treading carefully. 'If you have no objections, I could talk to a few people—'

'I do object,' she says. A touch of feisty independence never does any harm with a man like Jack Taylor.

'Okay. Sure. I didn't mean to—'

'I know you didn't, Jack.' Holly remains firm. 'And I am grateful. It's just that I don't want your help. Not in that way. I may need it, but I really don't want it. You do understand, don't you?'

'Of course I do. You've made your own success.'

'Everyone needs help sometimes,' Holly says, soft again.

'But not mine, now.'

'As I said, not in that way.'

They play with their food for a while, Holly with her turbot, Jack with his roast pigeon. Neither of them have eaten much. That bodes well, too, Holly thinks. Fresh energy pulses through her in welcoming waves. She knows now that, at long last, she has picked the right man. Right man, right situation, right time. It's been so long, but here Jack Taylor is, right beside her and ripe for picking. Oh, life can be so *good* sometimes—or at least it can be when it isn't being a bitch.

Jack puts down his fork. 'I need a little help myself, Charlotte.'

'What with?'

He takes a moment. 'Nick Miller.'

The hurt is in Holly's eyes, but she keeps her gaze steady. 'What about him?'

'I know you said you've told me everything about him. About the way you felt about him.'

'I have told you everything.' Holly searches his face. 'You do believe it's over, don't you, Jack?'

'I want to.'

'It's been over for years.' Her voice is clear and steady. 'And it was never really going anywhere. If I'd only recognized that fact long before I did – if I'd only listened to my parents – especially my mother, who never trusted Nick – I'd have been much better off.'

'But you loved him,' Jack says.

Holly nods frankly. 'Yes, I did. But he never loved me.' She raises her chin a little. 'Unrequited love.'

Jack shakes his head. 'That's hard to believe.'

'It happened.' She keeps her eyes on his.

'But why did he keep on coming back to you? It makes no sense.'

'None at all.' Holly gives a little shrug. 'He kept coming back to make trouble, I guess.' She manages a smile. 'He was good at that.'

'He hurt you very badly, didn't he?' The question is tender.

'Yes, he did.'

Jack shakes his head again and stares into his wine glass. 'You know, a part of me wants to find Nick Miller and break his legs for the way he treated you, but another part just wants to shake him by the hand.'

'Why?' Holly asks, startled.

'Because though I can't stand to think of anyone hurting you, Charlotte—' He breaks off. 'You know, I still can't seem to think of you as Holly—'

'You don't have to.' Holly touches his arm. 'I was Holly to Nick. I'm Charlotte to you.' She pauses. 'Why did you say that, about wanting to shake Nick's hand?'

Jack is unsmiling. 'Because if he wasn't such a loser, and if he hadn't done all those terrible things to you, you might not be here with me now.'

Holly waits a moment. 'So what do you need help with, Jack?'

He picks up his glass. 'I guess I just have to know if you're over him. I mean, really over him.'

The energy hits Holly again, the excitement. She knew, before they sat down at their table one hour and ten minutes earlier, exactly what she hoped to achieve today. It's coming now. As sure as an orgasm. Just a touch more foreplay, a little more stroking, a few more strong, bold touches—

'Nick Miller is in my past, Jack,' she says, taking her time. 'I won't deny I may have been a fool in those bad old days, but no more.'

'I'm sorry, Charlotte. Don't feel you have to—'

'No, Jack.' She loves seeing his guilt. 'Let me. Please.'

He falls silent. Holly knows he's thinking.

'I haven't heard from Nick in six years,' she goes on, building up

27

slowly. 'I'm in love now for only the second time in my life. But this time, it's real. It's grown-up, mature love.' Her voice strengthens and warms. 'And I need you to know, Jack Taylor, that when I fall in love, that's it for me. No game playing. I'm in it for the long haul, and it's vital you understand that, because I don't think I could bear to be hurt again.'

Jack can't remember the last time he wept. He's an almost forty, hard-assed, hot-shot attorney with a double corner office on Avenue of the Stars, for Christ's sake! (When his mother died – that was the last time.) But looking at Charlotte now – listening to the remarkable openness with which she's pouring her heart out to him – he can feel his throat tightening.

'I'll never hurt you, Charlotte,' he says.

'I think you mean that.'

'I do, believe me.'

Nearly there.

'If we're going to go on, Jack,' she says, 'our relationship has to be honest, and it has to be all the way. That's the kind of person I am, Jack.'

Jack takes the napkin off his lap and dumps it on the table. His heart is beating fast, the way it usually only does when he's nearing closure on a big settlement, or when he's on the treadmill at his gym.

'Marry me, Charlotte.'

Holly hears it, but remains still. She feels her triumph, physically *feels* it, down inside her pelvis, writhing and surging.

'I want all those things, too,' he goes on. 'The honesty, the permanence, the trust. That's why I realize now that I don't just want you to come to LA to live with me – to be with me part-time. I want you – I need you – with me *all* the time.'

The eavesdroppers to left and right of them are growing ever more interested. The moment is entirely perfect. Holly shifts in her seat, feels her wetness, wonders if she's en route to a public orgasm. In Le Cirque, of all places.

'All the way?' she asks, very softly.

She watches Jack's throat work for a moment with emotion.

'Every last inch,' he says.

28

APRIL

4

Nick had made the move to California six years ago, at around the time Holly had been about to start law school in New York. The West Coast had never figured in his plans till then; as an aspiring painter, he'd set his sights on settling in SoHo or the Village. But right then, in the middle of the summer of 1990, going West suddenly seemed the only sanity-saving thing for him to do – his best chance of putting the past behind him and moving forward.

Fantasies of living right by the Pacific drew him to Venice Beach. He got lucky, found a second floor walk-up one bedroom apartment in a pink-painted house right on the boardwalk near Sunset Avenue, and beat some hot competition from much cuter Hollywood wannabees to get himself regular lunch and dinner shifts waiting on tables at Figtree's and the On the Waterfront Café. The rest of the time he spent going to the movies and painting: clever, instant portraits for tourists right there on the boardwalk and more serious stuff up in his apartment, some of which he managed to sell to a couple of the local galleries, steadily carving a small niche for himself as a talented – and cheap – landscape and portrait painter.

After what he had been through in New York, Nick's new way of life felt soothing and easy. He seldom ventured much farther afield than Santa Monica, avoided downtown Los Angeles like the plague, grew his hair and a beard, the way he had for a while in college, and melted into the Venice scene. New friends passed gently through his days and nights, and pretty, amiable, spirited girlfriends came and went without fuss or storms. Periodically, Kate's and Ethan's letters from Bethesda tried to nudge him towards reality and permanence (Kate's invariably more sharp and pointed than Ethan's) but Nick never much resented his parents' proddings because he was well aware that Venice Beach could only be a temporary bolthole for him.

He knew that his escape from the 'real' world was an indulgence, but he figured he was due some drop-out time, and the new life seemed to be bringing him luck as well as respite. When LA rioted and when Malibu and Topanga Canyon burned in wildfires, Nick stayed home, unscathed; when El Niño turned the weather nuts and the Los Angeles River into a raging torrent, he stayed dry, painting the surf; when movie moguls joined their neighbours to shore up hillsides and stop their homes from sliding into the ocean, he watched them on TV. And even in January of '94 when the big quake sent all of his books tumbling off the shelves in his own living room, Nick was out of town – in San Francisco of all places – checking out fresh pastures.

Almost four years – four decent, *sane* years – had passed before he finally stopped waiting for the other shoe to drop; before he felt confident enough to believe that he really had left his past behind him on the East Coast and that the time had come for him to put down new roots.

San Francisco seemed, to him, the perfect choice.

'You can't move to San Francisco,' Kate Miller said on the telephone when he broke the news.

'Why not? It's a wonderful city.' Nick had visited four times before making his final decision.

'Earthquakes.' That one word seemed enough to Kate.

'Mom, I've been living in LA for four years and it hasn't worried you that much.'

'It's scared hell out of me and your dad,' Kate enlightened him, 'but at least you kept saying it was temporary so we just crossed our fingers and tried not to think about it more than we could help.'

'What about when I was at NYU? There are fault lines under Manhattan.'

'Don't try snowing me with science, Nick,' his mother said drily. 'In New York, we figured you were more likely to be mugged or murdered.'

Not to mention arrested, Nick thought.

32

'So why not focus on how much more civilized San Francisco is?' he asked.

Kate was silent for a moment.

'You've made up your mind,' she said.

'Come and visit, Mom. You'll love it, too.'

'I don't doubt I'll love the city,' Kate said. 'It's the San Andreas fault I'm never going to feel comfortable with.'

He made the move in the spring of 1994. He packed all his belongings into his red Toyota Land Cruiser and drove up the Pacific coast on State Highway 1, taking his time heading north, spending a day around Big Sur, wanting to experience the wild, precarious sensation friends had tried to describe to him of being right on the western edge of America with nothing but ocean between him and Japan. He hung out for a few hours in Carmel (a place, together with Big Sur, that he would always – stemming from his NYU days of movie passion – associate with *Play Misty for Me*), then a few hours more in Monterey (*Cannery Row*, of course – the movie *and* the novel). And then, with a sudden, strong urge to reach his final destination, he got back in the Toyota and drove non-stop all the rest of the way to San Francisco.

He staged his arrival the way he'd promised himself he would – the way he'd planned it for the last several months – driving the car up to Twin Peaks, parking and climbing the steep footpath to the summit and gazing for a good long while at the panorama laid out far below. It was sunset, the most perfect time he could have picked, and it was all there – all the places he'd thought about and readied himself for were right *there*. He had binoculars with him and a map, and he could identify a whole host of movie locations: Russian Hill from the car chase in *Bullitt*; the Presidio from the movie of the same name; the big Hyatt hotel on Market Street that the Mel Brooks shrink had been phobic about in *High Anxiety*.

And, of course, the bridges. Golden Gate Bridge, rust red and delicate from this distance, glowing in the warmth of the sunset, then softly starting to sparkle as its lights came on. All there for him. His new city.

Home.

* * *

33

Nina Ford was the realtor who helped him find his new apartment. He had been staying at a small bed and breakfast inn close to Union Street. Once a Victorian farmhouse, it had a library and a garden and was charm itself, but Nick wanted his own space as soon as possible. He had chosen Ford Realty because of a piece about the company in the Real Estate section of the Sunday *Examiner*. Personally run by two British sisters, the article made it sound a cosy, caring set-up. It carried no picture, but when Nick had finished reading he had an image of two middle-aged, tweedy English types with a mission to make their clients as snug and content as they were.

How wrong could a man be?

They had arranged to meet outside a property on Fillmore Street (just a few blocks, Nick had noted, from the supposed site of the Victorian house where Keaton, Modine and Griffiths had slugged it out in *Pacific Heights*) that Nina Ford said she had thought of as soon as Nick had told her that he was an artist.

She was right about the proportions and light being ideal for his needs. But, as it turned out, the apartment was the least of it.

'Nick Miller?' was all she said, holding out her hand, and he was blown away. Instantly. Crazily. Just like that.

It wasn't just the looks. Honey hair. Great legs. Long, fine nose. Wide mouth. (All paintable, all gorgeous.) Grace.

He thought, maybe, it was the smile. That smile set off something behind the eyes (a shade between hazel and amber – tough to capture on canvas) that reached out and touched Nick in a place no one had ever reached before.

Things have happened to this woman, he thought. *Bad things*.

He knew that, suddenly, without question. And that was when he realized exactly what it was about her.

That look in her eyes reminded him of his own.

They ate lunch together at Alioto's on Fisherman's Wharf, one week after Nick had moved into the apartment.

'I'm an alcoholic,' Nina told him, right after she'd ordered a bottle of Calistoga water. 'I'm not exactly sure yet why I feel I have to tell you that, but somehow it seems important that I should.' She took a

34

breath. 'I've been sober for more than five years now, and my life's been in pretty good shape for the last three years, thanks to Ford Realty – thanks mostly, I think, to Phoebe, my sister. But whichever way you cut it, I am still a recovering alcoholic.'

A surge of admiration for her courage hit Nick at around the same instant as one of overwhelming pity, but, sensing that Nina would probably welcome neither, he took his time before responding.

'I'm glad you told me,' he said.

Her eyes flicked away from his, escaped for just a moment, then returned, steady again. 'I'll understand if you find it too much of a problem.'

'Why should I find it a problem?' Nick's question came naturally.

'Many men do,' Nina answered.

Nick looked at his glass of Chardonnay. 'Does this bother you?'

She shook her head. 'Not anymore. Not much, anyway. I'm used to it. I'm a working woman in a major American city – I have to be used to it.'

The power of suggestion hit Nick with a sudden, intense urge to take a long sip of the wine, and it took a ludicrous effort to tear his attention away from the glass.

'What made you start drinking? I mean—' He broke off.

'What made me a drunk?' Nina smiled a gentle, sad smile. 'My mother was an alcoholic for most of her adult life. She killed herself in 1987. On her fortieth birthday. I was nineteen, Phoebe was seventeen. We handled it very differently.' Nina paused. 'Phoebe's the kindest person I know, but she has a lot of straightforward common sense which seems to help her cope with bad things. It never occurred to Phoebe to think she might take after our mother.'

'But it did to you.' Nick no longer wanted his wine.

'Not consciously. Until our mother died, I'd always enjoyed a degree of social drinking, but afterwards, I simply seemed to blunder right on where she'd left off.' She grimaced. 'A bottle of vodka in a session. Very ugly.'

'Very painful,' Nick said.

'Oh, yes.' Nina paused. 'Maybe my becoming a drunk was genetic, or maybe it was more to do with learned behaviour patterns – or maybe it was just some kind of self-destructive fear or guilt – but for four years I did do my level best to follow her.' She looked

35

away from him, out at the bay. 'I'd almost managed to go all the way when my father and Phoebe stopped me.'

Their chowder arrived and they both picked up their spoons and made an effort to eat, to be normal.

'You don't look especially like an artist, you know,' Nina said.

Nick smiled. 'What do I look like?'

'Hard to say.' She made a little show of studying him. The thick, slightly wavy dark hair. The keen, gentle, toast-brown eyes. The straight mouth and slightly angular nose.

'You could be many things,' she said. 'Doctor, architect.' Her eyes danced just a little. 'Streetfighter?'

'You mean the nose.' Nick lifted his left hand to touch it. 'It got a little bent out of shape one night in New York.'

'A mugging?'

'Not exactly.' He offered no more details, and Nina didn't pursue it. 'My father's an architect,' he said.

'In New York?'

He shook his head. 'Bethesda, Maryland.'

'Washington clients?'

'Mostly.' Nick paused. 'Does your father live in San Francisco?' He wanted the rest of the picture.

'He lives in Scottsdale, Arizona,' Nina answered. 'His name's William, and my mother's was Joanna.'

'Both British?'

Nina nodded. 'My father's a pilot. He was a flier in the RAF, but he gave that up because my mother hated the long separations. He compromised by starting up a small civil freight aviation company outside London, but it was always a financial struggle – so when this amazing American came along offering Dad a partnership in his own company, my father couldn't resist.'

'Did your mother hate moving to the States?'

'I think my mother hated everything by then. She was a very unhappy person. Oh, she loved her family, but I don't think we were enough for her.' Nina shrugged. 'She wanted more. She claimed she wanted our father on the ground like most normal husbands, but Dad knew that if he gave up flying altogether he'd be miserable, too.' She paused. 'Phoebe doesn't think it would have made any real difference to our mother – she says that her unhappiness went right through to her core.'

36

Their entrées arrived, cold Dungeness crab for Nick and *cioppino* – a Sicilian shellfish stew – for Nina.

'I don't think you do take after her,' he said, abruptly.

'No, I don't think I do either. Not entirely, anyway.'

'Maybe I'm being presumptuous,' he went on, trying to choose his words carefully, 'but you don't seem an unhappy person to me. What happened to your mother was tragic enough to mess anyone up. But from what little I've seen of you, I'd guess you have quite a capacity for joy.'

Nina smiled. 'I think maybe I do.'

Nothing had become automatically easier, she confided in Nick, when she'd stopped drinking. There was a string of failed relationships with men – business types, professionals and academics who all seemed to expect, from her outer image, things that Nina could not and had no desire to deliver. Mostly, of course, what they did *not* want, Nina said, was a drunk on their hands, neither for the risk of a blemish on their own reputations nor for the constant, ongoing battle against the ugliness, the repulsiveness of relapse. And so Nina had made a decision to toughen up by building a wall around herself and allowing no one to enter her heart. At the time she met Nick, she had not accepted a date with a man for more than two years.

'What made me different?' Nick asked. 'My fighter's nose?'

'You really want to know?'

'If you want to tell me.'

'It was your eyes.'

Nick laughed. 'My eyes are plain, ordinary brown.'

Nina didn't laugh back. 'They're not ordinary at all. They're kind. And they're honest. And they seem to see a lot that other people don't.'

'I'm an artist. I need to see.'

'But none of those things were what made me agree to have lunch with you today,' Nina said.

Nick kept silent. He remembered his own thoughts about Nina's eyes the day they'd met at the apartment. He knew, suddenly, what was coming.

37

'There's pain in your eyes,' Nina said. 'The kind I've seen over the years in my own mirror.'

'Is there?' Nick said.

For three months, they spent every spare moment together, falling more in love with every passing week. Six months later, they had first pick via Ford Realty of a pretty, detached clapboard Edwardian house on Antonia Street between Pacific and Faber Avenues in Pacific Heights.

It was perfect for them both. Near the summit of a north-facing hill, close to Lafayette Park and the relaxed buzz of Upper Fillmore shopping, the house had big, high-ceilinged rooms, log-burning fireplaces, hardwood floors, a pretty back garden with a stone barbecue and weeping willow, a garage for Nina's Lexus (the Toyota could rough it on the street) and great views from the third floor. Nick had problems about accepting that, for the moment at least, the lion's share of the financing would be Nina's, but Phoebe Ford – physically dissimilar to Nina, with William's red hair, pale, almost pure white skin and a more fragile build – told him that since Nina had fallen so hard for the house, it would be little more than macho selfishness to ask her to settle for less.

'Besides,' Phoebe said, 'you're a terrific painter, and we all know you're going to be famous some day and hang in MoMA and get paid megabucks and be able to buy all the houses you want.'

Nick liked Phoebe a lot.

In April of 1995, five weeks after they moved to Antonia Street, they were married in their own garden under the willow tree. Kate and Ethan Miller came from Bethesda, William Ford from Arizona, and the Millers' pleasure at their son's and new daughter-in-law's happiness was transparent. But the mistrust in Nick that Ford had displayed, equally openly, from their first encounter, continued right through the simple marriage service and beyond – though Phoebe's patent joy for both Nina and Nick went a long way towards making up for her father's grudging behaviour.

* * *

Places in and around San Francisco ceased to remind Nick of old movie locations, and became landmarks and lodestars of another kind. Maiden Lane, off Union Square, was where he and Nina had first walked hand in hand; California Street was where they'd shared their first Vietnamese dinner; Golden Gate Park was where they'd played their first game of tennis; Sausalito's waterfront at night was where they'd had their first kiss.

Life with Nina was all Nick had ever hoped for. She was warm and considerate, sexy and humorous, gentle and intuitive. Even in her down-times, when her mood swung low and she became darker and went to more AA meetings – sometimes with Nick, sometimes alone – and when only Bill Regan, her AA sponsor, seemed wholly to understand her needs, Nick still knew that he loved her more than he'd ever loved anyone.

He came across *Firefly* when he was searching for glue in the bottom drawer of an oak dresser that Nina had brought to their kitchen from her former home on Telegraph Hill.

'What is this?' He held up what seemed to be a manuscript, and looked at his wife, who was making garlic bread to accompany the fresh pasta they were having for dinner. 'Nina?'

She glanced over. 'It's nothing.'

'Doesn't look like nothing.'

'It's just something Phoebe and I wrote a couple of years ago.'

Nick was looking at the front page. 'Is it a novel?'

She shook her head. 'A children's story. About a girl who's haunted by a strange spirit creature who glows in the dark. It's a little bizarre in places. It's nothing.'

'May I read it?'

'Sure.' Nina laid a cloth over the warm, fragrant bread. 'If you really want to.'

Nick began to remove the elastic band that held the pages together.

'After dinner,' Nina said.

'This is not nothing,' Nick said, a little before midnight.

'What do you mean?' Nina, beside him in bed, closed her new

Patricia Cornwell mystery and turned to look at him. The light in the bedroom was soft and flickering with flame from the fireplace. Nick's face, tough enough in daylight, seemed almost delicate in the firelight, his bone structure more clearly delineated. He looked, Nina thought with a pang, vulnerable.

Nick put the manuscript carefully down on the quilt. 'This is a truly *wonderful* children's story.'

'Really?' Nina was startled.

Nick sat up. He felt intensely excited and stirred. 'Really,' he said. 'It's dark and it's warm and it's just dangerous enough to get them scared and intrigued and longing for more.'

'I don't know.' Nina lay back against her pillows. 'Phoebe and I both agreed when we finished it that it was more of a cathartic exercise than anything else. It seemed like a harmless way of expressing our old childhood nightmares. We certainly never thought it would interest anyone else.'

Handling it gently, Nick pulled the elastic band back around the manuscript. 'I'd like to try my hand at illustrating it.'

Nina stared at him. 'You're kidding.'

'I never kid about my work. Not when something really triggers me.'

She was silent for a moment, then shrugged.

'Go for it,' she said. 'If you really want to.'

'Do you think Phoebe would mind?'

'On the contrary,' Nina said.

The results of their collaboration were, Clare Hawkins – a literary agent who operated out of her home in the Russian Hill district – told them, fascinating: beyond-Rackham, sensuous and fragile, but deliciously close enough to nightmare realms to attract even the most precocious, horrorwise youngsters of the nineties. Looking at *Firefly* again alongside Nick's illustrations, Phoebe became ecstatic and even Nina – who still had reservations about the story being too much the product of the post-traumatic phase of their lives – began to admit that the package might have some potential.

It turned out to have considerably more than potential, attracting not only publishers and readers, but also the brains behind Meganimity, a fast-growing animation production company in Los Angeles.

'We want you to work with us,' Steve Cohn of Meganimity told Nick in the late fall of 1995, with the book about to hit the stores all over the country. 'I mean, we really want you on board with us for this one.'

'When are things going to start to happen?' Nick asked Cohn.

'Soon,' Cohn replied. 'Spring of next year. Be prepared to spend quite a bit of time with us here in LA.'

'That's fine for me,' Nick told him. 'But Nina and Phoebe have a real estate company to run in San Francisco.'

'No problem,' Cohn said. 'They're just the writers – you're the artist.' He paused. 'Though you might like to make sure they're ready to cook up a new story in their spare time.'

'My wife,' Nick pointed out, amiably enough, 'would probably want me to tell you what you could do with that last remark. My sister-in-law would simply come out and tell you that you're a sexist pig.'

Cohn grinned. 'And my wife would agree with them both.'

To the young artist and movie fan, accustomed to the small peaks and troughs of alternating creative triumph and gloom, all the attention that followed the publication of *Firefly* was a revelation. Suddenly, people of substance and influence were sitting up, taking notice and wanting more. Nick loved it, though not quite as much as he had loved the period of collaboration with Nina and Phoebe.

They all counted their blessings regularly. The book, already in its eighth printing, was so hot that six months after publication parents, aunts and uncles still couldn't get enough copies. Nick, Nina and Phoebe were in demand for signings and bookstore readings. Nick was flying to and from Los Angeles for meetings with Meganimity's Hollywood-based producers, and there was talk of spin-offs in the electronic games and multimedia markets – though Clare Hawkins was advising them to take much of this LA-speak with a handsome pinch of salt.

'What you guys should be thinking about is your next book,' Hawkins, a tall, slim, handsome woman in her late forties, told Nick, Nina and Phoebe when she came to 1315 Antonia Street for dinner in late April. 'Do you have any ideas?'

'No,' Phoebe said.

'Nor do we plan to have any,' Nina added.

'I told you,' Nick said, with a wry smile.

Clare shrugged. 'I thought you might have persuaded them.'

'Nina and Phoebe Ford are not easy women to persuade.'

'We're realtors,' Nina said, gently, 'not writers.'

'Tell that to your readers,' Clare said.

They were eating Nina's homemade ravioli stuffed with crabmeat at the round oak table in their dining room, an austere space softened by a warm Persian rug snared at a Jackson Square auction and by three glowing candelabra from an antique shop on Fillmore Street.

'I don't need convincing,' Nick told Clare. 'I'd love nothing more than to illustrate another Ford book.'

'Except that *you* understand,' Nina said, 'that *Firefly* was a once-only piece of therapy turned good fortune.'

'Maybe not,' Clare said. 'Have you tried?'

'We don't really want to try,' Phoebe answered for them both. 'We've had such a great time with this one – it's been the experience of a lifetime.'

'And it's done wonders for Nick's career,' Nina added.

'And there's nothing to stop him going on in the same vein,' Phoebe said. 'You've said yourself that you've had approaches from other writers wanting Nick to illustrate for them.'

'Nothing that's inspired him,' Clare said.

'Because there's been nothing to touch *Firefly*,' Nick explained simply. 'Nothing's even come close. Which is why I'm planning to paint some portraits, work on some of those good bread-and-butter magazine commissions you've got for me, and hold on for the right book deal.'

'Meganimity will be disappointed,' Clare said. 'Knowing you had another one on the way might make them even keener to promote *Firefly.*'

'There is another creation on the way,' Phoebe said, reaching out and touching her sister's still flat stomach.

'You're beaten, Clare,' Nick said. 'Face it.'

He was too content to care. If Nina and Phoebe ever changed their minds and wrote another story, no one would be happier than him, but there was always the possibility that they were right and that

Firefly had been a one-off feat. Besides, they did have a business they loved, and Nina and he would, before too long, be pretty much occupied with their child. And though all the attention and royalty cheques and talk of advances were more than welcome, and it was good to have been able to take over the mortgage repayments from Nina, he was a painter – an artist, for heaven's sake – not some big-league commodity.

Critics, publishers, movie producers and even agents would come and go. Love, warmth, sharing and, above all, sanity, were something else entirely. It had taken Nick most of his life to find them. He would not give them up without a fight.

5

Holly Bourne is in her final week at Nussbaum, Koch, Morgan. There will be a party for her at official close of business tomorrow evening, though almost everyone who attends – associates, partners, even secretaries – will be returning to their offices after a drink or two. Holly remembers her mother complaining sometimes about her father's long working hours. Eleanor Bourne has always taken great pride in her senior administrative job with the State Department, but Richard Bourne's regular fifteen-hour days in his DC law practice have often given her cause for grievance. Holly – along with some of the other ambitious associates at NKM – has already grown used to working eighteen-hour stretches, six or seven days a week. Holly's never been afraid of hard work, never been afraid of anything much that's necessary to get her where she wants to be.

From the end of next month – if she's passed the bar exam – which she will – she'll be working in Los Angeles for Zadok, Giulini & O'Connell in Century City offices just two blocks away from her fiancé's own law firm. She'll be taking a small salary cut to achieve that move, but her prospects are high. Michael Giulini and Alan Zadok, the partners who conducted her interview, were both aware at that time of her impending marriage to Jack Taylor, of Anderson, Taylor, and are prepared to wait for her until after the wedding (at the Hotel Bel-Air in LA, despite her parents' hopes of hosting her big day in Washington DC), and the Grand Cayman honeymoon. Holly knows that Giulini and Zadok are set to do far more for her in time if she meets their expectations. She intends to do that and more. Holly intends to work her small, exercise-tightened butt off to achieve her goals.

* * *

44

She has just emerged from Bergdorf Goodman with three shopping bags – the rest to be delivered – and is walking along Fifth past the Doubleday bookstore, when she sees the notice in the window.

Her throat tightens. Her pulse rate quickens.

She steps inside. The security guard at the door looks at her shopping bags, and Holly opens them to be checked and stapled shut to stop her from slipping unpaid-for merchandise into them. *As if.*

The book-signing is on the second floor. There's quite a queue. Mothers, aunts, a few small children, a couple of fathers.

The two women authors are sitting side by side behind a table, taking their time over each signing. Though seated, one of them seems petite, with carrot-coloured hair, white skin and green eyes, the other taller, an elegant honey-blonde with a long nose and unusual, not-quite-hazel, eyes. As each successive customer passes them a book, both women smile and chat for a few moments, then the blonde signs before the redhead, and the book is handed back. They make a good team.

He is not there.

Holly walks over to a table where the books have been stacked in an intricate pyramid-like edifice. She has already bought the book, did so last November soon after publication, when she read it carefully, studied each illustration at length, and then threw it away.

She takes another copy now and gets in line.

'Wonderful book,' the woman ahead of her turns around and says to Holly. She is holding three copies. 'My daughter loved it so much I thought it would be nice to get her an autographed copy.' She beams. 'The other two are for my friend's children.'

Holly's smile is warm. 'Mine is for my niece.' She has no niece, but it sounds apt.

'Boys seem to love it just as much as girls, you know.'

'Really,' Holly says.

The woman turns away as she reaches the table and hands over her copies with pride. The blonde is speaking to her, some comment about her buying three, but another woman in the line is coughing loudly, so Holly can't hear exactly what is being said.

Now it's her turn.

'Thank you very much,' the redhead says.

'You're welcome.' Holly places her copy of *Firefly* on the table. 'I'm glad to meet you both.'

'The pleasure's ours.' The blonde's British accent is more pronounced than her sister's. 'Is this for someone in particular?'

'It's for myself,' Holly says. 'I collect children's books.' Another invention.

The redhead smiles. 'That's nice.'

'Anything special you'd like us to write?' the blonde asks.

Holly takes an instant, still making up her mind.

'There's a Wordsworth quotation I particularly like,' she says. 'Some find it a little gruesome – I just find it moving.'

The blond woman picks up her Mont Blanc fountain pen.

Holly dictates, slowly and clearly.

> 'A simple child,
> That lightly draws its breath,
> And feels its life in every limb,
> What should it know of death?'

The woman hesitates for an instant, then finishes writing the verse and signs her name. She puts down her pen in silence, blots the words and passes *Firefly* to her sister. The redhead adds her own name, looks up at Holly and gives her a small, curious smile as she hands the book back to her.

'Interesting choice,' she says.

The blonde makes no comment.

'Have a nice day,' Holly says and gives way to the next in line.

Outside, back on Fifth Avenue, she crosses over Fifty-sixth Street and stops by a trash can. She slips the Bergdorf Goodman shopping bags over her left wrist, takes *Firefly* from the Doubleday bag and opens the book at the signed page. Very carefully, she tears out the page and places it back in the bag.

And then she throws the book into the trash can.

6

I look at my work sometimes, at my portraits, and I see in some of them the reflection of my memories, of my innermost emotions and responses to the people who have meant the most to me.

I look at Ethan Miller, my father, the quiet, gifted, successful architect, with his calm, concentrated face, his brown eyes and thick, wavy hair, so like my own, and at Kate, my mother, the high school art teacher, with her short, fair hair and her pretty blue eyes always so open and candid, like her personality, and I remember the early pleasures of watching them both at work. My dad hunched over his drawing board, my mother in another world at her easel. The smells of paint and turpentine and varnish. The sounds: of rapid, smooth sketching, of brushes and palette knives on canvas, the clear, clean swish of the draughtsman's pen. And I remember how, by the age of nine – when we moved to Bethesda from Philadelphia – I had become as content with a stick of charcoal or a paintbrush as most other boys my age were with a catcher's mitt or basketball.

I look at my portrait of Richard Bourne, distinguished, bespectacled, grey-templed Washington lawyer and gentle man, who loved Holly dearly yet half recognized, I always suspected, at least some of her problems. Unlike Eleanor Bourne. Such a fine-looking, tightly controlled, high-achieving woman, of whose dislike I was always aware, who had the capacity to slay with a single fire-ice glance from her dark eyes anyone who dared suggest to her that her child was less than perfect. A complex woman, Eleanor Bourne. Holly told me once that Eleanor blamed her for Eric's death, and because of that, for a while, Holly said she had blamed herself too. And yet, once Holly had started growing up and doing so well, Eleanor was the first

47

in line handing out accolades to her daughter and refusing to accept that Holly could do wrong. Blame where none was due; not where it was needed. A complex, difficult woman, Eleanor Bourne.

And then there's Holly's portrait.

I painted several of her through the years, but kept only one: the first, painted about three years after my parents and I first moved into Holly's street. How lovely she was back then. Hair the colour of roasting chestnuts, pale, smooth skin, calm grey eyes. Richard's eyes. And that smile. Holly's very own smile. The girl-next-door who everyone always said – then and in years to come – was such pure delight to look at and to know.

I believed that too, in the early days. Or I thought I did.

I still remember the first time I saw her, framed in her bedroom window: I remember a sad, sweet face gazing down at me, and I remember how that sadness seemed to vanish the instant I smiled back up at her. Light out of darkness. I heard, soon after that, what had happened to her brother Eric, and how desolate Holly had been since losing him, and I remember thinking – friendless new boy in town that I was – that it might be kind of a nice thing if I could help make her feel better again.

And I did. Even Eleanor was grateful to me back then for helping get Holly back on track. Not that Eleanor actually *liked* me, not even in those days. I was okay, I guess, for the boy next door, but Holly – well, it was obvious to Eleanor and just about everyone else that Holly, frankly, was in another league. She was a year younger than I was, but she was 'special'. With those looks, and with her high intelligence, there was never any doubting that Holly Bourne was destined for all-round success.

Special.

7

'I like you,' she said to Nick in the second week of December 1976, not long before his first Bethesda Christmas.

He grinned at her.

'I like you too,' he said.

'Do you love me?' she asked him.

He was startled. It seemed to him a weird kind of question. He loved two people: his mom and his dad. It had never occurred to him to love anyone else.

'I don't know.' He saw hurt in her face. 'I guess. Maybe.'

The hurt went away. 'I love you,' Holly told him. 'I love you a lot.'

He grinned again. Hearing her say that she loved him made him feel a little dumb, but glad, too.

'Thank you,' he said.

He didn't know what else he was supposed to say.

8

Our relationship was uneven from the beginning, and I guess it was always potentially dangerous, an unhealthy kind of see-saw. There are two ways of looking back at those early days, I realize that now. There was the way I used to tell myself I thought it was, and then there was the way I really, deep-down, *knew* it was.

I *told* myself back then that the bad things that happened were all Holly's doing – that I'd just let myself get suckered in. But that wasn't entirely true. How could it have been?

I was genuinely fond of Holly during those first few years, but Holly adored me. I guess that at the start I was a little awed by her tragedy, touched by her prettiness and sorrow, and impressed by her swift, clever mind. Holly thought that I was her big brother and best friend and, in moments of fantasy into the future – and Holly fantasized a lot – her husband-to-be and the father of her children, all rolled into one.

I make no excuses, not now, not from an adult perspective. But to a ten-year-old boy, it was all pretty damned flattering. I had never been one of a gang, not even back in Philadelphia, had always been happiest watching movies or sketching, always a little set apart, and here was this girl next door – a spunky, winning, beautiful girl – who honestly seemed to think I was the bee's knees. I tell you, it was more than good for my ego. It was, I realize now, intoxicating.

I guess I should have cut Holly out of my life as soon as she started getting me into trouble. Everyone thought Holly was so damned perfect – no one would have believed me if I'd told them the truth – but

50

the Holly I came to know as we grew up together was a secretive, frantic girl who craved action, excitement and risk. The real Holly played practical jokes on neighbours, smoked in the park and stole magazines, cigarettes and candy. The real Holly also had a great talent for ensuring that she never got caught, and because she was always talking me into coming with her on her adventures, more often than not I was the one who ended up taking the rap. Once it was vandalism at school; another time it was trespassing in a neighbour's back yard; a couple of times it was trying to sneak into the movies without paying. By the time I was twelve years old, I was *that* close to getting in serious trouble with the cops, and my parents were miserable about what seemed to be happening to me, but I just couldn't seem to tell Holly no.

I got the blame for stuff because I was older and my face fitted. And because I was a prize schnook. One look from those pleading, trusting eyes of hers, and I just couldn't seem to bring myself to rat on her – and anyway, it made me feel like a hero.

That was all bull. I know that now – and I had to have known it then too, deep down, since I don't think I was a complete fool. The truth of the matter is that if I *really* hadn't wanted to get involved with Holly's schemes, I could have refused. If I hadn't wanted to be her scapegoat, all I had to do was go to my parents and tell them what was going on.

I wasn't such a hero. Holly was a girl and a year younger – though, believe me, it's true what they say about girls growing up faster than boys. But she was definitely smaller and physically weaker than I was. No one was twisting my arm. Holly might have masterminded our adventures, but because I was older and bigger than she was, I guess I ought to have been capable of assuming the leadership in our twosome. In those days, I *told* myself – and pretty much managed to believe – that it was all Holly's fault, that I was going along with her because she was vulnerable and a little crazy and she needed me to take care of her.

It was a lie. I think now that the truth was that I found Holly's wickedness the most exciting thing I'd ever known. There I was, this artistic, gentle, well-brought-up kid, yet there was a side to me back then that enjoyed all those bad-boy deeds.

Normal stuff, perhaps, for a healthy, growing kid. Not really harmful, if it had ended there.

But it didn't.

51

9

Sex seemed the next, natural step.

If Holly Bourne had been exciting at twelve, how infinitely more thrilling she seemed to Nick almost three years later, when his own hormones were racing, surging, powering his body and far too much of his mind.

'Wouldn't you like to kiss me now?'

Holly asked that question on September 25th, 1982. It was a Saturday afternoon, and she and Nick were in the Bethesda Mall hanging out near a lingerie boutique named Angel's, while Holly debated whether or not she should buy or steal the pair of tiny lacy bikini panties she could see hanging on a rack inside.

She didn't wait for Nick's answer.

'Or maybe you'd rather wait until I'm wearing those new panties before you kiss me.'

Nick glanced around, felt the heat on his cheeks. 'Holly, for Pete's sake, someone's going to hear you.'

'I don't care,' Holly said.

'Well, I do. We're not supposed to even be here.'

'I told my mom I was going to the mall today.'

'To buy a book,' Nick pointed out.

'So I'll buy a book.' Her eyes sparkled. 'Or steal one.'

'Holly, you have to quit stealing stuff.' He'd told her over and over. 'If you don't stop, I'm going to tell your parents and they'll do more than stop you.'

'You sound just like Eric used to.' She was still smiling.

'I'm not Eric.' Nick tried distraction. 'Let's go get a shake.'

'Uh-uh.' She was not to be diverted. 'I'm going in there now – are you coming?'

'No way.' Nick was adamant. 'It's a bad idea, Holly.'

'So kiss me instead.'

Holly puckered up and closed her eyes. Nick looked around for familiar faces, saw none, and bent to brush her lips with his own. Holly opened her eyes at the same time as her mouth, and her right hand came up to draw his head closer. He felt the moist softness inside her lips, felt her small, firm tongue pushing against his teeth—

'Holl-*ee*.' Nick pulled away.

'What?' The grey eyes were dancing. 'Didn't you like that?'

'No.'

'Liar.'

His face was hot again. 'Okay, so I liked it. Big deal.'

'So do it again,' Holly urged.

'No way.' Nick started to move away, but she caught at his hand and held onto him. 'Holly, this is not the place.'

'So let's go somewhere else.'

'Like where?' Nick felt a throb of undeniable arousal down inside his jeans. Holly had been teasing him this way for quite a while now, but mostly she'd been easy enough to divert towards some other kind of game. Lately, however, he was beginning to realize that she meant business. Holly wanted Nick to kiss her properly, the way they did in the movies and on TV and in the books she had taken to reading in bed late at night when Richard and Eleanor thought she was sleeping. Until right now, Nick had wanted to divert Holly because something told him, *warned* him, that kissing her was not a hot idea. They were like brother and sister, after all, had been for more than six years now. A brother did not kiss his sister, not that way. Everyone knew that.

Suddenly, though, he found he was not so sure.

Kissing was only the beginning. Touching came next. Holly enjoyed touching Nick and describing how that felt and what effect it had on her.

'Your skin feels so *different* to mine. Not as soft, but it's really warm, and oh, it smells so good – I think I want to kiss that spot – maybe I'll just lick it, see what it tastes like . . .'

53

Her touching moved downward.

'So *that's* it. Oh, it's so soft and sweet . . . you like that? I can tell you like that. Oh, Nick, you're so bad, and that feels so *good*, and oh, look, just look at the way it's growing! It makes me feel almost scared, like it has a life all of its own . . .'

He preferred not to talk while he touched her – was, in fact, incapable of speech most of the time, partly because Holly and he were kissing, partly because, when he felt the thrust of her little hard nipples against the palms of his hands, or when she let him push his fingers down inside her panties, down into the dark, wet mysteries of her, it was all he could do not to cry out loud.

They went all the way for the first time on Christmas Day, her fifteenth birthday. They had spent most of the day in their own homes, doing all the traditional family eating and present-giving and other normal stuff. Ethan and Kate gave Nick a handsome leather portfolio to use when he wanted to maybe start showing his work to galleries or graphics companies or whoever. Nick gave Ethan a new book on Frank Lloyd Wright and Kate a set of acrylic paints and some perfume. Richard and Eleanor gave Holly a fine gold necklace from Tiffany with a small diamond-studded H pendant and the yearbook for her leather-bound set of Encyclopaedia Americana. Holly gave Richard a pipe she'd ordered three months earlier from the Dunhill catalogue, and she gave Eleanor a grey cashmere scarf that she'd stolen from Lord and Taylor in DC.

Nick had done his best to discourage her.

'What if she wants to change it?' he'd asked her after the deed had been done and it was too late to change her mind.

'She won't – she's too polite. And if she does, I'll say I lost the receipt.'

'You never lose things – she won't believe it.'

'She'd believe I stole the scarf even less.'

Holly couldn't get away until after five, and Eleanor didn't want her going out at all, but Richard agreed that it was only fair she have an opportunity to exchange gifts with Nick.

'I could always ask him to come over here,' Holly said to her mother, knowing how much Eleanor would hate any visitor at this time on Christmas Day when her home was still in disarray from dinner and present giving.

'No, that's all right. You run along, dear.'

'What do you have for Nick?' Richard asked.

'A pair of gloves.' Holly held out the package.

'You'd better take something for his parents,' Eleanor said.

'I don't need to, Mother. They won't expect anything.'

'If you're intruding on their Christmas Day, you can't go empty-handed,' Eleanor insisted.

Richard sucked on his new pipe. 'She could take one of those bottles.' He nodded at the small stack of pre-wrapped bottles of whisky and champagne that his wife insisted they keep in stock for last-minute gift emergencies.

'Holly can't give liquor,' Eleanor said. 'What would the Millers think?'

'They'd probably think it was very nice and open the bottle,' Richard said.

'It'll have to be chocolates.' Eleanor pointed to another pile of tastefully wrapped boxes. 'One of the medium-sized ones, Holly. They're all Godiva – just so you know what you're giving.'

'Thank you, Mother.'

'You won't be very long, will you, dear?'

'Not very, Mother.'

'Have fun, Holly,' Richard said, and winked at his daughter.

'Merry Christmas, Daddy,' Holly said, and winked back at him.

'Happy Birthday, sweetheart,' he said.

The atmosphere in the Millers' house was sleepy, Ethan having eaten and drunk too much and Kate having worked too hard, and even Matisse, their collie-cross, appearing to be hung over. Holly had told Nick once that she would love to have had a dog, but because both her parents worked right through the week, Eleanor said they couldn't keep any animal. It wasn't fair on the creature or the family, she said, and even if Carmelita, their housekeeper, did claim that she would love the company of a dog, Eleanor pointed out that Carmelita was unlikely to stay for ever, and then there would be nothing but trouble for everyone.

'Happy Birthday, Holly,' Nick whispered at the door. 'Everyone's half asleep. We'll have to go up to my room.'

'Good,' Holly whispered back.

From her armchair in the living room, Kate Miller raised her arm to wave limply at her and mouthed festive greetings, while her husband snored gently and Matisse wagged his tail languidly.

Nick's bedroom was smaller than the room next door that he used as a studio. There was a· writing desk, computer and chair, a walk-in closet, an en-suite shower room, a bookshelf – bowing a little in the centre from overloading – and a bed covered with a patchwork quilt. There being no lock on the door, Nick moved the chair to about an inch away from the handle, not quite close enough to merit an accusation that they were barricading themselves in, but near enough to give them at least a moment's warning if either of his parents decided to enter the room.

'It's okay,' Nick always said to Holly when she asked him to jam the chair right up under the handle. 'Mom and Dad always knock before they come in.'

'Do you want your present,' Holly asked him now, 'or do I get my Christmas kiss first?'

Nick put both arms around her and kissed her, giving it his best shot, his most practised and deep French kiss. He felt Holly move tight up against him, felt her moan a little as his tongue thrust in her mouth.

'That,' he said, coming up for air, 'was your birthday kiss. This is your Christmas kiss.'

More than a minute passed.

'Just as well,' Holly said, breathlessly, 'I chose your present carefully.'

Nick drew away. 'I want to give you yours first.'

'Okay,' Holly said. 'But we don't have too much time. My mother wants me home soon.'

'You've only just come.'

'I know.' Holly fastened her gaze on his mouth. 'But we have a lot to get done.'

Nick felt a kick down below and knew he was already hard.

'Here,' he said, and handed her a small square box.

'What is it?'

'Open it and see.'

It was a powder compact.

'It's lovely,' Holly said.

'That's just your official present,' Nick said. 'My mother was with me when I bought it, so I had to get something safe.'

'Where's my unofficial present?' Holly looked around.

'Under my pillow,' Nick said.

Holly wasted no time tearing it open. When she saw the tiny, lace-trimmed silk panties, her eyes brimmed with tears.

'You remember,' Nick said. 'In the mall. Our first kiss.'

'Of course I remember.' Her face lit up. 'Did you steal them?'

'No, I did not steal them! God, Holly, you're terrible.'

'But you love me.'

'More than ever,' Nick said, meaning it.

'Now your present.' Holly got her package from the writing desk. 'Your unofficial one is inside the official one.' She handed it to him. 'Be careful how you handle it.'

He tore off the paper, found the gloves. They were brown suede with sheepskin lining. He lifted them to his nose, sniffed them with pleasure.

'These are great. My old ones are shot.'

'I know.' She had been with him when he'd dropped one glove in the street after they'd gotten off the school bus one November morning and a truck had run right over it. 'I was with you, remember?'

'Sure.' Nick was looking in the torn paper.

'I said inside the official present.'

Nick looked intrigued. 'Inside the gloves.'

'The left one.'

Nick felt inside the glove and pulled out a gift-wrapped parcel no more than an inch square.

'Be careful,' Holly said again. 'It's fragile.'

He squeezed the little package, puzzled. 'It's soft.'

'Open it.'

He took it out of the paper and stared at it, lost for words.

'You're blushing,' Holly said triumphantly.

'Jesus,' Nick said, softly.

'It's a condom.'

'I know what it is,' Nick said.

'Don't you want to?'

57

Nick's throat was tight and dry. It was not the first time he had held a condom in his hands. At school they'd all fooled around with them any number of times. A lot of kids claimed they'd used them. Nick thought a few of them probably had.

'They're weird looking things, aren't they?' Holly said.

'Sure are.'

'I don't mind—' Holly stopped.

'What?' Nick looked at her.

'I was going to say, I don't mind if we don't use it. I just thought you'd say we should wait until we had one. Knowing you, Mr Better-Safe-Than-Sorry.'

'You're right,' Nick admitted. 'I would have.'

'So now we have one.'

Nick was silent.

'Don't you want to make love?' Holly's voice wavered a little for the first time, hurt getting ready to make its entrance.

'Sure I do,' Nick said. He swallowed. 'More than anything.'

'Really?'

'I think about it all the time.'

'Me too.'

'I'm just—' He hesitated.

'Scared?'

'A little.'

'You don't have to be,' Holly said. 'Not with me.'

Nick looked into her face. 'No. I guess I don't.'

'I love you, Nick. So much.'

'Me too.'

'How about it then?'

'Now?' He was startled. 'Here?'

'It is my birthday,' Holly said. 'And that is my Christmas present to you. Don't you think this should be the day?'

'Yes. In a way.' Excitement began to shove anxiety out of Nick's mind. 'But what if someone comes in?'

'You said they won't.' Holly was confident.

'They might come upstairs.' Anxiety returned in full force. This was not a good idea, Nick decided. It might, in fact, be one of Holly's worst ever, but he didn't have the nerve to tell her that in case she got too upset. 'My mom's bound to come up any second now and ask us if we want anything.'

'Then we'll tell her we don't.' Holly sat on the edge of Nick's bed and patted the quilt. 'Come on.'

'Holly, it's crazy.'

'No, it isn't.' She looked at the door. 'Just jam the chair under the handle. That way the worst your mother could get is suspicious.'

Nick looked at the chair and back at Holly, at her beautiful eyes with their enormous black pupils, at her lips. A sudden, curious, rushing, physical kind of hope shot through his body like a flame. 'Maybe you're right. Just this once.'

'Do it,' Holly urged him.

By the time he'd moved the chair, carefully and almost silently, Holly had already pulled her sweater over her head. It was not the first time Nick had seen her in her bra – they'd been fooling around at the very edge of this for a couple of months now. Nick had meant what he'd said about thinking about it all the time. He thought about sex with Holly just about every minute of every day.

'Come here,' Holly said, softly.

He walked towards the bed.

'Take off your sweater,' Holly said. 'That's good.' He was sitting beside her now. 'Now undo my bra.'

Nick's fingers were clumsy, trembling a little as he reached behind her and unhooked the flimsy cotton and lace brassiere. He had touched Holly's breasts many times, but up until now he had only caught glimpses of them as he'd fumbled in darkness, pulling up the sweaters or blouses that had been in his way. Now, though, there they were, naked and bold, pale and soft with perky pink nipples, and Nick wanted to kiss them, to suck those nipples, to bury his face between them.

'Go on,' Holly whispered, urged. 'Go *on*.'

Once it began, there was no stopping it. The mutual nakedness was so different, so much more fantastic than all the half-blind groping around had been, and as Holly unzipped his good Christmas Day trousers, Nick needed no more urging to do the same for Holly's skirt, and then he was dying – just *dying* – for more, and her pantyhose were on the floor, and then her panties, too, and her hands were dragging off his own shorts. His penis sprang free, and they lay down together, and Holly's hands were all over him, on his chest, on his back, on his buttocks, and, oh, *Jesus*, that felt unbe-*liev*-able, and they started kissing then, such deep, glorious, wet, probing kisses, and they just got him harder and harder, and he could hear himself groaning right into her mouth.

'I want you,' Holly moaned, pulling her mouth away. 'I want you right *now* . . .'

'Me too.' Nick was panting. 'Oh, God, me too.'

Holly opened her legs, and Nick stared down at the magical V, at what nestled between – the sweet mound of dark, curling hair – and a brand-new panic flared up inside him; for how in the name of sweet Jesus was he going to put his enormous, pulsating penis inside that scarcely visible place that he'd only played with until now with his fingers?

'Come on, Nick.' Holly's grey eyes were huge, pleading. 'Come *on*.' She held out her arms to him. 'Come on, I'll help you.'

She knew she could help him, knew the way better than he did, for hadn't she been playing those games, practising alone in her room under the covers late at night, thrusting a finger into her hungry wetness the way she'd read in her mother's old copy of *Scruples*? – and then, as she became more skilful and more avid, bunching first two and then three fingers together, pushing them as high up into herself as she could – though she'd known it wasn't the same as the real thing would be. And now there it was, her darling Nick's cock was right there, plump and juicy and quivering, and she just couldn't bear to wait another *second*.

'The condom,' Nick said, suddenly, remembering.

'Oh, God,' Holly moaned. 'Forget the condom.'

'But it's important.' Frantically, Nick looked around for it. 'We have to—'

'No,' Holly told him firmly, her voice suddenly louder, more commanding. 'We don't.'

Nick looked down at her, at her pretty face, changed now with her wanting, cheeks flushed, eyes almost foxy, lips swollen, and he stopped panicking about the condom or about how he was going to find his way into her. Instinct was going to take over now, he knew it, and they did love each other, so it had to be okay, and anyway, like Holly, he couldn't, he *wouldn't*, wait another second.

Their bodies came together again, and her soft tautness beneath him was heaven on earth, and they kissed again, and he reached down with his right hand and took hold of himself and started trying to find the place, and he couldn't at first – oh, Christ, he couldn't *find* it – and then Holly's hands were helping him, and she was opening herself further, and there it was – oh, God, oh, Jesus, here it *was* – and he was pushing a little, and he heard Holly gasp and give a small, soft cry of pain, and he started to pull out, afraid of hurting her—

'Don't,' she hissed at him. 'Don't stop, it's okay.'

So he didn't stop. He pushed again, and it was tight in there, tight and smooth and warm, and suddenly Holly made another of those weird, wonderful sounds, and it all started to change; she was moving her hips, and he was moving too, and it became impossible to differentiate the sensations on and around his penis and testicles from the feelings he was experiencing throughout his entire body.

'Holly,' he said. Just her name, nothing else, but the single word was filled with wonder and glory.

'Oh, yes,' she said, rocking back and forth.

'Oh, God,' Nick said, knowing he was coming – any second now he was going to come right there inside her – and some vague, blurry thought about the condom came back into his mind for an instant, but he shoved it away and plunged right on—

The sound at the door froze them both.

Nick stared down into Holly's face, saw his own terror mirrored in her eyes. He was still deep inside her, could feel her trembling, but he didn't dare move a muscle.

The sound came again.

A kind of snuffling.

'Who?' Nick mouthed at Holly.

She shook her head.

Another snuffle.

Holly started to laugh, very quietly.

'What?' Nick whispered, appalled. '*What*?'

'It's the dog,' Holly said, still laughing. 'It's your goddamned *dog*.'

Nick listened. Half of him wanted to laugh too; half of him wanted to scream.

'Matisse,' he hissed, 'go away.'

The dog scratched at the door.

'Get *lost*, Matisse,' Nick commanded, not daring to shout.

The dog went on scratching.

'Oh, Jesus,' Nick moaned. 'Matisse, will you go *away*.'

The animal scratched harder, and the door rattled.

'He's not going anywhere,' Holly said, still laughing.

Nick groaned. Slowly, carefully, aware that he'd lost his erection, he withdrew from Holly's body.

'Oh.' Holly grinned. 'Poor baby.'

'Jesus, Mary and Joseph,' Nick said, collapsing beside her. 'Damned dog.'

Holly thought for just a second.

'*Canis interruptus*,' she said, with pride.

Nick looked at her with a mixture of disgust and admiration.

Only Holly Bourne would speak in goddamned *Latin* at a time like this.

10

Sex was like electricity to me at sixteen, all-enveloping, a rush a million times greater than smoking, drinking, truanting or shoplifting. I might have found those things more of a turn-on than I had wanted to admit, but at least I had always recognized that they were wrong, bad. Sex didn't feel bad to me. Sex felt pretty damned fantastic. And it was, of course, Holly who had initiated me into the wonders of it – as it had always been Holly who had initiated me in every great or small illicit adventure – her fifteen-year-old body so soft, so tight, so uninhibited, so *irresistible*.

By the time I came to the uncomfortable awareness that having sex with an underaged girl was probably more heinous a crime than stealing, it was too late. I was hooked. If I'd thought about sex with Holly a lot before we started doing it, now I thought about it every waking moment. I dreamed about her at night when I was *able* to sleep, lay awake in bed fantasizing about her when I was not. It was disturbing and it was wonderful. It was incredibly uncomfortable and disruptive and amazing all at the same time.

I guess I was a kind of an addict. All the good things in my life – all the safe, normal things – began to suffer. My painting changed. Up until that time, no matter what had gone on in my world, more than anything else it was beauty that had turned me onto painting. People told me they liked my work because it made them feel good. My sketches of them; my watercolour landscapes; my pen and ink drawings of Washington DC. But the more I screwed around with Holly or *thought* about screwing around, the darker and weirder my work seemed to get. Instead of painting the dreamy rural scenes I'd always liked – still liked, but couldn't seem to manage any more – I produced a Maryland landscape that looked as if a tornado was about to rip its way out of a purplish, bruised, wild sky. Rather than portraying people in a kindly way, as I almost always had, I went abstract, presenting my poor art teacher, Miss Stein, with a picture of a man's head split horribly in two. I didn't like it any more than she did, but there didn't seem to be much I could do about it. I guess I didn't know anything about testosterone highs in those days.

It went on and on. Holly and I couldn't get enough of each other. She was a natural. She read raunchy books, but I'm not sure she needed them. At fifteen years of age, Holly Bourne was managing to work out for herself the mind-blowing variety of things a boy and girl could do to each other for pleasure. And even if some kind of suppressed guilt was tarnishing the love affair a little for me, not only was I not arguing with Holly against it, but I was drinking at her well like the thirstiest of young savages.

Until the afternoon of August 18th, 1983.

11

The day was hot and humid. Nick and Holly had been swimming in the Bournes' pool. Carmelita had brought them lemonade and cookies. Nick had rubbed suntan oil into Holly's back and shoulders, and she had returned the favour. And then, hungry for one another, they had adjourned to the small, cool summerhouse behind the pool.

'I want to try something new,' Holly said.

The by now familiar shiver of excitement stroked Nick's spine, making him tingle. 'What?'

'The French call it *soixante-neuf*,' Holly said, softly, and her eyes gleamed in the dim light. 'Sixty-nine to you.' Nick was not much for foreign languages.

'What is it?' Nick was avid.

Holly came very close. He could smell chlorine and perfume and suntan oil and the other, very particular, scent that always came off Holly when they made love.

'We both go down on each other at the same time,' she whispered in his left ear. 'It's called sixty-nine because we're both kind of upside-down, so that's what we look like.'

'Jesus,' Nick said, breathing fast, already hardening. The things that Holly was willing and eager to do never ceased to astound him. He thought about them later, sometimes, and a sense of shame almost threatened to overwhelm him, but then he would start to remember the way it had actually *felt*, and the shame would slip away again as perfectly as something disappearing under a quicksand. 'When?' he asked.

'Now.'

'We can't,' Nick said. 'Carmelita might come out again.'

Holly shook her head and stepped away. Her hair was still wet, slicked tightly back over her scalp, and her body shone with oil. She had an idea she looked exotic and impossible to resist, like something out of a magazine. She knew by now that Nick would not resist her, and she loved the sense of power that gave her.

'She won't come out again,' she said. 'She likes taking a nap around this time. Her siesta.'

'What about your parents?'

'They're still at work. You know that, Nick.'

'I still think it's dangerous,' he said, half-heartedly, more than open to persuasion.

'You love danger,' Holly said, coming close again.

'Not as much as you do.'

'You love me,' she said, nuzzling his neck.

'Jesus, Holly.'

'You want to suck me off, don't you?' She took his right hand and guided it down to the bottom of her swimsuit. 'You want me to do that to you, don't you?'

'*Jesus*, Holly.'

They were devouring each other so intently that they didn't hear a single sound until Eleanor – back home early from work for the first time in months – opened the summerhouse door and walked right in on them.

'Holly,' she said, 'go into the house.'

That was all she said. Not another word. No screaming or cursing or making threats. Eleanor merely waited in absolute, deafening silence as Holly wrapped herself in a towel and Nick, his face aflame, scrambled to pull on his trunks. And then, very coldly and deliberately, Eleanor swung her right hand, striking him hard and noisily on his left cheek and catching his mouth with a gold ring, drawing blood.

Holly ran out of the summerhouse, sobbing, and Nick skulked home, managing, thank Christ, to avoid Ethan and Kate who were both working in their respective studios.

He knew, of course, that it could only be a temporary reprieve. He knew it was only a matter of time – maybe minutes, maybe an hour – before one or both of Holly's parents came to their front door and

66

brought the full force of their wrath down on his miserable, aching head.

He knew, too, right there and then, that it was all over. Holly and Nick were finished. No more glorious, painful, confusing secret explosions of fire and juice. If he got horny, he was back to taking care of that on his own under the covers or in the shower.

Though frankly, remembering Eleanor Bourne's face, he could not imagine ever getting horny again.

Eleanor and Richard stood together later that hot August evening before the Millers' dead fireplace, refusing to sit, fearsomely united in their condemnation of Nick, who was upstairs in his room. Holly, too, was upstairs in the Bourne house, confined to quarters.

'Your son's very, very lucky,' Richard Bourne, pale and shaken, told an appalled Ethan, 'that we care too much for our daughter's good name to have him arrested for raping a minor.'

'Don't you think that rape is overstating it somewhat?' Ethan asked.

'Of course it is,' Kate said, hotly. 'Surely neither of you believes that Holly's been blameless in all this?'

'Holly is most certainly the victim in this situation,' Eleanor said. 'Holly is only fifteen years old.' She was majestic in her quiet, digni-fied outrage. 'Your son is almost seventeen. Holly is a slender, light-boned young girl. Your son is a tall, strong young man. There is,' she said, her tone final, 'nothing to argue about.'

'There is,' Kate pointed out, 'if you're going to use words like rape.'

'This is a perfectly clear-cut situation.' Richard Bourne was sud-denly business-like, very much the confident lawyer. 'Either Nick stays right away from Holly from now on, or the police will be called and charges will be brought.'

'And I promise you,' Eleanor added, 'whatever the legal outcome, none of your family would ever recover from that scandal.'

'Please,' Kate appealed, shocked. 'Can't we try to—'

'Facts are facts, Kate,' Richard cut her short. 'I'd say, once again, that Nick is getting off very lightly.'

'He ought,' Eleanor said, 'to be whipped.'

'He certainly ought,' Richard added, 'to be in court.'

'We're so very sorry,' Ethan told them, taking Kate's hand and squeezing it tightly for moral support. 'You must know – you *have* to know – that we're just as horrified as you.'

'I seriously doubt that,' Eleanor said.

'We will, of course,' Richard pointed out, 'be taking Holly to see our doctor. If there are any long-term ramifications—' He paused, his attorney's composure deserting him, unable to go on.

Kate saw that his hands were trembling, and experienced a fresh surge of rage against her son. Nick had to have realized, damn him, what he was getting himself into – and given what he and Holly had apparently been up to in the summerhouse, this could hardly have been their first time. Changes she had been noticing in him swept suddenly, shockingly through Kate's mind. She thought about the strange developments in his work, recalled a conversation with Beatrice Stein, Nick's anxious and suddenly disappointed art teacher, three months ago – three *months* ago – and the abrupt realization that Nick and Holly might have been this deeply, this crazily entangled for so long, made her feel physically sick.

Richard had rallied and was continuing. 'If the doctor finds any signs of long-term repercussions, either physical or emotional,' he said, 'then we may still be forced to bring in the police.'

'We understand,' Ethan said, numbly.

'I hope you do,' Eleanor said.

Repercussions.

Kate stared miserably at her husband, and then back at the Bournes.

'Yes,' she said, quietly. 'We do.'

Though he couldn't hear the actual words, Nick, listening from his open bedroom door upstairs, put together a pretty fair picture of what was happening down in his own living room. But he never found out exactly what went on inside the Bournes' house that night or in the days that followed.

Kate and Ethan were perfectly clear with him on their own stance. They could try – with a great deal of difficulty – to empathize with him, they said, on the grounds of youth and passion and first love. But the law was plain, making those feelings, and most certainly the act itself, simply and utterly *wrong*; and threats of prosecution

68

notwithstanding, Nick was going to have to comply exactly with the Bournes' wishes, or face the consequences.

'Which would mean juvenile court at best,' Ethan reminded him.

'They could lock you *up*, Nick,' Kate added passionately, desperate to make him realize the direness of his situation.

'I don't see that they could prove rape,' Ethan said, struggling for a scrap of comfort.

It was the first time Nick had heard that word used. Horror filled him like sickness. 'Holly didn't say I raped her! I don't believe that.' It was a plea. 'Holly could *never* have said I raped her!'

Over in the corner of the living room, Matisse whined.

'No one exactly said that she did say that.' In spite of himself, a wave of compassion gripped Ethan.

'You can be damned certain that's what Richard and Eleanor will be claiming if it comes to prosecution,' Kate said, anger and fear still keeping her from gentleness.

'Not necessarily,' Ethan said. 'Holly's a minor – that would be enough on its own.'

Nick stared at both his parents' faces. 'She did want to,' he said, quietly, pleadingly. 'She always wanted to. You have to believe that.'

'We do believe that,' Kate said, allowing him that much.

'We know you would never force yourself on a girl,' Ethan added.

'We also know that you've broken the law,' Kate went on, relentless again, 'and you've betrayed the Bournes and us. To say nothing of Holly.'

'Holly *wanted* it,' Nick said again, desperately.

'Stop *saying* that,' Kate yelled at him, suddenly. 'For heaven's sake, Nick, it isn't as if it's the first time you've broken the law! We thought all that trouble, all that crazy wildness, was behind you – behind *us*.' She shook her head despairingly. 'My God, Nick, I always thought we'd brought you up to respect the rules, to respect *people*, but you've let us down so badly I can hardly believe it.'

Matisse whined again, stood up and then lay back down, his head between his paws. And at that instant, Nick understood, for the very first time, what an outsized fool – what a *jerk* – he had been all those times when he hadn't told his parents that Holly had been the brains behind his brushes with authority. Even if he had been guilty of going along with her, if he had only *talked* to them in those days, confided in them instead of playing the dumb white knight, they might have stopped him from seeing Holly; and at least, even if they still blamed him now, they might understand that she wasn't the wide-eyed innocent the Bournes were claiming she was.

'I guess there's no point trying to explain about those other times now,' he said, knowing how lame he sounded.

'No point at all,' Kate said.

'I don't see that there's much *to* explain,' Ethan said, softly, and somehow his father's gentler disappointment was infinitely more wounding to Nick than his mother's anger.

'I guess not,' Nick said.

'Promise us one thing,' Kate said.

'I'll stop seeing Holly,' Nick said quickly.

'That has to go without saying,' Ethan told him.

'Promise us that Holly couldn't be pregnant.' Kate's blue eyes were fixed intently on Nick's.

He said nothing. He couldn't speak.

'Oh, my God,' Kate said, her face whitening.

Ethan's voice was even softer than before. 'You did take precautions, son, didn't you?'

'For the love of Christ,' Kate said, her horror growing, 'tell us you're not as irresponsible as that.'

'We did,' Nick said, hearing his feebleness and nauseated by it. 'Sometimes.'

'Nick, how *could* you let us down like this?' his mother asked.

'How could you let yourself down?' his father said, and, without another word, walked out of the room.

12

Holly remembers that day, too, and what came after.

Of course she does.

If she closes her eyes, even now, all these years later, she can still conjure up the old memories, can vividly remember the hunger and the fabulous, ferocious, sweating feeling of being with Nick at that time when their bodies and all their senses were so young and raw and bursting with life.

She remembers her parents, too. Especially the naked, blazing fury on her mother's face when she found them in the summerhouse.

Oh, how she hated Eleanor that day.

Not just that day.

She remembers her mother taking her to a doctor, making her lie on a table while the stranger in a white coat told her to open her legs and then clamped her open with cold steel and put his gloved fingers up inside her. Eleanor thought that she was so mortified by it all. Eleanor didn't realize that the whole time the doctor was examining her and Holly was lying there, eyes shut, cheeks hot, she wasn't really *there* at all – she was thinking of Nick, imagining that the fingers inside her were *his*, and it was all she could do to stop herself having an orgasm right there on the examination table.

It was all over now, Eleanor told Holly.

It wasn't over, Holly told her mother, because they loved each other.

That was nonsense, Eleanor said. If Holly believed that Nick loved her, she was a fool. He had taken cruel advantage of her innocence, Eleanor said. He was no better than a beast and he deserved to be punished for it, though Eleanor and Richard were mindful of Holly's reputation, which was why – for the moment, at least – they would take no action.

Unless he came near her again.

'*You and he are finished.*'

Holly remembers those words.

Remembers weeping over them. And then laughing, too, secretly in her bedroom. Because they were, of course, a lie, and a measure of her mother's ignorance, because Nick was her destiny.

Holly knew that, and so did he. It might take weeks or even months, but it was only a matter of time before they would be together again.

It never occurred to her back then – not even for a single second – that Nick might betray her, any more than Eric ever had.

But it is true what they say.

One lives, and one learns.

72

13

I swore to my parents that I would do what the Bournes were demanding and stay away from Holly, as far as that was possible, given that we were still next-door neighbours. I felt so bad about everything – almost everything, at least. That was the weirdest part of the whole catastrophe, in a way. I had expected to feel terrible about breaking up with Holly, yet now that it was over, now that I had been given no choice but to stop seeing her, I felt a kind of relief. I don't know, maybe – I wonder now, more than a decade later – maybe I had been hoping to get caught. Maybe I had wanted to be stopped.

The fact was, as the first week passed, and then the second – and Holly was not pregnant, and the full wrath of the Bournes did not descend on me – I found that, while I did desperately miss having sex with Holly, I wasn't sure how much I actually missed *her*.

That thought made me feel guiltier than any of the crimes we had committed together over the last several years. It made me wonder if I was, at heart, a shallow, selfish, callous person, and the very fact that I was now spending more time worrying about my own reactions than about what Holly might be going through next door, made me dislike myself even more.

Thanks to our parents' vigilance, I had only one brief encounter alone with Holly during that initial period of disgrace, when I was out walking Matisse one Saturday afternoon in October in the woods behind Leyland Avenue. Holly was sitting on an old tree stump staring at the pond – the same pond in which her brother had drowned –

when she saw me. She cried out, jumped to her feet and came running over, flung her arms around my neck and kissed me on the mouth, and I confess that I was startled enough and glad enough to kiss her back for a good few moments before I remembered myself and pulled away.

Holly told me that she knew I was staying away from her because I had no choice. She said that she knew I wanted us to be together every bit as much as she did, that parental power alone – God *damn* them, she said, crying a little – was keeping us apart.

And what did I say to her? Did I seize that opportunity for honesty? Did I tell Holly that I thought maybe our parents were right? Of course I didn't. I was too cowardly for that. Oh, sure, I excused myself by imagining that I was saving her feelings, but all I was really being was a lousy, stinking coward.

Holly didn't realize that it really was over. Holly loved me, God forgive me. That seems an egotistical thing to believe, but I do believe it was true. As long as we were having those incredibly hot, passionate, secret meetings, my need for Holly had been all-consuming. Now that that had been ended, I think she needed me far more than I needed her. I cared about Holly, I had a lot of complicated feelings about her – I guess I probably had genuinely been *in* love with her – but I don't believe now that I ever really *loved* her.

Shame on me.

MAY

14

Holly has been having a brief post-honeymoon visit with her parents at home in Bethesda. She and Jack left Grand Cayman airport a few days ago, parting with loving, newly-wed embraces before boarding their separate early morning flights to Los Angeles and Washington DC.

It's been a pleasant trip back home, with both Richard and Eleanor patently delighted by her happiness. Holly knows that in marrying Jack Taylor, the perfect, conventional choice, she has sealed yet another of Eleanor's ambitions for her: a wealthy, attractive, professional husband. Eleanor Bourne likes life to be neatly mapped out. The next of her goals for Holly will be a partnership at Zadok, Giulini & O'Connell. Then a first child – ideally a son – for Jack.

It's different with her father. Richard likes and respects Jack Taylor, but his greatest concerns are for his daughter's well-being and happiness rather than for her status or wealth. Holly spent almost twenty minutes in the washroom on her United flight from Grand Cayman perfecting the right expression to convince her father of the joys of the honeymoon. Richard has, after all, spent a lifetime seeing through people on the witness stand and is not an easy man to fool. But then again, Holly knows that she's a better actor than most – and anyway it's to her advantage that Richard *wants* to believe that she's happy with Jack.

And she almost is – at least, happy enough to cope. So long as she can go on dreaming about Nick. So long as she can go on fantasizing – as she did every night of her honeymoon – that it's *him* making love to her, not her husband.

* * *

It's the last day of her visit. Richard and Eleanor have a fund-raiser to attend that evening in Georgetown, so Holly has told them that she will take a cab to Dulles in time for her six o'clock flight to Los Angeles.

'Are you sure you're going to be all right, darling?' Eleanor asks her before they leave. It's Carmelita's day off. 'I feel so bad leaving you alone like this.'

'I'll be fine.' Holly smiles at her mother. 'It's been a wonderful few days, Mother. Just like old times.'

'I know your father's loved having you home again.' Eleanor's expression is uncommonly tender. 'And so have I.' She pauses. 'I'm very proud of you, Holly. You do know that, don't you, darling?'

'I do, Mother,' Holly says.

Holly does know it. So far as Eleanor is concerned, she is now a substantial success story, but then again, anything less, Holly also realizes, would in her mother's eyes be evidence of some failure of her own. Had Eric lived, it might perhaps have been different; with a golden son, there might have been room in Eleanor's heart for an imperfect daughter. As it is, Holly knows that her mother has long since blocked out the nightmarish Holly-blaming months following Eric's drowning, just as she thinks that Eleanor has probably by now almost entirely blotted out the sight of her daughter sucking Nick Miller's cock in their summerhouse thirteen years ago.

'Do you ever hear anything about Nick Miller?' Holly asks Eleanor now, casually, as Richard descends the staircase, attractive and dignified as always in his dark suit.

'Only more about the success of his little book,' Eleanor says disparagingly.

'I hear there's going to be a movie,' Richard says, adjusting the knot of his grey silk tie in the Queen Anne hall mirror.

'Just a cartoon,' Eleanor says. Nick Miller could win an Oscar or a Nobel Prize and Eleanor would still dismiss it. Nick has, and always will, represent only three things to her: mediocrity, crudeness and trouble for Holly.

'You don't ever discuss me with the Millers, do you?' Holly asks her parents suddenly.

'Of course we don't,' her father answers. 'You asked us not to.'

Holly looks at her mother. 'Neither my career nor my marriage?'

'Kate Miller asks about you, of course, from time to time,' Eleanor

78

says, 'but I tell her as little as possible. They know that you're married, and they know that you're doing well, and that's all.'

'So they don't know I'm living in Los Angeles?'

'Certainly not,' Eleanor assures her. 'At least, not from us. We hardly ever really see the Millers. We never did have anything much in common.'

'It's just,' Holly goes on, 'that Nick and I have made such a complete break now, and it's so clearly been the best thing for us both.'

'You don't need to explain it to us.' Richard pats her arm.

'The only pity is that it didn't happen long before,' Eleanor says.

'Water under the bridge,' Richard says.

'Now you have Jack,' her mother adds.

'Looking forward to getting back to him?' her father asks.

'More than anything,' Holly answers.

She waits until their black limousine has turned the corner at the end of the street. Quietly, gently, she closes the front door and walks over the lawn to the house next door. She knows they're home, saw them through her parents' drawing room window when they returned, loaded with shopping bags, two hours earlier.

Ethan Miller opens the door.

'Holly,' he says. 'What a nice surprise.' He says it as easily as Holly remembers him saying most things in the past, but she sees a wariness in his brown eyes. Nick's eyes.

'I've been visiting,' Holly explains. 'I thought it might be nice just to say hello. It's been a while.'

'A long while,' Ethan says.

He invites her to come inside. Nothing much, she sees, has altered. The house smells, as it always did, of painting, though the old reek of dog has gone.

'No Matisse,' she says.

'Matisse died.' Kate Miller comes out of the kitchen, wearing jeans, T-shirt and white moccasins. 'Hello, Holly. What brings you here?'

'Holly's been visiting with her parents,' Ethan reports.

'I know she has.' Kate smiles at Holly. 'We hear congratulations are due. On your marriage,' she adds, to jog her husband.

'Of course.' Ethan remembers. 'It's great news, Holly,'

'Still in New York?' Kate asks.

'Where else?' Holly says.

They move into the living room. It, too, seems much the same. Shabby in comparison with Eleanor Bourne's perfection, but many times more comfortable. A home for artists. Holly can feel ghosts shifting inside her. She has a desire to be left alone in this room. In this house. She wants to go up the staircase to Nick's old room, to lie on his narrow boy's bed, and to remember. Not that she has forgotten.

'Can we get you something to drink?' Kate is asking her.

Holly shakes her head. 'No,' she says. 'Thank you.'

'Why don't you have a seat?' Ethan offers.

He removes a book from one of the armchairs, stands holding it. Holly sees that it's *The Catcher in the Rye*, old and dog-eared. She remembers Nick loving that novel.

'I won't stay,' she says. 'I just wanted to say how glad I am about Nick's success with *Firefly*.'

'Have you read it?' Ethan asks.

'Of course,' Holly answers, but offers nothing more.

'It's been very exciting for them all,' Kate says.

'I'm sure it must have been.'

No one mentions Nina by name, or Phoebe, or Nick's marriage, but the moment is as strained and awkward as the rest of the encounter.

'Are you sure I can't get you anything?' Kate asks. 'A glass of juice or some coffee?'

'No, thank you,' Holly says again. 'I'm about to leave for Dulles.'

'Back to New York,' Ethan says, just for something to say.

'Back to my husband,' Holly says.

She can see a photograph on a table behind Ethan Miller. Nick and the blonde, presumably in their own living room. He is standing behind her, not much taller than she is. His thick, wavy hair is shorter now than it used to be. The art student is long gone. He looks older. His arms are around his wife; his hands, covering hers, are resting on her stomach. Her stomach is flat, but their faces are both filled with pride. There is no doubt.

The shock almost fells Holly. It takes every ounce of strength to stay standing upright. To keep from screaming.

'I must go now,' she says, suddenly.

She gives Kate her cold hand and smiles.

'Have a safe journey home, Holly,' Kate says. 'And take care of yourself.'

Holly shakes Ethan's hand too. He walks her out to the front door, hesitating briefly, as if debating whether or not he should kiss her cheek. He does not. They have both been pleasant and polite, but she knows they are relieved that she's leaving.

'Tell Nick I wish him and his wife well,' Holly says.

'We will,' Kate says.

As the Millers' front door closes behind her, the cab Holly booked earlier draws up outside her parents' house. The driver, a middle-aged, tired-looking man, gets out.

'I have bags,' she tells him.

She gives them to him, asks him to wait for her outside.

The entrance hall of her parents' house is cool. Holly's cheeks are burning hot. She leans against the closed front door and shuts her eyes.

Nick is going to be a father.

Nick's baby.

The sickness overwhelms her so swiftly that she only just makes it to the powder room in time. Afterwards, she finds that she's shivering and perspiring. Slowly she gets up from her knees, rinses her mouth, splashes her face, dries herself with one of Eleanor's fluffy white monogrammed guest towels.

She looks in the mirror. Her face is white. She closes her eyes again, takes a few deep breaths. She's beginning to feel better. The desire to scream has left her. Completely.

Miraculously.

She keeps her eyes closed, and images float into her mind. From a dream she had on her wedding night in Los Angeles.

Nick, loving her.

She thinks she knew, even then, that it was too vivid, too *real*, to have been a dream – that Nick was actually *with* her. She doesn't understand how, but maybe in life there are some things it's better

81

not to understand or rationalize. All she's certain of is that now, at this very minute, she knows for sure. She *knows*.

She opens her eyes. Everything seems brighter. Clearer than before.

A baby.

Nick's baby.

Holly smiles into the mirror.

JUNE

15

'You're seven months pregnant, Nina.'

'I think I know that, Phoebe.'

'You get backache, you're tired, you pee all the time.'

'I hadn't noticed.'

'You won't be able to sit still for hours on end, and you can't go in and out of a courtroom because you have to keep on peeing.'

'I suppose I can't.'

'The doc said you shouldn't travel unless you really need to.'

'Okay, Phoebe.'

'And it isn't as though I can't do this without you.'

'I said, okay, Phoebe. You can go without me. You *should* go without me. I'll stay at home and keep house.'

'You'll stay in the office and keep Ford Realty running.'

'Okay, Phoebe.'

'And Nick can keep house.'

'Don't you just love new men?'

Ever since her sixth month, when she'd had an episode of light bleeding – which her obstetrician had reassured them had been minimal and of little concern – it had been an almost ceaseless battle for Nina to stop both Nick and Phoebe from over-cossetting her. They didn't seem to realize how great she felt, how unimaginably *wonderful*. Some of that well-being, she accepted, was due to hormonal changes, but she knew, too, that it was far more significant than chemistry. This new life growing inside her, this constant companion, was bringing her a tranquillity she had never known before. Not even Nick, who had given her so much joy and confidence and ease, had brought her such extraordinary *peace* as this unborn child of theirs.

'I can understand Nick fussing,' Nina had said to her sister more than once, 'but you're usually so sensible.'

'Since when?' Phoebe asked.

'Since always.'

'I've never been an expectant aunt before.'

'Well, all I can say is thank God Dad's in Arizona,' Nina said. 'If he were here too, driving me crazy, I don't know what I'd do.'

'You should make the most of it,' Phoebe told her. 'Once the baby's born, we'll all ignore you.'

'I look forward to it,' Nina said.

The trip to Los Angeles was necessary because Ford Realty was having to sue Bradley, Pearce, Dutton, an LA-based corporation, for reneging on a property deal. It was not either of the Ford sisters' idea of fun; they both tried to avoid legal tussles whenever possible, but there was just no avoiding this one because there was simply too much money at stake. BPD had, initially, been Nina's client, but since she and Phoebe pooled information at the close of almost every business day, it was perfectly feasible for Nina to give a deposition to Michael Levine, their attorney, and for Phoebe to make the journey from San Francisco without her.

'You know I don't really like LA,' Phoebe reminded Nina.

'I know you don't.' Nina's sympathy was ironic.

'I suppose I'll just have to make the most of things.'

'I suppose you will.'

'Think I should stay at the Beverly Hills?'

'Oh, definitely. Where else *could* you stay?'

'And I suppose I should drag myself out to Rodeo Drive at least once.' Phoebe sighed. 'Maybe look out for something gorgeous for you to wear in the last couple of months.'

'Don't waste money on me,' Nina said. 'I'll be skinny again soon enough.'

'Maybe I'll just pick up something wacky for the baby.'

'You're going to be in court, remember?'

'Not all the time,' Phoebe said. 'They always have a million adjournments – think of the OJ trial.'

'This is not murder, Phoebe.'

Phoebe sighed again. 'I know.'

16

The other side has won, but neither Holly nor Stanley Pearce, her client, was expecting any other outcome, and Holly knows that she has at least succeeded in keeping BPD's financial pain well below the threshold they can afford.

'Pearce may give you a rough ride after the verdict,' Alan Zadok warned her a week ago, 'but that's only because you're new.'

'And I'm not a partner,' Holly said then.

Zadok shook his balding head. 'Pearce knows this is small potatoes. And I've told him you'll do a fine job.'

'Not a bad result, Ms Taylor,' Stanley Pearce concedes now, shaking her hand. 'I'd have preferred an outright win, of course.'

'As would I, Mr Pearce,' Holly agrees.

She doesn't apologize for losing; she knows she has nothing to apologize for. Holly hates losing at anything, but this case was cut and dried long before the file was dumped on her. Besides, she has other, more important things on her mind.

She looks across the courtroom at her opponents. She's been wondering ever since being assigned the case which of the partners would show.

Stanley Pearce takes his leave. Holly spends a minute or two assembling her papers and files, keeping one eye on Michael Levine and his client.

She waits for the right moment. And then she stands and walks across the room.

'Ms Ford?'

The redhead looks up. 'Yes?'

'Charlotte Taylor.'

'Yes, I know.'

'Congratulations,' Holly says. She nods at Levine. 'To you both.'

'You, too,' Levine says. 'Good job.'

'You won.'

'Sure did.' Levine grins.

'Shall we?' Phoebe Ford rises from her chair, ready to leave.

'Ms Ford,' Holly says, 'do you have a moment?'

'Of course.' Phoebe looks a little puzzled.

'It's a personal matter,' Holly assures Michael Levine.

'Fine with me.' Levine checks with his client. 'See you outside?'

'Sure,' Phoebe says.

Holly waits for the other lawyer to go. She wonders if Phoebe's going to remember her face. She makes a mental wager that even if she does, the other woman won't make the connection to the New York signing.

'I'm sorry to hold you up, Ms Ford.'

'Not at all.'

'I just wanted to tell you how much I loved *Firefly*.'

Holly watches the other woman's pale face light up with genuine pleasure. It's so easy to make people feel good.

She goes swiftly on. 'I'm expecting a baby and I'm really looking forward to the day when I'll be able to introduce my own child to the book.' She pauses. 'I just wanted to let you know that. I hope you don't mind.'

'Hardly,' Phoebe says. 'It's a wonderful thing to hear.'

'*Firefly*'s a wonderful creation,' Holly tells her.

'Only partly mine,' the other woman points out.

'I know.' Holly pauses. 'It must have been a happy collaboration for you and your family.'

'It was,' Phoebe confirms.

'Not every woman gets along so well with her brother-in-law.'

Phoebe smiles. 'Nick Miller's very special.'

'He must be,' Holly says.

She can see Phoebe looking at her with a touch of renewed curiosity, and knows that her memory has been jogged.

'Is something wrong?' Holly asks.

Phoebe shakes her head. 'For a moment I had a feeling we'd met before.'

They say their farewells and begin to walk out of the courtroom.

Another wager won, Holly thinks.

Near the door, Phoebe stops.

'The Wordsworth quote,' she says, softly. 'It was you, wasn't it?'

Holly smiles. 'Yes, it was.' She wonders if the blonde would have been as sharp.

'When's your baby due?' Phoebe asks her.

'Not for a long time yet,' Holly answers.

'I'm happy for you, Ms Taylor,' Phoebe says.

Holly's pleased with the way things have gone. It doesn't bother her at all that Phoebe Ford remembered her. Moments like that only serve to sharpen the game. Holly loves games.

She started devising this one soon after she realized that she was pregnant during her visit home to Bethesda. Though, of course, it all really began about eight months before that when she met Jack – her perfect excuse to move West. There are many more games to come. Games within battles within her own special war. Holly especially likes games with risks attached to them. They are, after all, what have always made her function best, even as a child; the risk-taking, the gambles against the odds.

If only Nick hadn't betrayed her, it would all be so much simpler, so much more straightforward. Holly would not have been forced to marry Jack, would not have felt compelled to make love to another man. But Nick has taken this other woman, this *wife*, and though Holly knows, without question, that, ultimately, she will forgive him, there are punishments to mete out first.

The eventual outcome, of course, is not in doubt.

Nick will come back to her.

Her prize.

This is not Ford Realty against BPD.

This is the real thing.

17

'The strangest coincidence,' Phoebe told Nina later on the phone.

It was early evening in her room at the Beverly Hills Hotel. The 'pink palace', as it was fondly known, had been renovated from top to toe since Phoebe had last found reason to stay there, and what had been exquisite before was even more so now. Outside, the evening air was soft and fragrant with bougainvillaea, oleander and jasmine. Somewhere, not too far away, someone was partying. Phoebe could hear a piano and laughter, and gossip and the chinking of glasses, none of it intrusive, simply adding more delicate layers to the whole.

'Remember the woman at one of the book signings in New York in April?'

'I remember a lot of women,' Nina said.

'The one who dictated the quotation you thought was bizarre.'

'The Wordsworth?' Nina did remember.

'She was the attorney for the other side.'

'For BPD?' Nina was surprised. 'She's a lawyer in LA?'

'And a good one,' Phoebe said.

'Did you speak to her?'

'She came over after the hearing and told me she was pregnant, and that she was looking forward to introducing her child to *Firefly*. Wasn't that nice of her?'

'Very nice,' Nina agreed. Her hands moved automatically to her own belly.

'How're you feeling?' Phoebe asked.

'Wonderful.'

'She-he kicking much?' Phoebe refused to call the baby 'it'.

'Not too much. More when you're around.'

'Eager to see Aunt Phoebe. Wise she-he.'

'What are you doing tonight, Aunt Phoebe?'

'Room service. I've ordered just about everything there is. I'm starving.'

'Enjoy it,' Nina said.

In the background, Phoebe heard Nick's voice.

'What's Nick saying?'

'He says well done, and he sends his love,' Nina transmitted.

'Give him a hug from me,' Phoebe said.

'See you tomorrow, darling,' Nina said.

'Don't forget to tell Nick about Wordsworth.'

18

Holly and Jack are in the tub in the master bathroom of Jack's house, a few blocks from Brentwood Country Club on San Vicente Boulevard.

About five hours have passed since the resolution of Ford Realty v Bradley, Pearce, Dutton. The Taylors have eaten dinner, and now they are reading briefs in the tub. They both love their bath. It's large, round, gleaming black and doubles as a jacuzzi, and since Holly installed a splash-proof reading stand on a gilt arm which swivels to any chosen position to suit the bather, Jack has decided that it's the closest place to heaven.

Holly stops reading.

'I'm going to go into private practice,' she says, as calmly as if announcing a shopping trip to Rodeo Drive.

'What?' Jack is startled.

'You heard me.'

'What are you talking about? You've only just joined Zadok, Giulini.' Most people skip the 'O'Connell' when they talk about the firm. 'I thought you were happy there.'

'Not really,' Holly says. 'You know I've always wanted my own criminal law practice.'

'It's news to me, honey.'

'I told you when we first met,' Holly says, though she knows she told him nothing of the kind. She could not have done because she only decided it herself at six o'clock this very evening.

Jack reaches out to switch off the air jets. He's frowning, he looks concerned. 'Honey, I remember I asked you if you'd considered joining the DA's office, and you made a point of telling me then that you wanted to stay in corporate law.'

'I didn't say that exactly,' Holly says and switches the jets back on.

92

'Yes, you did.' Jack smiles at her, his indulgent smile. 'Don't you remember? You told me you graduated third in your class and made Law Review and passed the bar exam first try, and I told you you were probably the stuff to go to the top as a prosecutor if you had a mind to, and you told me you preferred the cooler cut and thrust and impersonality of corporate law. Too much humanity in crime, you said.' He nods, pleased. He takes pride in the agile, retentive memory that has served him so well as an attorney. 'Those were your exact words, Charlotte, honey.'

Holly leans back, reaches for her Chanel soap and begins washing her left leg, starting at the foot. 'Well, if they were,' she says, steadily, 'maybe I wasn't quite ready back then to share my inner ambitions with you.'

Jack watches her for a moment, the arched foot with its painted toenails, the strong, slender calf and thigh. His wife has the capacity to turn him on with the slightest effort. It appears now that she also has the capacity to take him completely by surprise.

'Okay,' he says. 'So what's your plan?'

Holly smiles. 'Look for suitable premises, commission my sign—'

'Charlotte Taylor. Attorney at law. Just like that.'

'Just like that.' Holly begins soaping the inside of her left thigh, then stops and hands the bar of Chanel to Jack. 'Feel like helping me?'

'Always,' he says softly, taking the soap.

'Look for clients,' Holly goes on.

'Want my help with that?'

'I don't know. I'd rather go it alone, if I can.'

Jack nods and leans forward, reaching between his wife's legs. 'What about your father? He'll want to support you too.'

'I expect he will.' Holly shuts her eyes as Jack rubs the soap over her clitoris, imagining, as she almost always does, that his hands are Nick's. 'I hope I won't need him.'

Jack stares at her, half perplexed, half admiring. This is a wild, and probably unwise, idea of hers, but then, of course, potentially brilliant as Charlotte is, she does seem to have a track record of making spur-of-the-moment decisions. And since one of those was to abandon a perfectly healthy career in Manhattan to come West with him – and since he makes more than enough money for both of them – he decides he isn't about to rock their marital boat by arguing about this new scheme.

Especially not when he's as iron-hard as he is right now.

19

It comes back to me sometimes in fragments: bright, painful flashes of feeling. But the memories themselves, alas, are all too whole. I wish they were not.

When Holly, the teenager, first realized that I was surviving too well without her, she decided to take her revenge by spreading a rumour around our high school that I had sexually assaulted a thirteen-year-old girl. Being mercifully unsubstantiated by real accusation, the rumour died a natural death, but it was a frightening and ugly time for me. My parents backed me up, knew it was all lies, yet they still blamed me indirectly. I had, after all, been guilty of the crime the Bournes had accused me of, and I had hurt Holly badly – and I was *damned* lucky she hadn't gotten pregnant – so I had no choice, Ethan and Kate both said, but to put up and shut up.

At least one thing was clear, I figured: Holly's love had turned to hate. It wasn't right for me to hate her back, I realized, since she'd only been lashing out with lies because of her own wounds. But Holly hated me now, for sure. And yet the next time I had anything resembling a conversation with her – about eighteen months after the summerhouse disaster – and told her that I would be leaving Bethesda soon to study fine art and film art at NYU, you might have thought, from the shock on her face, that I'd told her I had two months to live.

I had been in New York for a little over a year when, in the fall of 1986, Holly showed up one Sunday morning at my apartment on Christopher Street in the Village. She had changed a lot. The nymphet was gone, and in her place was a composed young adult law student. She was only there, she told me, to say hi, because we were both at NYU now and it seemed foolish to pretend we weren't. She was living in a dormitory and content. She liked the way I looked, liked my hair long and tied back in a ponytail, liked my new beard. She said I looked like a pirate. She also said that she couldn't stay long because she was meeting friends, but that it felt good to know she had a big-brother-type to turn to if she ever needed help. If I didn't object.

Of course not, I said.

The past was all forgotten, apparently. I thought I believed her. I *wanted*, I guess, to believe her. So when, a few months later, she came back begging to be allowed to stay a while and share the rent because she was having such a bitch of a time in her dorm, I swallowed my doubts. *Big brother*, she had said, hadn't she, in her new, laid-back, grown-up way? She offered to sleep on the couch, but I told her if she found a fold-away bed she could sleep in my studio. She said that would be great, but if ever I was painting up a storm late at night she'd take the couch instead – and really, if we stopped to think about it, maybe this was fate pushing us together, and it would be almost like old times. Only almost, she added, and laughed.

I told myself it would be okay. It might even be fun having her around again. And anyway, I still owed her, didn't I?

And for six whole months it *was* fine, because Holly had grown up big-time. We both had. I could not have wished for an easier lodger.

I should, of course, have known better.

20

On April 11th, 1987, a Saturday night, Holly and Nick brought a Chinese take-out back to the apartment, drank a bottle and a half of cheap Chardonnay while watching a TV rerun of *Un Homme et Une Femme*, and ended up in Nick's bed.

'Are you sure this is such a hot idea?' Nick asked Holly, right after she had pulled her T-shirt up over her head, exposing her well-remembered pale, uptilted, pink-nippled breasts and the tender, sweet valley between them.

'How can you *ask* me that?' she answered.

And after that, of course, it was too late.

He knew, the instant he awoke to see the dark outline of her head on the pillow beside him, that he had made a bad mistake. And when Holly woke up just a moment later and saw the look in his eyes, Nick knew that he had just compounded that mistake by hurting her again.

'It's okay,' she said, quickly, lightly.

'Holly—' He started to sit up.

'No, really, it's okay.' She turned her head away, but it was obviously she was close to tears.

'God, Holly, I'm sorry.' Her hurt, his guilt, dismayed him. 'I mean it, I'm so sorry. I should never—'

'I told you, it's okay. It took two, remember?' She was already out of bed.

'But I should have—'

'Leave it, Nick.' She was pulling on her clothes. 'I agree with you. It was dumb of us both. We've got a great friendship going here. We

96

should forget it happened.' She forced a smile. 'See? I've forgotten it already.'

The downhill slide began. Holly said one thing but did another. On one level, she was perfectly amenable, never failing to do her share of chores and immersing herself in her prelaw freshman studies – but at the same time, on a more insidious level, she became increasingly hard to live with, frequently turning on displays of possessiveness in front of Nick's friends, and often actively insulting them in a clear attempt to push them away.

'She's more like a nagging, dominating wife than a room-mate,' Jake Kolinsky, a fellow art student, commented once after a particularly unpleasant evening at home with them both. 'Why don't you ask her to move out, Nick?'

'I've dropped hints,' Nick told Jake. 'I've suggested she might be happier living someplace she'd have more space to call her own, but she always says she's perfectly happy with me and then changes the subject.'

'I'm sure she is happy,' Jake said, 'but you're not.'

'No, I'm not,' Nick agreed, 'but I don't really want to hurt her again.'

Then his mother wrote to him. Generally, Kate wrote about once a month, warm, chatty letters written in a straightforward, easy style.

This one was strained from the first line.

Dear Nick,

I'll come straight to the point, because I've learned through the years that that's the best way. Your father thinks we should mind our own business. But I'm afraid I disagree.

Holly wrote to Eleanor and Richard about your new love affair, and I'm sure you won't be surprised to learn that Eleanor, for one, is not pleased with the news. I think that the only thing preventing her from employing some sort of hit squad to wipe you off the face of her personal world is that Holly made it so clear that she's happier than she's ever been in her life.

I'm not writing to try to put you off Holly. Far from it. It might, I suppose, have been to be expected if you and she had both stayed home. But with all the wealth of choice there must

*be in New York City, your father and I both feel that this has to
mean there must be something very special between the two of
you.*

*Just so long as you're not sticking together because one or
both of you has been lonely. That would be a sad and foolish
reason to embark on something that clearly means a great deal
to Holly.*

*So what I'm saying, Nick, is this. You're both over eighteen,
but that doesn't mean you aren't still very young. Holly has had
to get over losing you once. Be very careful that neither of you
gets badly hurt again.*

Your father and I both send you special love.

    As always.

Your mother.

It was the last straw. The clincher. Holly telling her parents that
they were in love, sleeping together and happily living together as a
real couple. The other stuff had been irritating, difficult and uncomfortable, but Nick had felt guilty enough about sleeping with her
again to put up with it. This was just plain weird.

And there was only one cure.

He told her that same night.

'This can't go on,' he said. 'I should never have let you stay in the
first place.'

'No,' Holly said, quietly. 'Perhaps you shouldn't have.'

He couldn't believe it was so easy. She started packing right away,
told him she'd be fine, that she had money and could go to a hotel
until she found a new place, and Nick was on the brink of telling her
that he hadn't meant she should go instantly – but then he stopped
himself. If he changed his mind now, who was to say he'd ever be rid
of her?

'Why did you *do* that?' he asked, almost curiously, as she hurried
to and fro in the apartment, assembling her belongings. 'Why did
you tell all those lies about us to your parents?'

'I'm sorry if it caused you embarrassment,' Holly said.

'For Christ's sake, Holly,' he said, and stopped.

And she went on with her packing.

JULY

21

Nina is eight months gone now and beginning to admit to feeling it. Her back aches, she doesn't sleep much at night, she gets cramps in her legs and has swollen ankles, but worst of all, from her point of view, she says she feels clumsy as a cow.

To me, she's lovelier than ever. She protests, but I try to sketch her whenever I get the chance, hungry to catch every change, every fragment of miracle. Her breasts, full and wondrous, ready to sustain our child. Her belly filled with the still unknown mysteries of 'she-he,' as Phoebe calls the baby. I try all I can to help, but I'm constantly aware of my uselessness. I can only rub her back and massage her legs to ease the cramps, and fight with her when she does too much around the house and in the office.

'You should be letting Phoebe handle all the valuations and outside appointments from now on,' I told her last week.

'Phoebe's busy enough,' Nina said.

'She wants to help,' I reminded her.

'She also knows that I hate sitting still in the office all day,' Nina argued. 'And you know it, too.'

My wife is a stubborn lady.

My heart feels a little, I imagine sometimes, like Nina's belly: close to bursting, but with purest joy and anticipation. I dream of 'she-he' almost every night now. I never quite see the baby's face, but I feel its essence, and the air in my dreams seems filled with my pride and love.

Nina wanted so badly for us to make love last night, but I was too afraid of hurting her or the child.

'I want to,' she said. 'One last time, while we're still as we are.'

I saw the yearning in her face, and wanted her more than ever, but nothing would sway me; nothing she nor any doctor might say would persuade me to take even one scrap of a risk with my beloved wife or my fragile daughter-son.

'We'll always be as we are,' I told Nina.

'Do you promise me that?' she asked me.

I promised her.

22

Holly has her practice. An average kind of office suite on the eighteenth floor of one of the steel and concrete giants on Figueroa Street: a neat waiting area where her secretary can double as receptionist, and two decent-sized rooms, one of which houses her law library, the other, with its limited downtown LA view, providing her own office. The discreet plaque on the outer door reads:

TAYLOR, GRIFFIN
ATTORNEYS AT LAW

Griffin is a silent partner in this practice, because he or she does not exist, but Holly likes the ring of substance in the name, and the touch of anonymity it affords her. Taylor is not an uncommon name. No need to blare this particular achievement to the world.

She has no permanent secretary yet, just a temp to answer the phone, take messages, write letters and open junk mail and bills. She also has no clients. That's fine for now, because this is part of Holly's learning curve. Holly has decided to be a fine defence lawyer. She doesn't care if she never gets to be Clarence Darrow, but she wants to learn to be as good, manipulative, cunning and useful a defender as possible. Her library is what counts most in this office. And the telephone. And the television set and computer. Holly is currently in the business of discovering what's going on in the world of small-time crime in western California. She reads every newspaper, watches every news bulletin, regularly downloads the contents of the news-database service the firm's subscribing to, spends a lot of her time in court – observing, listening, studying – and what time there is left talking to those who know all about the things she wants to learn.

Holly learns fast. She always has. And what she's learning right now is how Charlotte Taylor, defence lawyer, can best persuade the legal network to spill its secrets for her. Cops are good sources, though she knows enough to pick those too new to have grown hostile to defence attorneys, or those old and ugly enough to be too grateful to give a shit. Assistants in the DA's office are particularly fruitful, as, of course, are crime reporters. So long as they're men and heterosexual, and have plenty to lose if they brag about laying a married lawyer.

They love the tightness of her ass, the pertness of her breasts, the size and colour and perfection of her big, pregnant nipples, the softness of her still almost flat stomach. They love the way she uses her hair, grown longer since her marriage, the way she lets it down and trails it over them. So long as Holly shuts her eyes and pictures Nick beneath her, she can bring a man to climax using nothing more than her hair.

Her mouth, of course, is even better.

Jack thinks she was nuts to leave Zadok, Giulini. Holly knows he thinks she's gone a little nuts, period. She also knows that he'll go on indulging her because he's still crazy about her. Here's this brilliant, beautiful woman who does things to him no other woman has ever done, and she's his wife, for God's sake, his *wife*, which makes Jack Taylor, in his own eyes, one of the luckiest sonofabitches in greater Los Angeles. What does he care if she doesn't bring in big bucks into the bargain? Jack didn't marry Charlotte Bourne for her money or her talent as a lawyer. So, for the time being at least, he'll go on being an easy-going husband, indulging this whim, maybe even patronizing her a little now and then.

Holly doesn't give a damn about being patronized, but she's only just managing to hold it together with Jack. She's always been a pretty fine actress, but there are limits, even for her. She can cope with sex in a good cause with men only too happy to find a gorgeous, classy woman prepared to fuck their heads off without any demand for commitment – but this constant nightly sham of not only loving but *wanting* her husband is starting to prove almost too much for her to bear. Sex with Jack was endurable for a while, but in the first place he kisses too wet for her realistically to go on pretending she's kissing Nick; and in the second place Jack prides himself on being able to keep pumping away at her for so goddamned long that Holly's been torn between throwing up from motion sickness or going to sleep. She could, of course, simply tell him that she's having a baby and that she's nervous about hurting it which is why they can't have sex any more for a while, but, since – apart from her nipples – she doesn't really show at all yet, she has no intention of telling Jack about the pregnancy. What he doesn't know can't hurt him, after all, and ignorance has to be a happier state for him than finding out that she's having another man's child.

She'll be gone before he notices anything, but in the meantime, she's stuck with him, for better or worse. Though knowing what she wants out of life, and what she is, ultimately, going to achieve, makes things just about bearable for now. She wants what she's always wanted.

Plus ça change . . .

Holly has her plan, after all.

And it's about time to make her first major move.

23

Phoebe was alone at the Ford Realty office on Union Street when the fax came in.

> To: N. Ford, Ford Realty
> From: G. Angelotti
> *Confidential*
> (Sent via Fax Modem, therefore unsigned)
> 17 July 1996
> Dear Ms Ford,
>   I've recently inherited a house at 2020 Catherine Street in Haight Ashbury which I wish to sell as soon as possible. Your services have been particularly recommended to me, which is why I'm giving you first opportunity. If you're interested, please visit asap to value and prepare details. I've left the keys inside the large crack to the left of the porch, and I'd be grateful if you'd post them through the mailbox when finished.
>   I'm out of town until next week, so would you please fax my secretary by return at the above number to let her know if you're going to attend today.
> Yours sincerely,
G. Angelotti

Phoebe glanced at her watch. It was getting close to three-thirty. Not much time to get everything done and drive over to the Haight, and with Nina finally agreeing to take some rest, and Betty Hill – their office manager – and Harold, their secretary, both down with the flu, it was tempting to toss the fax to one side. G. Angelotti, whoever he or she was, certainly wasn't allowing Ford Realty too much time.

Phoebe ran a check on the computer and found no Angelotti, though of course the fax had mentioned a recommendation, not previous dealings. She considered calling Nina at home to check with her, but decided against it, since it had taken her and Nick a whole lot of time and energy to persuade her sister to stay put for once. And she certainly wasn't going to trouble poor Betty, not when she was running a fever and aching from head to toe.

She and Nina tended to avoid viewing unoccupied properties alone – but then again, Phoebe hadn't seen anything worthwhile on Catherine Street in a very long time, and some of the Victorian houses in one section of that winding, rather characterful street did have great sales potential. She certainly hated the idea of letting those keys sit there where anyone might find them, and not taking a look today was tantamount to telling G. Angelotti to take the business to another realtor . . .

She faxed back her reply, waited for confirmation that it had been sent, and then she switched on the answering machine, locked up the office and headed for Haight.

2020 Catherine Street stood in a section of row houses that were clearly on the verge of being beyond help. Further down the hill, some of the well-kept, almost immaculate properties that Phoebe had remembered, only served to emphasize the sad contrast between them. 2020 was dingy and neglected, its paintwork flaking, its woodwork rotting, its once handsome stonework crumbling. No wonder G. Angelotti was hoping to unload her or his inheritance as quickly as possible.

Phoebe parked her Mazda the way all San Franciscans were taught to (by law and by necessity) on the steep hills – wheels to the kerb facing downhill, to the road when facing up, handbrake tight – and got out of the car, heaving her overladen canvas shoulder bag off the passenger seat.

She checked over the house and its neighbours from where she stood. Most of them looked uninhabited, and the property two doors along from 2020 sported DANGER warning signs at the first-floor windows and across the front steps. At least the Angelotti house wasn't quite in that category.

'One thing's for sure,' she said, softly. 'Your new owner's a bit of an optimist, thinking we can sell you as you are.'

Phoebe often spoke to houses, particularly those that struck a chord in her. Which this one did, in its own dismal way. Maybe some client on Ford Realty's lists might feel similarly, might be prepared to take on 2020 Catherine at the right price and nurse it back to health. She and Nina both loved these intricate Victorian houses with their pillars and arches and elaborate, complicated cornices and unexpected twists and turns. Both Ford sisters felt protective about the old properties and the history they represented, reasoned that if they had survived a century, a monster earthquake and a great fire, then no one had the right to allow them to crumble into decay.

She took a few more moments looking around, trying to get a handle on the present residents of Catherine. Parked vehicles aside, there weren't many clues. Four houses along from 2020, two casually-dressed young women stood chatting at the front door of one of the better properties, and on the other side of the street a middle-aged, too-thin man in shorts and sandals walked slowly and breathlessly up the hill. A black and white cat lay, sunbathing, on the fourth step of the house immediately opposite where Phoebe stood.

Nothing and no one else.

'Okay,' Phoebe said, addressing 2020 again and hitching her bag up onto her shoulder, 'let's go see what you're really made of.'

She started up the crumbling steps towards the front door and, she hoped, the crack sheltering Angelotti's keys. Halfway up she stopped, suddenly unsure if she'd remembered to bring along her electronic measuring gizmo. She opened her bag and rummaged through. No gizmo.

'Oh, phoo,' she grumbled at the house. 'That means I'm going to have to pace out every one of your damn rooms and corridors. Happy now?'

She started up again, her mind and hands still buried in the bag, only half-concentrating on where she was planting her feet. Her fingers closed on something metallic caught in the bag's lining – she paused again to look and leaned back against the balustrade for balance.

She heard the sound about one second before it gave way.

A cracking. 2020's own private quake.

The rail was the only thing there was to grab on to.

It and Phoebe fell together.

24

From across the street, out of sight behind the steps of the empty house opposite 2020, Holly watches for a long while. Her heart is pounding too hard and her palms are moist with a kind of panic and confusion. Holly is not accustomed to feeling like this, unable to think properly, smoothly.

She thought she had prepared so carefully, so thoroughly. She made sure that the blonde was still going out on valuations despite her advanced state of pregnancy – only *yesterday*, for heaven's sake, Nina Ford Miller was valuing an apartment in Presidio Heights. Holly has taken care every step of the way, inventing G. Angelotti but sending the fax from a public machine on Market Street so that it bore a San Francisco fax-back number for added credibility.

She checked in at the Huntington yesterday afternoon, having told Jack she was coming to meet a prospective client's business partner. She told Jack she couldn't tell him much about the case, and Jack scarcely raised an eyebrow, simply kissed her long and hard and told her to be careful and that he was going to miss her. Jack doesn't know that his wife has already come to San Francisco twice this past month, taking an early flight up and returning late the same afternoon. He doesn't know that on both occasions she spent several warm, tiring hours, shielded by large sunglasses and a hat, blistering her toes on a cross section of the city's less than immaculate streets in order to choose the most workable site for her plan. Holly steered clear of Pacific Heights and Cow Hollow, knew they were too close to both the Millers' home and Ford Realty's office, aware, in any case, that she was unlikely to find suitably neglected properties in those districts. She was beginning to think that she might never find the right house, that she might

109

even have to go with her Plan B (taking a sound building and rendering it unsafe herself), but sabotage was a much riskier scheme and one with which she would have been far less at ease.

And then she found Catherine Street and its crumbling, potentially lethal row houses.

She knew, late last night when she left the hotel and came to Catherine Street and took away the DANGER signs at 2020, that someone other than Nina Miller might be the first up those treacherous steps and into the house – that someone else might get hurt. But somehow she didn't picture it happening so swiftly, before they even reached the front door.

And she did not picture it happening to the redhead.

Time passes. On the other side of the street, Phoebe Ford lies very still in the rubble at the base of the steps of 2020. There is no one else around. The two women who, not long before the collapse, were standing at a front door four houses away, have vanished inside. The thin man who was walking up the hill turned a corner and disappeared before Phoebe fell. Even the black and white cat that was sunbathing on the steps behind which Holly is waiting has skulked away.

The wheels of Holly's mind are starting to turn again.

There. There. You're you again. No need to panic.

Her heart rate slows. Part of her brain, she realizes as she calms down, is simply registering a degree of guilt at having involved an innocent party, and irritation at having missed her target. But another, more dominant, part is already beginning to calculate how best to utilize this new, unexpected situation.

After all, she reasons, everyone knows there's more than one way to skin a cat.

And maybe there's more scope to this particular skinning than she might, at first, have thought.

She goes on watching.

Phoebe does not move.

25

They were sitting in the garden, watching the charcoal on the barbecue burn, waiting for it to turn white, when the telephone rang.

'I'll go,' Nick said.

'No, you cook.' Nina struggled to her feet. 'I'm too hungry to wait much longer.'

'If it's Phoebe, tell her we've plenty if she wants to join us.'

Nick watched his wife walk into the house, thought, with one of his frequent rushes of pleasure, how graceful she managed to remain in spite of her size, and then he looked back at the charcoal.

'It's ready,' he called out. 'I'm starting.'

He put the chicken pieces on first and basted them with marinade. The aroma sprang into the air immediately, making his mouth water. He reached for his white wine spritzer and took a sip.

He heard a sound from behind and turned around.

Nina's face was white as chalk.

'Sweetheart?' Nick put down his glass. 'What is it?'

Her mouth moved, but no words came. Quickly, Nick went to her, put his arms around her, tried to push her down onto one of the garden chairs.

'*No!*' She pushed him away, the word shrill, alarming.

'Nina, tell me – what's happened?'

Her eyes were torn wide, staring at nothing.

'Phoebe,' she said.

They waited at People's Hospital for a long while, knowing nothing more than that Phoebe had met with an accident at a house in Haight Ashbury and had sustained serious injuries. A doctor, young, harried

111

and tired looking, came to see them, explained that Phoebe had two badly broken arms requiring urgent attention, and some head injuries, extent as yet unknown.

Nina, as next of kin, signed the papers consenting to surgery, but asked unnaturally few questions.

'These head injuries,' Nick said, quietly, reaching for Nina's arm. She felt stiff, like a doll. 'Are they bad?'

'As I said, we can't assess that yet.' The doctor paused. 'She's unconscious, and we've put her on a respirator—'

'She's on life support?' Nick was horrified.

'It isn't as bad as it sounds,' the doctor reassured him. 'We often put head injury patients on a respirator simply because it breathes quickly for them and helps decrease any swelling on the brain.'

'So there's no immediate danger?' Nick asked.

'That's right.'

Nina moved away from Nick.

'What about brain damage?' Her voice was quite loud and hard, not at all like her normal voice.

'It's too soon to say, Mrs Miller.'

'When will you be able to say something?' Still that harshness.

'This is an inexact science,' the doctor answered. 'Until your sister regains consciousness, or we've run some tests, we won't be in a position to answer any more questions. I'm sorry.'

The waiting began again. Nick watched Nina's face growing more strained with each passing half-hour and knew that there was nothing he could say or do that would persuade her to go home or even lie down.

'You want to go home, you go,' she said once, unfairly.

'I'm going nowhere,' Nick said.

Twenty minutes later, she went into labour. Nick stayed with her while things got underway, ascertained that her own obstetrician was en route, and then went to make the call he had been dreading.

'William Ford.'

Nina's father always answered in that clipped, crisp way. Phoebe had joked once about it being a pity that her dad's time with the RAF had come after World War Two because his manner, even sight unseen, was enough to scare a Messerschmitt out of the sky.

'William, it's Nick.'

The silence was fleeting, but telling.

'What's happened to Nina?'

'She's gone into labour.' Nick's chest felt tight.

'It's too early,' Ford said.

'Thirty-six weeks.'

'Are the doctors concerned?'

'They seem pretty confident.' It was hard to find the words. 'Phoebe's had an accident.'

'What do you mean?' Ford waited a second. 'What do you *mean*?'

'She had a fall.' Simple was the only way to tell it. Simple and stark, the way it was. 'We don't know exactly what happened. She went to see a property, and a wall collapsed.' Nick's heart wrenched, but he forced himself on. 'Phoebe's badly hurt, but they don't know yet how badly.' He decided against specifically mentioning head injuries – time enough when the man arrived. 'They're operating now to set some broken bones in her arms,' he said.

The new silence did not mask Ford's anguish.

'I'm on my way.'

'Good,' Nick said, as gently as he could. 'I'll tell Nina.'

The line was cut.

Shortly after one in the morning, not long after Phoebe's surgery had ended, Dr Judith Liebowitz, one of the investigating physicians, diagnosed a subdural haemorrhage. Within a half-hour, while Nina laboured on another floor of the general hospital, a team of surgeons were drilling burr holes in Phoebe's skull, draining the blood clot that had formed, and clipping the ruptured vessels.

A nurse, coming in to the labour ward to report to Nick what was going on in the OR, made the error of speaking in earshot of Nina. Her blood pressure shot up and her pulse began to race.

'I want to know everything that happens to Phoebe,' she said between contractions, gripping Nick's hand so tightly that her fingernails cut into the palm of his left hand. 'Don't you dare let them keep anything from me. You tell me *everything*.'

'I will, sweetheart,' Nick soothed her, silently cursing the nurse.

'You swear it.'

'Don't worry.'

'*Swear* it, Nick.'

'Cross my heart and hope to die.'

'Phoebe's okay,' Liebowitz, petite, black-haired and energetic, reported to Nick ninety minutes later outside the delivery room. 'The surgery went beautifully.'

'Is she conscious?' Nick asked.

'Not yet, but that's to be expected with this type of injury.'

'Is she still on a respirator?'

'For the time being.'

'What can I tell my wife?'

'Tell her to worry about giving birth and leave the rest to us.'

'You don't know Nina,' Nick said.

'So tell her the truth.' Liebowitz smiled and patted his arm. 'It's good news, after all.'

Their daughter was born at six minutes to five next morning. She weighed four pounds and twelve ounces, was placed in an incubator, given oxygen and humidity and fed through a nasogastric tube.

'She's what we call moderately premature,' a paediatrician told Nick. 'She has a few problems right now, but nothing we can't deal with.'

Nina – who had been so calm through every stage of her pregnancy, who, even through her labour pains had been so distracted by her sister's plight that she had seemed scarcely to register her own physical state – now began to come apart. Nick, afraid for her, sat by her side, held her hand, stroked her hair, tried every way he could think of to allay her fears, but knew it was impossible to do so.

'She'll be all right,' he told her. 'I know she will.'

Nina stared at him wretchedly, bitterly. 'Our daughter or my sister? Who's going to be all right, Nick?'

'They both are,' Nick said.

'How do you know that?'

He held fast to her icy hand. 'I know it because Dr Liebowitz said Phoebe's surgery was successful, and I know that our little daughter's going to be strong, just like her mother and her aunt.'

'You don't know that,' Nina said. 'You can't know it.'

'I can, Nina,' he said forcefully. 'And so can you.'

114

'I want to see my baby again,' Nina said.

'She's sleeping. The nurses say that preemies really need their sleep, and we should fit in with her natural patterns.'

'I hate that word – preemie.'

'It's just a word, sweetheart.'

'I want to see her now.'

'Soon,' he said.

'She's so *tiny*.'

'She's beautiful,' Nick said.

Nina shifted restlessly in the bed. 'I want to see Phoebe.'

'You have to get stronger, sweetheart.'

'I'm strong enough now.'

Nina tried to sit up but fell back again. For just a moment, she seemed, at long last, on the edge of tears, and Nick almost longed for the release, for her sake, but it was not to be. Nina lay back against the white hospital pillows, and stared at the ceiling, and though her lips moved a little, she made no sound.

Nick's fear for her grew.

William Ford came, and Nina did give way then, wept in her father's arms while Nick, feeling suddenly, disturbingly, like an outsider, looked on. To him, Ford said hardly a word, but the hostility in his eyes was unmistakable. It was shockingly apparent to Nick that the older man blamed him in some irrational way for what, in the space of twenty-four hours, had befallen both his daughters – as if Phoebe might not have fallen, and Nina might not have gone into premature labour if Nick had taken better care of his girls.

'How exactly did it happen?' Ford asked him later, outside the ICU.

'No one knows exactly,' Nick answered. 'Phoebe was at a house over in Haight Ashbury and she fell from the front steps.' He paused. 'One of the paramedics said it looked as if a supporting wall had crumbled away. He thought maybe Phoebe was leaning against it—'

'What in God's name was she *doing* at a place like that?' Impotent rage and despair blazed from Ford's green eyes. 'My daughters are in real estate, not demolition. Why was she looking at a derelict house in the first place? Tell me that.'

'I don't know, William.' Nick stayed gentle, feeling for the man in spite of his own pain. 'I don't know any more than I've already told you.'

'Nina's falling apart,' Ford said, unnecessarily.

'Yes, she is,' Nick said.

'And do you understand what that could mean to her?' Ford challenged.

'Of course I do,' Nick said steadily. 'But I don't think Nina's going to start drinking again,'

'And what exactly do you base that on?'

'On being her husband,' Nick answered.

'You weren't there,' Ford said, and all the remembered agony of his wife's and Nina's alcoholism were in those three words.

'No, I wasn't.' Nick paused. 'But I am here now.'

The initial crises passed, and both Phoebe and the baby were pronounced in a stable condition. People kept asking the new parents what they were naming their baby, and Nick and Nina had been leaning towards Zoë for a girl several weeks ago – a lifetime ago – though they'd agreed to wait until they were certain that it suited her.

'You decide,' Nina told Nick now.

'We'll both decide,' Nick said.

'I can't.'

'I don't want to make that kind of decision without you, Nina.'

'Tough,' she said, and closed her eyes.

The baby, who had been diagnosed with jaundice on her sixth day of life and was being treated with phototherapy, was still in an incubator in the premature baby unit. Nick crouched beside his daughter and stroked her tiny right hand through the porthole with one of his fingers and wondered how in God's name he was supposed to know what name suited this fragile, pitiful scrap of mottled flesh and blood?

'Zoë?' he asked her softly through the glass. 'Is that a good name for you, sweetheart? Will you be happy with that?'

The infant squirmed and cried and Nick felt his heart contract at her helplessness and the thin, plaintive rage of her wail.

'I love you, Zoë,' he told her, and the sensation within him was so powerful it took his breath away. 'You get strong now, for your mommy and daddy.' There were tears in his eyes, but he made no attempt to brush them away. 'You be healthy and you grow, Zoë, my love, do you hear me?'

* * *

Flowers and messages of support came flooding in – from friends and relatives, from publishers, from Clare Hawkins, from Meganimity, from Betty and Harold at Ford Realty – but they were hardly noticed. At what should have been a time of profoundest joy, Nick felt only hopelessness and inadequacy as he watched Nina, discharged but refusing to leave the hospital, going back and forth between the ICU and the prem ward where she, like Nick, for the most part, could only gaze and touch through that damned porthole, without even the warmth and comfort of holding or nursing her fragile daughter.

Phoebe remained unconscious, yet Judith Liebowitz seemed optimistic.

'The scans have all been positive,' she explained, patiently, for the third time, to Nick, Nina and William Ford, in the corridor outside the ICU.

'Then why hasn't she woken up?' Nick asked.

'That's hard to say.' Liebowitz shrugged. 'At times like this, the body can develop all kinds of protective mechanisms. Recovery sometimes takes longer than expected. It could be that Phoebe just isn't ready to wake up.'

'But she will wake up?' Ford asked the question tightly.

'There's no reason to believe that she won't,' Liebowitz answered.

'Oh, God,' Nina said.

Nick reached for her hand. 'The news isn't bad, sweetheart.'

'But they don't know that, do they?' Nina said. 'They don't know anything for sure.' Her voice pitched higher. 'And what about her poor arms? Both in plaster like that – maybe she doesn't *want* to wake up.'

'Take it easy, my darling.' Ford put one arm around her shoulders and Nina let go of Nick's hand and leaned against her father. 'Of course she wants to wake up. She's going to be all right, I know she'll be back with us soon.'

'It's hard all round,' Liebowitz said, gently, to Nick, and smiled at him. 'You need to be very patient.'

Nick looked at Nina and William, at their closeness.

'Yes,' he said.

26

An investigator for the insurance company checking into Phoebe's accident, came to talk to Nina, Nick and William at the hospital on the eighth morning after Zoë's birth. They found an empty waiting room on the same floor as the premature baby unit.

He handed Nick his card. 'Lawrence Dinkin,' he said. He looked around for somewhere to put his raincoat. It hadn't rained for a while; it seldom did rain much in July in San Francisco. There was an antiseptic smell about him and the expression on his thin face was doleful. He would, Nick thought, have made a fine funeral director.

'What can we do for you, Mr Dinkin?' Nick asked.

'Why don't we all sit down?' Dinkin suggested.

'Will this take long?' Nina wanted to know. 'I want to get back to my daughter.' She was restless all the time, never settling in one spot for long, only sleeping when sheer exhaustion overcame her.

'I understand that, Mrs Miller.'

Everyone except Ford sat down, Dinkin with his briefcase on his knees. It was a nice enough waiting room, its walls almost covered with photographs of parents and their babies on the point of leaving People's Hospital.

'Have you found out what made that damned wall collapse?' Ford was seldom slow in coming to the point.

'The wall collapsed, sir,' Lawrence Dinkin answered, 'because that's what it was ready to do.'

'What does that mean?' Nick asked.

'It means,' Dinkin said, 'that the wall, front steps and much of 2020 Catherine Street were in an unsafe condition, and that this was known, to the owner and to the building firm which was getting ready to move in to start work.'

'Are you telling us the house was going to be demolished?' William Ford stood close to Dinkin, bending slightly from the waist and looking more than a little menacing.

'Not demolished, sir, no.' Lawrence Dinkin, accustomed to hostility in his line of work, was unfazed by the older man's manner. 'But much of the stonework, and the steps and porch in particular, were scheduled to be strengthened or rebuilt.'

'Then what was Phoebe doing there?' Nick asked.

'She went to value the house,' Dinkin answered.

'She wouldn't do that,' Nina said.

It was the first time she had spoken since they had all sat down. She had been very quiet – too quiet – too much of the time since the accident and Zoë's birth. Nick watched her sometimes when she was being particularly uncommunicative, sensing the constant thoughts and fears churning around inside her mind like a laundry overload in a tumble drier.

'Phoebe and I seldom take on houses in such poor condition,' Nina explained, 'unless we have a client we know is especially keen to take on renovation work – and even then we'd discuss it first and probably go together. We hardly ever go to empty properties alone.'

Mr Dinkin opened the briefcase resting on his knees, and pulled out a piece of paper. 'This was found in your sister's purse, Mrs Miller.' He leaned forward and handed it to her. 'It's a copy of a facsimile sent to the offices of Ford Realty shortly before Ms Ford went to Catherine Street.'

Nina read it. 'It's addressed to me,' she said.

'Yes, it is.'

'May I see it?' Nick asked. Nina passed it to him. 'Who's this G. Angelotti?' he asked right away, reading the fax and then passing it on to William Ford.

'I've no idea,' Nina said.

'A prospective client, it would seem from the fax,' Dinkin said.

'What does he have to say about it?' Ford asked. 'You have spoken to this Angelotti character, haven't you?'

Lawrence Dinkin looked up at William Ford, still standing over him. 'We haven't been able to trace any such person, sir.'

'What about the fax-back number for the secretary?' Nina asked.

119

'That number belongs to a machine in a public fax bureau on Market Street,' Dinkin replied. 'Unfortunately, they don't keep records of customers, so it wasn't much help.' He paused. 'Ms Ford did send a reply, by the way, Mrs Miller.' He checked his notes. 'At three forty-seven – probably just before she went to see the house. Your manager, Mrs Hill, found the original on her desk, and the bureau confirmed receipt, but no one ever came to pick it up or called about it.'

'So we don't even know know if Angelotti's a man or a woman,' Nick said.

'Not yet,' Lawrence Dinkin confirmed.

'Maybe you'd better try a little harder to find out,' Ford suggested.

Dinkin gave a thin smile. 'We've been very thorough, sir. The property at 2020 Catherine Street is owned by a woman named Mary-Anne Brown.'

'So what does she say about it?'

'Nothing at all. Mrs Brown is ninety-eight years old and lives in a nursing home in New Mexico. Her affairs are handled by a law firm by the name of Dwight, Abraham and Shapiro. I've talked at length with Joseph Shapiro, and it would seem that neither the fax nor G. Angelotti has anything to do with either the law firm or with Mrs Brown.'

'How can you be sure of that?' Nick asked.

'Mary-Anne Brown owns several properties in that section of Catherine Street,' Dinkin explained. 'Five of them are in roughly the same state of disrepair as 2020. Neither Mrs Brown nor any member of her family has expressed a wish to part with any of the properties, the intention being to renovate, restore and rent.'

There was a brief silence as Dinkin's information sank in.

'You're saying someone, under false pretences, deliberately got Phoebe to go and inspect a dangerous house,' Nina said slowly.

'The fax was addressed to you, Nina,' Nick reminded her.

'Indeed it was,' Dinkin agreed.

William Ford sat down at last, suddenly pale.

'You're telling us this was no accident, aren't you, Mr Dinkin?'

Dinkin nodded. 'It would seem to look as if that might be the case.' He paused. 'All Mrs Brown's other properties on Catherine Street have danger signs clearly displayed on their windows, and tapes marked DANGER tied across the steps to alert people to the risks.'

'What about 2020?' Nick asked.

'The passer-by who found Ms Ford after the accident,' Dinkin said, 'told the police that he didn't remember seeing any danger signs. He was correct – there were none when the paramedics arrived. But according to Joseph Shapiro, the builders swear the signs were on 2020, just as they were on all the others. If the builders are telling the truth, then that means the signs were removed.'

'By this Angelotti?' William Ford stared down at the copy of the fax still in his hands.

'By someone,' Lawrence Dinkin said.

27

Lawrence Dinkin spent a while longer with us this morning. He seemed to want to talk about us as a family, about how we relate to one another, the time we spend together, working and otherwise. He seems a dry kind of a man, not the type of person to be particularly interested either in art or in the world of children's literature, yet he expressed fascination in the way *Firefly* came into being and how we all felt and still feel about its great success.

Nina stood Dinkin for about another five minutes after she'd established that he had nothing more to offer on the cause of Phoebe's fall. 'If you don't need me,' she said, 'I have a new baby who does,' and then she simply walked out of the room. That left William, Dinkin and me. If I say that Lawrence Dinkin spent the next fifteen to twenty minutes pumping me about my relationship with my sister-in-law, and if I say that he gave me a nasty feeling that he was trying to decide if I might have some deep, dark reason for wanting Phoebe to take a dive off a derelict building, that probably makes me sound paranoid. But it is the way I feel – or rather, it's the way I *would* be feeling if I had the time and space in my brain to give a fuck what Dinkin thinks about me. Not to mention William, who spent the last portion of that interview staring at me with blatant suspicion, all his paternal antennae bristling, while the investigator asked his irritating, insulting, *crazy* questions.

My personal priorities right now are clearly sorted. I need my baby daughter to be released from that incubator into her parents' arms. I need Nina's sister awake and functioning and back to being Phoebe again, not this terrifyingly pale-faced, sleeping woman on white sheets. And then, after those two top-priority prayers have been granted, I need someone to find out who on God's sweet earth sent that fax, took away those danger signs and tried their damnedest to steal Phoebe away from us.

Except that G. Angelotti, whoever the hell he is – if he even exists – didn't send that fax to Phoebe, did he? He sent it to Nina. And as I told Lawrence Dinkin, that's just as wild, just as improbable as if it had been aimed at Phoebe, because everyone who knows Nina loves her, and Ford Realty is in the business of buying, selling and renting property, not making serious enemies.

'This has to be a mistake,' I told Dinkin. 'It *has* to have been an accident.'

'Under the circumstances,' the insurance man came back smoothly, 'that hardly seems possible, given that neither the owner of 2020 Catherine Street nor anyone connected with her, either knows a G. Angelotti or has even considered putting the house on the market.' He paused. 'Unless you have some alternative explanation, Mr Miller.'

I had none then. I have none now.

What Dinkin says is patently right. There is no mistake. Whoever sent that fax to Nina meant her to go to Haight Ashbury and, presumably, to climb those steps. And to fall.

I guess that gives me another priority, every bit as overwhelming as the others.

I need to protect my wife.

28

Not long after Holly moved out of my Christopher Street apartment in 1987, my mother wrote to me again to report that Holly had been back to Bethesda on a visit, and had told Eleanor and Richard all about our 'break-up'.

> *Your father and I* – Kate wrote – *are both surprised and disappointed in you for the shabby way you've treated Holly. We can't help wishing you could have acted with a little more sensitivity.*

It's hard to say who I was more angry with right then: Holly, for her lies, or my own parents for believing them. I called home, told my mother very coolly that in future she might consider asking me for my side of a story before accepting someone else's version. Startled and defensive, Kate asked me a few loaded questions and instantly concluded that I was older, that Holly was all alone in the big city in her freshman year, and that it was, therefore, my fault.

Why didn't *that* surprise me more than it did?

Less than three weeks later, my next-door neighbour Frank Zilotti moved out of his apartment. That same night I got home late after working my shift as a waiter at Bradley's (cash had been tight enough even when Holly had been sharing the rent, but now I was waiting tables and tending bar at the Village Gate to make ends meet) to hear the unmistakable sounds of a new tenant moving in. Furniture being moved around, doors opening and closing, soothing music playing. For a while it was Mozart, then Bach, then Sinatra and Jimmy Van Heusen took over with '*All the Way*'.

I was not particularly unhappy. It was late, but at least their taste was okay.

The song ended, there was silence for a second or two, and then it began again. I looked at the clock, saw it was almost two, thought about knocking on their door, decided to give my new neighbour a first-night break and went to bed. I was bushed anyway – I was generally tired enough to sleep through almost anything in those days.

I'd lost track of how many times Sinatra had told me someone loving me was no good unless they were going to love me all the way, when mercifully, I crashed.

Next morning there was blissful silence and I figured, as I poured my first cup of coffee, that the obsessive Sinatra-fest had probably just been some moving-trauma-related coping device. I forgot about it. I put in an hour's sketching, assembled my notes in readiness for that day's lecture on Chinese painting in the Yuan Dynasty, and was just closing my own front door when the door to Zilotti's old place swung open.

'Good morning.'

Holly was standing there in the doorway wearing frayed cut-off denims and a white T-shirt with red strawberries printed over the right breast. She looked like someone who's fixed up a surprise party and expects the recipient to be ecstatic.

I was not. I was shocked.

'Isn't this great?' Holly said.

'What are you doing here?' I asked, though it was, of course, perfectly obvious.

'It was all such a big, fabulous coincidence,' she told me, 'Zilotti's place being up for grabs just exactly when I was looking, and I decided it had to be fate dragging me back here. Don't you think it must be?'

I didn't think I ought to say exactly what I thought, so I kept silent and let her ramble on.

'And all our problems – *your* problems really, since I never had any – were mostly because of our living together in the *same* apartment. This way,' she went on, 'it'll really be almost like the old days

125

in Bethesda, don't you think? Best friends and neighbours. Could anything be more perfect?'

It was borderline alarming. It was so much like listening to an echo of what Holly had said almost a year before when she'd talked me into letting her become my lodger. All kinds of thoughts swerved through my brain and veered away again: thing I ought to say to her about her lies, and about her nerve in coming back, and about how she shouldn't bother unpacking because I had no intention of letting her stay there.

But there was no point saying any of those things, because it was no business of mine whether she lived in Zilotti's old apartment or not. Holly had presumably signed her lease and paid her rent.

And short of either breaking the law and physically throwing her out, or making my feelings blindingly clear and making an enemy out of her, there wasn't a single thing I could do about it.

As it had when we'd first shared my place, it started out well enough. We led different lives. I was in my junior year, Holly was a sopho-more. I was majoring in fine arts with film arts as my minor; she was studying prelaw. Much of my time – when I wasn't at the Tisch School – was spent uptown in and around the Duke and Chan houses and museums; Holly's working life centred around Washington Square and the law library in Vanderbilt Hall. If her evenings were free, I didn't know or care, because I was invariably working.

It seemed to be working out. Several times in the first month or two, Holly asked me to come in for a cup of coffee, and when I told her I was either working, painting, studying or planning to sleep, she showed no signs of taking offence. Yet by the end of 1987, I knew that Holly's outward breeziness was masking the return of her old, almost-but-never-quite-forgotten craving for risk-taking.

I knew it, because Holly made sure I did.

29

Holly rang Nick's doorbell one December morning.

'I got you a present.' She handed him a parcel wrapped in blue paper printed with bright yellow balloons. It was a cold morning and the heating in their building was notoriously inadequate, but she was wearing a white man's shirt and her toenails were painted scarlet. 'Let me know if you like it,' she said, and went right back home.

It was a brown Ralph Lauren sweater.

Nick rang her bell a few minutes later.

'I can't accept this,' he said and held it out.

'Why not?' Holly was peaceable about it.

'Because you shouldn't be buying me expensive gifts.'

'I didn't.' She took a step back. 'Coming in?'

'I don't have time,' Nick said. 'Holly, Ralph Lauren doesn't come cheap, even on sale.'

'It wasn't on sale,' Holly said.

'All the more reason.' Nick held it out again, insistently. 'Come on, Holly, take it back, please. It's much too expensive.'

'No, it isn't.'

He got tougher. 'You have to realize we don't have that kind of relationship any more. We're neighbours, nothing else.'

Holly smiled. 'Nick, it wasn't expensive because I didn't buy it.'

'What does that mean?'

'What do you think it means?' She paused. 'How did I always used to pick up little things I wanted in the good old days?'

It took him a moment. 'You stole it?' He was incredulous.

'Sure I did.'

'Jesus, Holly.' For the third time Nick thrust the sweater at her.

127

'Take it back right now.'

'It's not my size.'

'So take it back to where you stole it from.' He threw it hard past her and it landed on the rug behind her.

Her grey eyes were calm. 'You never used to be so fussy.'

'I was a *kid*. I grew up.' Nick shook his head as he turned away.

'Pity,' he heard her say.

That was just the start. Holly knew that Nick was determined not to get involved, but that didn't stop her trying to tell him about the stuff she got up to. He refused to spend time with her, so she took to ambushing him on the stairs, or she would just happen to be coming out of the building when he was coming in, or she waited for him outside the Tisch School or wherever she knew he was going to be working. He did his best to ignore her, began to realize that she was sick in some way, but one of the most remarkable and disconcerting things about it was that he knew that Holly's image with others was as intact as ever. Only Nick knew that she hung around crazy, dangerous places to buy dope, that she shoplifted, that she got a huge buzz from eating at expensive restaurants and skipping out without paying.

Months passed. Holly went through quiet weeks of introversion and apparently devoted study, then switched back to wild, uncontrollable periods during which she drove him almost nuts playing '*All the Way*' over and over for nights on end. Once, Nick stormed out of his apartment wearing nothing but his shorts and pounded on her front door, threatened to break it down and smash her hi-fi system if she didn't stop, but all that happened was that the other resident on their floor poked her grey head out through her own front door, and a man from the floor below yelled up the staircase for Nick to shut the fuck up or he'd call the cops and have him arrested.

'One of these days,' Nick told Holly the next time he saw her, '*I'm* going to call the cops, and the hell with you and your career as a lawyer.'

'What makes you think they'd believe you?' she asked him simply.

The bitch of it was he knew she was probably right.

* * *

She suckered him in just twice more, in the space of twenty-four hours during October '88, not long after the start of her junior year.

It was Saturday lunchtime, the second weekend of the month. Nick was just making himself a hero sandwich when his phone rang and a man identifying himself as Marty King, the manager of The Wheel, a pottery shop on Bleecker Street, told him that a young woman named Holly Bourne had been caught stealing a vase in his store and had begged him to contact Nick.

'It's normally our policy to prosecute,' King told Nick in a confidential tone, 'but it seems to me that your friend really needs some professional help, so if you can guarantee she gets that—'

'What do I have to do with it?' Nick wanted to know.

There was a brief hesitation. 'I understood from the lady that you are her fiancé.'

Nick was stunned. He, too, hesitated for just a moment, and into that silence came the unmistakable sound of Holly sobbing and pleading.

'Mr Miller?' King said.

'Yes,' Nick said.

He heard Holly again, begging now to be allowed to talk to him, and Nick could hear the manager weakening, and sure enough, an instant later, she was on the line.

'Nick—' Her voice was choked and soft. 'Nick, please, help me out of this.' He could barely hear her, and he could just picture her half covering her mouth and turning away from Marty King so that the poor guy wouldn't hear what she was saying.

'Nick, just get me out of this jam' – she was barely audible now – 'and I swear on anything you want I'll leave you in peace for ever.' She paused for just a fraction of a second. '*Please*, Nick, if not for my sake, then do it for my parents – this would kill my father, you *know* it would.'

Nick knew, deep down, that he was crazy to even think of bailing her out. He had thought any number of times over that past year – had really *believed* – that what was happening right now was what he wanted, what Holly deserved, maybe even exactly what she really needed. Yet suddenly the image of Holly under arrest, perhaps in a holding cell, her legal career ended even before it had begun – and all of that mostly because he hadn't lifted a finger to help her at this one low point – seemed too awful, too tragic, to contemplate.

'He's right, Holly. You know that, don't you?' he said into the phone. 'You do need treatment.'

'Yes,' Holly said, humbly. 'I know.'

'I'm talking about a shrink, Holly.'

'A psychiatrist, yes.' Holly's voice had grown clearer, and Nick knew it was for the manager's benefit. 'I'll do anything, Nick, I swear it.'

'And you'll stay out of my life from now on?'

'Yes, Nick. I swear.'

Nick hesitated one more moment.

'Let me talk to the manager again.'

Marty King insisted Nick came to The Wheel to fetch Holly, and she was white as chalk and trembling violently when he arrived, and outside on the street he thought he'd better take her arm because she still had that sick, ghostly look about her. And then, just before they reached their building on Christopher Street, Holly stopped and looked up at Nick. She was crying again, but she was smiling, too, the most brilliant smile Nick had ever seen on her face.

'You've proved it now,' she said.

'Proved what?' Nick asked, though he had an ugly feeling he knew.

'That whatever you say, whatever you do, deep-down you still love me.'

'Holly, stop it.' Nick shook his arm loose and stepped away from her.

The brilliance stayed in her eyes. 'It doesn't matter,' she went on. 'Whichever way you want to play it from now on, I want you to know that I'm here for you – friend, lover, sister. Whatever you want, Nick.'

He knew then that the whole scene – maybe even getting caught stealing the vase in the first place, because Holly had never let herself get caught stealing before – had been a sham, one of Holly's adventures, a kind of a dare with herself to see if she could hook him.

'You crazy bitch,' he said, softly, right there on the street. 'Don't you know yet that I don't want any of those things, not from you, not ever again?'

'I know you don't mean that.' Holly had lost her smile. 'You can say it, but I know you don't mean it.'

'You're a thief, Holly, and a manipulator, and a liar, and there's only one thing I want from you,' Nick told her, and his voice was very hard and clear. 'And that is never, *ever* to see or hear from you again—'

The grey-haired woman from their building passed them, and Nick saw from her shocked expression that she had heard his last few words to Holly – to that poor, sweet, hard-working, respectable law student with tears in her eyes – but Nick found that he didn't give a damn what she or anyone else thought.

'From now on,' he went straight on, 'you are welcome to go to jail or to stay in your apartment and play '*All the Way*' for the rest of your fucking mad life, because it won't make a scrap of difference to me, because I'm going to get the hell out of this place just as soon as I can and then I will never, *ever*, have to see you or think about you again.'

At three o'clock next morning, he was woken by the sound of frantic pounding on his front door. Disorientated, groping for the light switch and a robe, he stumbled out into the hall.

'Who is it?'

The pounding went on and with it the sound of hysterical sobbing.

'Holly, go away,' he said.

'I need *help*,' she sobbed and went on pounding.

'Oh, shit, Holly,' Nick hissed through the door, 'you're going to wake the whole goddamn building. Just take a pill or something and go to bed like a normal person.'

'Nick, *please*—' It was almost a scream. 'They're going to *kill* me – you have to let me in.'

Gritting his teeth, mindful of the neighbours, Nick opened the door. Holly, dressed in a heavy sweater and jeans, ran right past him, through into the bathroom and locked the door.

'What are you *doing*?' Nick called after her, confused.

He only half registered the sound of feet running up the stairs, and by the time he turned to close the door it was too late. Two men shoved past him into the apartment, one of them slamming the door right out of his hand.

'What is going *on*?'

They were white and tough-looking. One of them, a guy with

dyed-blond long hair and a mean mouth, held a big, ugly, serrated knife in one hand.

'Where is she?' he demanded.

Blood rushed fast through Nick's head. What the *hell* had she gotten herself into now? What the hell had she gotten *him* into?

'Where *is* the fucking bitch?' The man with the knife pushed Nick up against the wall and his head hit the corner of the Andrew Wyeth print he'd hung there the previous spring. The other man, darker, his head almost completely shaven, stalked around the hall saying nothing.

'We want our money,' the knife man said.

'What money?' Nick's voice was thin with fear.

'The money she owes us for the *dope*, dope,' he said, and stuck the knife blade against the side of Nick's neck, not far from his jugular. 'Bitch snatched it and ran, thought we'd let her get away with it.'

Holly's voice came loud and clear from behind the bathroom door. 'I got it for *him*.'

'Is that so?' The shaven-headed man wheeled around and came up so close to Nick the rankness of his body odour was right in his nose.

'I don't know what the hell you're talking about,' he said, terrified to move or even breathe with the other guy's knife still tickling his neck.

'Give them the money, Nick!' Holly yelled from the bathroom.

'For Christ's *sake*, Holly!'

'You heard the lady,' the blond said.

'Nick, I *told* you it wasn't worth trying to get away with it,' Holly called out. 'Just *give* it to them.'

That was the moment when Nick really, finally, understood exactly how dangerous Holly Bourne was, just before the two low-lives bouldered their way into the bedroom dragging him with them, found his wallet and took his earnings before rampaging through his studio, slashing four of his paintings and, as a parting gesture, beating the crap out of him.

He must have passed out for a few moments, because next thing he remembered the thugs had gone and Holly was there beside him on her knees on the living room floor dabbing iodine on his cuts, her mascara all over her cheeks but otherwise apparently quite calm.

'Are you *nuts*?' Nick struggled up, dizzy and in pain, but in almost too much of a rage to care. 'Are you completely out of your warped little *mind*?'

Holly ignored him, just went on trying to fix him up.

Nick shoved her away hard and she fell on her backside.

'I'm only trying to help you.' She looked wounded.

A pain shot through Nick's left arm from the effort of pushing her. He got onto one knee and managed to get to his feet. 'Get out, Holly.' His voice was trembling.

'Please, Nick, let me take care of those—'

'Get out before I lose it, Holly.' He was shaking with anger. 'I mean it.'

'Calm down, Nick.'

He stared at her. It was almost impossible to believe how normally she was acting, sitting there on her ass on his floor with a bottle of iodine in one hand and gauze in the other like Florence-fucking-Nightingale.

'I *mean* it, Holly,' he said again. He bent down, smacked the bottle out of her left hand, not caring that iodine spilled over the rug. He grasped her upper arm and dragged her up off the floor, his own muscles shrieking with pain. 'I'm warning you. If you don't get out of here right this minute, I won't answer for what I may do to you.'

'I wouldn't do anything if I were you,' Holly said, quietly.

Nick became aware then of the sounds outside in the hall. Voices calling to each other. Neighbours.

'Oh, great,' he said. 'Just *great*.'

He got to the front door and ripped it open. Three men stood in the hall, two young, one old. The old one, the man from the floor below, was carrying a baseball bat. They all jumped back at the sight of Nick.

'It's okay,' he said, still breathing hard. 'There was some trouble here, but it's over.'

Wielding his bat, the old guy peered around Nick, trying to see inside. 'Miss?' he shouted. 'You okay in there? We called 911 – the cops are on their way.'

'She's fine,' Nick said, wanting to scream. His face felt like it might have been pulped. He was suddenly afraid to look in the mirror. On the other hand, he figured, no one here was exactly offering to get him to the hospital.

Holly came out from behind him. 'I'm okay.'

One of the younger men, a guy Nick had never seen before, winced as he saw Holly. 'Jesus Christ, the bastard hit her.'

Nick turned around. Holly, whose face had been mascara-smudged but otherwise unblemished, now sported a nasty scratch on her right cheek.

'You bitch,' he said, softly. 'You lousy bitch.'

And then he heard sirens.

It was one hell of a night. Nick told the cops exactly what had gone down, but with Holly contributing her own version of the story, and with traces still clinging to the sides of the lavatory bowl in Nick's bathroom testifying to the fact that someone had tried to flush marijuana down into the New York sewer system, no one was listening to him.

'He's probably going to be charged with possession, ma'am,' one of the cops said to Holly before they took Nick to the station. 'Do you want to add assault?'

'No, thank you, sir,' Holly said, fingering her scratch.

'Look at her nails,' Nick said. 'Check her *nails*.'

The cop threw him a sour look. 'Why would we want to do that, sir?'

'Because she gave herself that scratch, so you'll probably find her own skin and blood under them.'

'This isn't homicide, sir.' The cop smiled a *don't-be-such-a-jerk* kind of a smile and shook his head.

'Do you have to charge him with possession, officer?' Holly asked. 'I mean, there isn't really much evidence, is there? And it's not as if he was planning to sell it. Couldn't you just forget it?'

'There isn't much evidence,' Nick exploded, 'because she flushed it down the goddamned john herself.'

The policeman grinned at Holly sympathetically.

'You got yourself a real white knight here, ma'am.'

Nick made his call from the police station that night to his friend Jake Kolinsky, and it was Jake who got a lawyer to him two hours later.

Liza Montgomery was a short, skinny African-American aged around thirty-five, with tired but sharp eyes and a matter-of-fact

134

attitude. In a cold, miserable room at the station, Nick told her everything he could think of about himself and Holly and their history, and the crazy way she'd been acting during the last few months. In particular, he told her about Marty King, the pottery store manager, who, Nick suggested, could be called to testify that Holly was a thief and, therefore, not to be believed. Liza Montgomery pointed out that, at the end of the day, Holly having allegedly stolen a vase the previous lunchtime was not relevant to Nick's present situation, and did not, alas, manifestly alter the fact that traces of marijuana had been found in *his* john, in *his* bathroom, in *his* apartment.

'It's going to be her word against yours, Mr Miller.'

'But she's a liar,' Nick said. 'And a thief.'

'Maybe so,' Montgomery said.

'All I did was open the door when she was banging on it and yelling for help. The neighbours must have heard her.' He knew he was clutching at straws. 'You could get them to testify to that. I only opened the door to help her.'

'According to the police report, it was one of your neighbours who called 911 and reported that *you* were disturbing the peace, Mr Miller,' the lawyer said, 'not Ms Bourne.'

'Jesus.' Nick shook his head in anger and despair. 'This is all so nuts – I mean this is really *nuts*. Holly buys marijuana off these two low-lives but doesn't bother to pay them so they'll chase her right into my apartment, and then she tells them the stuff is for *me* – and I don't use dope, Ms Montgomery, I don't even smoke *tobacco*, for Christ's sake—'

'Take it easy, Mr Miller—'

'And then these guys beat me senseless, and when I wake up Holly's all over me like the measles, and when I tell her to get lost she puts a big scratch on her own cheek – her own *face*—'

'Which she claims you put there.'

'I told them to check her fingernails, for fuck's sake – I should have told them to check mine.'

'And I told you to take it easy,' Montgomery said again. 'At least she's not bringing assault charges against you – unless she has a change of heart.'

'Great,' Nick said. 'Just peachy. How am I supposed to take it easy when that bitch is one step away from putting me in jail?'

'No one's going to jail right now, Mr Miller.' Liza Montgomery reached over and patted his left hand. 'Let me go do some talking,' she said, 'see if I can make this thing go away.'

'What do you mean "go away"?' Nick was half-choked with outrage and disgust. 'I don't want it to go away. I want Holly to get what's coming to her. All I did was try to help her, and this is what she does to me. I mean, I told you she's a law student – is she the kind of lawyer you want in your profession?'

Montgomery made no comment. She was up on her feet, putting forms and papers back into her briefcase. 'I wouldn't hold your breath about what's going to happen to Ms Bourne, Mr Miller. I'd say the best you should be hoping for is that the DA's office agrees to drop the charges against you.'

'And what about Holly?'

The lawyer was already at the door. 'If I were you,' she said, 'and if we do manage to get you out of this mess, that is one young woman I'd get myself as far away from as possible.'

'We live next door to each other,' Nick pointed out.

'You said you were thinking of moving out. So move.'

'We're still both going to be at NYU.'

'NYU's got to be one of the most spread-out campuses in the country,' Liza Montgomery said. 'Try losing yourself in it.'

Montgomery achieved exactly what she had said she might. The DA's office had agreed to decline prosecution, but she wanted to make Nick understand that he was on a kind of unofficial probation: that his arrest was on record, and that if he got into trouble again any time in the next few years, he'd be unlikely to get lucky a second time.

'I know you think the whole thing sucks,' the lawyer said on the street outside the station just after two o'clock that afternoon, 'but it might very well have gone to court, and you might have ended up with a conviction, so you just be grateful. More important, remember what I told you about being careful.'

'And meantime Holly gets away with the whole thing,' Nick said, raising his voice over the din of traffic, too exhausted and, frankly, too relieved to make much more fuss.

'Not entirely.'

'What does that mean?'

'It means she's had a warning, too.' Liza Montgomery flagged down a yellow cab. 'It means that she's been noticed, just like you have.'

'Except she doesn't have an arrest record,' Nick pointed out.

'No, she doesn't,' the lawyer agreed, opening the cab door. 'But it's better than nothing, expecially if she's on her way to law school, not to mention a moral character screening.'

Nick supposed that it was, probably – hopefully – better than nothing. That at least Holly Bourne had, for the first time, been drawn to the attention of the police, which meant that surely, from now on, it would be in her own interest to stay out of trouble and away from him.

It wasn't much, but it was something.

30

I'm coming to it now. The worst part. The thing that stopped me, right at the beginning, from telling Nina the whole truth about Holly and me. That still stops me, even now.

It's strange, really, and sad, because I realize, looking back, that Nina would have believed my side of the story. Nina would even have understood. I know that now. Now, when it's too late to tell her. And it is too late, simply because we've loved each other now for what feels like the whole of my life. I feel, sometimes, you see, that my life – the life I want and need so badly that the fear of losing it *chokes* me – only began that day on Fillmore Street when I first saw Nina.

I love my wife, but, unlike her, I haven't shared all of my truths. I know, therefore, that Nina ought not to trust me completely. And I am so afraid that the day will come when she discovers this. I am so desperately afraid that we will be damaged by that discovery.

I can face many things.

I don't think I can face losing Nina.

31

After the fiasco in Christopher Street that had resulted in Nick earning an arrest record with the NYPD, he moved out of his apartment and went to stay with Jake Kolinsky at his home on Mulberry Street. It wasn't far enough away from the old place – and Holly knew where Jake lived – but it suited Nick well enough while he was looking for a new apartment.

At Thanksgiving, when Jake went home to Brooklyn, Nick turned down his parents' invitation to go to Bethesda, certain that Holly would be heading for the Bourne household. He was right. Holly did go home and reported, in a neighbourly kind of way, to Ethan and Kate that she was concerned about the company Nick had lately been keeping, which prompted Ethan to call Nick to express his and Kate's own anxieties for him. Nick erupted on the phone and told his father the whole truth and nothing but the truth about butter-wouldn't melt Holly, and Ethan said that he believed him. But not quite before Nick had heard a tiny worm of doubt in his dad's voice, and although Ethan Miller had always been a good, decent father, and Nick loved him without reservation, he found that moment or two of wavering hard to forget.

Nick didn't go home for Christmas either. He was busy moving into a Chelsea apartment on Twenty-third and Ninth. A big, old, anonymous building. A fresh start.

Except that, in February, Holly came to live there too.

She never put a foot wrong, never even tried to speak to Nick, but she was *there*, in his face. He tried talking to Liza Montgomery about getting some kind of an injunction against Holly, but Ms Montgomery wasn't any too hopeful. Or helpful, come to that. Holly moving into the same building as Nick hardly constituted any kind of a crime. He'd admitted himself that she wasn't actively *doing* anything to disrupt his life; she had neither assaulted him nor trespassed on his property – she hadn't even *spoken* to him. If Nick was keen to throw cash down the john in the same way that someone (he didn't care for the way Ms Montgomery said that '*someone*') had tossed the marijuana down his Christopher Street toilet, then she was prepared to approach a judge on his behalf. But when it came down to it, unless Holly Bourne seriously overstepped the line, Nick would be advised to remember that he was the one with the arrest record, and Holly was still the law student, with no rap sheet.

'So what am I supposed to do? Move again?'

'I can't think of a better idea,' Liza Montgomery said.

So much for Holly having been warned off.

Nick broke his new lease and found a place in a small brownstone in Gramercy Park. He could barely afford the rent, but he figured it was worth every ounce of sweat and exhaustion he was going to have to go through to pay for it, because there were only two other apartments in the house, both fully occupied by long-stay residents, and so, even if Holly did track him down and try to move in, there was no vacant space for her.

This time, he really thought he'd cracked it. Months passed. He took his finals, went home for a week, came back to Manhattan, and there was still no sign of Holly, and Nick knew she was starting her senior year that fall and facing her own finals and her Law School Aptitude Test, and maybe – just maybe – even Holly knew when she was beaten.

And then he met Julie Monroe, a black music student who taught jazz aerobics part-time, and life became pretty special for several months. Until, not long before Christmas 1989, Julie told Nick that she had been hassled in the park by a young woman claiming to be his ex-fiancée and wanting to warn Julie that Nick Miller was a racist.

He knew it was Holly even before she described the woman. Julie assured him that she had shrugged it off, but the other woman had persisted, had claimed that if Nick was spending this much time with a black woman it had to be for some kind of warped pleasure – or was he just going through some African art period? Julie swore that she hadn't believed a single word of it, and Nick thought that was probably true, yet he knew, too, that from that moment on, every time he so much as lifted a stick of charcoal to sketch Julie, a little splash of Holly's poison would inhibit them both.

It was too much.

He went looking for Holly that evening.

She was still living in the Chelsea apartment. Nick stood in the lobby while the doorman buzzed Holly, a part of him hoping she might not be home because maybe he was too angry to think straight.

She was home.

'I knew you'd come,' were her first words as he came out of the elevator on the tenth floor.

She had grown her hair longer, and was wearing it off her face in a simple pony-tail. She wore no make-up and she was more beautiful than she had ever been.

'I've been expecting you,' she said as she stood back to let him in.

She was wearing a pair of silky, black pyjamas, the kind some women wore for entertaining and others wore for bed, and she smelled of one of the perfumes he still vividly remembered from their days of sharing, a soft but penetrating jasmine scent. He wished, already, that he had not come.

The door closed, and they were in Holly's small, square, dimly lit entrance hall.

'Coffee?' she offered.

'I'm not staying,' Nick said.

'I didn't ask you to stay,' Holly said calmly. 'I just asked if you wanted coffee.'

'No coffee,' Nick said.

She led the way into her living room. There was no overhead lighting, just two table lamps that came on as Holly touched the switch by the door. She had furnished minimally, a few expensive-looking matte black pieces and plain off-white walls. No paintings.

'I've come to warn you to lay off,' Nick said straight off.

'Warn me?' Holly said softly.

141

'Yes.'

'Have a seat,' she said.

'No.'

'Mind if I do?'

'I don't mind what you do, so long as you stay out of my life.'

Holly sat down on one of her straight black chairs. It looked uncomfortable. She looked up at him. Her naked face, the candour in her grey eyes, made him edgy.

'Don't you know?' she said.

'Know what?' He was aware that he sounded aggressive, which was good. Aggressive, he had concluded a while back, was the only way to be with Holly. Aggressive and then gone.

'That I only said those things to Julie to provoke you.'

'Of course I know.' Nick paused. 'How come you even know her name?' he asked, then shook his head. 'No, don't tell me, I don't want to know.'

'I knew if I said enough,' Holly went on, 'made you angry enough, you'd come and see me. I knew calling you up and asking for help wouldn't work this time – we've been through that one before, haven't we? So I figured anger would do it.' There was unmistakable sadness in her smile. 'And I was right.'

Nick sat down on the chair furthest away from Holly. It was as hard as it looked. He wondered, fleetingly, why anyone would choose a piece of furniture this uncomfortable for their home.

'I like them,' Holly said, reading his mind. 'I do a lot of my reading in this room. These chairs keep me awake. I'm doing pretty well in school, but there's so much to learn. I can't afford too many hours' sleep, you know?'

'What did you hope to achieve by getting me here?' Nick asked. A little of the aggression had drifted away. He felt almost bemused. 'I mean, what is the *point* of it? Knowing that there's no other way someone's going to agree to see you, unless you make them mad enough to want to hit you. Why would you want that?'

'Is that what you want?' she asked. 'To hit me?'

'Of course not.'

'It must be, or you wouldn't have said it.'

'Violence isn't my style, Holly.'

'Are you sure?' Her eyes goaded him.

Nick stood up again. 'I came here for just one thing, and that was to tell you, one last time, to leave me alone – to stay out of my life.'

'To *warn* me,' Holly added, emphasizing the word as if the idea of it was giving her a buzz.

'If you like.'

'It's what you said when you came in.'

He sighed. 'That's right.' He looked down at her. 'I'm warning you to remember that I could make it hard for you to get as far as law school, let alone as far as getting admitted to the bar.'

Holly looked back up at him, her eyes unwavering. 'How would you propose doing that, Nick?'

'I could tell people about you. The right people.'

'You think they'd listen to you?'

'Enough to give them cause for a few doubts about you.'

'They wouldn't listen for long if you were in jail,' Holly said.

He stared at her. 'I won't be in jail.'

'You might be if you get into any more trouble,' she said. 'I know your lawyer told you that.'

Bemusement vanished and anger returned, but he held it steady and under control. 'Just leave me alone, Holly,' he said, one more time. 'Just concentrate on getting your own life together and forget that we ever knew each other.'

Holly said nothing for a few moments. She sat quite still and very straight, her black silk-covered legs uncrossed, one hand on each knee.

'Don't you understand how much I miss you, Nick?' she asked, at last, looking directly ahead at the wall, not at him. 'How much I regret driving you away?'

He couldn't believe the switch.

'You have to forget all about that, Holly,' he said. 'It doesn't matter any more.'

'It does to me.' She raised her face, looked at him again. 'Surely you must realize by now, Nick, that no one else – not Julie Monroe, not anyone – is ever going to love you as much as I do.'

Nick shook his head. 'You're sick, Holly.'

Hurt filled her eyes. 'Sick because I love you?'

'Sick if you don't realize by now that you're the last woman on earth I could ever love.' It was no harsher than what he'd told her once before, standing on Christopher Street after the business at the pottery store, but he knew that he had to say the words again, had to hope that this time they might get through to her.

Holly stood up and walked over to him. Nick thought, for just an instant, that she was going to slap him, but he didn't flinch. She was small, after all. He'd forgotten how small she was.

She came at him, not to hit him, but to kiss him.

Her arms snaked around him, and she kissed his mouth.

Startled, Nick pushed her away. 'For God's sake, Holly.'

'Why?' Holly asked. 'You know you want to.'

She reached out, grabbed his right hand and laid it over her left breast. He snatched it away. 'Cut it out, Holly.' He turned away, feeling stifled, claustrophobic, wanting suddenly to get out.

'Why don't you want me?' she asked, baiting him. 'Wrong colour?'

He was at the living room door.

'Is black cunt more thrilling? Is that it?'

He turned around and she was right there, right up against him, one arm going round his waist again, one hand pulling at his head. He tried to draw back, tried hard to resist the temptation to shove her – he knew that with one single hard push he could send her flying, but that wasn't what he wanted. All he wanted now was to get *out* of there.

'Oh, come on, Nick,' she said. 'You know you want this.'

'No, Holly, it—'

She cut him off with a kiss, right on his mouth. He backed off, but the door was at his back, and she started kissing whatever she could reach – his face, his hair, his neck. He felt her tongue, hot and hard, in his left ear, felt one of her hands sliding down his back, gripping his buttocks – and, for just an instant, for just one hideous, unbelievable instant, he felt his body involuntarily responding to her—

Oh, Jesus, no! This is not *what I want.*

'You see?'

Her other hand was at his zipper, and she knew – he could see that she *knew* – what had happened, and his anger upped another notch, and thank God – *thank you, dear Christ* – obliterated that brief, disgusting flicking of desire—

'*No*, Holly.' He grasped at the invading hand, pulled it off him.

'Don't you want me any more? Don't you want to be in my mouth

144

again, Nick?' Her eyes were wide, wild. 'Is Julie Monroe better? Is that it? Is that why you want her?'

'Shut *up*, Holly.' He let go of her hand and pushed her away, pulled his zipper up, felt his hands shaking.

'Do you like sucking her off more than you did me, Nick? Is that it?' She was relentless. 'I'm just trying to understand, don't you see? To understand exactly what I'm up against—'

'Shut up, Holly!' He got out of the living room, backing into the little square hall, but it was dimmer than the room had been and it took him a moment to get his bearings, to figure out where the front door was.

'Is it because she's an athlete, Nick?' Holly was right behind him. 'Does Julie teach you new things? Is she stronger than me? Does she know how to keep you harder for longer than I did?'

He turned round again, faced her. 'Holly, I'm warning you—'

'More warnings. Why?' Holly moved swiftly, got between him and the door. 'What's wrong with my asking a few questions? Aren't I entitled to be curious about the woman who stole you from me?'

'I wasn't yours to steal, Holly.' Nick was fighting one of the hardest battles of his life to stay in control, to stop himself from grabbing at her and slamming her against the wall to get her out of his way – but it was getting tougher, it was getting close to *impossible*.

'Of course you were, Nick.' She flicked the light switch near the door and an overhead lamp dazzled him with brightness. 'You can't have forgotten, you can't have.' She unbuttoned the black silk top and exposed her breasts. 'You remember these, surely. You loved them for long enough—'

An ugly, panicking sense of suffocation overwhelmed Nick again. For the second time he did push her away, harder than before, and her right shoulder hit the wooden frame of the living room door. She flew at him, pressed herself right up against him, and this time he couldn't tell if she was kissing or biting. He could feel her teeth and her tongue on his ear, on his neck, and he could hear himself shouting at her to stop, yelling at her in a voice that was scarcely his own, and her perfume was all over him, and he thought he was going to explode with anger or maybe pass out with it . . .

He hit her.

The shock stopped her for just an instant – stopped them both in their tracks. It seemed to Nick that a light sparked sharply in Holly's eyes – half fear, half exhilaration, and then she came back at him again, tilting her pelvis so that she was rubbing against his groin—

'I said *no!*' he yelled. And hit her again.

All his life, Nick had believed – even after the two drug pushers had beaten him up and Holly had driven him almost to breaking point – that real violence was not in his nature. He was a gentle man. He had never, in his wildest dreams, thought that he could hit a woman and – dear God in heaven, forgive him – that hitting her could feel like some kind of *release*.

Yet there Holly was, down on the floor, and, crazy as she was, she'd dragged him down on the carpet with her – and even now she was still pulling at him, still *wanting* him, and – oh, *Christ* – he slapped her again, and he could hear panting and a kind of moaning, and sweet Jesus, that was *him* . . .

With a final, terrible groan, he tore himself off her.

And knew what he had done.

Holly lay on her black carpet, gasping. Her lower lip was bleeding, her face flushed, one mark from his hand vivid on her left cheek, another on the white skin just above her naked right breast.

She stared up at him. For several long, hideous seconds, Nick thought that he might have hurt her badly, and his whole being jangled with horror and terror.

But then he realized that the look in Holly's grey eyes was not of fear, or pain, or even of hatred.

The look in her eyes was of triumph.

'Oh, Nick,' she said, very softly.

He thought he was going to throw up. He looked at the door, then back at her. More than anything on earth, he wanted to be out of there, away from her.

He tried to speak, but no words came out.

'Oh, Nick,' Holly said again, still lying absolutely still.

He took a deep, shuddering breath, held, for a moment, onto the wall, needing support, and the worst of the nausea went away. He took another breath.

'Are you hurt?' His voice was throaty, strange. 'Do you need a doctor?'

Holly shook her head, yet still she didn't move.

Nick's terror came flooding back.

'Oh, Christ, I have hurt you.' He fell on his knees beside her.

'Holly, where's the pain? What have I done?'

'Nothing I didn't want you to,' she whispered.

'Holly, try and get up.'

'No,' she said.

And then, with a slow, flowing, almost theatrical movement, she held out her arms to him, and Nick realized, with a fresh jolt of shock, that even after all that had just happened, she still wanted him.

'Oh, God,' he said, and got back to his feet, trembling again. 'Oh, God, Holly, you are so sick.'

He turned his back on her and went back to the door.

'Don't go,' he heard her say, still from the floor.

He turned the handle.

'Please,' Holly said.

He opened the door.

'Stay,' she said, 'or I'll make you sorry.'

He ran.

32

That was the long and dreadful night during which I made my decision to leave New York and come to California.

Fear drove me. Nothing more compelling or honourable than that. I was just so damned afraid. Of what I had done to Holly. Of what I might have done to her if I hadn't stopped when I did. Of what might happen the next time I saw her. Which I would, no matter what care I took, if I stayed in that city.

I was scared of the cops, too. Liza Montgomery had made it clear enough, when I'd sought her opinion on getting a court order to keep Holly away from me, that I had next to no chance of getting a judge to look at my situation with sympathy – and that was *before* I'd laid hands on Holly, for God's sake. The DA's office might have dropped those possession charges, but I already had an arrest record and a verbal warning to stay out of trouble for several years at least. If, just fourteen months later, Holly decided to accuse me of assault – and I hated even to *imagine* what embellishments she might add to her personal version of events – then there was every chance I'd end up in jail.

I didn't want to go to jail.

I didn't want to stay in the same city as Holly Bourne.

The arrangements, simple and inadequate as they were, still took time. Almost thirty-six hours passed before I was able to get on my flight to Los Angeles. I sweated while I broke yet another lease, while I packed up my things, made my airline reservations, organized freight for those canvases too precious to me to leave behind, and resigned from my three jobs.

I shared my plans with no one, not Jake, not even my parents. I don't think I slept more than a half-hour in total before I got on the plane. I was waiting for a knock on the door. From the police with an arrest warrant. From Richard or Eleanor Bourne. Or Holly herself.

No one came. Not in those last hours in Manhattan, nor at La Guardia while I was waiting to board my flight. Not in my first weeks or months in Venice. And finally, as time passed, I stopped being afraid altogether of the cops, or even of Holly Bourne.

The fear only comes back when I think about Nina finding out.

My wife has herself a real hero.

I could have coped with telling Nina that I was a damned fool for ever having let Holly back into my life once I'd left Bethesda. I could have coped with telling her about all the stuff that happened after Holly followed me to New York. I could have told her about the sex, the anger, Holly's machinations, my trouble with the police. I could even have told her that it was cowardice that brought me to California.

But I could not tell her about the violence.

Nor could I tell her that, for at least a few seconds of the time that I was hitting Holly Bourne, it felt like the right thing – like the only thing – to do.

There is no way I ever want to tell her that.

AUGUST

33

Phoebe has been off the respirator and conscious now for several days, thank God. Out of danger. But she hasn't spoken since the fall. Not a single word. Between her silence and her two broken arms, that makes her almost completely helpless.

The doctors assure us over and over again that there's been no permanent brain damage, that there's no reason why Phoebe shouldn't talk again, given a little time. But time is passing, and I know that neither Nina nor William really believes their assurances, and so the continuing spectre of some awful, still undiagnosed injury looms over us all like a terrifying, depressing fog.

There is some good news, wonderful news. Our sweet baby girl is clear of respiratory problems and jaundice, and has gained just enough weight to satisfy Sam Ellington, her paediatrician, that she's almost ready to come home with us.

I've already painted Sam holding Zoë, because he's a big, broad, black guy who looks more like the Refrigerator than a doctor, but he has these angel-tender hands, and he's helped save our daughter, and he touches me immensely. I haven't yet attempted even a sketch of Nina breastfeeding Zoë, though observing this as I regularly do seems to me the most perfectly beautiful experience of my life. I think maybe I'm reluctant to try to paint it in case I fail to capture what I feel. It's so much more than I dreamed it would be. It's purest warmth and safety. It's giving, and taking, and giving back more. It's a perfect, elemental circle, it's love and life, the whole shebang, everything that counts or matters. And it takes us both away, for a blessed while, from our continuing fears and anxieties over Phoebe.

William's mistrust of me seems not to have diminished at all. Lord knows he didn't care much for me before Lawrence Dinkin came to call on us, but though he's made no actual accusations (William is no fool, he knows how Nina would react), I get the distinct feeling that, in the absence of any other contenders, I am my father-in-law's number one suspect.

I've tried talking to Nina about it. I've been to enough AA meetings with her over the last couple of years to know that trying to keep anxieties from her is neither good for her, nor what she wants. But where this nonsense with her father is concerned, Nina doesn't want to know.

'You're imagining things,' she told me only yesterday morning in the hospital when I broached the subject again after William had refused to talk to Nina about Phoebe while I was in the room.

'I imagined what just happened?'

We were in that same waiting room we'd used when Dinkin had paid his visit. I have grown to detest that room, as I have come to hate the sight and sounds and smells of People's Hospital.

'Dad's a little over-sensitive about privacy, that's all,' Nina said. 'He's always been the same with—'

'With outsiders?'

'No, of course not,' she protested quickly. 'He just got used to it being only the three of us.' She looked at my expression – I guess it must have been a little on the wounded side. I was certainly angry at William, but trying to damp it down for Nina's sake. 'I think maybe it's taken him longer than it ought to let someone else in,' she added, unconvincingly.

'I'm your husband, Nina.'

'And Zoë's father,' she added.

'Who Zoë's grandfather doesn't trust,' I said.

'Nick, please, don't do this to me,' Nina said.

'Do what?' I asked, though I knew exactly what she meant.

'Don't put me in the middle like this.' She shook her head. 'I can't cope with any more right now.'

* * *

Guilt stabbed me, as it so often does these days. Of course she couldn't take any more. She had more than enough bad stuff going on without me adding to her burden. I told her I was sorry, told her she could forget all about it. I pretended to agree with her that I believed William would come around, would in time have as much faith in me as Nina did.

And Phoebe did. If only she could tell him.

The bitch of it is, of course, that William Ford's instincts about me aren't that far off track, are they? I don't mean about harming Phoebe. I'd sooner cut off both my own arms than have had this happen to her. I adore my sister-in-law. Nina knows that, and so does Phoebe.

But then they don't know what I did to Holly.

34

Holly knows. Holly will never forget. Not a single moment of it.

And yet she still loves him.

Strange, perhaps. Considering what he did to her. The way he walked out on her.

But then Nick always has been misguided.

She thought, after he ran out on her that night – after he'd hit her and left her bleeding on the floor – that she would call the cops, do what she had told him she would. Make him sorry.

But time passed, and she went on lying there on the black carpet – not because she was too hurt to stand up, but because she found she needed to stay there, where Nick had left her, needed to replay the scene that had just ended, to relive it in her mind, over and over again.

The physical contact, the closeness of that last struggle between them. The smell and feel and taste of him. The shocking exhilaration of being slapped by him. The victorious awareness that she had made him wild enough to do that.

She spent most of that night lying there on the floor, fell asleep in that same spot, right there where they'd shared their last embrace. She dreamed of her brother during those hours – the same, terrible, depleting dream she always had – and when she did, finally, wake up from that wretched sleep and struggle to her feet, all the passion and triumph had vanished and she was cold and aching, and more deeply depressed than she could ever remember feeling since Eric's death.

* * *

156

Holly still remembers that feeling: that sudden, terrifying, paralysing realization that she truly had lost Nick. That he had really gone. And when, a week later, she discovered that he had, indeed, left New York City and that no one seemed to know (or was telling her) where he had gone to; and when, another week on, she went home for her Christmas birthday, and Kate and Ethan Miller said they had no idea where Nick was spending the holidays, that feeling of terror, trapped deep inside her heart and mind, grew even more intense, more agonizing. She didn't let anyone else see what she was enduring. She had to go on with her Holly-about-to-take-law-school-by-storm façade, she *had* to go on being the perfect daughter of whom her parents were so proud, however torturous it was.

She just about held it together until, on January 2nd, she escaped back to New York.

She sat very still and quietly on the flight from Dulles to La Guardia, and then she did the same on the cab ride into Manhattan. And she let the doorman at her building carry her bags up to the tenth floor for her, and gave him five bucks, and then she closed and locked her front door and waited until she heard the sounds of the elevator taking him back down to the lobby.

And then she let go.

When she came back to herself, she saw that she had ripped the stuffing out of the seats of her straight black wooden chairs, and that she had smashed her two matte black end tables almost to matchwood, and that her hands were bloody and bruised.

But she felt better.

Better enough to go on.

Nick's leaving did her a favour. That was what she told herself when she surfaced from the darkness. She had emerged from this kind of blackness once before, with Nick's help, with his outstretched hand of friendship. But this time, there would be no Nick to help her – but that was okay, too, she told herself, *promised* herself, because she was going to grow stronger and more capable without him, was going to stand alone, fight her battles alone.

Holly forced herself to examine, for a little while, the events that had brought her to such a low ebb, that had turned such a pure love into obsession. The introspection brought her few answers, but at least, she thought, with a degree of satisfaction, she had made herself recognize and accept that that *was* what had become of her love: that it was obsession that had taken her over and almost ruined her.

Almost.

Nick's going away was the best thing that could have happened. Holly repeated that to herself several times each day, turning it into a kind of mantra. His presence in Manhattan had sapped her independent forces, diverted her energies, diminished her. Now that he had vanished from the face of the earth, she could be herself again, be Holly Bourne, up-and-coming.

That was the start of the period of her life when Holly began to feel – began to genuinely *believe* – that she had freed herself from Nick Miller's spell. The period when her love of what she was learning, the awareness of what she was striving for at law school, took over from the wilder, more destructive side of her personality. When the vast, swirling ocean of jurisprudence, the great bog of corporation law and the magnificent imbroglio of criminal justice began, slowly, but with the most thrilling precision, to crystallize for Holly Bourne. Student and lover of law. Above all men. Even Nick Miller.

And then, about three years into her new life, Holly went home on another visit, ran into Ethan Miller in the street, and he let slip that Nick was living in California.

That news, the sudden location of the object of her obsession, shook Holly up badly, wrecked her concentration, whacked her new-found clarity out of focus for a couple of weeks, but then things seemed to settle back down again. So what if Nick hadn't vanished off the planet after all? she told herself severely. So what if he had washed up on the other side of America? It was still another world. Not her world.

But then she learned about the existence of Nina Ford.

And a matter of months after that, in April of 1995, she learned that Nick had married her.

After that, it was all ruined. It was like being sucked down into a blind, endless spiral, all the protective layers – the studying, the successes, the making of friends – the comparative *normality* – melting away as if they had been part of a single absurd delusion that Holly Bourne really *could* contemplate life without Nick Miller. And from then on all her thoughts, waking and sleeping, all her energies, all her concentration, began to focus on Nick again.

On his betrayal.

And on getting him back.

She knew when she stole the danger signs from the house in Haight Ashbury and sent his wife the fax, that there was a chance Nina might escape completely or that she might sustain only minor injuries. It was a gamble, but almost risk-free from her own point of view. And the gamble failed. Though, of course, even if she had succeeded in removing Nina from Nick's life, Holly knows that would only have been a first step.

After all, Nina living or dying is not what's important here and now. Nick coming back to Holly is what matters. And, not being a fool, Holly knows that Nick will never do that, not without a push or twenty.

Holly knows what she wants now.

She has learned a few things along the way.

What she wants is for Nick to need her.

Need is almost more important than love.

35

Nina and Nick took Zoë to visit Phoebe before they left People's Hospital to go home to Antonia Street to start their new life together as a family.

William was there in Phoebe's room, as he was most of the time (standing guard, Nick was almost beginning to feel, lest the evil son-in-law crept in alone and pressed a pillow over her face), and Phoebe managed one of her strange, vague, disturbingly absent smiles when she saw them walk in, but that was all. Nina laid Zoë very gently on Phoebe's stomach, and not for the first time, Nick found himself silently praying that this might be the breakthrough they all longed for; as if the simple sensation of touching her baby niece might heal whatever mysteries were keeping Phoebe from wholly returning to them.

There was no healing. Instead, Phoebe started to cry. Tears bloomed in her eyes and fell down her ghostly cheeks, and her nose ran, and Nina tugged two tissues out of the Kleenex box on the bedside table and gently dabbed at her sister's face, and then she, too, was weeping.

'It's all right,' William told both his daughters. 'It'll be all right.'

Zoë, who had been sleepy and compliant until then, wriggled and whimpered and Nick bent down and laid his hands either side of her, ready to pluck her up if she rolled or showed any sign of kicking.

'I'll take her,' William said, swiftly, and bent, too.

Nina looked up sharply, her eyes still wet. 'No, Dad,' she said. 'Nick can manage.'

Nick was just picking up his daughter, when there was a knock, and Sam Ellington poked his head around the door.

'Nick,' he said, softly, awkwardly. 'Someone to see you.'

'Who is it?' Nick felt Zoë's body warmth snug against his chest, cradled the soft spot on her head protectively with his right palm.

'I think you should come outside,' the paediatrician said. 'Let mama have a cuddle with Zoë.'

'Nicholas Miller?'

Two men waited in the hall outside Phoebe's room.

'Yes.'

'Inspector Abbott, SFPD, Narcotics Division.' One of the men, stocky, with dark too-slick hair and sweat above his upper lip, flashed a badge.

'Inspector Riley.' The other man was taller, slighter and fair, his hair razor-cut. Both men wore dark suits.

Nick looked at Sam Ellington. 'Is this about Phoebe?'

Ellington shook his head. 'I don't know, Nick.'

Abbott removed a document from an inside pocket of his jacket and held it out. 'We have a warrant to search your house, Mr Miller. We'd like you to accompany us there now.'

The panic hit him like a body blow. Old times from another life came back, vivid and scary. His arrest in New York. Liza Montgomery warning him to stay out of trouble. The overwhelming, blessed relief at being freed to walk.

And his terror after that last evening with Holly Bourne, just before he'd escaped to Venice. Six years – more than six years, for fuck's sake – how could they be coming for him now?

Narcotics Division. Drugs. Still maybe related to the old arrest, but not assault, at least.

A crumb of comfort.

'I don't understand,' he said.

'Which part?' Inspector Riley asked, belligerently.

'Why do you want to search my house?' Out of the corner of his eye, Nick saw Ellington's troubled, puzzled face.

'Just come with us, please, sir,' Abbott told him.

Riley laid a hand on Nick's shoulder. Tough, mean fingers.

The comfort was gone. 'My wife,' Nick said, and his tongue felt suddenly thick in his mouth. 'We're taking our baby home today.'

161

'They're welcome to join us.' Riley's breath smelled of chewing gum and cigarettes.

'Personally,' Abbott said, 'I'd advise against it.'

The door to Phoebe's room opened, and Nina emerged, holding Zoë. Instinctively protective, Sam Ellington stepped between her and the inspectors.

'You can come with us and unlock the door,' Riley told Nick, 'or we can break it down.'

'What's going on?' Nina stared at Riley's hand on Nick's shoulder. 'Nick?'

Nick shook his head. 'This is insane.'

'Go with them, Nick,' Sam Ellington said. 'I'll explain to Nina, and we'll get you a lawyer.'

'Why does he need a lawyer?' Alarm pinched Nina's face. 'Explain *what*?'

'They want to search the house,' Nick told her. 'For drugs.'

'That's ridiculous,' Nina said.

'Of course it is,' Nick agreed, 'but they have a warrant.' He looked at Ellington. 'I won't need a lawyer.'

'Of *course* you need a lawyer,' Nina said. 'I'll call Michael Levine – he'll know the right person—'

'No,' Nick said sharply. 'No lawyer. It'll be okay.' He moved towards her and Riley let go of his shoulder. 'They won't find anything – we both know that. It's a mistake.'

'I don't understand.' Nina's bewilderment was growing with every second. 'Why are they doing this?' She turned to the policemen. 'Why are you *doing* this?'

'Sooner we start, sooner we finish,' Abbott said, gentler than his partner.

'I'm coming too,' Nina said.

'No,' Nick said, sharp again. He looked at Zoë, nestling against her mother's shoulder. 'You stay here with the baby and your family. Don't come home till I call you.'

'We may need you later on, too, Mrs Miller,' Abbott told her.

'They won't need you.' Nick looked at Nina's eyes, wide with shock and fear. 'They're not going to find anything, sweetheart.'

'This is *really* ridiculous.' Nina was caught between anger and tears. 'Zoë's ready to leave.'

'I know,' Nick said, 'and I'll be coming back for you both when this is over.'

'Go on,' Ellington urged quietly. 'Go take care of this nonsense, Nick, and we'll take care of Zoë.'

By the time they reached Antonia Street, there were two other cars, and from the instant Nick unlocked the front door, what seemed to him like a cascade of police officers of all shapes, colours and sizes flooded past him and took over their house.

It was almost a rampage. Everything that could be taken apart was. Nina, going out of her mind at the hospital, called right in the middle of it, and Nick told her on the kitchen phone that the situation was under control, but right then a plate dropped onto the floor and smashed, and two men began noisily dismantling their oven, and Nick knew that she could probably hear more than enough to know that *nothing* was under control.

'I called Michael Levine,' Nina said. 'He says he recommends a criminal lawyer called Chris Field – he's going to try to get in touch with him.'

'We're not going to need anyone, Nina,' Nick said again, tautly, watching the two officers unscrewing the oven door. 'I told you, they're not going to find anything.'

'Then why are they *looking*?' Nina wanted to know.

Good question.

Packs of flour, pasta and sugar were split and spilt all over the kitchen counters. Pillows and a quilt in their bedroom, seat cushions and curtains in the living room were all ripped at the seams, and a table lamp got knocked over and broken. Tube after tube of oil and acrylic paint in Nick's studio was squeezed out, and precious framed works were cut out with a semblance of care. Nina's bottles of make-up, jars of cosmetics and cartons of tampons were messed up.

Worst of all, they hit the nursery. Zoë's mattress, the packs of her diapers, containers of baby powder, and every last one of the soft, clean, cuddly animals that Nina and Nick had placed carefully, strategically around the room for the gentlest, snuggest, long-awaited welcome home for their daughter.

Nothing was found.

* * *

163

'I told you,' Nick said to Inspector Abbott as they were all leaving.

'Everyone does,' Abbott said.

'I can't answer for everyone,' Nick said. 'I just want to know why you would think you'd find drugs in our house.'

'You have a prior arrest,' Riley said.

Nick stared at him. 'Seven years ago, in New York. It was a mistake. They dropped the charges. I was set up.'

'Aren't you all?' Riley's comment was dry.

'It's still on file,' Abbott said.

'So what's that supposed to mean?' Nick was struggling to keep his temper. 'That you have the right to go round breaking up every house belonging to anyone who ever got arrested?'

'We had probable cause,' Abbott said.

'What does *that* mean?' Nick asked.

Riley opened the front door. 'It means a judge agreed we had enough cause for a search warrant.'

'That's no explanation.' Nick's frustration burst into his voice.

'You got lucky, sir,' Abbott said. 'If I were you, I'd settle for that.'

'And what about the mess your guys made? My wife's about to bring our baby daughter home from the hospital.'

The two detectives stepped outside.

'I guess I'd start cleaning up,' Riley said.

'It's over,' Nick told Nina on the phone. 'Everything's fine.'

'They didn't find anything?'

'Of course they didn't find anything. There was nothing to find.'

'But why did they think there would be?'

'I don't know,' Nick said. 'They wouldn't tell me.'

'Maybe they'll tell a lawyer.'

'I doubt it.' Nick tried to sound more positive. 'The main thing is it's over.'

'Are you sure?'

'It has to be over. They didn't even find a cigarette.'

Nina's voice was still shaky but relieved. 'Do you want me to bring Zoë in a cab?'

'I don't think you should bring her at all. Not today, anyhow.'

'What do you mean?'

'They messed up the place, sweetheart.' Nick looked around their

164

living room, at the cushions slit open, the curtain linings unravelled, the books strewn everywhere. 'It looks like we were robbed.'

'I want to bring her home,' Nina said softly. 'I don't care what it looks like.'

'They searched Zoë's nursery,' Nick told her.

'Oh, Nick.'

'Honestly, baby, I'd rather clean things up before you come home.'

There was a moment's silence.

'I'm not leaving Zoë in this hospital one second more than I have to,' Nina said. 'Aside from everything else, I don't really want to give my father any more ammunition against you.'

'Didn't you tell him what was going on?' Nick asked.

'No, not exactly, but he knew something was wrong. I told him it was a plumbing problem at the house.'

'Good,' Nick said. 'Thank you.'

'I still don't understand how it could have happened.'

'Obviously someone made a mistake.'

'Some mistake,' Nina said.

He thought, for just a moment, of telling her about his New York record. *Yeah, great idea, on the day your daughter comes home for the first time.*

'I wish you'd let me take care of the cleaning up before you bring Zoë home,' he said again.

'No chance,' Nina said. 'You've been through enough on your own already. We're coming home to help. No arguments.'

They took the baby with them all over the house, keeping her in her carrycot for safety while they worked quietly, tackling the nursery as their first priority. Nick scrubbed the floors and walls, while Nina did her best to fix and mend and generally cleanse. She wept for a few minutes in the kitchen while she sat at the table and stitched up the old-fashioned teddy bear she had found at FAO Schwarz on Stockton Street and which she'd hoped might become a great love of their daughter's, but then the phone rang and it was Chris Field, the lawyer, wanting to talk to Nick.

* * *

'What did he say?' Nina asked as Nick put the phone back on its hook on the wall.

'That the police had some kind of a tip-off.'

'What?'

Nick kept his voice low, mindful that the baby was asleep in her carrycot on the floor. 'Apparently someone claimed I had heroin in our house which I was planning on selling – *heroin*, can you believe that?'

Nina's pale face grew even whiter. 'Who would say such a terrible thing?'

'Field doesn't know,' Nick answered, bitterly. 'He says the police don't have to tell him. The only person who needed to know that was the judge who signed the search warrant. According to Field, the search was righteous. "*Righteous*" – how's that for a bizarre choice of word?' Anger raised his voice. 'And I almost forgot – he also told me that the cops are pissed off because they didn't find anything. *They're* pissed off.' He shook his head. 'Jesus.'

'Take it easy.' Nina nodded towards Zoë.

'I'm sorry.' He shook his head again and sank down on one of the other chairs beside her. 'I am so sorry about everything.'

'Why should you be sorry?'

'It was me they suspected.'

'What else did Field say?'

'He asked me if I had any idea who might have given that kind of information to the cops.'

'And do you?' Nina asked.

'Of *course* not.'

'No need to yell at me,' she said.

'No,' he agreed. 'I'm sorry,' he said again.

'I don't blame you for yelling. I feel like screaming myself.'

They both sat in silence for a while, alone with their thoughts, and then Nick looked down at Zoë. 'How can she sleep through all this?'

'She's such a good baby,' Nina said. 'We're very lucky.'

'Yes.' Nick nodded. 'We are.'

They stopped talking again.

'It was all so beautiful,' Nina said, after a few minutes.

'It will be again, sweetheart,' Nick told her, his heart aching for her. 'I promise you it will be.'

'It feels dirty.'

166

She stood up wearily and went into the utility room, over to the tumble drier, and Nick got up, too, and went after her.

'However much we scrub the house,' she said, switching off the machine, 'I think it's always going to feel tainted.'

'No, it won't. Of course it won't.'

She looked at him while she removed Zoë's warm, soft laundry and held it close to her chest. 'Do you really have no idea why this happened? Who might have done this to us?'

If we were in New York, Nick thought, *and if it weren't so crazy, I might have a candidate.*

'No idea at all,' he said, and paused. 'Field said stuff like this happens sometimes. Mistakes.'

'That word again. So convenient.'

'Yes.'

'Perhaps we should think about suing?' Nina suggested. 'For harassment, maybe. Don't people do that sometimes?'

'I don't know,' Nick said. 'I don't think it's such a hot idea.'

Not with a prior arrest for possession.

'Maybe you should ask Chris Field about it?'

'No,' he said.

'Why not?'

'Because I think he would have suggested it if he thought it was an option.'

'Maybe,' Nina said.

She was still holding Zoë's laundry in her arms.

'Why don't you give me that stuff to put away,' Nick suggested, 'and you go take a nap?'

'Not until we've finished cleaning,' Nina said.

'I think a nap might be just what you need.'

Nina looked into his eyes for a long moment. 'I'll tell you what I do need, Nick. I mean, what I honestly, seriously, want.'

'Tell me,' he said, though he thought perhaps he knew.

'A drink,' Nina said, and walked out of the room.

36

She didn't take a drink, thank God. I suggested we might go together to an extra AA meeting or two to help us through, but Nina gave me this strange, disquietingly frosty look and told me she had less time to spend on herself now than ever before, so she was just going to have to depend on her own inner strength, such as it was. I told her that if it helped at all, I thought she was the strongest woman I had ever known. She told me that it didn't help at all.

Moments like that make me afraid. The big fear, the one that clutches at my vital organs and won't let go. The fear of losing Nina. Only now, of course, that fear has grown in stature, since if I lose my wife, I may lose my daughter, too. I have no words for how that prospect – no matter how remote a possibility it may seem – makes me feel.

Same old fear. Same regret. I should have told Nina everything about Holly when I met her. That way, I could have brought Holly into the picture on the day of the drugs search, could have set my wild, unsettling, niggling doubts before my intelligent, intuitive wife. I could have said: *'This just went through my mind – now tell me I'm nuts, tell me that it couldn't be.'*

Of course, it couldn't be. Can't be. Not anything to do with Holly, because everyone knows she's happily married with a great career in New York City. Thousands of miles away. In my past.

I did make one phone call home, just to be sure that was still the case, and my mother assured me that it was. Is. So I put away those doubts, shoved them where they belonged – in my history, the lousy part – and put the day of Zoë's awful homecoming down to the perils of being an American in 1996.

* * *

Our daughter has been home with us for two weeks now. If I thought that I knew about love and completeness before, I know now that I had no idea. This little bundle seals our union, has transformed what was already a happy home into the real thing. This piece of squirming, wailing, sucking, sleeping, diaper-filling humanity is what Christmases and Thanksgivings are all about. Except that Zoë seems able to inject that spiritual high into me every single day.

The fear is receding again.

Phoebe's arms are still in plaster, her hands useless due to the nerve damage sustained through her compound fractures, though the surgical team have high hopes for an improvement in time. She still has not spoken, and no one has been able to find any more physical reason than before for what they refer to as aphonia and we lesser mortals call loss of speech. It may be a residual effect of her head injury, or it may be some psychological problem. There is certainly no reason that they can find that Phoebe will not, at some point, speak again. In the meantime, it's vital to her long-term physical recovery that she spends some time in a specialist rehabilitation centre. With the Waterson Clinic, one of the finest places of its kind, located in Arizona just a dozen or so miles away from William Ford's home in Scottsdale, there seems no more sensible alternative.

So come the end of August, my father-in-law will ride off into the desert with our beloved, still-silent Phoebe.

No doubt he would be a much happier man if he could snatch up Nina and his granddaughter, too, and get them away from the son-in-law he no longer trusts.

SEPTEMBER

37

Things would be moving along a whole lot more swiftly, Holly realizes, if she could have seen to the planting of a few ounces of smack inside the Miller household to be found by the narcotics inspectors. As it was, it had been pretty much of a gamble (another gamble) as to whether or not her anonymous phone call to the Narcotics Division was going to be heeded.

She made the call in San Francisco from a pay phone in the Moscone Convention Center, her voice made unrecognizable and untraceable by an electronic filtering device she'd stolen a week earlier from an amateur spy shop in downtown Los Angeles. (It was the first time in quite a while that she'd stolen anything – it was harder to motivate yourself to shoplift when you were an adult with enough credit and chargecards at your disposal to stretch the width of Rodeo Drive – but the old buzz was still just as potent as it had always been.)

'I'm not going to give you my name,' she said, 'just the name and address of an artist with a New York drugs history living in Pacific Heights with a stash of China White for sale. And you might want to bear in mind this guy's not only married with a new baby, but he's also a big-time illustrator of children's books,' she threw in for good measure. 'Nice, huh?'

More than enough to give Nick a good tough time if the cops bought her dime-drop and went in, and anything more at this stage than the hassle and unpleasantness of a smack search would have been counterproductive from Holly's point of view. This one, she calculated, was merely intended to drive a wedge between the loving couple. Just a little one for openers.

She'll do better next time.

Something that Nina Miller will find much harder to ignore or to forgive.

Something spicer.

It's remarkably easy to squeeze information out of the average man when he has a hard-on and a beautiful, skilful woman is promising him whatever his particular pleasure is. In the past two months, Charlotte Taylor – managing to pay Taylor Griffin's bills well enough with a small cluster of unspectacular, low-life clients – has learned a good deal about how to make the right men give her the kind of unauthorized information she's looking for.

Details, for instance, of ongoing investigations into certain unsolved crimes in the San Francisco and northern California area. Sexual offences, for example, against minors. Not full-blown rape cases, but vile, reprehensible, unforgivable crimes nonetheless.

The last kind of crime that the illustrator of *Firefly*, the soon-to-be major animation release, is going to want to be accused of.

Holly still remembers, sometimes, those years when she thought she was completely over Nick, free of him. At law school, after he had left New York. When she wanted, more passionately than anything – for just that brief, beautiful time – to serve the law, to serve justice, even fantasizing that maybe, in some hazy, Utopian future, she might love again and *be* loved, the way ordinary people seemed to manage.

That's all in the past now, vanished almost without trace. Now, ever-increasingly, Holly's thoughts, waking and sleeping, are revolving around Nick Miller again. Now, in bed at night with her husband, all Holly's fantasies are about Nick. A Nick behind bars. A desperate Nick, abandoned by all those who have ever loved him. Except one.

The one person left who can help him.

Alone in her office on the eighteenth floor, inside the almost entirely fabricated world of Taylor, Griffin, Holly daydreams about sitting beside Nick in court: his lawyer, his lifeline. Sometimes, driving out to some deserted beach, or alone at home in Brentwood when Jack's at the office and Vita, their housekeeper, is out shopping, Holly rehearses her defence strategies, considers the witnesses she'll call on her client's behalf when the time comes. She even acts out her closing argument and her rebuttal: the manner in which she will finally, systematically, *brilliantly*, wipe out the evidence against him.

Evidence she will have created in the first place. Enough to indict – not enough to convict.

'*The last woman on earth I could ever love,*' he said to her that last night in Manhattan.

And her last words to him:

'*I'll make you sorry.*'

It would serve him right if she simply built a case against him and then left him to stew. But the way Holly sees it now, if she plays this ultimate game perfectly, she will, at long last, achieve her goal. Nick will have to understand, will finally have to realize that when the chips are truly down there's only one woman who's going to stand by him, to protect him. Defend him.

Love him.

And he will be so grateful.

He'll have to be so damned grateful.

175

38

On a Saturday morning, two weeks after Phoebe and William had left for Arizona, a manuscript addressed to Nick arrived at the Millers' home and, for the very first time since reading *Firefly*, Nick found himself utterly captivated by a proposal.

'It's a translation of an Italian children's story called *Graziella*,' he told Nina later that afternoon after she had closed the Ford Realty office and they were strolling with Zoë – now two months old – in her baby carriage in Lafayette Park, 'and it's very beautiful.'

'What's it about?'

'It's an adventure, I guess, only it's just a dream. A child from a boring, ordinary kind of a home in Milan goes to sleep and finds herself lost in Venice in wintertime.' Nick smiled. 'It's very dark for a children's story – a lot darker than *Firefly* – but there's this incredible, swirling sense of atmosphere and fantasy right through it. I mean, can you imagine how scary Venice in the depths of winter could be for a lost child?'

'Sounds like *Don't Look Now* for children,' Nina commented.

Nick nodded. 'But there's not exactly a sense of horror, just this compelling, deliciously creepy sense of fear.'

Nina stopped walking and looked into his face. 'It's really grabbed you, hasn't it?'

'Yes, it has,' Nick agreed. 'I want to illustrate this one, Nina. I'm not sure if it's going to appeal to the American readers in the same way as *Firefly* did, but it's the only thing I've really been excited by since I first read your story.'

The sun came out. Nina pulled the hood further over the carriage to protect the baby. 'Did you hear that, Zoë?' she said. 'Your daddy's

176

going to paint another book for you to enjoy when you're a little bit bigger.'

'If I get the job,' Nick said.

'Who sent it to Clare?' Nina asked him.

'It didn't come via Clare. It came direct from a guy called Bruno Conti. Says he owns the English language rights and he's looking for an illustrator for the US edition, and he thinks I may be it.'

They walked on. They both loved this flowery, pine-scented park that felt so safe, Nick often thought, in contrast to Central Park. Until Phoebe had gone to Catherine Street that afternoon in July, in fact, Nick had felt safe all the time in San Francisco. Sure, the ground beneath them did shake periodically, and each tremor was a salutary warning, made Nina and he discuss every now and again the possibility of relocating one day for Zoë's sake. But on the whole, even with Phoebe still sick and too far away in Arizona, and despite the big trauma of the heroin search last month (the worst of its jagged edges now, mercifully, fading into the past, with no further contact by the SFPD), Nick knew that he and Nina both still felt much the same warmth for their home.

'Thing is,' he said, getting back to the new manuscript, 'Conti says he's staying in Carmel, but he only just saw *Firefly* for the first time, and he's leaving the country in two days' time.'

'What will you do?' Nina asked.

'Go see him, I guess.'

'What about Clare?'

'I'll call her as soon as we get home.'

Clare Hawkins was against him going to Carmel.

'I'd rather check Conti out first, Nick.'

'Go ahead. I don't plan on meeting him till tomorrow.'

'It's almost Saturday evening,' Hawkins pointed out. 'I'm not going to be able to find out anything about him till Monday afternoon at the earliest.'

'Too late,' Nick said. 'He's leaving Monday.'

'In any case,' the agent added, 'it would be wise if I come with you to meet him.'

'Be my guest. I'd be delighted.'

'I'm not free tomorrow, Nick. I don't really have any time for almost a week.'

'Then I guess I'll have to go without you.'

Hawkins sighed. 'He's really got you steamed up, hasn't he?'

'Not him. *Graziella*. You'll love it too when you read it.'

'Don't make any kind of a deal, Nick.'

'I won't.'

'If Conti tries to talk money—'

'I'll tell him I leave all that to you.' Nick grinned into the phone. 'Stop worrying, Clare. All I want to do is work on some rough ideas tonight, and take a drive down there tomorrow to show the guy. If he likes my sketches and suggestions, then you and he can talk business when he's back in Italy.'

'Where's he based?' Hawkins asked.

'I don't know.'

'What's the name of his company? Does he have a company?'

'I don't know.'

'You don't know much, do you, Nick?'

'I guess not.'

'Be careful.'

His rough, swiftly executed sketches in a portfolio, Nick kissed Nina and the baby goodbye just after eight on Sunday morning, chose the scenic ride and headed in the Land Cruiser towards Pacifica and Highway 1 south en route for Santa Cruz. He'd only made this trip twice since moving to San Francisco, both times with Nina, once with Phoebe on board, and that occasion had been a special pleasure. They'd stopped at Ano Nuevo State Park where they'd booked a hike with a ranger, and though they'd all been thrilled as big kids to see the elephant seal colony on the beach, Nick would never forget in particular the unadulterated joy on Phoebe's face. If – *when* – she got well again, he promised himself as he passed Pigeon Point now, he would make sure they all took a quiet fall trip to Yosemite together.

He made only one stop at Monterey for a cup of coffee to clear his head of driving fuzz, and reached Carmel just before midday. The little hillside town was, as he'd thought it might be, crowded with late-summer-Sunday visitors, so Nick (who, like most Californian residents, generally chose to take his pleasure trips off-season) felt few regrets at having to forego the galleries and quaint streets in order to locate the address Bruno Conti had given him.

178

It was just outside the town, almost a mile towards Salinas. Steinbeck sprang into his mind – was seldom far away when Nick made these forays out of San Francisco. The house where Conti was staying was prettily Spanish, its roof toasted by sun, its solid white-washed stone promising coolness within.

Nick parked the truck, grabbed his portfolio, found a bell push and rang. The door opened almost immediately, and a young woman, almost certainly Mexican, stood smiling at him, combs pulling her jet black hair so tightly off her face that Nick felt sure, in spite of her smile, that it must be painful. Her white, starched apron and flat, sensible black shoes made her, he guessed, the housekeeper.

'I'm here to see Mr Conti,' Nick said.

'Yes, sir.' Her accent was strong.

She stood back to let him through. The hallway was dim and cool, as Nick had known it would be, and there was a faint scent of jasmine and of cooking (probably last night's lingering) in the air. The housekeeper led the way out of the hall through a narrow, white-washed corridor, past three closed doors and under a stone archway into a sun-drenched back yard.

There was a small swimming pool, an even smaller paddling pool and a cobbled patio with a white wrought iron table and four match-ing chairs. No one seemed to be around.

'Please wait here, sir,' the Mexican woman told Nick, and indi-cated one of the chairs. 'Would you like something to drink?'

Nick felt the heat of the midday sun. There were two palm trees at the other end of the pool, but there was no shade over the patio, not even a parasol. He nodded and smiled at the housekeeper. 'Something cool would be good, thank you.'

'Please sit,' she said, and went back into the house.

He sat.

The garden was bordered on all sides by flowering bushes, their per-fume thick in the air, their colours pleasing. As an artist and man, Nick was appreciative of nature, but he was no botanist, could identify few species much rarer than a rose, had not even, he mused as he waited in the heat, painted a single flower for its own sake since leaving college.

The housekeeper returned with a jug of iced tea, a tall glass and a little ornate silver dish of sugar cookies. Nick thanked her, and she went away again.

179

He poured some tea, drank a little, and waited. The light was very bright. He closed his eyes. He felt sleepy.

Children's voices woke him. Little children, laughing, chattering.

Startled, Nick opened his eyes as they ran, barefoot, past the patio on their way to the paddling pool. There were three of them, two girls and a boy, all aged about six or seven, colourful towels tied around their waists. The boy, his hair white gold, clutched a big beachball, which he threw into the water. One of the little girls, a pretty little dark-haired charmer, looked in Nick's direction and waved a hand, beaming at him. He smiled and raised a hand in response, then glanced back to see who else was coming out to join them. There was no one.

The children shed their towels simultaneously and hovered for a moment at the edge of the paddling pool. They were all naked. The second girl, a blonde not quite as pale as the boy, turned around to smile at Nick before she and the others got down into the water. He smiled back. The dark child waved at him again, and for the second time he responded.

He did not hear the small click and whir of the Nikon camera.

Nor did he see the figure crouching at the edge of the garden, concealed by hibiscus, scarlet lobelia and California fuchsia.

He took another drink of his iced tea and settled back to watch. Small children unsupervised around water made him nervous. He wondered if they were Bruno Conti's own family, wondered how much longer it would be before the man arrived.

The children played for quite a while, in and out of the pool, tossing their plastic beachball back and forth to each other, before the boy held onto the ball for a longer moment than previously and then threw it out of the pool towards Nick.

Nick stood up, happy to oblige, retrieved the beachball and tossed it back into the water.

The camera clicked and whirred again.

The game continued. From time to time the boy – always the boy – threw the ball, quite deliberately, in Nick's direction, and each time

180

Nick got up out of the chair and tossed it back, always making a decent-sized splash and eliciting shrieks of laughter from whichever child got wettest. They were beautiful children, especially the dark-haired girl, and Nick thought, for a moment or two, of pulling out a pad and pencil and making a few sketches of them, but then he decided against it. None of them had yet spoken to him – which he figured probably stemmed from parental lessons about caution with strangers – so aside from throwing the ball back to them every now and again, he kept an eye on them for safety's sake but left them otherwise alone.

He was hot. The main pool looked cool and smooth and tempting. Nick picked up his portfolio from the ground by his chair, started to open it, wanting to remind himself of *Graziella*, the reason he'd come, but then that seemed too much effort and he put it down again.

He looked at his watch. It was almost one o'clock. A wave of irritation passed through him and he stood up and wandered over to the paddling pool.

He crouched down near the edge.

'Will you kids be okay on your own for a moment?'

'Sure, mister,' the boy answered, and the two girls giggled.

Behind the flowering plants, the Nikon took several more shots.

Nick straightened up, turned around and walked slowly back towards the house, stepped through the white stone archway and stopped.

'Hello?' he called.

No one answered. Nick listened, but heard nothing. He wandered a little further inside.

'Is anyone here?' He pitched his voice a little louder.

There was no response at all. He knocked on one of the closed doors, waited a beat, then opened it. A sitting room, painted white, with cane furniture and pink cushions that matched the curtains. It looked almost too clean and free of clutter to be a home. He closed the door again and walked through to the dim, square front hall.

'Mr Conti?' he called, much louder this time. 'I've been waiting almost an hour.'

Not a whisper. Nick's irritation grew.

He remembered the kids in the pool. What in hell was he supposed to do? Sit out there, baking and nursemaiding them for the rest of the afternoon?

181

Quickly, he walked back out into the garden.

The children were gone, their ball and towels with them. Not a trace remained except for their wet footprints on the smooth stone by the pool, and those were fast drying in the sunshine. The surface of the water in the paddling pool was perfectly smooth.

'Curiouser and curiouser,' Nick said aloud to himself.

He looked around. There was a little too-warm tea left in the jug, but at least it was still there, otherwise he might have begun to feel that the whole last hour had been a figment of his imagination, some kind of noon heat illusion. But the tea *was* there, which meant, instead, that either Bruno Conti had been unavoidably detained and that his housekeeper was unreliable, or that Conti was himself both ill-mannered and undependable.

Either way, he knew he should have listened to Clare.

39

I took my portfolio, left a terse note for Conti on a small round table in the hall, drove into Carmel, had a sandwich and a Coke and called Nina to let her know what had happened.

'I'm going to take 101 on the way back,' I told her. 'I should be home by around five.'

'Don't rush,' Nina said. 'Drive safely.'

'I love you,' I told her. 'Kiss the baby for me.'

We sat at home all that evening anticipating an apologetic call from Conti, but there was no word either that night or the next day. I felt rattled, not so much because of the wasted journey, but because the Italian story had really got my creative juices flowing, and being jerked around that way was frustrating.

'I'll make some calls,' Clare Hawkins told me on the phone.

'Aren't you going to say you told me so?' I asked her.

'I never expected him not to show,' she said.

Clare is a kind woman.

The cops came to the house two afternoons later while Nina was upstairs in the nursery feeding Zoë.

I opened the door to them myself. Three this time. Two inspectors from Juvenile Division and a detective from Carmel. Bad dream time again, only worse than before.

They told me they wanted me to go with them for questioning.

Nina came into the hallway, the baby in her arms. I looked at her face. She looked confused, sick. She looked the way I felt.

They took me away.

They let me go home again after a few hours. The events of that afternoon are blurry, which is the only mercy. If the drugs thing was crazy, this was beyond insanity.

They have pictures. Of me playing with naked children by a pool at a house in Carmel. They have to warn me, they said, that I fit a description – as near as damnit – that they have on file of a multiple child molester. And so, these photographs having come into their possession, they want to talk to me.

You wouldn't believe the way those pictures make me look.

All I did was smile, wave my hand and toss them their ball.

I look like a genuine dirtbag.

Nina called Chris Field, the lawyer who had spoken with the Narcotics police on my behalf in August. We hadn't met back then, but now, faced with his youth, efficiency and ice-blue eyes, I couldn't shake off the uncomfortable sense that he wasn't as totally convinced of my blamelessness as I needed him to be.

According to Field, the fact that I have the translation manuscript and Bruno Conti's letter means little to the police. Paedophiles, the cops say, are adept at creating smokescreens. *Paedophiles*!

The bleak fact is that there is no one who can conclusively prove my innocence. Nina did what she could to back up my account of what had led me to Carmel, and then alerted Clare Hawkins, who dropped everything to come and do the same.

Except, of course, neither she nor Nina was actually *there*.

On the good news front, such as it is, the cops don't have anyone on their side who was there either. The house belongs, Field tells us, to a seventy-three-year-old sculptor who spends most of every summer and early fall on the Côte d'Azur in France. The property stands empty and unstaffed, except on Fridays when a maintenance company cleans and checks out the place.

There's no evidence that I – or anyone else – broke into the house. No neighbour to even back up the police's notion that I might have obtained keys and let myself in. There's also no Mexican house-keeper, no children, no parents, and definitely no Bruno Conti. Just a bunch of maybe-indecent-looking pictures sent to them anonymously and untraceably.

So they had to let me go, didn't they?

Like I said, I don't remember – prefer not to remember – every detail of my afternoon with the Juvenile inspectors and the detective from Carmel, but I do know that, some time before Chris Field arrived and told me to keep my mouth shut, I told the officers that it was clear to me I'd been framed. And I told them what had happened last month.

'That was a set-up too,' I said.

I knew, as soon as I saw their expressions when they returned from checking my claim with Narcotics, that I'd made another mistake, that I had just voluntarily dived from the rank of 'possible sleaze' to 'unproven major-league scumbag'. The kind they were not likely to have an ounce of sympathy for.

The kind they were even less likely to forget about.

The alarm bells that started ringing softly – too softly – in August when Inspectors Abbott and Riley arrived at the hospital with their search warrant, are by now shrieking in my head fiercely enough to give me a force ten migraine.

Prior arrest. Riley pointed that out, as I recall. Yes, I do have that prior. And I had a beating, too, just before that, from two ugly sono-fabitch drug pushers in my New York apartment.

Another memory zeroes in, from way back. A nasty, dirty little rumour going around my high school that I had sexually assaulted a thirteen-year-old.

It can't be Holly, I tell myself again.

How can it be?

It *has* been more than six years. She *is* a happily married attorney living in Manhattan. We've both moved on.

It *cannot* be Holly.

* * *

Clare Hawkins – having failed to find any trace of Bruno Conti, and having also ascertained from Lisa Cellini, the Italian author of *Graziella*, that she and no one else owns the English translation rights to the story – thinks that *Firefly* may be at the root of this craziness.

'We're in California, Nick,' she said yesterday evening when she came over to Antonia Street for a bowl of vegetarian chilli and a pow-wow at the kitchen table. 'We have more than our fair share of sickies who thrive on child pornography.'

'What does *Firefly* have to do with porn?' Nina jumped in before I could, her expression scandalized.

'Not a thing, to you or me or Phoebe,' Clare said. 'But there are weirdos around who may have found those fragile, sensuous illustrations of Nick's some kind of turn-on.'

'I don't believe it,' Nina said.

'You don't want to believe it,' Clare told her. 'And even if that's not it, there are plenty more low-lives who get their kicks out of stirring up gossip and innuendo – the dirtier the better. Any one of them could be looking to try to make big bucks out of selling this story to the media.'

'That makes no sense,' I said. 'I'm not famous, so no one would buy the story – and if they were going to try blackmail, surely they'd have sent the photos to me, not the police?'

'So what does it mean?' Nina stirred her chilli disconsolately.

'I'd go with my sickie theory,' Clare said.

'It's horrible,' Nina said.

I said nothing more. I didn't believe in either of Clare's explanations last night and I still don't this Thursday morning.

It is crazy even to *think* of linking my troubles with the cops to Holly Bourne. Yet I do. Suddenly it seems perfectly feasible to me that she might have let me alone for a few years because she knew I was just treading water, buying time. Until I met Nina. Or maybe Holly was happy for a while herself, with her career, with her husband. God knows what it is that makes Holly do the things she does. What made her lie and steal as a child and then lay the blame like a gift at my feet, all the while telling me how much she loved me.

* * *

This morning Nina talked to William in Arizona and found out the latest news on Phoebe – no significant change, more's the pity – and now she's gone to Ford Realty and I'm in charge of our daughter.

Zoë is in perfect shape, according to Sam Ellington. He's trained us to get used to calculating her 'corrected' age when we're studying her physical and behavioural development. Zoë may have been born just over two months ago, but because she came along four weeks early, we should be expecting her to react the way she would if she were only one month old. It's just an infancy thing, Sam assures us. In time, he says, we'll be able to forget all about corrected age and the other vestiges of prematurity. In many ways, I think Nina and I have almost forgotten them already. To us, all that counts is that Zoë's here with us and that she's healthy. Her mother aside, I have to tell you that I truly believe our daughter is the most beautiful human being I've ever laid eyes on. Her hair seems to be turning from golden peachy fuzz to an unmistakable red, just like her aunt's, and her skin – that disturbingly mottled born-too-soon appearance long gone – is exquisitely, delicately pale.

Light of our lives.

I've been afraid of the past for a long time. But until now there was at least always a blanket of certainty that it *was* the past that I could throw over my fear to douse my nightmares. And now that blanket has been snatched away.

By Holly.

I do know that it's Holly. Everything points to her, no matter how hard I try to fight the suspicion. Nothing else makes real sense to me.

Which means that, finally, I have to tell Nina the whole story. Every last, ugly piece of it. There's no choice left to me. This is more than phoney drugs charges and damning photographs.

Because if Holly is behind those things, then doesn't that have to lead on to far worse, far more monstrous suspicions?

I think back to Julie in New York and remember Holly trying to destroy that relationship. And that was just a relationship, not lasting love. Not a marriage.

I hope to God that I'm wrong. That Holly really is the happily married, stable and responsible lawyer her parents claim, who has long since put the past behind her. But I can't go on ignoring the possibility that I may be right. Nina and Zoë are the most precious people in my life, and Phoebe is the closest thing I've ever had to a sister.

Except for Holly, of course, who used to call me her big brother. When she wasn't calling me her lover.

That is why, when Nina gets home this afternoon, I will have to sit her down and tell her the whole truth.

And risk losing everything.

40

Holly is finding the waiting frustrating. Keeping things together with Jack at home and at Taylor Griffin is getting harder every day. She lost one of her few clients only yesterday because she allowed her attention to wander during a meeting, and he walked out on her. Not that she gives a damn. He was nothing, a petty fraudster, a nobody.

If only she could have been at the Juvenile Division on Valencia during Nick's questioning. If she could have seen for herself the shock on his face when they first picked him up and later, when he saw the photographs. Her photographs. Best of all, if she could have seen him talking to his wife about it. Seen Nina's face.

But you can't have everything. Not all at once, anyhow.

The rest was all so simple to organize. A few calls and a little action. Not so hard with the contacts she's been making. No shortage of hungry, vulnerable, desperate people willing to help out an anonymous woman with ready cash to hand over.

It was hearing Dina Stimson, the wife of one of Jack's friends, talking about *Graziella* that sparked this particular idea. Dina, who fancies herself something of a linguist, told Holly at a party that she'd been reading to her daughter from a veritable suitcase of French and Italian children's books brought back from a recent trip to Europe, and that this particular story had really captured her attention. A telephone call to Rizzoli in Rome, a platinum American Express card and Federal Express brought Holly her own copy within forty-eight hours.

She chose Carmel partly because its artistic nature made it an

189

appropriate location for the fictitious Bruno Conti to stay while on the West Coast; and partly because one of her most grateful clients (a married hospital orderly who'd been caught performing indecent acts with a hooker in his wife's old Mustang in West Hollywood – a catastrophe which Charlotte Taylor had contrived to keep both from his wife and employers) had a cousin living in Santa Cruz who worked for the postal service on the Monterey Peninsula and who was, therefore, in a good position to pinpoint a suitable empty house in or around Carmel. For one thousand dollars, the same man in Santa Cruz saw no problems in arranging for another cousin – an illegal – to pose as a housekeeper for a few hours one Sunday, and to bring along three of her children to help. Naked would cost another five hundred, the cousin told the orderly to tell Holly. She handed over another three.

Taking the pictures was the hardest part.

Seeing him, after so long, and having to stay silent and invisible.

He looked wonderful. Older, but still handsome, still lean. Better than ever, in spite of the fact that he was hot and uncomfortable. He had cut his hair and shaved his beard, which emphasized the strong lines of his face and chin and the seductive bend on his nose that was the legacy of the night the dope pushers had beaten him up.

Christ, she wanted to touch him.

The father of her unborn child.

Their miracle.

But then she remembered Nina.

And got down to business.

He didn't have any idea she was there. The sounds of the children, laughing and splashing in the pool, covered the sounds of her Nikon. He didn't hear her, didn't see her, didn't sense her. Which was good, of course, since his finding her there would have ruined everything, *everything*, for ever. Yet it wounded her, at the same time, that he didn't somehow feel her presence in that backyard. If it were the other way around, if she were that close to him, in a garden, in a house, even in a *park*, she would know he was near, she would just *know* it.

She thought she'd screwed up once. Just after she had captured a great, really compromising shot of Nick tossing the beachball back to the naked boy, just at the moment when the water had splashed the blond girl and made her shriek, the other little girl's huge dark eyes had veered suddenly away from the pool. Right at the California fuchsia. Right at *her*, Holly thought, holding her breath, getting ready to run.

And then she saw that what had caught the child's gaze was a tiny lizard resting in some droplets of water under the bush a few feet in front of where she was squatting. Holly waited to see if the girl would be sufficiently intrigued to get out of the pool and come over to try to touch the creature, but then the lizard darted away and disappeared somewhere behind the scarlet lobelia, and the child's attention returned to the game with the ball.

It was all over too soon after that.

She watched Nick getting hotter, losing patience; snapped a few more shots when he went over to the pool and crouched down to talk to the kids; and then he walked back into the house, and the boy, the leader of the pack, remembered his instructions and got the girls out of the water, grabbed their towels and headed for the gate at the back of the garden.

Holly heard Nick calling for Bruno Conti.

She saw him come back out, saw his confusion, his irritation, watched him pick up his portfolio.

And vanish back inside the house.

The photographs were developed and on their way to the Carmel and San Francisco police departments twenty-four hours later.

Holly knew that Nick's height, weight and appearance were a close enough match with a sleazeball who had been molesting small children in San Francisco and all points in Northern California for the past several months.

Knew that the photographs would give the cops more than enough cause to pull him in.

Easy.

She imagines Nina's reaction over and over again. The wife. The other woman. That's how she thinks of her. The elegant blonde with the long nose.

She was sitting down when Holly saw her that time in the book store in New York, so Holly doesn't know what her legs are like. Long and shapely, she supposes. Her own legs are pretty damned perfect, of course, but in her case, in the eyes of men, it's the whole package that counts. It certainly used to count where Nick was concerned. And will do again, when the time is right.

Holly remembers that when she dictated the Wordsworth quote to Nina Ford, the pregnant blonde made no comment. But Holly caught the flicker in her eyes. It was tiny, but there just the same.

Fear.

She enjoyed doing that to Nina.

41

I'm going for a walk,' Nina told Nick after he had finished telling her.

Nick looked at her. 'It's past midnight.'

She looked right back at him. 'In more ways than one.'

Nina got up from their sofa, her movements slow and weary. He watched her, not moving, not wanting to crowd her. She walked out of the living room into the hall, and he hoped she would turn left and head up the stairs, but she turned right instead, towards the front door.

He jumped up. 'Nina, you can't.' He followed her into the hall.

She stopped and turned around. 'Why can't I?' Her face had grown very pale again, the way it had with each of the successive blows she had been dealt in the last several months. There was defiance in her eyes. Defiance, anger and shock.

'It's late.'

'You said that already. This is a city. People go out at night.'

Nick felt sick, as if something had died.

'You're not wearing shoes,' he pointed out, very gently.

Nina looked down at her feet. She had kicked them off hours ago, she couldn't remember where. They had begun talking in the kitchen, she remembered that, and she thought they'd gone upstairs for a while, but she wasn't certain. It suddenly seemed too much of an effort to think about her shoes.

'I'll go to bed,' she said, and walked past him to the foot of the staircase, where she paused for an instant. 'Please don't follow me,' she said, without looking back. 'I'll check on Zoë.'

'Nina, we need to talk.' Desperation made his throat tight.

'I'd have thought you'd talked enough,' she said.

And went up the stairs.

Nina did not sleep. She feigned it when she heard Nick coming into the bedroom three separate times. She kept her eyes closed and her breathing even, and she sensed him looking down at her. Probably, she thought, he knew she was faking, but he wasn't going to challenge it. If she was pretending to be asleep, then that was as clear a message to him as a turned back or a walk-out.

She lay in their bed and tried to analyse how she was feeling. She wanted a drink – she knew that much. The rest was harder to figure out. Nick had told her so much during that endless ugly evening that it had seemed, at times, like listening to someone reading aloud from a journal, telling tales from his life in precise order, relating every remembered detail, whether his audience wanted to hear those details or not.

Not. *Not*.

He could have told it so swiftly and concisely. *I fell off a mountain*, a person with a broken back could say. No need to give chapter and verse on how they climbed the damned mountain, or whether they knew it was a bad idea to climb the thing in the first place but they did it anyway.

'*I got involved with Holly Bourne again even though I said I didn't, only she didn't like it when I broke it off with her, and she turned into a crazy lady and followed me everywhere and made my life a misery until I finally lost my mind and beat her up.*'

That was all there was to it, really.

'*Oh, yeah, and she half-flushed dope down my john and got me busted for it.*'

That was all he would have needed to say. If only he had said it a couple of years ago when they met and were telling each other their secrets. Or at least *she* was telling him her secrets.

She wondered, for a little while, how she would have reacted back then if he *had* told her everything about him and Holly. But then she stopped wondering, because it was irrelevant now. What counted now was that he had not told her. Had not trusted her.

Was only telling her now because he had no choice.

God, how she needed a drink!

*   *   *

194

Nick checked on Nina a few times in the night, and on Zoë, but he never went to bed. He was too afraid that if he got into bed with Nina, she might get out. He was afraid that if she stopped pretending to be asleep and got out of bed, she might leave the house.

Maybe even go to some illegal, after hours bar. It was against the law to serve liquor after two AM in California, but even if Nina had never been the kind of alcoholic who cared to go to private clubs where they broke the law behind closed doors, Nick figured she must have spoken to enough drunks over the years at AA meetings to know about those places.

Of course, she could just get drunk downstairs. They didn't keep much in the house, but Nina insisted they always had enough stock to ensure visitors could drink what they wanted.

She had been sober for more than seven years. Even through the terrors of Phoebe's fall and its repercussions and Zoë's precarious early days; even when the police had destroyed Zoë's homecoming. She'd come close then, but no more than that. And after they had taken him in after Carmel, she had been more outraged for him than for herself.

Nina was such a brave person. She deserved so much.

Nick sat on a straight chair in the kitchen, a cup of coffee going cold in front of him on the table, his mind numb.

Words his mother had spoken to him years ago, after Eleanor Bourne had found him with Holly in their summerhouse, came back.

How could you let us down like this? Kate Miller had asked him.

He was good at letting down people he loved.

How could you let yourself down? Ethan Miller had added.

He was good at that, too.

He didn't mean to fall asleep at all, just to lie down for a while on the sofa in the living room, just to rest his eyes and brain a little. But he did sleep, and when he woke it was morning, and when he ran barefoot up the stairs and found both their bedroom and the nursery empty, he panicked, raced to pull on jeans and sneakers and a sweater, ready to go out in search of them.

Nina was in the kitchen sitting at the pine table, holding Zoë.

The relief was overpowering.

'What did you expect?' Nina asked quietly. The baby lay in her arms, staring intently up into her mother's face, the picture of contentment.

Nick sat down opposite them. 'I don't know.'

'That I'd have gone?'

'Maybe.'

Nina's expression gave nothing away. 'We have a daughter. A home. A marriage of sorts.'

Fresh pain knifed through him.

'I'm so sorry, Nina.' He didn't know what else to say.

'I know you are.'

'That isn't enough, is it?'

'Not really.'

'I don't know what else I can say,' Nick said.

'Probably because you've said it all.' Nina paused. 'Finally.'

Nick got up again, went over to the coffee pot. 'Want some?'

'No.'

He poured himself a cup. The pain was still there. Nina was here, in their house, with Zoë, with him, but he wasn't certain how much that meant any more. A bottomless, infinite ocean had opened up between them. All the ease had gone, the closeness.

'You didn't trust me, Nick,' she said from the table.

'Oh, yes, I did,' he said, coming back and sitting down again. 'That wasn't why I didn't tell you.'

Her eyes met his. 'You didn't trust me to understand. Or to accept you, warts and all.'

He put his right hand around his cup and squeezed it tight. It was hot, but not enough to burn. 'I thought I'd lose you.'

'You might have.'

'I couldn't bear to risk that.'

'You should have,' Nina said.

'Yes.'

In Nina's arms, the baby kicked her little legs and gave one of her small squealing pleasure sounds. Any other morning, Nick knew he would have stood up and peered down over his wife's shoulder, grinned foolishly at his daughter, stroked her golden carrot hair or tickled her tummy. But the ocean was still there and he was afraid of drowning.

'I'm going to take Zoë to Arizona,' Nina said, suddenly.

The knife again.

'We're leaving this afternoon,' she said. 'Just for a visit.'

More reassurance than he deserved.

'I miss Phoebe too,' Nick said.

'I want to take this trip without you, Nick. I need to get away.'

'I know.'

Silence fell.

'Will we get past this?' he asked her after a few moments.

She was a while answering.

'Maybe,' she said.

He knew it was the best he could hope for.

'Do you really believe Holly's behind all the things that have been happening to you?' Nina asked a little before lunchtime in their bedroom, where she was folding nightdresses and skirts into a beige canvas suitcase. 'Obviously you do, otherwise you wouldn't have told me what you did.'

'I can't think of anyone else it could be.'

'What are you planning to do about it?' She looked down into the case which lay open on the bed, picked up her small make-up bag from the quilt, zipped it up and tucked it into a corner.

'Other than trying to find out exactly what Holly's been up to, I don't know yet.'

'You could tell the police,' Nina suggested.

'I tried telling them I'd been set up – they didn't want to know.'

'But they didn't charge you with anything.'

'That doesn't mean they believed me,' Nick pointed out. 'And why would they? I have two strikes against me already, neither of them exactly in the parking fine league.'

'Three,' Nina said, 'if you count your New York arrest.'

'Thanks for reminding me.'

'You're welcome.' She paused. 'What about Chris Field?'

'I don't think he believed me any more than the cops did.'

'If you say so.'

'What about you?' Nick asked, suddenly.

'What about me?'

'Do you believe me?'

197

She didn't answer right away.

'It's a lot to take in,' she said.

Nick felt a sick, sinking feeling in the pit of his stomach. 'You don't believe me, do you?'

Nina stopped packing and sat down on the side of their bed. 'Are you honestly trying to tell me that you think this woman might even have been behind the fax and Phoebe's fall?'

'I don't know,' Nick said. 'It's pretty hard to imagine.'

'It's insane,' Nina said.

She got up again and went on packing.

'Do you need all that?' It looked to Nick as if she was taking enough for a month at least. The panic rose again.

'It's not so much.' Nina looked down into the suitcase. 'You're right,' she said, and shook her head wearily. 'I don't know what I'm doing.'

'Can I help?'

'No,' she said. 'Thank you.'

In the nursery next door, Zoë started to cry.

'Shall I go?' Nick asked.

'Please.'

Nick went to the door and stopped. 'Are you sure you want to take the baby to Arizona?'

Zoë was happy now to take a bottle, which had freed Nina for longer hours at Ford Realty – almost a necessity given that Phoebe looked like being out of the office for the foreseeable future.

'It might be more of a break for you,' Nick went on, 'if you leave her with me.'

The bleakness in Nina's eyes floored him.

'It isn't Zoë I need a break from,' she said.

42

I sat in my empty house, in the desolate bedroom, and made the call. It was five o'clock that same evening in San Francisco. Eight in Bethesda.

'Mrs Bourne? This is Nick Miller.'

'Oh, yes.'

Her voice hadn't changed a bit. I could picture her, hair swept up, make-up understated but perfect, wearing something 'comfortable' and probably silky for an ordinary evening at home with her husband.

'I'm calling from San Francisco,' I said.

'What can I do for you, Nick?'

I was almost surprised to hear her call me Nick. From the chilliness in her tone, 'Mr Miller' would have been more in keeping.

'I need Holly's address – or her telephone number.' Straight to the point, that was the only way with Eleanor. 'I know she's in New York, but I don't know her married name.'

'No,' Eleanor said.

'I thought you might give me the information.'

'No, Nick. I won't do that.'

'Why not?'

'I should have thought that was perfectly obvious.'

'The past is long gone, Mrs Bourne,' I tried pointing out. 'We're both settled now, both happily married. I just thought it might be nice to make contact again.'

'Then perhaps you could write to her.' Eleanor paused. 'At our address. We'll pass it on to her.'

I knew I wasn't going to get anywhere.

'How is Holly?'

'Very well. Thank you for asking.'

I waited until six in the morning to try to catch Richard Bourne (without Eleanor) at his office. Nine AM in Washington DC. It was a Saturday, but I remembered that in the past Holly's father had more often than not worked on Saturday mornings.

Nothing had changed. Richard accepted the call and was a touch warmer than his wife had been, but gave away nothing much more useful.

'Holly asked us some time ago not to pass on anything more than general information about her to you or your parents, Nick,' he said. 'I'm sorry.'

'I see.'

'She's happy now,' Richard said. 'Settled. You understand, I'm sure. We all feel it's better this way.'

'I guess you do.'

I did understand. Perfectly. It would, under other circumstances, have been the best news possible.

As it was, it still got me nowhere.

I caught a late Sunday morning United flight to DC, arriving mid-evening, too late to do anything but check into a hotel. Any hotel would do – something to eat, a bed for the night, a place to shower and drink coffee before bearding the protective father in his law office first thing next morning. I didn't want too much time to think or to prepare; if I was going to break down Richard Bourne's barriers, whatever I said was going to have to come straight from the heart and from as clear a mind as possible.

Not that, on past record, I've done too well with protective fathers, but I had considered the alternatives and there really weren't any, since the cops obviously weren't going to listen to me. So I was going to have to try my damnedest with Bourne.

At least, finally, I was going to do *something*.

And with Nina and Zoë away, what did I have to lose?

* * *

200

I thought I'd beat Bourne into his office, an impressive, tasteful affair – old wood, antique rugs, fine art and more than a hint of the lawyer's pipe tobacco, smoothly blending with the electronic trappings of the new age – in a sleek building on Connecticut Avenue in downtown DC. But when I got there just after eight o'clock, Bourne's secretary, Mrs Eileen Ridge, another early bird, told me serenely that her boss had already been hard at work for over an hour. Without an appointment, the middle-aged and affable Mrs Ridge told me, she very much doubted there was any chance of my seeing Mr Bourne. I gave her my most courteous, most humble smile and asked her to point out that I'd flown from the West Coast just to see him, and she said that she would do what she could for me.

She ushered me through a pair of tall, broad, oak doors less than fifteen minutes later. Richard Bourne, formal and easily elegant – just as I remembered him being in the old Bethesda days – was up on his handmade-shod feet beside his handsome desk, waiting for me. If he was angry, he wasn't letting it show. On the other hand, he wasn't exactly wreathed in smiles either.

I couldn't blame him.

'Mrs Ridge tells me,' Bourne said, shaking my hand firmly, coolly, 'that you've come to Washington specifically to see me.'

'Yes, I have.'

'I see.'

We both sat down in leather chairs, and Richard Bourne took off his small half-glasses and laid them carefully on the desk blotter in front of him. A small, polished wood pipe rested in a heavy marble ashtray and I waited for Bourne to pick it up, tuck a little tobacco into the bowl and light it, slowly and pleasurably, the way I remembered him doing in the old days, but he did not. He shook his head just a little. Not even a ripple from his immaculately cut grey hair.

'I had hoped,' he said, 'that I'd made my position clear, Nick. On the subject of divulging Holly's whereabouts to you.'

'You did, sir,' I said. 'Perfectly.'

'Then why are you here?'

'To make my own position clear.' I looked the other man in the eye. 'And to make sure, at last, that you understand the situation that led to my calling you in the first place.'

'I can't see that it's going to make a difference.'

'I think it may,' I said. 'But you'll have to be the judge of that.'

Richard Bourne's small sigh was regretful, polite. The sigh of a man too innately courteous to want to send someone who'd come thousands of miles just to see him, back on his way without even a hearing.

'Would you like some coffee, Nick?'

'I don't want to put you to any trouble, Mr Bourne.'

Bourne smiled ruefully. 'Somehow, I suspect that having Mrs Ridge bring us a pot of coffee may be the least of the trouble you intend to cause me.'

Coffee came, stylish as everything else in the office, in a silver pot on a silver tray complete with sugar tongs and tiny cookies. Bourne asked Mrs Ridge to cancel his first appointment and to hold his calls, then poured for himself and for me, and invited me to go right ahead with whatever it was I wanted to say.

'Before I start,' I said, 'I want to thank you.'

'No need,' Bourne said.

'You're prepared to listen to me.'

'You're an old friend of my daughter's,' Richard Bourne said.

'Not for a very long time,' I said. 'Longer than you realize.'

I skipped childhood, since Bourne knew all about that – or thought he did. I began with the NYU years, with Holly's lies to others and to herself about the status of our relationship. I told Bourne about her obsessive dogging of my every move, about behaviour patterns that had become tantamount to stalking. About the day she'd deliberately got herself caught shoplifting so that I would come bail her out. And about the night that had followed, when Holly had had me beaten up by drug pushers and arrested for possession of dope she had herself stolen.

I even told him – because I had no choice, because I knew I had to tell the whole truth and nothing but, if I had a snowball's chance in hell of being believed by this skilled jurist and father – about the night I went looking for Holly after she'd tried to poison Julie Monroe's mind against me. The night Holly pushed me too far.

'I'm not proud of that,' I said, softly, harshly.

'Of what exactly?' Richard Bourne's grey eyes were intent. Father's eyes.

'Of losing it.' I paused. My whole body was growing tenser.

'You struck my daughter?' Bourne's face was pale now.

'Yes, sir.'

I didn't want to go on, but I knew I had no choice.

'It appalled me. I didn't think I was capable of *thinking* about, let alone actually hitting a woman.' I veered away from Bourne's eyes. 'But Holly—' I stopped again. How could I tell this decent man that his daughter had *enjoyed* being hit by me? 'Holly wanted me to stay, regardless,' I pushed on. 'I couldn't believe it. I knew I had to leave, right then, for both our sakes, but she begged me not to go. And then, when I wouldn't, she said that if I didn't stay with her, she would make me sorry.' I faced up to Bourne again. 'I was already sorrier than you can imagine.'

The office was very silent. Over on the mantelpiece above the unlit fireplace, an antique French carriage clock ticked smoothly, and beyond the splendid doors Eileen Ridge's fingers tapped keyboard symphonies on her computer, but otherwise there was nothing except for our breathing. The coffee in both our cups was untouched and, I imagined, cold.

I waited a few moments before I went on. I think I was half expecting Bourne to throw me out, maybe even to throw a punch. But he just sat there, like a stone.

'That was the night I decided to go to California,' I went on. 'To get away from Holly. I could say it was for both our sakes, but it was really for my own. And I managed pretty well. Well enough to believe that after six years, and after being happily married to my wife for two of those years, I could forget about the past.' I took a breath. 'But I know now that's not true. Because Holly definitely has not forgotten.'

'Sounds to me, Nick,' Richard Bourne said, 'as if you might be the obsessed party in this story.'

'Does it?' I sat forward, allowing fresh anger to pump adrenalin, to keep me alert and tightly focused. 'Then maybe I'd better tell you what's going on *these* days, Mr Bourne. Let's forget the past and concentrate on what's been happening to me and my family now – this very year – and then you tell me just how else I should feel.'

I told Richard Bourne about the fax addressed to my pregnant wife enticing her to the house in Haight-Ashbury, and about what had happened after Phoebe had gone in Nina's place, and about the insurers finding out that it had been no accident and about them coming to me for answers. I told Bourne about the narcotics search on our house the day we were due to bring Zoë home from the hospital. And I told him about Carmel and the photographs. And about remembering, suddenly, out of nowhere, the time Holly had spread lies around school about me and an assault on a thirteen-year-old girl.

I took a sharp, swift glance at Richard Bourne's face then; saw discomfort, even shock, briefly exposed in his eyes.

'I didn't want to believe it either, Mr Bourne,' I went on. 'I told myself, more than once, that Holly couldn't possibly have anything to do with the things that were happening to me. Holly's happily married, I told myself. Holly's an attorney now, like her father. It couldn't be Holly.'

'But now you think it is.' Bourne's voice was stiff.

'Yes, I do.'

For a moment or two, I thought I saw the practised, unflappable lawyer starting to drown beneath the father's swamping fear of the unthinkable. But then the father disappeared again, and the attorney returned.

'And this is why you want me to give you Holly's address?' Bourne asked. 'So that you can confront her, make these accusations face to face?'

'So that I can check out the happy, married, New York lawyer for myself,' I told him, staying steady.

'I don't think so.'

'Why not?'

'Because I don't want my daughter's life disrupted.'

'Then you'll know why I feel the same way about my own family,' I said.

Richard Bourne picked up his glasses but didn't put them on. 'Your accusations are very serious, Nick.'

'Yes, they are.'

'I assume you have no proof to back them up.'

'Not yet.'

'Then I suggest you're very careful not to make them again to anyone else.'

'Are you going to sue me if I do?' I asked him.

'It's certainly a consideration,' Bourne answered.

I shook my head. 'You won't.'

'Why not?'

'Because you're too close to believing me.' I was staring right at him. I felt, at that moment, as if I had pinned him down, in emotional terms, the way an entomologist might pin down a butterfly on a board. 'You don't want to believe me, but you're certainly afraid there's a chance I'm right.'

Bourne rose from his chair, walked slowly over to the floor-to-ceiling oak bookshelves on his right and stared at nothing in particular for a while. I gave him the time he needed. I felt for the man. Though nowhere near as much as I felt for Nina and Phoebe and Zoë.

Finally, he turned around.

'Do you trust me, Nick?' he asked.

'Yes, I do.'

'Enough to leave this with me?'

'That depends on what you plan to do with it,' I said, aware suddenly that I had won at least the first round of the battle. Holly's own father, a man of influence and some power, was not dismissing my suspicions outright. That was almost more than I'd dared hope for.

'I need you to leave that up to me, too, Nick.'

'I'm not sure that I can do that.'

'Do you have much choice?' Bourne smiled, a joyless, tired smile.

I shrugged. 'I can go looking for Holly.'

The lawyer sat down again, steepling his manicured hands. 'I don't want Holly harassed, Nick. I assure you I will look into everything you've just told me.'

'And then?'

I could not afford to let him off the hook. I needed as much out of this encounter as I could get, because I knew I might never get another chance. If Eleanor Bourne got to know about our talk, for example, she would tear everything I'd told Richard to shreds, make him swear to ignore all I'd said and to protect only Holly. But if Bourne had given me his word, as a man of law, then I figured – maybe naïvely, maybe not – that there was a chance he would stand by it.

'And then, if I find there's any truth in any part of it – and I must tell you that I don't believe, for a second, that there is—'

Sure you do, I thought, but managed not to say.

'– but if I find even a scrap of truth, I promise you that I will deal with the problem, and that, after today, my daughter and her whereabouts need be of no more concern to you.'

'Simple as that? Concern?' The anger flooded back, rich and hot. 'My sister-in-law is still hospitalized. The San Francisco police have searched my home for drugs. I don't *use* drugs, Mr Bourne. They've pulled me in for questioning about molesting *children*.' I got to my feet and focused down on him hard. 'As it happens, I'm not all that *concerned* about myself – I sure as hell don't care to be unjustly accused of outrageous crimes, but if all this were just about me I could probably deal with it.'

'I do understand, Nick,' Bourne said.

'Do you?' I stayed on my feet. '*Do* you? Do you understand that I'm afraid for my wife? For our baby?'

'I don't believe that my daughter would ever hurt anyone.'

'Yet Phoebe still has two broken arms and a head injury, and hasn't been able to speak a word since the fall. Someone did that to her, and I have a terrible feeling that that someone may be Holly.'

Bourne was paler than ever.

'You said that you trusted me,' he reminded me.

'Yes, I did.'

'Then I'm asking you – for all our sakes, your family as well as mine – to let me deal with this. I give you my solemn vow that I will do that. That if – and I repeat *if* – there is the slightest evidence that you are right in any part of your accusations, I will take appropriate action.'

I knew that was the most I could hope for. I didn't expect the man to cave in, to cut up his daughter and serve her to me on a plate. I don't think I even really expect him to denounce her, to the cops or anyone else, if he does find out that I'm right. But I did think that there was a reasonable expectation that Richard Bourne would do what he had said he would. Look into it. Deal with it.

'Okay,' I said. 'All right.'

There was relief in the other man's eyes.

'Thank you, Nick,' he said.

'I'm sorry,' I said.

I was.

* * *

Now that I'm back again in my deserted, Holly-damaged home, I think about all the other things I wanted to say to Bourne, to ask him. How does he plan to go about finding out the truth about Holly? Does he realize just how devious his daughter is, what a great *actress* she is?

How very, very sick she is?

But I know I have to leave all that to him to work out for himself. And I believe now, at least, that there is a chance that he will.

43

The day after Nick came to Washington, Richard Bourne cancelled forty-eight hours' worth of meetings, appointments, lunches, dinners and games of golf, and flew to Los Angeles to see Holly.

Eleanor thought he was going on business. Richard had not told her about Nick Miller's visit, nor did he plan to until after he'd talked to Holly by himself. Eleanor would not have believed Nick. Eleanor would not have forgiven Richard for giving Nick's claims even a hint of credence. God only knew Richard didn't want to believe them either. Yet something deep inside told him that it would be an even greater betrayal of his daughter to ignore them completely.

It was just after five in the afternoon when the cab dropped him and his overnight bag outside Holly's office building on Figueroa. Like Jack Taylor, Bourne had had some difficulty comprehending Holly's decision to leave Zadok, Giulini, O'Connell and set herself up as Taylor, Griffin – yet Bourne, too, had seen that Holly was determined to go her own route. Holly had been that way ever since she was a little girl; soft and vulnerable and appealing some of the time, unmalleable iron when she chose to be.

If Bourne was honest with himself, he knew that he and Eleanor had lost true insight into their daughter's psyche long ago, certainly once she'd changed direction and chosen NYU over Harvard. If he was even more honest and looked back at the earlier years – at the time when she and Nick Miller had first become intimately involved without any of their parents having the slightest suspicion – he had

208

to admit that they couldn't have known as much as they ought about Holly then either.

That admission made him shiver now, as he took the elevator up to the eighteenth floor of Holly's building.

It was the first time Bourne had visited her there. It was, he could not help feeling as soon as he stepped through the door, a deeply ordinary office, a world away from the plush comfort, atmosphere and pace she must have grown used to at Zadok, Giulini and at Nussbaum, Koch, Morgan in New York City before that. Still, he reminded himself, if Holly was happy with her decision, that was all that mattered.

She was waiting for him in the outer office.

'Daddy, this is such a lovely surprise,' she said, coming straight into his arms. She looked and smelled wonderful, the way she always did, always had. Her secretary, she told him, had left for the day and she had no more appointments, so they had the place all to themselves – though she still didn't understand why he had insisted on coming to Taylor, Griffin rather than meeting her and Jack at home or in a restaurant. Because, Richard told her right away, (partly because he thought his nerves mightn't stand too much prevarication), there were matters they needed to talk about that were strictly private.

Holly led her father into her own office and drew him down onto her small leather sofa.

'You're not sick, Daddy, are you?'

The anxiety in her lovely eyes touched him and stabbed fresh guilt in his gut and heart.

'No, Holly, I'm not sick.' He glanced around. This office, too, was neat and practical, but oddly devoid of atmosphere; no artwork on the walls and not a single photograph on the desk.

'Is Mother all right?'

'Your mother's fine.' Bourne paused. 'Though she doesn't know I'm here.'

'I know. You told me that on the phone. You asked me not to tell Jack either.' Holly smiled. 'So what's the big secret?'

Bourne took another moment, looking his daughter over. She was wearing a charcoal linen suit with a white silk blouse, and her hair was tied back off her face with a black ribbon. She looked sophisticated, innocent and very beautiful. He felt, abruptly, like weeping.

'Daddy, what's the *matter*?'

He shook his head, dragged himself together.

'Long flight,' he said. 'I'm tired.'

Holly put a hand on his arm. 'Then why not go to the hotel and take a nap?' She knew that he'd reserved a room at the Beverly Wilshire. 'Or come home with me?'

'No, not yet,' Bourne said. 'What I could use, though, darling, is a drink. Do you keep any scotch here?'

'Naturally I do.'

Holly kept it in a small walnut reproduction cabinet that matched her desk: not quite up to her father's style, but good enough for her purposes.

'Dewars,' she said, pouring for him. 'All right?'

'Perfect.' He took the glass from her. 'What about you?'

'Not right now.' Holly considered briefly, as she had once or twice before, telling her father about the baby, but decided, yet again, that the time wasn't right. She looked at Richard's face, saw the tension in his jaw and on his mouth, thought she saw a kind of sadness in his eyes. Perhaps even a touch of fear. She experienced a sudden jolt of apprehension herself.

'Tell me.' She sat down again beside him. 'Tell me what's wrong, Daddy. Please. You're scaring me.'

Bourne took a drink of scotch, then crossed one leg over the other, cradled the glass in both hands, and prepared himself.

'When did you last see Nick Miller?'

Holly blinked. Otherwise, she prided herself, apart from mild surprise, there was not a flicker of reaction.

'Years ago,' she said, vaguely. 'About six, I think. In New York City.' She paused. 'Why?'

'He came to see me,' Bourne said.

'When?'

'A few days ago.'

'In Bethesda?' Holly stood up. She needed to do something with her hands. She went back to the cabinet, found a bottle of tonic, opened it and poured.

'In DC. He came to my office.'

210

'What for?' She could feel her father's eyes on her, but she didn't look back at him.

'He's been having some problems.'

'Really?' Holly took her glass over to her desk, ran her right hand idly through a sheaf of paperwork, then sat in her working chair. 'I thought everything was great for Nick these days. The book and his marriage and so on.'

'That's what I thought, too,' Bourne said, and waited.

He was suddenly aware of his too-rapid heartbeat. Jolting in his chest the way it had often done when he was a much younger man reaching the end of one of his early solo cases, when judgment was nearing and his own performance was on trial. Victory had always seemed so earthshakingly important. He thought now how trivial it had all really been.

'Nick told me that some things have been going wrong in his life recently,' he said. 'Badly wrong.'

'What sort of things?' Holly asked.

Her father didn't answer right away. He was looking at her in a strange and disturbing manner. As if he were trying to see into her. A man seeking clues.

'What *sort* of things, Daddy?' she repeated.

Bourne seemed to come to a decision.

'I'm not going to beat around the bush, darling,' he said, and his voice was strained.

'Okay.' Holly found suddenly that she felt very calm.

'Nick has a theory that you might be behind his problems.'

'Me?' Still the calm, the sense of being in control. Her father was the one struggling. It was easier for her, she thought, for she was in possession of the facts. She was, she realized with satisfaction, ready for this. It had taken her a few moments to understand that, but she was ready.

'Is he right?' Bourne posed the question softly, while blood seemed to surge in his head.

'About what, Daddy?' Equally soft, but far more tranquil. 'I don't understand what it is you're asking me.'

He told her. As briefly as he could, all the time watching her reactions, waiting for her to save him, feeling like a drowning man, choking on his own words, on the doubts that filled him. The telephone on Holly's desk rang a couple of times, but a machine in the outer office picked up, and Holly made no move to go check her messages, merely sat there and went on listening to what her father was telling her.

Richard wasn't sure what he had hoped for. Denial, of course, vehement and instantaneous denial – that went without saying. But that alone might not have been enough, that was the nightmare of this awful confrontation with his own child. He needed her to convince him, to *prove* to him that it was all lies, some bizarre, perhaps deranged invention of Nick Miller's.

Someone else's problem. Someone else's sickness. Please, God.

Not his daughter's.

In the end, she just confused him. Even more deeply than he had been at the outset.

'Poor Daddy,' Holly said.

Pity. In her voice and in her face. Nothing else. Neither anger nor indignation nor reproach.

Oughtn't there to be shock? Outrage?

'Nick shouldn't have done that to you,' she said.

Dismay at the oddness of her response hit Bourne like a mallet to his solar plexus.

'He should have come to me,' Holly said.

Bourne moistened his lips with his tongue. 'He didn't know where to find you. You told us not to tell him where you were.'

'Yes,' Holly said, softly. 'I did.'

'Because you were happy. With Jack. With your life.' Bourne paused. 'Aren't you happy, Holly?'

'You know I am, Daddy.'

Still that gentle pity. Still no outrage.

Bourne felt a great rush of shame flood his face. Why did he need her to deny the accusations of a man who had become a stranger? A man who, on his own admission, had hit Holly on at least one occasion.

And yet he still longed to hear her denial. Longed for it with all his soul.

Holly left her drink, stood up from her desk, walked around it to the sofa and looked down at her father.

'What do you want me to say, Daddy?'

He turned his face up to hers, but said nothing.

'Do you want me to say that Nick's a liar?'

Bourne kept his eyes on hers. 'If that's the truth.'

'Don't you know that without hearing it from me?' Holly waited several seconds. 'Oh, Daddy,' she said, reproachfully.

Swiftly, Bourne reached up, grasped at Holly's right hand and drew her down to sit beside him. 'I want you to listen to me, Holly. Okay?'

She nodded. 'Of course.'

'I'm just going to say this once, all right? And then, if that's the way you want it, you'll never hear me say it again. Deal?'

Holly gave a small, wry smile. 'Deal.'

Bourne's cheeks were still hot. His chest hurt and he felt nauseous, but he knew neither sensation was a symptom of illness.

Get it said. Get it out.

'Holly, my darling,' he said, very quickly, 'if there is any part of Miller's story that has the slightest truth in it, you must tell me.' He didn't wait for any reaction from her now, just plunged straight on. 'I'm not going to judge you – I only want to help you. There is nothing we can't deal with together – *nothing*, do you understand?'

Holly took her hands out of his.

She was staring at him.

'Holly, I have to say these things to you. You see that, don't you?'

'I see that,' she said, quietly.

'I wish—' Bourne stopped.

'What do you wish, Daddy?' The words were cooler now. The pity was almost gone.

He said it, at last. 'I wish that you would deny it.'

'Why should I?' Holly asked, simply.

Because it would give me hope.

'I don't know,' he said, wretchedly. 'I'm not sure.'

He had never in his entire life felt so lost, so much like a man stumbling around in the dark. He had always been blessed with conviction about most things, capable of extricating tiny grains of truth from the messiest risotto of lies, of recognizing and accepting when there were no grains of truth to be found.

'Holly, please, try and help me out here,' he begged.

'How would you like me to help you?'

'Tell me there's nothing to it. Tell me that Nick Miller's deluded, or that he's just a damned liar.' His desperation grew, and he fought to contain it. 'I know this must be shocking for you, darling – that you probably think I shouldn't even have felt the *need* to ask you this – that I should just have told Miller to get the hell out of my office—'

'What did you tell him?' Holly asked, suddenly.

Be honest now, or you'll lose her.

'I told him that I didn't believe for an instant that there was any truth to his accusations,' Richard answered as steadily as he could, 'but that I would look into them.'

'And?' Holly pushed him.

'And that, if there was any truth in them, I would deal with them.'

'How?' she asked.

Her father stared at her.

'*How* would you deal with them?' she persisted.

'I was assuming there would be nothing to deal with.' *Praying.*

'Were you?'

The coolness became chillier. His daughter still sat beside him on the sofa, yet Richard thought he could almost feel her sliding away from him. Emotionally detaching.

And then another realization struck him.

She was toying with him. He had felt, until this moment, that she was merely punishing him for his disloyalty, but suddenly he sensed that Holly was playing some sort of a game with him.

'Holly, please,' he said.

'What, Daddy?' she asked, still coldly.

'Tell me that Miller's stories are lies. Just *tell* me.'

'You haven't answered my question. About how you would deal with the situation. If they weren't lies.'

Tell her, man.

'I'd ask you to see someone,' he said, softly.

'What kind of someone?' Holly asked.

'Someone who could help. A specialist of some sort.'

'A psychiatrist?'

'Perhaps.'

Holly stood up, slowly. She smoothed the linen skirt of her suit with the palms of both her hands. The hands were perfectly steady, without so much as a tremor. That was a hell of a lot more than Bourne could claim.

It ought to have made him feel better. But it didn't.

Because he had seen the look in her calm grey eyes change as she stood up, just after he had answered her question about the psychiatrist. The change had been fleeting – was already gone – but it had been there nonetheless.

Rage. Terror. Despair.

All three had been in her eyes for those few short moments while she had been smoothing her skirt.

'Lies, Daddy,' Holly said, abruptly. 'Nick's stories.'

Richard said nothing.

His daughter looked down at him, her eyes calm again. Normal.

'Don't you believe me, Daddy?'

Oh, God.

'Daddy?'

Richard nodded. 'Yes. Of course I believe you.'

'I mean, the stories may well be true – those things may well have happened to Nick and his family,' Holly went on. 'But they've certainly nothing to do with me.'

Richard nodded again. 'Good.'

'You do believe me, don't you?'

'Yes, Holly.'

She smiled down at him. 'I'm glad.'

'Me, too.'

'So why don't we lock up here, and then I can drive you to your hotel? You look very tired.'

'I am.'

Tired enough to lie down and die.

'Maybe we should skip dinner this evening,' Holly said, gently, the coldness all gone. 'Maybe you could use some good room service – spoil yourself for one night.'

Bourne got to his feet. He felt a hundred years old. Drained and oddly dirty. He longed to stand under a good, hot shower. 'I was hoping to have dinner with you and Jack.'

'Jack doesn't know you're here, Daddy. You asked me not to tell him, remember?'

'Yes. Of course I did.'

'Unless you want me to tell him now. About our chat.'

'That's your decision,' Bourne said.

'I think perhaps not,' Holly said. 'What about Mother?'

'What about her?'

215

'I don't think she'd understand too well, do you, Daddy?'

Bourne shook his head. 'I don't suppose she would. It would certainly upset her.'

Holly put out her right hand and patted her father's arm. She was perfectly composed again. As she had been when he had arrived.

'Just between ourselves then?'

'All right, Holly.'

She opened a drawer in her desk and took out her purse, then picked up her attaché case from a chair.

'So, room service for you this evening, and an early night?'

Bourne nodded again.

'Yes,' he said. 'That sounds good.'

Holly went ahead of him to the door and turned out the light. 'It's a pity you have to leave in the morning.'

'Yes, it is,' Richard said.

He had felt her urgent desire to have him gone, even while she had been so superficially calm and considerate. He thought about that off and on all that evening and all that night – when he wasn't thinking about the other aspects of their conversation.

If he could call it a conversation.

He didn't know what to make of his feelings, how to analyse them, judge them. He had arrived in Los Angeles with dreadful suspicions in his mind and a vast yearning to rid himself of them, and though he had, ultimately, got the denial he had craved, the fact that he had been forced to beg for it rendered it rather impotent as denials went.

He could understand Holly's anger with him – he could certainly understand that – he was deeply, desperately angry with himself, after all. He understood, too, her need to toy with him as a punishment for believing such things about her.

If only – if *only* – she hadn't looked at him that way after he'd talked about having her see a psychiatrist. The rage he could have accepted, under the circumstances; but the despair and, most of all, the terror, had seared his soul.

What to do now?

What to do next?

Nothing? Something? What *was* there to do, given that she had denied point blank having had anything to do with Nick Miller for six years? She was his *daughter* – surely he owed it to his own child to believe what she told him?

Of course he did.

Without honesty between father and child, there was nothing.

He had to believe Holly. He *did* believe Holly.

After all, he was hardly going to take the word of a man who'd been in trouble even as a boy, a man who'd abused his and Eleanor's trust when he was a teenager, who had admitted striking a young, vulnerable woman. He certainly could not take Nick Miller's word over his own daughter's.

Damn Nick Miller, he thought, over and over again, lying sleepless in his big, comfortable hotel bed.

And damn me for my doubts.

44

The Western Union telegram arrived at Antonia Street on Wednesday morning.

> GLAD YOU CAME TO ME. BE ASSURED I SHALL KEEP MY
> WORD. ANY PROBLEM THIS END I WILL DEAL, SO SET
> YOUR MIND AT REST. APPRECIATE YOUR TRUST. RICHARD
> BOURNE

Nick, who had already called a disturbingly unresponsive Nina in Arizona to tell her about his trip to Washington DC, called her again about the telegram.

'Do you trust him?' Nina asked.

'I think so.'

'He's her father. And a lawyer.'

'He's always seemed a decent man to me, Nina.'

'Good,' she said.

That was all. Just *good*.

Nick gritted his teeth.

'How's Phoebe doing?'

'The same. No change.'

'Is Zoë okay?'

'Zoë's beautiful.' A slight softening.

'What about you?' Nick asked. 'How are you doing?'

'As you'd expect,' Nina answered.

Nick gripped the phone tighter.

'I could catch a flight – join you.'

'I don't think that's such a great idea.' She paused. 'We won't be away too long.'

'I love you, Nina,' Nick told her.

'I know you do,' she said.

Nick looked at the Western Union telegram again after the call. He thought about the manner in which Bourne had elected to contact him. In this high-tech, high-speed era, the telegram seemed to Nick to spell out old-fashioned urgency mixed with confidentiality. Bourne was, at the very least, confirming to him that he recognized their predicament was not of the run-of-the-mill phone or fax variety.

ANY PROBLEM THIS END I WILL DEAL . . .

Nick thought, on greater reflection, that he probably did still believe that Bourne would do his best. That, if he was forced to accept that he had no real moral choice, Bourne might even face up to the awful, unpalatable truth. Which he would, as a good, responsible father, surely *have* to deal with.

. . . SO SET YOUR MIND AT REST.

Sharing his load with Bourne had, Nick decided, been the right thing to do. He did, at least, feel a little lighter in some ways than he had before his trip to DC. Someone else – *perhaps* the person in the world with the most influence over Holly – now knew about his suspicions.

But as for setting his mind at rest, Nick knew that his mind would not be fit for any real kind of rest until Nina and Zoë were back home with him.

45

About twenty hours have passed since Holly left Richard at the Beverly Wilshire. They haven't spoken again. Holly supposes that her father didn't like to call her at home in case Jack was around, and by the time she got in to Taylor, Griffin this morning, Richard was already back in the air, Washington-bound. Holly knows he's left LA, knows which flight he's taken, knows he went directly from Dulles to his office. She knows all those details because she's been checking up on him. Oh, yes, she's aware that she's going to have to do a lot of checking-up on her father for quite a while.

That's what happens when fathers tell their daughters they don't trust them anymore. Oh, yes, that's what happens. *Of course I believe you*, Richard said, but she looked into his eyes and knew it wasn't true.

Quite a shock.

Quite a blow.

Especially the stuff about the shrink.

Quite a shock.

That's the only piece of this whole incident she would quite have enjoyed her mother hearing. Eleanor would have been shocked, too. Eleanor would have hit the roof and then probably have refused to speak to Richard for about a month.

Holly thinks – correction, Holly *knows* – that she covered up pretty smartly. Oh, sure, she lost it for a second or two, gave away a little more than she liked, betrayed her feelings, but so what? So the fuck *what*? She regained control again almost immediately and kept it from then on to the end.

Matter of fact, she can't even really seem to recall now exactly *how* she felt during those few weak moments. Not that it matters now. It's no longer important how she felt then.

All that's important now is getting things moving quickly.

A whole lot more quickly than she was anticipating.

Lots of planning. Lots of legwork and rapid-fire action. But nothing quick-and-dirty. Everything from now on will have to be meticulously organized. Nothing left to chance.

It isn't all bad by any means. There is an upside to what Richard told her. An upside so wonderful Holly can almost hear her blood humming.

Nick has been trying to find her. Nick wants to talk to her. Maybe even see her.

It is, of course, too soon. He doesn't need her. Not yet.

Nick is only trying to track her down because he's made the connections between past and present a little more swiftly than she expected him to. He is, from what her father has told her, already mad at her. Suspicious that she may have had something to do with what happened to the redhead. Probably raging.

The thought of that doesn't alarm Holly. It excites her.

There's nothing to be alarmed about. Not really. He may have taken his suspicions to her father, but Holly knows that she (and Eleanor, if necessary) can control Richard. And no one else is going to believe Nick. If anyone else does even *listen* to him, ultimately no one will take his word over hers. He's the one with the record. She's the lawyer.

If it comes to that. Which it will not.

But her blood is humming.

She really was not intending to make her next move yet. She was planning to wait a while longer before leaving Jack, and she has succeeded beautifully in keeping her condition secret from him. Dieting to keep her figure for as long as possible, but taking vitamin supplements for the baby's sake. Only letting Jack see her naked in the dimmest light, in case he notices the subtler changes in her body. Controlling her morning sickness so that she never throws up when he's anywhere around. He has been surprisingly easy to fool.

She's always known she was going to have to go when she really starts showing. In case Jack gets the idea that the baby is his.

She laughs, quietly, to herself. As if.

Holly knows she can't stand much more of him anyway. Oh, he's still the best of husbands, but being with him – even when he isn't trying to play the great stud – has started to make her flesh creep. She's always had a low boredom threshold with men.

Except for Nick.

She locks up the office, catches an elevator down to the lobby, walks out onto Figueroa, crosses the street, heading for the Westin Bonaventure Hotel a couple of blocks away, strolls into the Flower Street Bar and orders a vodka martini.

She knows right away that she's going to get lucky.

The bar is dark after the sunshine on the street. Dark and busy. Four businessmen, two of them Texans, are sitting at the curved, marble topped bar, drinking beer, eyes on the TV ball game, their jackets draped over their bar seats.

One of them with a Nokia phone, switched on, in its left-hand pocket.

Holly pays the bartender for her martini, sips just a little of it (thinking of the baby), eases Mr Mobile's phone out of his pocket and into her purse, leaves a two dollar tip for the bartender and walks straight out, her high heels clicking on the marble floor around the bar.

Back in the sunlight, she makes directly for Fourth Street, turns the corner, steps into a doorway, checks that the phone has a sufficiently strong signal, and makes her call.

She memorized the number earlier that afternoon. Holly has never had any problems with her memory.

'San Francisco Police?'

She pauses.

'I have some information for you.'

Still humming.

222

46

First Narcotics, then Juvenile. Now Personal Crimes.

So much for setting his mind at rest.

They came for him, without warning, at four-fifteen that afternoon. For the first time since Nina and Zoë had left, Nick was overwhelmed with gratitude that his wife was not home.

'Just a few questions, Mr Miller.'

Now what? *Now* what?

There were two of them. Inspector Norman Capelli, who looked uncannily like the tall, doleful husband in *Married With Children*, only a whole lot less funny, and Inspector Helen Wilson, who looked like a harassed, untidy, stressed out mother of at least four, but was so sharp beneath the surface that talking to her was almost like walking on broken glass.

'About your sister-in-law's accident.' That was Capelli.

'The insurance company don't think it was an accident,' Nick said.

'What do you think, Mr Miller?' That was Wilson.

'I think they're probably right.'

Nick looked around the interview room they had brought him to in the Hall of Justice. It was almost identical to the one that the Juvenile cops had quizzed him in on Valencia Street. Dingy linoleum on the floor, stained, splintered table, chairs that didn't match. Bare walls. If he thought back a few years, he remembered that the room in the station in Greenwich Village had been much the same. He felt trapped in some kind of time warp.

'Why do you think they're right?' Capelli asked.

'Mr Dinkin – that's the guy from the insurance company – made a good case,' Nick answered. 'Danger signs taken down. That kind of thing.'

'How do you and your sister-in-law get along, Mr Miller?' Wilson pulled out a chair and sat down next to him. Her fair hair was curly and smelled of cigarette smoke.

'We get along fine.' Nick sighed. 'Why do you want to know?'

'Why do you think we want to know?'

'I don't know. I'm beginning to assume you're going to ask me something crazy – like if I had anything to do with her fall.'

'Did you?' Capelli stood a couple of feet away, between the table and the door.

'Of course not.'

Nick tried to swallow the anger that was uncoiling in his gut. Losing his temper with these two officers was going to get him nowhere except maybe locked up.

'Have you ever been to Catherine Street?' Capelli asked.

'No.'

'You didn't go to see the house after the accident?'

'No. My wife went into labour the same night.' Nick looked up at Capelli. 'I'm sure you know that.'

'So you've never seen Catherine Street.' Still Capelli.

'Never.'

Capelli came to sit at the table, facing Nick, and Wilson rose and took up a position leaning against the wall. They seemed very smooth to Nick, a practised team. He thought about asking for a lawyer, but wasn't sure who to ask for, Chris Field having failed to inspire his trust.

'You never even went there after what happened?' Wilson asked. 'Not even to check it out for yourself?'

'I didn't have time,' Nick said. 'I told you, my wife went into labour the night of the accident – our daughter was born four weeks premature.'

'How's she doing now?' Capelli asked.

'Fine. She's doing great.'

'So you don't even know where Catherine Street is?' Wilson said.

'I know it's in the Haight, but that's about it.' Nick turned back to Capelli. 'Look, what *is* this?'

'What is what, Mr Miller?'

He knew his temper was about to get the better of him, but he couldn't do anything about it. Besides, he was starting to figure that maybe it was about time he got mad at someone.

'All this – *crap*,' he said hotly. 'I am getting so *sick* of being hassled by you people.'

'Excuse me?' Inspector Wilson leaned away from the wall in an attitude of mock curiosity. 'Have we met before?'

'No, we haven't,' Nick answered, 'but I'm sure you're aware of my other dealings with your colleagues in Juvenile and Narcotics.'

'You do seem to have had a lot of *dealings*, as you put it, with us lately,' Capelli agreed mildly.

'None of which have led to any charges,' Nick pointed out.

'Not yet,' Wilson said.

'Not *ever*,' Nick hit straight back, 'because there's never going to be any genuine evidence against me—'

'Because you're innocent, right?' Wilson again.

'Because it's all been part of a set-up,' Nick told her. 'I tried telling the Juvenile guys the same thing, and they didn't want to know, but it's all starting to get way out of hand now, so someone's going to have to start listening to me.'

'So who's been setting you up?' Capelli asked.

Nick didn't answer right away. Richard Bourne had asked him to leave the situation in his hands, and he'd agreed. But he hadn't known then that less than three days later he was going to be dragged in yet again by the SFPD.

'A woman named Holly Bourne,' he said to Capelli.

'And who exactly is Holly Bourne?' Wilson wanted to know.

'An old acquaintance. Someone I knew when I was a student in New York City.' He was sweating. 'We used to be neighbours when we were kids, back in Bethesda, Maryland.'

'And what makes you think this old neighbour is setting you up now?' Capelli asked.

'Because she's—' Nick hesitated. *Crazy? Obsessed?* Which word was most likely to make these police officers pay attention to what he was telling them? 'Because she's sick,' he said, finally.

'What kind of sick?' Wilson asked.

Nick ignored her and concentrated on Capelli. 'Why am I here? I mean, why am I here now, today? What happened to make you come pick me up?'

'We have a witness who says they saw you on Catherine Street.'

'That's impossible.'

'How so?' Capelli asked.

'Because I told you, I was never there.' Nick paused. 'Who says I was?'

'Someone who seems very sure.' Wilson, still over by the wall, smiled. 'A concerned citizen.'

'Have you met this citizen?'

'We have a witness.' Wilson stopped smiling. 'That's all you need to know.'

'What was it?' Nick went on pushing. 'A phone call?'

'Why don't you let us ask the questions, Mr Miller?' Inspector Capelli said.

'Was it a woman who called?' Nick asked.

'Why?' Wilson asked right back. 'Did you notice a woman when you were on Catherine Street?'

'I've already told you I wasn't there.'

Nick stopped talking. Holly. Almost certainly Holly. But when exactly had she made this call? Since he'd talked to her father? Or had she given some 'information' to the cops before Richard Bourne had become involved?

I WILL DEAL . . . SET YOUR MIND AT REST . . .

The message on the Western Union telegram was still clear in his mind's eye. Had Bourne lied to him, plain and simple? Nina, on the phone, had swiftly pointed to Richard being Holly's father and a lawyer and maybe, therefore, not the right man for Nick to take at his word. Was she right, after all? Or had Holly done this to him either before Bourne had contacted her, or afterwards, because she didn't give a damn what her father thought.

'Tell us a little more about you and Phoebe.' Capelli broke into his thoughts.

'Would you like a cup of coffee?' Wilson asked from the wall.

'No, thank you,' Nick answered, distracted.

'How about a cigarette?'

'I don't smoke.'

'Mind if I do?' Wilson pulled a pack of Merits and a matchbook from her skirt pocket.

'Not at all.'

She lit up and inhaled deeply. Nick wondered if smoking was still permitted on police property. He thought again about the wisdom or folly of being here right now without a lawyer. Maybe Chris Field might be better than no lawyer at all.

'You worked with your wife and Phoebe on your book, didn't you, Mr Miller?' Capelli asked.

'Yes, I did.' He felt anger starting to spiral again. 'It was a very happy time for all of us, before you ask.'

'And since that happy time?'

'May I say something else, please?' Nick leaned forward, put his right hand on the table top, just to the side of where someone had carved a few creative words.

'Go ahead,' Capelli said.

'Lawrence Dinkin – the man from the insurance company – made it clear he thought the accident was meant for my wife.'

'Because the fax about the house on Catherine Street was sent to her.' Inspector Wilson, still smoking, came to join Capelli and Nick at the table, sitting beside Nick again.

'Yes.'

'Doesn't seem conclusive to me,' Wilson remarked.

Nick said nothing.

'Given that the sender might have known your wife was out of the office,' Wilson added. Her lips were too thin, but her eyes were very blue and compelling.

'Meaning me?' Frustration balled Nick's hand into a fist.

'As you know,' Capelli contributed, 'the fax was sent from a public fax bureau in the financial district at three twenty-one that afternoon.'

'Where were you at that time, Mr Miller?' Wilson asked.

Nick thought, as he had a number of times before, about the possibility that Holly had been in San Francisco that day – unless, of course, she had hired someone else to send the fax on her behalf. Both thoughts made him sick.

'Answer the question, please,' Wilson said. 'Where were you at three twenty-one on July 17?'

Nick stared at her. 'I'm not sure.'

'Think about it.'

He tried, but it was a fuzz. He knew where he'd been when the call came about Phoebe: out back at home with Nina, waiting for the charcoal to turn white on the barbecue. But that had been later, around six-thirty . . .

'Were you at home?' Capelli prodded.

Nick shook his head. 'I can't remember.'

'Take your time.'

'I know I was home for most of that day. My wife was resting – she was tired.' Nick forced himself back to the afternoon in question. 'I went out for some supplies – I think it was just after lunch—'

'Supplies?'

'For my work.'

'Paints?' Wilson asked.

Nick shrugged. 'Paints and other stuff. I went to Flax, on Market Street. It took a while, but not too long.'

'So were you still out, do you think, between three and three-thirty?' Capelli was pushing harder now.

'I'm not sure. If I had to guess, I'd say I was home.'

'In which case your wife would be able to confirm that.'

'Not necessarily,' Nick said, then cursed himself.

'Why not?' Wilson asked.

Cold eyes or not, he ought to have called Chris Field.

'She may have been asleep.' He paused. 'Or not.'

Wilson smiled. 'Or not.'

'Why not ask her?' Nick said.

'We will,' Wilson said.

'She's out of town at the moment.'

'We know.'

Nick knew he needed to stop this before it got out of hand. He knew it, but there was another question he had to ask while he had the chance.

'Tell me one thing,' he said, looking at Capelli. 'Why the hell do you think I would want to hurt Phoebe?' He was breathing too fast and there was a pain across his chest. 'She's my wife's sister. I love her.'

'Are you saying you had no motive for wanting your sister-in-law hurt, or maybe dead?' Wilson asked.

'Of *course* I had no motive!' Outrage rang in every word.

'Not even if she knew something you were afraid she might talk about?' Wilson was cryptic. 'To your wife or someone else?'

'I don't understand.'

'Something maybe connected with your visit to Juvenile Division last month,' Wilson said. 'Something that Phoebe might have become upset with you about? Maybe threatened to expose?'

'Jesus,' Nick said. '*Jesus.*'

He stopped listening.

Holly. God damn her to hell, and maybe her father with her.

'I want a lawyer,' he said. *Any lawyer except Richard or Holly Bourne.*

Inspector Wilson stood up. 'You're free to go.'

Nick sat very still. 'So that's it?'

'For now.'

Slowly, Nick got up. His whole body ached. He felt as if he'd gone twelve rounds with Mike Tyson.

'Do I need a lawyer?'

'That's up to you,' Wilson said.

'If it were me,' Capelli said, wryly, 'I'd have got one a while back.'

Punch-drunk as he was, Nick knew he couldn't leave yet.

'What about Holly Bourne?' he said.

'What about her?' Capelli asked.

'I told you I think she's the one behind all this. Aren't you going to at least follow that up?'

'Could be,' Wilson answered.

'According to her parents,' Nick said, fast and desperate, 'she's an attorney now, married and living in New York City.'

'So Holly Bourne's an attorney, huh?' Wilson commented.

'Supposedly,' Nick said. 'Maybe you could check her out?'

'Because she's sick,' Capelli said. 'That was what you said about her, wasn't it?'

'That's right.' Nick glanced at the door. The temptation to escape while they were still telling him he could go was almost overwhelming, but the need to get through to them about Holly was even more powerful.

'You want to talk to us some more?' Wilson asked. 'Or do you want to speak to your lawyer first?'

Nick sat down again.

'I want to tell you about Holly Bourne,' he said.

'Are you sure about this?' Inspector Capelli double-checked.

Nick nodded.

'Very sure,' he said.

47

When I got home soon after seven o'clock – too late to contemplate calling Richard Bourne in Washington – I found a message on the machine from Nina.

'Call me, please.'

So brief it hurts.

Now what do I do?

What I would like – what I would *love* – is to keep this new horror from her. What I want is to believe that Inspectors Wilson and Capelli will follow the lead I gave them and bring Holly to justice – or failing that, that they'll at least have the decency to melt away into the same SFPD black hole that Abbott and Riley and the Juvenile guys seem to have dropped back into. What I want is to be able to kid myself that this one slipped in under the wire before Richard Bourne got in on the act and put a stop to all the craziness.

But, number one: I don't believe this is over. Number two: I know that Wilson and Capelli are going to be getting in touch with Nina anyway to check on my whereabouts during the afternoon of Phoebe's fall. And number three (and most compelling of all): if I keep just one more thing from my wife – whether my secrecy comes under the guise of funk or of trying to shield her – I know I will lose her.

So I make the call.

She tells me that Mary Chen, a psychologist at the Waterson Clinic, believes that Phoebe's speech loss may, at least in part, be of a post-traumatic nature. Chen's conversations with William and Nina having persuaded her that, until her fall, Phoebe was always a rock to them both, it now seems possible that this personal physical and emotional shock may have created a kind of mental pile up of old, partly suppressed nightmares.

'First our mother's alcoholism, then her suicide,' Nina says. 'Then my drunkenness.'

She sounds matter-of-fact listing the Ford family horrors, but I know my wife better than that. I know that the implication that her own problems may have contributed to Phoebe's present condition, must feel to Nina like a hot poker jammed into her heart.

'Dr Chen accepts that Phoebe's head injury alone was serious enough to have a temporary effect on her brain's speech centre,' Nina goes on, 'but then, when Phoebe first woke up and found herself trapped by the casts on her arms and all those tubes, unable to communicate with anyone—' She breaks off.

'Nina?' I almost ask her if she's okay, but I stop myself. Of course she is not okay.

'What?' Nina's voice is desperately strained.

'So they still believe there's no permanent physical damage,' I say. They say they've done every test there is.'

'So it must be temporary.' I'm fighting to push her uphill again.

'So they say.'

'Do they say how long it might last?'

'They just don't know.' She's close to tears now. 'Her voice might come back any time, or it might take weeks or even months. All they can do is persist with the speech therapy.'

'It won't take months.'

'You don't know that, Nick. You don't know more than the doctors.'

'No,' I agree. 'But I know Phoebe better than they do.'

Nina is silent for a moment, and I picture her gritting her teeth, refusing to give way.

And then the question comes. The one I've been dreading.

'Where were you?' she asks me. 'I called twice.'

Reprieve over.

'Nick?'

So I tell her.

Two good things come out of our miserable, lousy conversation. Actually, one good thing and one wonderful thing.

First, Nina sounds relieved that I've told the cops about Holly.

Second – better than anything – she and Zoë are coming home.

48

Holly's getting ready. To leave Jack and the house on San Vicente that has never felt like her own home. And Taylor, Griffin, and Los Angeles.

There's no sadness in her. Not an ounce. Except just a fragment, perhaps, for Richard. And maybe, curiously enough, for Eleanor. They both love her, in their own, different ways. So does Jack, of course – but Jack Taylor only loves the Charlotte shell she created specially for him, for the purposes of making him fall in love with her at the right time. That time is over now. Spent. Past.

Now is the time for moving on.

For ceasing to be Jack's wife, or Richard and Eleanor's daughter.

For disappearing.

Until the moment comes to magic herself back again.

For Nick.

This point has arrived sooner than anticipated, but that's okay. She's good at planning, at dealing with unexpected contingencies. Richard's unannounced visit has, without question, made her present position untenable – and in making her own anonymous witness call to the SFPD when she did, Holly realizes that she, too, has made staying in LA impossible.

She ought perhaps, she admits to herself on reflection, to have waited just a little longer, given herself a little more time to go underground, to make herself invisible – untouchable. After all, Nick's not likely now to hold back from the police what he's already told her father. And if – just *if* – they believe him, then that means the cops will come looking for her, at least for the answers to a few questions.

Which she has no intention of answering.

So Mrs Taylor regrets that she won't be able to go on play-acting as Jack's wife any longer. And Taylor, Griffin, of course, has been every bit as much of a convenience as her husband: part sanctuary from Jack and his increasingly claustrophobic adoration, part high-speed, on-the-job criminal law school. That, too, has served its purpose now. And Holly is almost ready.

To stage the rest of the battle from a new hideaway.

Until Nick finally has to admit that he can't go on without her.

It is coming, sooner than she thought it would.

Holly knows that Nick Miller still believes that hell will have to freeze over twice before he'll ever need her.

He is wrong.

49

According to Eileen Ridge, Richard Bourne had been in court when Nick had tried calling him first thing Thursday morning. Of course, she'd said, she would ask Mr Bourne to get in touch as soon as possible.

At two that afternoon (five in Washington DC) Nick had called again. Mrs Ridge had been friendly and courteous in telling him that she'd spoken with Mr Bourne, who had asked her to assure him that he was, as previously agreed, dealing with the matter, and that he would be in touch again only if there was anything further to report.

'Dealing with it how, exactly?' Nick asked, his stomach tight with frustration. 'As in doing precisely nothing?'

'I'm not familiar with the matter concerned, Mr Miller' – the courtesy hardly wavered – 'but if Mr Bourne says that he's dealing with something, then you can be certain that he is.'

'You tell Mr Bourne that while he's *dealing* with it, I'm still being harassed by the San Francisco police.'

Eileen Ridge's manner changed instantly from Message Fielder to Action Woman. 'Are you in custody at present, Mr Miller?' she asked him crisply. 'Do you need us to get in touch with a San Francisco lawyer on your behalf?'

'No, I don't need you to get me a damned lawyer,' Nick snapped.

Mrs Ridge remained silent.

'I'm sorry,' he said, embarrassed. 'I'm just upset.'

'That's perfectly all right, Mr Miller.'

'The only person I need you to get in touch with on my behalf is Richard Bourne,' Nick said. 'Just please pass on my message to him – can you do that for me?'

'Of course I can.'

Eileen Ridge was right, of course. He did need a lawyer. That was what he'd promised Nina last evening on the phone. That in the absence of anyone better, he would give Chris Field another call and bring him up to speed. Nina had told him that she and Zoë were coming home, but that she hoped he would put his new troubles in Field's hands before they got back. Nick had wanted to put it off, had said that all he wanted was to go to the airport and fetch his family, but Nina had been insistent that he get professional advice as soon as possible.

'You've waited long enough,' she'd said.

'Then surely a few hours more won't make much difference,' Nick had tried to convince her.

'Michael Levine still swears by Field.'

'Okay. I'll call him.'

'First thing?' Nina had pressed him. 'We'll catch a cab from the airport. I'd rather you were onto this, Nick.'

So he'd promised.

Nina and Zoë arrived back in Antonia Street just after six, after Nick had spent two hours with the frosty-eyed, waspish young attorney.

'What did he say?' Nina asked as soon as they came through the door, giving Nick the baby to hold but offering him nothing warmer than her own cheek to kiss.

'All the right things, I guess.' Nick held Zoë close, smelt her dirty nappy and was grateful even for that.

'But?'

Nina stayed where she was in the hall, made no move to go through into the kitchen or living room, either to grab some coffee or to sit down and relax, as she would ordinarily do. She seemed to be wearing the same blue jeans, white cotton blouse, navy blazer and loafers she'd left in last Friday though they looked as crisp as if they'd all been freshly cleaned. Nina almost always looked perfectly turned out, no matter what she was going through.

Nick answered her question.

'I told him that I'm sure Holly Bourne is behind everything that's been happening to us, including Phoebe's fall. I told him I've confronted her father with my suspicions. I told him that I've informed

235

the Personal Crimes inspectors about Holly and the past, and that I want him to check her out for me. Field said that he wished I hadn't gone to see Bourne, that I should never talk to the cops again unless he's with me, and he advises me to stay away from the whole Bourne family from now on.'

'Is he going to check Holly out?' Nina asked.

'I don't know. I didn't push it.'

'Why not?'

'I still don't think he really believes me.'

'Is that what he said?'

'No, of course not. It's just the feeling he gave me.'

'Isn't that the way all defence lawyers are with their clients?' Nina said. 'Surely it doesn't really matter if they believe you or not, so long as they can make other people believe you're innocent?'

Nick stared at her, startled. 'It matters to me whether my own lawyer believes me or not. It matters a hell of a lot.'

Nina nodded slowly. 'Then I suppose you'd better find someone else.' She held out her arms for Zoë. 'I'm going to put her down for a while.'

'I can do that.'

'I'd rather do it myself.'

Nick gave her the baby and watched her walk towards the staircase.

'Nina, what's going on?' he said.

'What do you mean?' She did not turn around.

'I mean, you've come home, but it feels like you're not here.'

'I'm here.' She started up the stairs.

'Nina.' His voice was sharper with apprehension.

She stopped on the third tread. 'Yes?'

'You do believe me, don't you? You do know I'd never hurt Phoebe?'

'Yes, of course I believe that.' Still she didn't turn around to face him. 'I think it's the craziest thing I've ever heard.'

'And what about Holly?' Nick's heart was pumping too fast. 'Do you believe I may be right about her?'

'I don't know Holly.'

And she went on carrying their daughter up the stairs.

* * *

William telephoned while Nina was bathing Zoë. Given no choice but to speak to Nick, he answered questions about Phoebe cursorily and with minimal politeness.

'Please tell my daughter that I'll be flying in tomorrow.'

'You're coming to San Francisco?' Nick was surprised, given that Ford had hardly left Phoebe's side since the accident.

'I am.' He offered nothing further.

'Will you be staying with us?' It was an effort, but for Nina's sake Nick was prepared to stay courteous.

'I don't think so.' William paused. 'Ask Nina to call me, please.'

'Of course,' Nick said.

He went upstairs to the nursery. Nina was bent over the baby bath, supporting Zoë with one arm, rinsing her gently with her free hand.

'Your father called,' he said. 'Did you know he was planning on coming to San Francisco tomorrow?'

'No.' Nina remained focused on the baby, who was kicking her legs. Zoë had liked warm water from day one at home.

'He is. He wants you to call him.'

'Does he want to stay here?'

'I asked him. He said he didn't think so. He wasn't very communicative.'

'I'll call him.'

Nick looked at her. 'You don't seem surprised that he's coming.'

'I'm not, especially.'

'I thought he wouldn't want to leave Phoebe.'

Nina lifted Zoë out of the bath and rested her on the pink towel laid out on the changing table. 'He's concerned about me too.' She patted the baby gently, then wrapped the towel snugly around her and was rewarded by delicious cooing sounds.

Nick leaned against the door frame. 'I gather you told him about the cops hauling me in.'

'He asked me what was wrong. I wasn't going to lie. I hate lies.'

'I've never lied to you, Nina.'

'Maybe not,' she said. 'But you haven't exactly shared the whole truth either, have you?'

She shook baby powder onto the palm of her left hand and patted it gently over the baby's body. The pleasure sounds continued, and Zoë's little arms waved. Nick felt one of those powerful rushes of love that sometimes made him go weak at the knees. This evening it made him feel like crying.

'So your father's coming here to protect you,' he said, quietly.

'Don't be silly.' Nina looked up at last. 'That's not true, Nick.'

'What else have you told him?' Nick asked.

'As little as possible,' she answered.

50

William checked in at The Fairmont, presumably, Nick surmised, as an unspoken statement that he didn't care to stay with his son-in-law. Which made little sense, given that his intention was clearly to spend most of the time he was in the city at their house.

For the first several hours after his arrival on Friday, he was ensconced in the living room with Nina, grilling her for information about her husband's relationship with the San Francisco police. Once or twice Nick, who had been painting in his studio and keeping an eye on Zoë, wandered into the room, was rewarded with a poker-faced look from his father-in-law and a weary expression from his wife, and wandered back out again. He thought, a couple of times, about asserting his rights more aggressively, confronting William directly, but this situation was placing more than enough strain on Nina's shoulders as it was, and he wasn't about to make it any worse for her than he already had.

At around five o'clock, while he was sitting on the window seat in Zoë's nursery trying to absorb a little of her enviable baby calm, Nick heard raised voices and recognized tones of unmistakable anger and distress in Nina's.

'Enough,' he said, and headed downstairs.

Zoë began crying at the precise moment that Nick reached the hall and Nina came out of the living room. She was wearing cotton slacks, a pale blue T-shirt and sneakers. Home clothes, nice and easy and cool. She looked anything but cool.

'What's happening?' Nick asked.

'Nothing.' Nina put one foot on the first step. 'Zoë needs feeding.'

'I've fed her, and bathed her. I heard yelling.'

'We weren't yelling.'

'As near as damnit,' Nick said.

Nina ran a hand through her long, loose hair. 'Nick, try not to get too angry with him,' she said, tiredly.

'You seem angry enough for both of us.'

'I'm allowed. He's my father.' Her eyes pleaded with him.

'I won't get mad,' he said softly. 'Do I take it I'm *persona grata* in our living room now?' He couldn't help the irony.

'Dad wants to talk to you.' Her embarrassment showed.

'Oh, happy day.'

'Nick, darling, please take it easy.'

It was the first time she'd called him 'darling' since Thursday. It wasn't much, but it was – he hoped – something.

William looked tired to the point of haggardness, but Nick found it hard to dredge up much in the way of sympathy for him. If this undisguised antipathy had only begun when he'd learned about Nick's encounters with the SFPD, it might have been understandable, but as it was, Ford had been hostile and suspicious towards him from the day they'd first met.

'I'm going to tell you what I told Nina,' he said from his armchair, attacking as soon as Nick entered the living room.

Nick held onto his temper. 'A drink, William?' he offered.

'It's too early for me.' Crisp and cold.

'I was thinking of coffee.' Nick sat down on the sofa. 'So what is it you told Nina?'

Ford had on his hard-nosed, air-force expression. 'That whatever she chooses to think about you, I'm still a believer that there's no smoke without fire.'

Nick looked right at him. 'What "smoke" exactly are you talking about here, William? Heroin, child molestation, or attempted murder – or all three?'

The dislike in Ford's green eyes intensified. 'I don't find the attempted murder of one of my daughters especially funny.'

'Nor do I,' Nick said. 'I think you know that.'

'Maybe I do, maybe I don't.' Ford sat forward. 'Here's my point of view. The drugs thing on its own could have been an error, maybe just a mistake, or maybe something spawned by someone's malice. The child business – in isolation – *might* be a disgusting invention, too – except that there's no escaping those photographs. You were playing with those children.'

'They threw a ball to me.' Nick felt the suppressed anger heating up in his stomach. 'I threw it back.'

'Those children were *naked*, man. Which means that at the very least you showed extraordinary lack of judgment.'

'What Nick showed was innocence.'

Nick and William both turned around. Nina stood in the doorway, holding Zoë in her arms. She came in and sat down on the sofa beside Nick, and that small declaration of solidarity sent a wave of gratitude washing over him. At least, for now, thank God, she was by his side.

'He's a grown man,' Ford persisted. 'Those little children were the innocent ones.'

'Nothing *happened* to the children, for heaven's sake,' Nick said.

'Maybe not,' Ford allowed, 'though we only really have your word for that.' He paused. 'But even if we forget the photos and the drugs, we can't – *I* certainly can't and won't – forget about Phoebe.'

'No one's actually accused Nick of having anything to do with hurting Phoebe,' Nina pointed out. 'And if they did,' she went on hotly, 'I'd tell them they were crazy – just as crazy as they were accusing him of keeping drugs in our home or of being some kind of pervert.'

'Can he prove his innocence?' William demanded.

Zoë started crying again, and her cheeks grew red.

'Shall I take her?' Nick asked Nina, ignoring Ford.

'Please.' She passed the baby over.

'If all this is just a pack of lies' – William stood up and glowered down at them both – 'then why did the police believe those 'lies' enough to question Nick three separate times?'

'Twice,' Nina amended. 'With the drugs thing, they just searched the house.'

'*Just*.' William loaded the word with scorn.

'They've had to question me,' Nick answered, staying steady, 'because someone's been feeding them false information.'

'And you claim this someone is that woman you used to know – this Holly person.'

241

'I've told the police I think there's more than a good chance it's Holly Bourne.' Nick propped Zoë against his left shoulder and stroked her head and back, and her crying promptly ceased. 'Good girl,' he murmured into her tiny ear. 'Good, sweet baby.'

'Sounds like hogwash to me.' William's eyes glittered. 'And if it isn't, I'd like to know what you could have done to make that kind of an enemy out of a woman.'

Nick glanced at Nina, who shook her head slightly but decisively. The confirmation that she had not told her father the whole ugly story warmed Nick again.

'Well?' William hectored.

'Dad, what happened in the past between Nick and Holly is none of your business,' Nina said.

'If it's put my daughter – your sister – in the hospital, I'd say that makes it very much my business.' William turned impatiently away and walked over to the window, gazing out, for a few moments, at the street. 'If you want my opinion,' he said slowly, measuring his words carefully, 'I think that until he can prove his innocence, your husband should have the decency to move out.'

'Excuse me?' Nick said, startled.

'Over my dead body.' Nina's voice was quiet but steely. 'Nick has done nothing wrong. He has nothing to prove.'

For the second time in two days, Nick felt like a stunned boxer on the ropes. Zoë wriggled against his shoulder and dribbled on his T-shirt, but he made no move to wipe either her face or his clothes.

'And what about Zoë?' Ford asked.

'What *about* Zoë?' Nick asked straight back.

'You have to consider your child's safety,' William said to Nina.

'Please don't ignore me, William.' Nick's voice cut through the air. 'I'd like to know just exactly what you're suggesting?'

Nina stood up, her hands balled into fists down by her sides. 'If you are suggesting,' she said to her father, 'that Nick would ever harm so much as a *hair* on Zoë's head, then *you* may as well leave right now and don't bother coming back.'

'Take it easy, sweetheart.' Nick got up too, still holding the baby.

'I mean it,' Nina said.

'Aren't you lucky to have such a loyal wife,' William said nastily.

'Yes, I am,' Nick agreed, as Zoë squirmed in his arms.

'I suppose I'd better go back to my hotel,' the other man said.

'I suppose you had,' Nick agreed.

'Dad, you're the lucky one round here.' Nina was close to tears of rage and frustration. 'I can't believe Nick's being so *reasonable*.'

'He's your father,' Nick said, still holding tightly to the baby. 'If he weren't, I'd probably have decked him by now.'

'Just try it,' William said.

'For God's sake, *stop* it, Dad,' Nina insisted furiously. 'This whole thing is getting out of control – I wouldn't blame Nick if he did hit you.'

Nick saw that she was trembling violently.

'I think maybe you should leave now,' he told Ford quietly.

William looked at Nina. 'It's not my intention to hurt you, my darling.' He made a move towards her, put out a hand to touch her arm, but she stepped away out of his reach. The heavy furrowing on his face grew deeper. 'I'm sorry, Nina,' he said.

'It's not me you should be apologizing to,' she said.

'I disagree.'

'Then there's nothing more to be said, is there?'

And Nina turned away from her father.

William flew back to Arizona next morning and a semblance of normality returned to the house on Antonia Street. Except that on both Saturday and Sunday night, Nick found Nina in Zoë's nursery at around three in the morning, weeping over the baby's crib. She tried her best to fob him off, said she was having bad dreams, claimed she was simply overtired from the general strain and not sleeping properly – but when the same thing happened again in the early hours of Monday morning, Nick knew he was going to have to drag the truth out of her.

'This has to stop, Nina.'

He stood behind her at the crib and put his arms around her, and she let him hold her but would not turn around.

'I'm going to ask you something,' he said, 'and I want you to answer me honestly.' He went on holding her, needing the feel of her against him, even though tension and fear were tautening every muscle in his body. 'Nina, do you want me to move out for a while?'

'*No.*' She pulled away, shocked, barely managing to keep her voice low because of the baby. 'Nick, of *course* I don't want you to leave. That's the last thing I want.'

'I don't mean just because of your father,' Nick said. 'I mean because of the things I told you.'

'I know what you mean,' Nina said. 'I told you, your going anywhere is the last thing I want or need.'

He drew a grateful breath.

Nina left his arms, walked over to the dresser on which she had placed a photograph of herself, Nick and Phoebe, arm-in-arm, and a copy of *Firefly* together with a set of tiny silver brush, comb and mirror that Phoebe had bought for the baby.

'Dad's been driving me crazy,' she confessed. 'He's been calling all the time since he got back to Scottsdale, nagging at me.'

'Saying what?' Nick paused. 'Or don't I need to ask?'

'Not really.' Nina's sigh was drawn out and miserable. 'He keeps telling me not to leave Zoë alone with you. It's unbelievable, I know – you *know* I know, Nick – but Dad seems obsessed. He reminds me over and over – as if I *need* reminding, for Christ's sake – that Phoebe's still in plaster, that she still can't talk.' She paused. 'He says that even if you didn't directly cause that, if Holly was involved, then that still makes it your fault.'

'He's not wrong about that, is he?' Nick said quietly.

'I didn't want to tell you,' Nina said. 'I know how bad you feel already – I didn't want to make it even worse for you.'

'Of course you had to tell me.' Nick came over to her, put out his right hand and stroked her bare arm. 'You're cold, sweetheart. Why don't you come to bed?'

'I'm fine.'

'No, you're not.'

She shook her head. 'No, I'm not,' she admitted.

Nick saw the awful strain in her eyes and in the tight set of her jaw. 'Have you been thinking about taking a drink?' he asked, gently.

'Oh, yes,' she said.

'How bad?'

'Bad enough. I've been coping, just about.'

'You're very brave,' Nick told her.

'Not brave at all.' There were tears in Nina's eyes again. 'I'm *afraid* to drink, Nick. I'm too bloody scared to go through all that again.'

'Brave and wise,' Nick said.

* * *

244

They went back to bed, and Nina fell asleep with surprising ease, but Nick stayed awake till after dawn.

He had already arrived at the decision that he was going to have to take some kind of action himself. He might have turned the facts over to the police and Richard Bourne, but all his instincts were telling him that even if the cops *did* locate Holly, she would convince them that *he* was the crazy one, the villain, the one with the record. And Richard still hadn't gotten in touch, which seemed to indicate to Nick pretty clearly that that was a closed avenue.

He couldn't just go on sitting around, waiting for the next blow to fall. Although this was probably the worst imaginable time for him to consider leaving Nina alone, if he wanted to call a halt to all the madness, it was pretty clear that he was going to have to leave town again to try to track Holly down. He knew, without even broaching the subject, that Nina wasn't going to agree with him about that – was not going to want him to go anywhere, least of all after Holly.

He was right.

'You can't be serious.'

Nina had slept late, had woken to find Zoë with a clean nappy and Nick at work in his studio on the third floor. He was working on an abstract using acrylic paint, taking out some of his fear and anger on canvas. He had been psyching himself up to tell Nina what his plans were for more than two hours.

'I'm very serious,' Nick told her, cleaning the brushes he'd been using. 'God knows I didn't want to ever have to see her again – and the last thing I want to do is leave you and Zoë right now—'

'Then don't.'

'I don't see that I have a choice.'

'Of course you have a choice, Nick.' Nina sank down onto a stool near the big window. 'You can leave it to her father and the police.'

'I don't believe anymore that I can trust Richard Bourne to help me,' Nick said. 'And I'm not convinced that the cops are going to see through Holly if they do talk to her.'

'Then hire a lawyer to find her for you,' Nina suggested. 'It doesn't have to be Field – there must be scores of good lawyers in San Francisco.'

Nick dropped the brushes into a glass jar. 'None of whom are guaranteed to take me any more seriously than Field did.'

'So hire a private investigator.'

'I talked to three of those yesterday,' Nick said. 'New York agencies.'

'You didn't tell me.' Nina looked startled.

'Because there wasn't much to tell. I told them I'd already tried the obvious places – directories and the State Bar—'

'When did you do that?'

'Over the last couple of days.'

'For God's *sake*, Nick.' Nina got up. 'How many *more* secrets are you going to keep from me?'

'They're not secrets, Nina—'

'Garbage.' She stared at him. 'Absolute, complete *garbage*.' She sat rigidly back down on the stool. 'What did the agencies say?'

'That it's clearly not going to be easy – which means it's going to take a lot of time and money, and without any solid place to start, it could even turn out to be a total bomb.'

'Surely a detective could at least find out Holly's married name.'

'So can I, with a little time and effort.' Nick picked up a second stool from behind his easel, put it down close to Nina and sat down on it. 'Though knowing Holly, I'm surprised she hasn't been using Bourne as her professional name.'

'Clearly you don't know her as well as you thought you did.'

Nick saw the anger still on his wife's face. 'You don't understand.'

'No, I don't.'

'You don't understand how convincing and respectable Holly can be.' He got up again, restless, walked back to the easel, stared unseeing at the uncontrolled chaos on the canvas. 'You can't even *begin* to understand – no one can, believe me – how great she is at climbing out of shit smelling of roses. She was like that as a child, and she was even better at it when she was a student.'

'And now she's a lawyer,' Nina said.

'Exactly.'

'Which can only make her more dangerous.'

'Which makes it more important than ever that I find out where she is and what she's up to – *really* up to.' He turned back to her. 'I can do that, sweetheart – I can see through her.'

'You couldn't in the past,' Nina pointed out.

'Not for a long time, no, you're right. Not till New York.'

'And then what?' Nina asked. 'When you've found her, seen through her, found out what she's up to – what then?'

'Then I go back to the police and leave it with them.' Nick came back, sat down again, reached for her hand and grasped it tightly. 'Nina, I'm not going to run any risks, not with you and Zoë here at home. I'm just going to track down a couple of people from NYU, try asking a few questions, find out what her first job was – at least get some place to *start*, so I can lose this awful feeling that she's just sitting someplace loving making our lives hell.'

Nina waited a beat. 'What about the rest of it?'

'The rest of what?'

'The other side of your relationship. With Holly.'

'There is no other side,' Nick said flatly. 'You know that.' He still held onto her hand, afraid to let her go.

'But there was.'

'When we were kids.'

'And in New York.'

'One night,' Nick said. 'That was all it was. A mistake.' He felt sick. 'I thought you believed that.'

Nina said nothing.

'Nina, talk to me.'

She took another few moments. 'I do believe it.' She shook her head. 'But that doesn't stop me being afraid for you. For us. Nick, if Holly did do that thing to Phoebe – whether she meant it for me or not –' The fear lay deep in her eyes. 'We're talking about attempted murder.'

'I know we are.'

'Then leave it to the police,' she said again.

'I can't do that.'

Abruptly, Nina pulled her hand away.

'This is all a waste of time, isn't it?' she said, coldly, standing up.

Nick was dismayed. 'Of course it isn't.'

'Oh, yes, it is.' She walked around him and the easel over to the door. 'You made up your mind to go after Holly before you even told me. You haven't been listening to a single word I've said.'

'That isn't true. I always listen to what you say.'

'Maybe you listen' – Nina turned the handle – 'but you don't hear. Forget it, Nick.' Her tone was harsher than he'd ever heard it. 'No more garbage – no more half-truths. No more wasting time.' She opened the door. 'I have better things to do,' she said.

And walked out of the studio without looking back.

OCTOBER

51

The atmosphere in our house is almost unbearable. It breaks my heart to feel Nina's coldness towards me, but I'm doing my best to stay calm and organized because there's nothing much more positive I can do. I've sworn to her that the instant I find even the smallest morsel of useful information – let alone actual proof of Holly's involvement – I will hand it straight over to one of my SFPD inspector buddies, but I'm not sure that she believes me. I can't blame her for her loss of faith, but that doesn't stop it hurting.

We've agreed, at least, on one thing: taking on a nanny to help with Zoë, which will give Nina greater peace of mind and freedom to visit with Phoebe and William in Arizona, as well as allowing her to spend more time at Ford Realty. Betty and Harold have been doing all they can to paper over the cracks, but with Phoebe away for so long and Nina still preoccupied, business is starting to suffer. Anyway, work – real work – may just be the one thing that's going to keep Nina sane and sober until all this is behind us.

Nina found Teresa Vasquez at the first round of interviews. Lucky. Lord knows we're due some. She's a small, light-boned, vigorous woman from Tijuana with great references, good enough English, and what seems to be a warm heart. Nina's only real problem with her – aside from her ten thousand doubts about leaving our baby with anyone, even the Nanny of the Year – is Teresa's tendency to talk the ear off anyone who'll listen, but I figure that means she's naturally friendly, which surely has to be good news for Zoë. Our daughter took to Teresa right away at the interview. Of course, Zoë takes to just about everyone.

So I guess I'm ready to leave. As ready as I ever will be.

Nina refuses to have any more substantial discussions about what I plan to do, her rationale still being that since I'm going to do what I want anyway, regardless of her objections or input, there's no point us talking. I have tried pointing out that I've still heard nothing from Richard Bourne, and that when I called Norman Capelli in Personal Crimes to try to nail him down about contacting Holly, he made it clear they weren't about to share any information with me.

'Maybe Chris Field could persuade Capelli to tell him,' she said.

She knows I have no more faith in Field than I did last time we talked about him. She knows – because I've told her repeatedly – that I will find another lawyer just as soon as I have something concrete to tell them, so that he or she will be standing by my side because they *trust* me, not just because I'm paying them to be there.

No change there either.

If Nina has told William about our disagreement – oh, Jesus, how I wish it were as simple as a *disagreement* – then she hasn't described his reaction. Of course, if her father does know I'm going away – anywhere away from Nina – he's probably cheering.

Damn Holly.

52

It is done.

Holly has locked the doors of Taylor, Griffin, emptied out her savings accounts, sold her platinum and diamond Rolex, and has left Jack and that whole phase of her life behind.

There was no fight, not even an argument, no pleading or anger, because she gave him not the smallest hint of what she was planning and left their home on a Thursday afternoon when she knew he was safely in court and Vita, their housekeeper, had the day off.

She was perfectly organized, her plans meticulously, exquisitely, laid. She and Jack have been married for less than six months, and Holly never did have any great urge to refurbish or to stamp any substantial personal marks on his home. Jack always seemed to regard that as an accolade to his fine taste and as a mark of her love for him. Holly simply knew that she would not be there long enough to make it worthwhile troubling with. So there wasn't all that much to pack up. Personal belongings. Books. Her computer. Her jewellery – including her beautiful three carat square-cut diamond engagement ring. The Tiffany tableware given as a wedding present by Richard and Eleanor. She was going to need dishes and silverware, after all, where she was going.

She knew exactly where she was going – though she did not, of course, intend letting anyone else know that. Neither Jack nor her parents. No one. Not even Nick.

Least of all Nick.

* * *

She did all the packing herself because it was safer that way. No moving company. No risk of gossip. No paper trail. No plane tickets. No car rental documents. No credit card charges.

Holly knows how smooth getaways are achieved. She fucked an inspector in Auto three times before she had all the details she needed. Which cars to pick and which to avoid; where and at what time of day or night to make the move; where to obtain a slim-jim – one of the habitual car thief's favourite tools of choice – or the kind of pliers to tackle locks, or the right sets of keys or whatever; how to hot-wire a car; where to get licence plates off wrecked cars and how to switch plates swiftly and safely.

Quite an education.

Holly has always got a buzz out of stealing, but breaking into the black Ford Taurus, getting the wheels and transmission unlocked and the motor started in the downtown underground parking lot – and then telling the attendant on the way out that she'd lost her ticket and grudgingly handing over the full daily rate – was the biggest and by far the most nerve-pumping theft she has ever undertaken.

Everything after that seemed easy – almost dull – by comparison. She drove to a second parking lot, still downtown, took her time switching the licence plates, careful, even with her hair tucked under a baseball cap and sunglasses hiding some of her face, not to be seen by anyone at all. The job completed and the original plates locked, for the time being, in the boot, she emerged from the parking lot, walked to the Holiday Inn, cleaned up in the powder room and then took a cab back home to Brentwood. Less than a half hour later, she called another cab, tipped the driver handsomely enough to persuade him to load all her belongings with few complaints (but not *so* generously that he would remember too much about her), told him she was going home to visit her parents and had him drive her to LAX. Once at the airport, she gave a skycap fifty bucks to take her and her worldly goods to a second cab, which transported her back downtown to the parking lot and the waiting Ford.

Four hundred and something miles later – the car's original licence plates long since ditched in a dumpster at a roadside diner – Holly has arrived at her destination.

It's night-time, and the house is dark.

It is so exactly, uncannily, what she was praying for. Karma. She was searching through a sheaf of San Francisco rental listings that she'd had sent to Taylor, Griffin when she found it.

Vacant possession. *'In need of work'* – which meant lousy condition, which made it affordable. No owner's regulations she couldn't meet. Perfect. The only thing that might have made it more amusing would have been the broker being Ford Realty's rental division, but then again, that might have been taking a risk too far.

Holly rented a post box and fax address, and took care of the whole deal long distance and fast, making an offer in the name of Rowe & Krantz (a dormant subsidiary of a law firm she had done some corporate work for in recent weeks and whose legal registered address was Taylor, Griffin's) and taking for herself the temporary identity of one of the firm's partners, Barbara Rowe. It was, of course, entirely fraudulent and another gamble, but Holly was working on the assumption that by the time – if ever – some accountant, or maybe even the IRS, spotted this chicken feed transaction on the firm's records, she would be long gone again and, thanks to her care and attention, there would be no reason to trace it back to Charlotte Taylor.

The Presidio Heights-based realtor had balked at first, uneasy about recommending that her client agree a lease with a company, rather than an individual. But then again, the realtor was hungry for deals and the situation was exceptional. The house in question had been empty for a while, mostly because the rental being asked by the owner was still pretty exorbitant for a property in comparatively poor condition; all Rowe & Krantz's references had checked out, and Barbara Rowe, the tenant-to-be, was an attorney, *plus* she was offering to pay six months' rent cash up front.

Holly lets herself into her new home, switches on the gas central heating and starts unloading the car. The street is quiet. A few cars drive up and down the hill. No one shows any interest in the woman carrying boxes and baggage from the Taurus into her house. The task completed, Holly gets back into the car and, a street map and torch on the seat beside her, makes for Candlestick Park, home of the Giants, and a good spot – she learned back in LA – to dump a stolen car.

She wipes over carefully inside and out, remembering to clean the rearview mirror – a prime site, the Auto inspector told her, for prints left by amateurs – as well as all the handles and the gas cap. The odds are heavily against anyone tracing this particular car. Pick the right kind of car, the cop said – nothing special – switch the plates, take it sufficiently far away, and no one's going to give a shit about getting it back.

She checks the Ford over one more time.

And takes a cab to her new home.

She stands outside for a moment or two, looking at her neighbours' house. There are only a couple of lights on: one upstairs on the third floor, the other on the first.

That's because two of the people who live there have gone away, and only the nanny and her charge are home.

Holly knows this because she has made it her business to know. She has been tracking these people's movements for a while now.

Of course, things are going to get a lot simpler from tonight.

Because the Millers live at 1315 Antonia Street.

And Holly now lives at 1317.

Neighbours again.

Just like in the good old days.

53

With Teresa Vasquez settled in at our house, and Nina in Arizona with Phoebe, I was in our bedroom packing a bag for my flight to New York on Monday, October 7th, when Chris Field called.

There's a surprise.

He said that he had been doing some checking, and had learned that Holly Bourne's marriage had not been registered either in Maryland or in the District of Columbia, or in New York City.

The United States being a big country, you might have thought that Field would have been justified in giving up the search at that point. But apparently, he thought about all the stuff that's been happening to me and my family in California, and had the marriage records checked first in San Francisco, and then in Los Angeles.

Bingo.

I sat down on the bed. I felt so sick that for a moment I could hardly speak.

'Of course,' Field went on, 'it might have sped things up a little if I'd known that her real name was Charlotte Bourne.'

That threw me for another loop. I had entirely forgotten, until that second, that Holly had once told me – soon after my family had moved to Bethesda, a *lifetime* ago – that the name on her birth certificate was Charlotte Holly Boume. No one had ever called her anything *but* Holly when I was around – not teachers, not classmates, not even Eleanor or Richard. It seems hard to believe, right now, that I could have forgotten something so crucial at a time like this, yet I *had*. I was only nine years old back then, and she was idly mentioning a boring detail on a piece of paper. Her name, so far as I and everyone else was concerned, was Holly.

257

'Who'd she marry?' I asked, finally, when I was ready.

'An attorney named Jack Taylor,' Field said.

'In LA.'

'That's right.'

'And is that where they've been living?' I asked.

'Yes, it is.'

I shut my eyes.

All this time, Holly was living in LA.

An hour by air from our home.

Playing games.

I opened my eyes again. From downstairs, I could hear the sounds of Teresa singing something Spanish to Zoë.

'What now?' I asked Field. My lawyer. Suddenly, Mr Ice-Eyes seemed like a regular prince.

'I think we should pass the information to the SFPD – if they haven't already obtained it for themselves.'

'What else?'

'We wait,' Field said.

'What for?'

'For the police to act on the information.'

'What if they don't?'

'Then we think again.'

That sounded more like the Chris Field I'd met and had no faith in.

'I'm not waiting,' I told him. 'I'm going to LA.'

'I'd strongly caution you against doing that,' Field said. 'It's not a good idea for you to approach either Taylor or his wife.'

'I'd like their address, please.'

'You really should be leaving this to the police, Mr Miller.'

'I just want to talk to Holly, face to face,' I said.

'Not a good idea,' Field repeated.

'I heard you,' I said. 'Now please will you give me the address.'

'Mr Taylor's home address is unlisted.'

'Then tell me where he works.'

'Why don't you just explain to me what you hope to achieve by going to see the lady,' Field suggested, 'and maybe I can take care of the matter on your behalf?'

The *lady*.

'Thank you,' I said, staying polite, 'but that's something you really

258

can't do for me. The 'lady', as you call her, will do a snow job on you, just as she's probably already done on the police.' I paused. 'The guy's a lawyer, right? Which means I can get his business address without your help.'

'I can't dissuade you?' Field asked, trying one last time.

'Not if you try till Christmas.'

54

Unable to reach Nina at the Waterson Clinic before his flight to LA that afternoon, Nick left a message saying that he had some new information and would be in touch again soon. The touch of relief he experienced at not having to speak to her just then, made him feel guilty. But then just about everything these days seemed to add another brick to his guilt load.

He checked in Monday afternoon at The Argyle – an early Art Deco hotel on Sunset Strip at which he'd stayed a couple of times courtesy of Meganimity – and had dinner that evening at Morton's with Steve Cohn, who wanted to talk about production delays on *Firefly*. Nick dropped the name of Jack Taylor's law firm casually into the conversation, and Cohn told him that Anderson, Taylor was a snappy Century City firm of entertainment industry lawyers employed by several of his acquaintances.

'Need an introduction?' Cohn asked him over his calves' liver and mashed potatoes.

'No,' Nick said, playing with his own food. 'Thank you.'

Luck of a kind was with him next morning. Jack Taylor was in the office that day, his assistant told Nick, and would have a half-hour free that afternoon owing to a cancellation. Taylor had Nick cool his heels in the waiting room for almost all of that thirty minutes, and when he did, at last, rise from behind his broad desk to greet Nick with a handshake, Jack Taylor's blue eyes held a pure hostility that was impossible to ignore.

'Mr Miller,' he said, curtly.

'Do you know who I am?' Nick wasn't planning on wasting any-one's time.

'I do,' Taylor said. 'Have a seat.'

Nick sat down, taking stock of the man Holly had married (the antithesis of himself: fair, smooth, older, probably much wiser and unquestionably more suitable) and then of his office. It was one of those LA power places, a spacious corner spot on a high floor, with a great deal of mahogany, old Persian rugs on polished parquet and a pair of horse paintings by the great British artist George Stubbs hanging on a wall to Taylor's left. It was all very imposing and grand and perfectly fine, yet it seemed somehow rather '*nouveau*' in com-parison with Richard Bourne's office which had, Nick felt, reeked of the genuine, venerable article.

'What can I do for you?' Taylor asked.

'I need to talk to your wife,' Nick answered.

'What about?'

Nick had no wish to be rude. 'Old times,' he said, 'and a little catching up.'

'I doubt very much that Charlotte wants to talk to you,' Taylor said.

'In my case,' Nick said, 'it isn't a question of wanting to. As I said, I *need* to talk to her. I've been trying to locate her for some time, but I've only just learned that she's been living here in Los Angeles. I was led to believe she – both of you – were in New York City.'

'I expect that's what Charlotte wanted you to believe.'

'I realize that.'

'So I ask you again, Mr Miller – what can I do for you?'

'Tell me where she is.'

'And why should I want to help you?'

'Why should you not want to?' Nick asked.

'Charlotte and I are separated,' Taylor said.

Nick took a moment. 'Since when?'

'I don't think that's any of your business,' Taylor said.

'I guess not.' Nick paused. 'Do you have a current address for her?'

'Even if I had,' Jack Taylor said, 'I wouldn't give it to you.'

'Why not?'

'I think you've done enough damage, don't you?'

Nick had a feeling he was unlikely to be granted more than

another minute or two. Taylor was freezing him out, swiftly and decisively.

'I don't suppose you're prepared to tell me why you've separated?' Nick said.

'I don't suppose I am.'

'Has Richard Bourne talked to you at all about my problems?'

'My conversations with Charlotte's father are also private.'

Nick sat forward, in a final attempt to arrest his attention, if nothing else. 'Mr Taylor, I have to tell you that Holly – Charlotte – could be in a great deal of trouble. If you still have feelings for her—'

'Enough to know' – Taylor cut Nick off – 'that all my wife's problems can be laid at your door.' The animosity in the blue eyes sharpened. 'Enough for me to be certain that I would not lift a finger to help you, Mr Miller, if a pack of hellhounds were snapping at your heels.'

Nick was out of there less than five minutes later. *No help there* – he thought as he left the building, found his rental car and drove away from Century City – *not today, not ever*. He could not feel anger towards Jack Taylor, who was, after all, just another casualty. Another of Holly's walking wounded.

Nonetheless, the new failure was a bitter pill to swallow. In the last twenty-four hours or so, Nick had discovered where and with whom Holly had been living for at least a part of that year – and yet still he was left with no more idea than before as to where she was *now*.

One thing was certain. He had to talk to Richard Bourne again. It was one thing for an estranged husband perhaps – just *perhaps* – not to know where his wife was, but it was a whole lot less conceivable that Holly's parents had no address for her.

Not that they were likely to share it with him, of course.

Especially not if the cops had been to see them because of the information he'd given the SFPD about their daughter.

It was too late to try reaching Richard Bourne in Washington that day, so Nick spent what was left of Tuesday afternoon randomly calling local law firms picked out of the directories in his hotel room, trying to find an attorney named Charlotte Taylor. He had telephoned less than one-third of the firms listed when office hours ended and he could no longer put off calling Nina in Scottsdale, where she was staying at her father's house.

'What now?' Nina asked, when he'd given her the day's news.

'I try Richard Bourne one more time.'

'He won't help you,' she said.

'I still have to try,' Nick said.

'If you say so.'

'I thought I'd fly to Phoenix tomorrow after I finish here.'

'Phoebe will be glad to see you,' Nina said.

That was all she said.

Nick didn't blame her. All he had achieved to date was hollow and useless. To Nina, Holly Bourne probably seemed like some kind of a phantom, an ugly shadow over their lives. Unless he could find a way of making her flesh and blood again – a real person to be focused on and accused – Nick could not see that changing.

He reached Bourne third time of calling next morning.

'I know that Holly's been living in LA,' he said, talking fast in case the lawyer cut him off. 'I know she's probably been calling herself Charlotte Taylor, and I know that she and her husband have split up.'

'So what do you want from me?' Bourne asked.

'Just two questions, then I'll back off.'

'No guarantee I'll answer them,' Bourne said.

'You gave me your word you were going to deal with this, Mr Bourne,' Nick reminded him, gripping the telephone tightly and staring out, unseeing, at the city view from his hotel windows. 'The least you can do is listen to me.'

'Go ahead.'

'Do you know where Holly is?'

'No, I don't.'

The answer was so flat and hard that Nick felt he could almost taste the pain and, more significantly, the truth in it.

'If you find out where she is, will you at least consider telling me?'

'I doubt that very much.'

Nothing Nick had not expected.

'Just one last question,' he said.

'If you must.'

'Are you afraid for Holly?'

Richard Bourne paused for only a moment.

'She is my daughter, Nick.'

Continuing all the way down to the Z's in the directory earned Nick the now maddeningly useless information that Holly – or rather, Charlotte Taylor – had briefly been in the employ of a firm called Zadok, Giulini and O'Connell. No one there, predictably, was prepared to give him any further personal information about Ms Taylor, other than to tell him that she had left them in July.

Back at LAX again, he called Nina at the Waterson Clinic shortly before boarding his flight to Phoenix.

'I can't wait to see you,' he said.

'Phoebe's definitely stronger,' Nina told him.

Nick's heart sank at her lack of response.

'Give her my love,' Nick said.

'I will,' Nina said, and put down the phone.

Nick thought about Holly a lot on that flight, about how much pain she had already inflicted and was still doing.

You've done enough damage. Jack Taylor's words. The husband, plainly injured by Holly, yet still defending her against Nick Miller, the great enemy.

He still had nothing more to tell Nina, and certainly he had a big fat zero so far as clearing his name with the San Francisco police was concerned. But two things, at least, had become very clear to him since he'd left home.

Richard Bourne knew now that his daughter was not the happy, high-flying picture that Eleanor Bourne liked to paint.

And Holly, cut off from her parents, separated from her husband – isolated and, presumably, unhappy – was probably even more of a loose cannon than Nick had previously believed.

55

Holly – in her new role as Barbara Rowe – has wasted no time in befriending Teresa Vasquez. The Mexican nanny, alone much of the time in the Millers' big house with just a small baby for company, is hungry for adult conversation and not at all shy about voicing her disapproval of Zoë's parents' ill-timed travel plans.

A lonely, middle-aged woman with a desire to be heard.

Easy prey.

'It is good to be given trust,' Teresa grumbles, 'and I know that both Mr and Mrs Miller have many problems right now, but a little baby needs her mother and father, and it's lonely for me with no one except the *nena* to talk to.'

'You can talk to me, Teresa,' Holly tells her.

She has invited Vasquez, with the baby, to tea in Barbara Rowe's living room: hastily and economically furnished with a cream-colored suite from a furniture showroom on Van Ness Avenue, two throw down rugs and a few knickknacks from Fillamento on Fillmore and some framed floral prints from Macy's. None of it exactly to Holly's taste, but she's been limited in both time (she can only shop freely while the Millers are out of town) and funds (since everything has to be paid for in cash, and she can't risk stealing right now in case she gets caught). Besides, this is Barbara Rowe's house, not Holly Bourne's.

'I'm going to be around a lot for a while,' she explains to the nanny, pouring tea, 'because I have a lot of work to do on the house. I'll be glad of your company, Teresa.'

'It's not proper,' Teresa says, reluctantly.

'Why ever not?'

'Because I am your neighbours' servant, Mrs Rowe.'

'You're a nanny, Teresa,' Holly corrects her firmly. 'I can't think of a more important job than caring for a helpless infant.'

She stirs her own tea and sips it, then glances at the stroller in which Zoë Miller is sleeping. Nick's daughter. She'd like to pick her up and examine her more closely, but instead she just sits there, on Barbara Rowe's sofa, drinking tea and chatting.

'You know, Teresa,' she says, 'I'm very keen to improve my Spanish vocabulary, and I'd love to learn Mexican cookery.' She smiles warmly at the other woman. 'So if you could maybe spare me a few hours whenever possible, I'd be very grateful to you.'

Vasquez's cheeks have grown a little flushed. She is flattered.

'I am not sure if Mrs Miller would approve.'

'Then let's not tell her,' Holly says conspiratorially. 'It can be our little secret.' She puts down her cup. 'When the Millers are home, we'll confine our lessons to your free time, Teresa, and neither of them need ever know.'

'I would enjoy it very much,' Teresa admits.

'And in the meantime, whenever you want to go out and have a little fun, I'll be happy to take care of little Zoë for you. After all' – Holly folds her hands over her own gently rounded stomach – 'it's only a matter of months before I become a mother myself, so I need all the practice I can get. You'll be doing me a favour.'

'You are very kind, Mrs Rowe.'

'I'm not at all kind.'

Holly passes Vasquez the plate of cookies she bought at a patisserie in Cow Hollow that morning, and the nanny – who's already had two – takes two more. If she eats like that all the time, Holly thinks, it's a wonder she stays so skinny. She makes a mental note for future reference to keep plenty of Vasquez's favorite items in stock.

'There is one more thing you could do for me, Teresa,' she says, thoughtfully, 'if you don't mind.'

'Anything,' Teresa says.

'It's very important that you don't speak about me to anyone – not even to Mr and Mrs Miller.'

'But they are your neighbours.' Vasquez is confused.

'Of course they are.' Holly goes on speaking slowly and carefully. 'But apart from you, Teresa – because I do need a friend – everyone needs a friend, don't you agree?—'

'Oh, yes, I agree.'

'Apart from you, the fewer people who know my name, or anything else about me, the better.' Holly pauses. 'It's because of my husband, you see.' She waits another beat, for full effect. 'He's a very violent man, Teresa.'

Vasquez's dark eyes become large. 'He hits you?'

'Oh, yes.'

'Have you told the police?'

'It was better for me to leave,' Holly confides in her. 'This way there's no trouble for him, and the baby and I will be safe.'

The nanny's left hand goes out instinctively towards Zoë's stroller, and touches the handle. 'Maybe you are right. You must protect your *bebé*.'

Holly smiles at her again, one of her warmest, most delightful smiles.

'So you do understand, about our little secret?'

'Oh, yes, Mrs Rowe,' the nanny answers. 'I understand.'

Being pregnant is the most wonderful thing that's ever happened to Holly, and not having to conceal it from Jack any longer makes it even more perfect. Even throwing up each morning while it lasted never really troubled her. She knows she's going to get fat as a cow – Lord knows she's eating at four times her normal rate. But then again, she is, as everyone always says, eating for two, and she figures that with all the vomiting she has to have been losing valuable nutrients, and Holly is not going to let her baby be deprived of anything.

Especially love.

56

Nina came into Nick's arms when he arrived at the clinic on Wednesday afternoon, and allowed him to hold her, but that was exactly how it *felt* to him: as if he were being granted a favour.

'Inspector Wilson called me here this morning,' Nina reported as they walked in the Waterson's lovely gardens. 'She asked a few questions about Phoebe's condition, but I'm sure she'd already spoken to the doctors, so she didn't need to ask me.'

'So what did she really want?' Nick's stomach gripped with tension. He was growing used to that sensation. He could hardly imagine his body or mind tranquil again.

The gardens were like an oasis in the dry desert heat, sprinklers constantly fanning fine sprays over the lawns and flower beds, smooth wide pathways between the lawns to ease the passage of patients in wheelchairs.

'She asked where you were. She seemed upset that you were travelling.'

'Don't leave town,' Nick said, wryly.

'I didn't tell her you were in LA.'

'Why not? I have nothing to hide.'

'I thought you might prefer me not to tell her,' Nina said.

They sat down on a bench. It was unpainted, natural blond wood, handsome and comfortable.

'Did Wilson say anything about Holly?' Nick asked.

'She didn't say anything much at all,' Nina answered.

Rather like Nina herself.

* * *

Nick used one of the public phones in the lobby of the clinic, failed to get hold of Capelli and had no choice but to speak to Wilson.

'Have you found Holly Bourne?' Straight to the point.

'Have you?' Wilson asked right back.

Nick assumed that meant they'd had no more luck than he had.

'I found out a couple of things,' he said. 'Her married name and where she was living, till recently.'

'Do you want to give me those details?' Wilson asked.

'I thought you might have found them out for yourselves.'

'I won't know until you tell me,' she said.

Nick gritted his teeth and gave her the facts, such as they were.

'So Holly Bourne's not even her name,' Wilson commented.

'It was the name she always used – at least until her marriage,' Nick said, 'so far as I knew. She always called herself Holly, which is actually her middle name.' He paused. 'So what now?'

'When are you coming back to San Francisco?' Wilson asked.

'Soon,' Nick answered.

'Okay,' she said.

'Inspector Wilson, I need to know what you're doing about finding Holly Bourne, or Charlotte Taylor, or whatever the hell she's calling herself now. I've just told you she's disappeared – that neither her husband nor her family knows where she's hiding.'

'You're assuming she is hiding.'

'Yes, I am. Aren't you?'

'Why don't we continue this conversation when you get back, Mr Miller?' Wilson suggested. 'Your daughter's at home, isn't she?'

'My daughter's being well cared for, Inspector.'

'I'm sure she is.'

'So why do you want me in San Francisco?'

A dark-haired woman in a blue suit was hovering in front of Nick, waiting to use the phone; he turned away from her and faced the wall and the small plaque that told him this telephone did not accept incoming calls.

'Am I still under suspicion?' he asked.

'Of what, Mr Miller?' Wilson asked, in her dry, unpleasant manner. 'Possession of heroin, child abuse or attempted murder?'

Fuck you, Wilson, Nick thought, but managed not to say.

'Do you still think I had something to do with Phoebe Ford's fall?'

'We're still investigating the case,' Wilson said.

'How? By trying to find Holly Bourne?'

'You know I can't divulge police business to you, Mr Miller.'

'But surely you must see by now that there's more than a chance I'm right about her? She's been living an hour away from San Francisco. She's walked out on her husband. No one knows where she is.'

'None of which constitutes grounds for suspicion of the attempted murder of a complete stranger,' Wilson said.

'It does in my book,' Nick said, and cut off the call before he said something he might regret.

He had known it before, but now he was more certain than ever.

No one really, wholly, believed him. Not the cops, not Chris Field, not even his own wife. Which meant that no one else was going to make any major effort to track down the woman he was now one hundred per cent convinced had lured Phoebe to that house.

Holly *was* in hiding. That was another thing he was sure of.

And it was still down to him to find her.

57

There's still no hope of getting poor Phoebe to try to convince the cops that I've never had any reason on earth to want to kill her.

She is, as Nina told me on the phone before I came, growing stronger, but she's undergone another bout of microsurgery on her arms and hands and is, consequently, still miserably plastered up from fingers to shoulder on both sides; and though she has started trying noticeably harder to speak, she's still not getting there.

We visited with her for a while after my call to San Francisco. William was there, like Nemesis, the whole time. Nina left the room to fetch a Coke, but William stayed put. I had the feeling that if I stayed in that room for seventy-two hours straight, William would remain glued to Phoebe's side for the whole time, doing without food or even the use of the bathroom.

My father-in-law won't even risk peeing if it means leaving me with his daughter for more than ninety seconds.

I am a dangerous man.

'I'm going home tomorrow,' Nina tells me now, after our visit, as we eat crisp salad and drink mineral water in the Waterson's restaurant. 'I can't bear to go another day without seeing Zoë.' She bites into a carrot. 'And you can appease Inspector Wilson.'

'How am I supposed to do that?' I ask her. My food is good, but I can't eat it. My stomach is cartwheeling for a change.

'By being cooperative.'

'How much more cooperative am I supposed to be? I've given them every piece of information I have, and they're still not listening to me.'

A teenage girl wheels herself into place at the table beside us. She has gorgeous, long dark hair and almond eyes. I think she may be paralysed from the waist down. She smiles at me and I smile back. I can't remember the last time I really smiled.

It was probably at Zoë.

'I'm going back to LA,' I tell Nina.

'What for?' She knows very well what for.

'To see a detective agency. They should have a better shot of finding her now.'

'So should the police.' Her voice is strained.

'I've told you, the police aren't interested enough in finding Holly. All they seem to want to do is pin Phoebe's fall on me. Wilson said it all, didn't she? Just because Holly's left her husband and her company doesn't mean she tried to kill Phoebe.'

'But that's true, isn't it?' Nina says.

'Which is why they should be out there looking for *proof*.' My exasperation is showing. 'Which is why they should be looking for Holly, not hassling me to go back to San Francisco.'

'We don't know that they're not looking for her.'

'Well, if they are, they're certainly keeping it a state secret.'

Nina's stopped eating.

'I don't want you to go to LA, Nick,' she says abruptly. 'I want you to come back home with me to our daughter.'

I can see a vein in her left temple throbbing, and part of me wants to stroke it, but another part of me wants to tell her that it's her fault if she has a headache because she ought to be understanding me, *supporting* me.

'I want us to get some normality back into our lives,' she says.

I stare at her. 'How in hell can we have any kind of normality until this is resolved?'

Nina tries one more time.

'Leave it to the police,' she says.

'I can't,' I answer.

I've never seen dislike for me in my wife's eyes before.

We may be in the desert. I feel the desert is in me.

58

Holly is watching from a third-floor window as Nina Miller arrives home from Arizona on Thursday. It's quite a heartwarming sight: nanny hurrying down the front steps, baby in her arms, to greet mother. Mother exchanging travel bag for baby as the cab driver carries her cases up to the house.

Holly knew that Nina would be getting back around this time, knew which flight she was taking. Just as she knows that Nick has returned to Los Angeles and that he and Nina were at loggerheads before leaving the Waterson Clinic over his decision to let Nina come home alone.

Holly's systems are all up and running smoothly now. On the home front she has Vasquez, the gabby nanny, hungry for treats and flattery, and in the world beyond she has Samuel Keitel. Keitel is a private detective from LA, whose greatest asset is that he's an honest-to-God chameleon. At the Waterson Clinic, Keitel knows how to pass for a doctor or anxious relative or cleaner; on the streets, he can stand right next to a person and still be virtually unnoticed. Holly has seen him in action. Keitel knows how to make himself invisible. As a consequence, between Vasquez – on whom she – as Barbara Rowe – has been bestowing friendship, food and gifts – and her man on the street, Holly has been keeping tabs on just about everything of consequence in the lives of Nick and Nina Miller.

By the time Nina Miller has been home for two days and two nights, Holly knows that Nick has employed his own LA detective agency – a firm called Interstate Investigations – and her reasoning is, therefore, that if Nick is prepared to throw enough time and money at the problem, he may ultimately track her down.

Right now, however, he still doesn't have the slightest idea where she is.

She, on the other hand, knows exactly where *he* is.

She knows which hotel he's staying at, and she knows that this time it isn't The Argyle. She even knows the number of his room.

And, thanks to a particularly nauseating one-night-stand with a middle-aged, paunchy LAPD detective in Burglary, she also knows three different ways to get inside that room.

59

Nick's downtown hotel was called the Mistral Inn and, whilst it wasn't exactly a hairshirt or even entirely a dump, nor was it the kind of place he had ever chosen to stay before. It was big, impersonal and dingy, and it was the sort of hotel where you had the feeling that if you died, no one would notice until you failed to settle your bill. Both Nina and Clare had asked him why he wasn't staying at The Argyle or at any of the other fine hotels in and around the city, and Nick had claimed full houses all over; but the truth was that, aside from the Mistral Inn being just a couple of blocks from Interstate Investigations on Flower Street, he was feeling so damned guilty about being in Los Angeles at all that sleeping in a great hotel would only have made him feel lousier.

'If you were planning on contacting Meganimity,' Clare had said to him when she'd heard he was going back to LA, 'I'd advise against it right now.'

'I wasn't,' Nick had answered, 'but why?'

'Because in the last twenty-four hours or so, they and the publishers appear to have gotten wind of your problems.' Hawkins had paused. 'No one's panicking, but you should be aware that you may have trouble if things get any worse.'

'What do my personal problems have to do with them?' he had wanted to know.

'Come on, Nick, you're not naïve,' Clare pulled him up. 'This is a children's product. Your problems have a great deal of relevance to that, like it or not.'

* * *

He did not like it, but in his present state of mind it seemed the least of his worries. He had been back in LA for two days now, and neither he nor the detective agency had achieved anything of significance in the search for Holly Bourne or Charlotte Taylor. He knew now that a company called Taylor, Griffin had belonged to Holly, but was no longer in operation, and he knew that both Jack Taylor and Richard Bourne were scurrying around trying to trace her too, but that was all.

Nina wanted him home. Nick wanted, more than anything, to *be* home. Nina's theory was that even if she accepted that he was right about Holly, it was clear that she had now gone to ground; which presumably indicated that she was afraid of being found out and was, therefore, more likely to back down than to risk trying any further mischief.

'Anyway,' Nina pointed out on the telephone on Saturday evening, 'you've done what you wanted to do. You've handed the case over to a detective agency – I don't see any reason for you to be hanging around in LA when Holly's probably thousands of miles away by now.'

'You realize that if I do come back,' Nick said, 'I probably won't *be* home for more than a few hours before the police haul my ass in for more questioning – maybe even charge me – and then I may never be able to come home again.'

'For God's sake, Nick, you don't know that,' Nina snapped.

'You've already told me Wilson called again.'

'Wanting to know if you were back, that was all.'

Nick looked around with distaste at the smoke-tinted walls of his bedroom, and was reminded of the interview room at the Hall of Justice. 'You don't believe that.'

There was a short silence before she replied.

'I don't know what to believe any more, Nick.'

She cut him off.

He called her back less than five minutes later.

'I'll fly home first thing in the morning.'

'Are you sure that's what you want?' Nina sounded as if she might have been crying.

'I know I want to be with you and Zoë,' he answered. 'I know I don't want to do any more damage to our marriage.'

'What if the cops do pick you up?' Suddenly she was uncertain.

'Then you'll have to call Chris Field again.'

'I thought you didn't trust him.'

'I guess he got me this far,' Nick said.

'All right.' There was a hint of warmth in those two words.

'I'll call you in the morning, to confirm my flight.' Nick paused. 'I love you, Nina.'

'I love you, too, Nick.'

He put down the phone. He felt better than he had in a while. He knew it wouldn't last, especially not once Wilson and Capelli got their teeth into him again. But right now, at least, for this short time, as he headed out of the bleak room in search of dinner, his soul felt just a few pounds lighter.

60

Holly is standing well back in the doorway of an office building just diagonally across the street from the Mistral Inn. It's quiet, with that kind of almost-dead feel that many downtown commercial districts assume at the weekends. People arrive at and leave Nick's hotel, most of them getting into cabs or driving away in their cars. Few leave on foot, except those heading into Sammy's Delicatessen on the next southwest corner.

The swing doors behind Holly open and close, and three gossiping women come out of the office building. Typists doing overtime, or maybe cleaners. One of them glances briefly at Holly as they pass her, but she has dressed unstrikingly in khaki pants, jacket and loafers – has taken pains to make herself unobtrusive – and the woman quickly returns to the chatter and vanishes with her friends.

Nick emerges from the Mistral Inn, wearing blue jeans and a plain white T-shirt. He stops for a moment at a coin-operated newspaper vending machine and picks up a *Los Angeles Times*. Even from across the street, Holly can see that he's looking tired. Tired and lonely. In need of company.

He tucks the newspaper under his left arm, strolls to the corner of the street, and disappears into Sammy's.

Holly waits another two minutes before she crosses the street and enters the Mistral Inn. '*Moon River*' is being piped into the medium-sized lobby, its notes slipping and sliding now and again on the over-used tape. There are two small clusters of people standing around,

278

one woman, on her own, sitting on a vinyl couch, waiting, and three guests standing in line at the front desk.

Holly doesn't hesitate, just moves right on through to the elevators at the back of the lobby beside the closed Olde Gift Shoppe. The left-hand elevator is standing empty, its doors open. She gets in, pushes the button for the fifth floor and rides up alone. Upstairs, the corridor branches two ways. An arrow with room number listings directs her to the right.

The corridor is dimly lit and smells unpleasant. Mustiness topped by air freshener, mixed with old food. Outside three separate rooms, trays of discarded meals stand uncollected on the carpet.

There's no one around.

She finds room 507 easily. Takes from her shoulder bag the card stolen earlier in the day from a chamber maid's apron pocket, slides it into the electronic door lock, waits for the green light, opens the door and removes the card again.

And lets herself into Nick's room.

61

Nick came out of the deli feeling even better than he had going in. One hefty corned-beef sandwich and a rib-sticking potato pancake, washed down with a cold beer and the decision he'd made to go home, and now he was looking forward to getting past this one last lonely night and heading straight out to LAX first thing in the morning.

The lobby at the Mistral Inn was almost deserted, but the Muzak was still playing, and shrieks of raucous laughter were filtering through from the Saturday-night crowd in the hotel bar. Nick hesitated for a second or two, wondering if one more beer might be better insurance against insomnia, but then he changed his mind and headed directly for the elevators. He would sleep tonight because he knew he'd made a good decision – perhaps the only decent decision he'd made in weeks – and even if he did toss and turn instead, he had the prospect of new beginnings with Nina and Zoë to fill the night, so who the hell cared about a few hours' lost sleep?

He knew the instant the heavy door closed behind him that something was strange in the room.

Perfume. Jasmine.

Familiar.

He flicked the light switch.

Holly was lying in his bed, under the sheets, looking straight at him.

Her shoulders were naked.

'Jesus *Christ*,' Nick said, his heart pounding like a jackhammer.

'Long time,' Holly said.

'Jesus *Christ*,' Nick said again. His legs – his whole body – seemed suddenly filled with lead. He couldn't move. He thought for a moment that he was going to pass out.

'Is that all you have to say, Nick?'

She sat up a little way and held out her arms to him. The top sheet fell away, exposing her breasts.

An old memory flashed like lightning through Nick's mind – Holly holding out her arms to him that same way on that nightmare last night in New York, just after they'd grappled and he'd hit her.

It was enough to cut through his paralysis.

'Get dressed,' he said, hard and sharp, and headed straight for the phone on the bedside table to her left. He picked up the receiver, his right hand shaking a little, and hit the zero button.

'Who are you calling?' Holly asked.

He didn't even glance at her. 'Who do you think?'

'I don't think you'll get security,' she said, softly.

Comprehension took another second to dawn. The phone was dead. Nick looked at Holly, and saw that she was holding the end of the cord in her right hand. She was smiling.

'Give me the cord,' Nick said.

'What's your rush?'

'Give me the fucking cord.'

'Take it.' She held it up a little higher, taunting. 'You could wrestle me for it.'

Don't play her game.

'What do you want, Holly?' He was finding it hard to breathe.

'I heard you were looking for me,' she said.

'Not just me,' Nick said. 'The police, too.'

'Aren't I popular?'

Nick held out his right hand. 'Give me the cord, Holly.'

'Okay,' she said, and gave it to him. 'It won't help. I cut it.'

He stared at it, saw she was telling the truth.

'I wanted to see you,' she said, soft again. 'I thought you might like to see this.' She pushed the covering sheet right down past her thighs. 'No, don't look away, Nick.'

Nick had turned away, was halfway to the door, passing her khaki-coloured clothes folded neatly over the back of the only chair in the room. If he couldn't call security or the cops from the room, he had no choice but to get back downstairs.

'Don't look away from our baby, Nick.'

He stopped in mid-step.

'Please look, Nick,' her voice said, half cajoling, half pleading. 'It's our baby. Your baby.'

Nick turned around. Both Holly's hands were resting on her stomach, palms down. He looked away from her stomach, up into her face. The grey eyes were wet with tears.

'Isn't it wonderful?' she said. 'Isn't it the most beautiful thing you've ever seen?' She paused. 'Our *baby*.' She lifted one hand from her belly and reached out towards him. 'Come and feel it, Nick.'

He thought he was going to throw up, right there and then on the cheap, stained oatmeal synthetic carpet. He had a great urge to scream.

He did neither.

Nina came into his mind.

And Zoë.

'Don't you want to feel your baby, Nick?' Holly asked him.

He looked her right in the eye. 'Sure I do,' he said.

'Then come on.' She patted the bed beside her.

'In a minute,' he said.

He went to the door and opened it. He was sweating, and his heart was still hammering in his chest.

'Where are you going?' she asked.

'To get us a drink,' he said, fighting to sound convincing. 'Something to help us celebrate.'

'I can't drink alcohol,' Holly said. 'Not in my condition.'

'Well, I need something,' Nick said, 'for the shock.'

'What about the mini-bar?'

'It doesn't carry my brand.'

'You never used to be so picky,' Holly said.

'You're right,' Nick said. 'I didn't. But things change.'

He started out through the door.

'Don't be long,' Holly said.

'I won't be,' he said.

The door clicked shut behind him.

Nick ran.

* * *

282

The party was still going on in the bar, but there was no one at the front desk. Nick spotted a brass bell and pounded on it, kept right on hitting it.

'Keep your shorts on.' A voice came through a door marked PRIVATE. 'I'll be right out after I finish this call.'

'No time,' Nick yelled across the counter. 'I need Security.'

A man of about fifty with greying hair and glasses stuck his head around the door. 'What do you need Security for?'

'And I need you to call the police,' Nick told him.

The man's eyes widened behind his glasses. 'What's going on? Have you been robbed?'

'Someone's broken into my room. They're still *in* there.'

'How do you know?'

'How the fuck do you *think* I know?' Nick thought of Holly, knew she was probably already dressed, knew she was maybe getting away while this loser was wasting precious time. 'Just get a Security guy up to room 507, and do it *fast*.'

'Right away.' The man vanished back behind the door.

'And don't forget the police!' Nick yelled, sprinting back to the elevators, accidentally pushing two women who were strolling arm in arm through the lobby.

'Hey, mister!' one of them, a skinny redhead in tight pants, objected. 'Ever heard of manners?'

One of the elevators opened its doors. Nick ran right in, jabbed the button for the fifth floor, and the doors slid shut right in the same women's faces. The elevator seemed slower than before. It stopped on the third floor, though no one got in, and then again on the fourth.

'Kids,' Nick said, under his breath. 'Damned *kids*.'

The doors slid open. Nick started running again, then made himself stop. The corridor was empty. Either Holly was still in the room, or he was too late. There was an overhead illuminated sign marking a Fire Exit at the far end of the passageway.

A sick sensation told him, even before he opened the door of 507 again, that if the room was empty, that was probably the route she'd taken.

It was empty.

Nothing. Not a trace of her anywhere, neither in the bedroom nor in the bathroom. She'd even tidied the bedclothes.

The only clues left as to what had gone on were the cut telephone cord and the jasmine fragrance – and Nick couldn't imagine *that* making much impression on a cop, let alone a judge.

He thought about going after her down the fire staircase, but knew there was no point. She'd had ample time to get down five flights, out of the hotel and into a waiting cab or car by now.

Too late.

Too fucking late.

'But nothing's actually been stolen, sir?'

'No.'

'And you weren't assaulted, or injured, in any way?'

'No, I *told* you that already.'

'I know what you told me, Mr Miller. I'm just trying to get a clearer picture of what went on.'

'I don't know how much clearer you want it.'

Nick had told Al Klein, the hotel security man, a short, squat man in a shiny brown suit, and LAPD Officers Santo and Leary, exactly what had gone on, together with a rapid, rough account of what lay behind the invasion of his hotel room by a crazy, dangerous woman, but none of the men appeared able or willing to grasp the gravity of the situation.

So what else was new?

'What exactly do you want us to do for you, sir?' Officer Santo asked, sitting down on the only chair in the room – the chair over which Holly had earlier hung her clothes. The smaller of the two cops, dark, slim and young, Santo's tone was full of exaggerated patience that came close to mockery.

'Arrest Holly Bourne,' Nick answered.

'What for?' Al Klein, leaning against the wardrobe, was smirking. 'Sitting naked in your bed or using jasmine perfume?'

Nick ignored Klein and kept talking to Santo. 'How about illegal entry for openers?' He was trying to stay non-aggressive, but it was becoming more of a struggle by the minute. 'And how about collecting some evidence?'

'What kind of evidence, sir?' Officer Leary was tall and overweight, and his skimpy mousy hair was combed sideways over his balding, perspiring scalp, but his manner was direct, and at least he looked as if he was still paying a degree of attention.

Nick looked around the room. 'She must have left prints,' he said. 'She wasn't wearing gloves.'

'You could try dusting for butt-prints,' Klein suggested.

Nick thought about punching the smart-ass, so-called security man in his mean little mouth, but that would really be playing into Holly's hands. And in any case, he felt a little like a car running out of gas. He was so sick and tired of people not lifting a finger to help him.

'You could call San Francisco,' he said, also not for the first time. 'Speak to Inspectors Capelli or Wilson in Personal Crimes. I already told you they've been looking for Holly Bourne.'

'We'll do that in the morning,' Officer Santo said.

Nick looked at his wristwatch, saw that it was after midnight.

'You know she's going to get away, don't you?' he said. 'If you don't even put out her description, she'll be out of LA before morning – she could be at LAX right now.'

'We've already reported the incident, sir,' Leary reminded him. 'There's not a whole lot more we can do, not without evidence.'

'What about the telephone?' Nick nodded his head towards the severed cord. 'Her prints have to be all over that.'

'Along with yours, the maids' and at least a dozen other guests,' Leary pointed out.

'But she's the one who cut the cord,' Nick said.

'We only have your word for that,' Santo said.

'You think I cut it?'

'No one's saying that,' Leary said.

'The phone cord's going to need paying for,' Al Klein remarked.

'So find Holly Bourne and send her the fucking bill,' Nick told him.

'It's your room,' Klein told him back. 'Your bill.'

'It's your goddamned hotel,' Nick said, his anger mounting again. 'You're supposed to take care of goddamned security, not let people walk in off the street and break into rooms.'

'There's no sign of a break-in,' Santo said.

'So she probably used one of those cards,' Nick said.

'They're definitely going to add the cost of the phone to your bill,' Klein said.

'Screw the phone,' Nick told him.

'Take it easy, Mr Miller,' Officer Leary said.

285

'Tell him he has to pay for the phone.' Klein wasn't giving up.

'Will you tell that fat little jerk' – Nick focused on Leary – 'that if he says one more thing about paying for the phone, I'm going to break his nose?'

'You going to let him threaten me?' Klein demanded, outraged.

'If I were you,' Officer Leary told him, 'I'd shut up about the phone.'

'And the hotel bill,' Nick added.

'That's gotta be between you and the hotel manager, sir,' Leary said.

Officer Santo's radio squawked unintelligible static into the crowded little room. 'We'd better wind this up, Mike,' he said to Leary.

'So how d'you want to handle this, sir?' Leary asked Nick. 'You want to come to the station, make a full report?'

'What for?' Nick said. 'You're not going to do anything, are you?'

'It's your right to make a full report, sir,' Leary said.

'Though all we're talking about here is an alleged illegal entry,' Santo pointed out, 'a damaged telephone cord—'

'Don't start again about the phone,' Leary reminded him.

'– and an alleged naked woman in your bed,' Santo finished.

'Shit,' Nick said, in disgust.

'Feel free to come to the station, sir,' Officer Leary said.

Nick thought about it. 'You have to make your own report anyhow, don't you?'

'We do,' Leary confirmed.

'So if I go back to San Francisco in the morning and tell the guys I know in Personal Crimes what happened here, they'll be able to access your report?'

'That's right,' Leary said.

'No one's going to claim nothing happened here?' Nick checked.

'No, sir, no one's going to claim that.'

'Tell him he has to pay for the damage,' Al Klein perked up again. Santo's radio screeched again.

Nick looked at Leary. 'Would you please do one thing for me?'

'If I can.'

'Get this little sleaze out of my room before I deck him.'

'No problem, sir,' Leary said.

* * *

286

Nick was out of the hotel an hour later and in a cab en route to LAX. His hotel bill had been cancelled – thanks to his threats to the night manager to publicize the hotel's lack of security – and Nick had had the minor satisfaction of witnessing Al Klein being told, for the second time that night, to shut up. Other than that, there was nothing on earth to be satisfied about.

For once in his life, Nick needed a stiff drink. He was pretty sure there would be no flights to San Francisco before around six a.m., and with the strict California liquor laws he doubted there would be any bars open at that time on a Sunday morning at the airport. But there was no way he was going to spend another hour – let alone the rest of the night – at the godforsaken Mistral Inn, and anyway, he might as well get himself checked in for his flight before he lost his nerve and changed his mind.

It wasn't that he wasn't longing to get home to Nina and Zoë.

That longing was greater than ever.

But he was going to have to tell Nina what had happened this night.

That Holly Bourne had been in his hotel bed. Naked.

Talking crazy stuff about having his baby.

Their baby.

And if he'd thought that telling Nina about any of the other stuff from the past had been hell, he had no words for how he felt about telling her this.

62

'Didn't you enjoy it? Having Holly naked in your bed again?'

That's the first question Nina asks after I've finished my humiliating tale. I was mortified before I began. Now I'm in ruins.

I figure the question should not be dignified with an answer. Not that I have much dignity left.

'When are you calling Wilson or Capelli to share this with them?'

That one I can answer.

'Later. I want to be at home with you and Zoë for a while first.'

'You needn't have bothered coming home,' Nina tells me.

It's around noon. Teresa is out, and the baby's asleep in the nursery. Nina and I are in the kitchen. I'm sitting at the table, feeling sorry for myself because my head aches from lack of sleep and because my wife hates me – feeling like a fucking idiot, if you really want to know. Nina, wearing jeans and a white cotton shirt, is pacing between the oven and the refrigerator, her hair swinging as she paces.

I look into her face when it comes into my view, though she won't stand still for long enough for me to really nail down what she's feeling or thinking. But I see enough. More than enough.

Nina's in pain again. And I'm the cause of it.

I hate myself more than she possibly can.

She stops pacing.

'I want you to go,' she says.

She has that pinched look she gets when things are really bad and twisted up in her mind. If I weren't in here, she would probably break down and cry, and maybe that would be good, though I'm not sure of that. Nina's rare tears always torment me.

288

'I'm not going anywhere,' I say.

I've heard what she said, but I'm choosing to believe she doesn't really mean it.

'I want you to *go*.' There's something approaching hysteria in her voice.

I think this shock is worse than anything I have experienced in my entire life. Worse than being set up by Holly with the drug pushers in New York. Worse than discovering that I was capable of hitting a woman. Worse than having the house wrecked by Abbott's and Riley's cohorts, or being dragged in for questioning by Capelli and Wilson.

It's hard to believe that anything could be more shocking than seeing Phoebe for the first time in the ICU at People's Hospital. Or coming into my hotel room last night and finding Holly naked in my bed.

But right this minute, this certainly seems like an all-time winner.

I get up from my chair, but then I feel suddenly weak and have to sit down again. I'm shaking.

'Don't you realize this is just what Holly wants?' My voice sounds loud, too loud, in the kitchen. I don't want to wake the baby.

'I don't give a *damn* what Holly wants,' Nina says.

She sounds and looks very strange. There's something there in her face that I've never seen before.

'But this is so *exactly* what she wants, Nina. To drive a wedge between us.'

'Then she's done a terrific job, hasn't she?' That look is still there. 'If you won't go, Nick,' she says, 'then I will.'

'This is crazy.' Christ, my head is going to burst.

She's standing at the door to the hallway, her back to me.

'Don't try to follow me,' she says, and now her voice is so hard, and she really is *going*. 'If you come after me, I swear I'll call the cops myself and have you arrested for harassment.'

Jesus.

I'm up on my feet again, and this time I'm staying upright, but Nina's moving a whole lot faster than me. She's gone through the door and upstairs, and as I hit about the fourth tread up, I can hear sounds from our bedroom, and then she's passing me on her way back down with a jacket and her purse.

I spin around and see she's already at the front door.

'Nina, for God's *sake*, where are you going?'

That look is still there.

'Leave me alone, Nick.' Her voice is trembling now. 'I mean it. Have enough respect for me to leave me alone.'

And now I realize what the look is. And this shock has to be the all-time record breaker.

She looks as if she hates me.

I mean, *really* hates me.

63

Being Sunday and Teresa's full day off, Nick was in sole charge of Zoë, and Nina hadn't called since she'd walked out, and he was getting way past apprehensive and well into full-blown alarmed. He'd called Bill Regan, Nina's AA sponsor, twice and left messages for him to phone back, and he had even begun thinking about calling the Waterson Clinic. But then William phoned at seven o'clock, and again at nine, and both times Nick told him that Nina had gone to visit a friend and that she might be late, and William asked for the friend's name and telephone number and sounded coldly suspicious when Nick was unable to give him either.

'Is the nanny there?' Ford asked.

'Teresa's gone out,' Nick told him.

'You're alone with the baby?'

Nick's hackles rose. 'Is that a problem?'

'Everything about you is a problem,' William said.

Nick put down the phone before he said something he'd regret after Nina got home. When she got home. *If* she got home.

The headache which had receded that morning after he'd taken a couple of extra-strength Tylenol, was back in full force, but he didn't care about the pain, and he didn't know what to *do*. He still couldn't go out looking for her – even without Zoë to consider, he wouldn't know where to start. Bill Regan called back just after ten, but said he hadn't heard from Nina, and he couldn't even help with suggesting any bars to try, because there were so many and because Nina had been sober for such a long time.

Teresa came home at eleven and went to bed, and Zoë woke up around midnight, and Nick gave her a bottle and changed her nappy

291

and rocked her to sleep, and taking care of the baby made him feel better for a little while. But not for long.

He hoped and prayed that he was wrong. He hoped that Nina had gone to see some friend he hadn't thought of, or maybe she'd just spent the day and evening doing ordinary-type things like shopping and going to the movies, or maybe she was spending the evening at an AA meeting.

But he didn't really believe in any of those possibilities.

Too many bad things had been happening to Nina. There had to be a limit to what she could handle, to how long she could stay strong.

Nick thought she was probably drinking.

The bars all closed, by law, at two in the morning. She came home just after two-thirty.

Nick was dozing in an armchair in the living room when he heard a cab door bang and a man's voice approaching their front door. He jumped up fast and his headache leapt violently back to life.

The driver was a decent guy, one of the old breed. He was holding Nina up with both arms, and Nick could see that one or two more drinks down the line he would probably have been carrying her.

'Your wife?' the driver said. He was white-haired, probably Italian, and strong looking for his age.

Nick nodded, not trusting himself to speak.

'Better put her to bed.'

Nina, transferred to Nick's arms, didn't smell like Nina. She smelled of beer, smoke, whiskey and vomit. Like a drunk.

'How much do I owe you?'

Nina realized whose arms she was in and made a weak attempt at a protest. 'Let me go.'

'In a minute,' Nick said, and stroked her hair. 'How much?'

The driver shrugged. 'Forget it.'

'No way,' Nick protested, softly. 'You've been to a lot of trouble.'

'No big deal,' the man said. 'I've been there, you know?' He started to turn away, walking down the steps.

'Please,' Nick called out. 'I'd like to give you something.'

'Just take care of your wife,' the driver said, got back into his cab and started the motor.

Nick closed the door.

* * *

292

She allowed him to undress her and guide her into the bathroom – only, he realized, because she was too weak to have much choice in the matter. But when she fell on her knees before the lavatory bowl and he bent down, ready to hold her head or mop her up or whatever she needed, she found the strength to look up at him briefly but fiercely.

'Go 'way,' she said.

He nodded and straightened up. 'Sure you'll be okay?'

Her face was chalk white. 'Go *way*,' she repeated.

He stood outside for a while, listening to the awful sounds of her heaving and moaning, waited till he heard the flushing and then, a moment or two later, the water running into the basin. And then he went into the nursery. Far enough away to give her privacy, but close enough to be aware if she got into trouble.

'Trouble,' he said out loud, wry at his splendid understatement, to Zoë's teddy bear. It was the old-fashioned one from FAO Schwarz that Nina had sewn up the night they'd brought the baby home from the hospital, the one Abbott and Riley's men had ripped apart searching for heroin.

'Big trouble,' Nick told the bear.

He had wanted to give Nina so many things, mostly love and peace. He thought he had managed the love pretty well, but lately the house on Antonia Street had become more of an emotional war zone than a peaceful home. He had known from the beginning that Nina needed stability. She had been so straight with him about that, about her drink problem, about her needs.

And he had let her down.

Seven years she'd been sober. And then Holly had climbed into his bed again – at least, that was the way Nina presumably saw it, and who could honestly blame her?

He heard the bathroom door opening, and went out into the corridor.

She still looked white and shaky and incredibly fragile.

'Going t'bed,' she said, slurring.

'Anything I can do?' he asked, softly.

'Leave me alone.'

Those words, at least, were clear.

* * *

He slept downstairs until six o'clock, thankful that he'd woken early enough to avoid embarrassing Teresa, who generally came down at half-past. His head still ached as he got up and straightened the cushions, but it was better than it had been the night before.

He went quietly upstairs and looked in on Zoë, who lay on her back in her pink romper suit, awake, kicking a little, contentedly, and smiling up at the new morning and her father. She really was smiling these days, corrected age and other preemie stuff notwithstanding. Nick gave her the index finger of his right hand for a moment, and his daughter grasped it with her own tiny fingers, and the warmth of her squeeze brought tears to his eyes.

'I love you so much, Zoë,' he whispered, and then, extricating his finger, he went out of the nursery and into his and Nina's bedroom.

It was still pretty dark, with the curtains drawn. Nina was dead to the world, sleeping it off, and Nick was glad for her. He couldn't know exactly what it would be like for her, waking up, remembering what damage she'd done to herself, but he could hazard a guess. The longer she was out of it, the better for her.

And for him, too, maybe, he thought with a terrible, conscious selfishness, since he hardly dared imagine what the coming day would hold for them as a couple.

'*Leave me alone.*'

She'd said that before she'd got drunk, as well as afterwards.

He was terrified in case she really meant it.

'Will you do something for me?' she asked him two hours or so later, after she'd woken and he had brought her a cup of coffee.

'Name it.'

'Tell Teresa to go out for the day.'

Nick sat on the edge of the bed. 'It's okay. I told her you have a virus or maybe the flu.'

'I want her out of the house.' Nina took a sip of coffee, gagged a little and handed it back to Nick.

'You okay?'

She nodded. 'I want her out so we can talk.'

'Oh.' Nick felt his own stomach contract. 'I'll tell her.'

'Thank you.'

He stood up, started walking towards the door and stopped. 'Would you like me to call Bill for you?'

'*No.*' She paused. 'Thank you.' The courtesy was an afterthought, the kind you might extend to a stranger or a colleague.

He turned the door handle.

'Nick?'

'Yes?' He turned around, craving an ounce of warmth.

'Is Zoë all right?'

'Yes.' He nodded. 'She's fine.'

They talked in his studio, where he had gone to try to drown his fears in work. Nothing had helped, of course, and the patchily, darkly-daubed canvas that stood on his easel testified to that.

'Wouldn't you be more comfortable downstairs?' he asked her.

'Here's as good as anywhere,' she said.

He cleared a space for her, sweeping some sketchpads off the wooden window seat and dusting it with his hands. No one else ever cleaned his studio; he liked to do it himself, since only he knew which scraps of paper might be fragments of future works. Generally, he took a pride in keeping the place clean and organized, but lately it just hadn't seemed a priority.

Nina sat down and leaned back at an angle against the window. She had showered and dressed in a baggy grey tracksuit, and she had tied her hair back, but she looked lousy, her face pasty, her hands shaking and her eyes ringed with shadow. Nick always loved seeing Nina in the mornings, liked her face without make-up, her mouth without lipstick, her hair uncombed. He had never seen her with a hangover before.

'I can't take any more,' she said.

Her voice was quiet and weak-sounding, yet there was an unmistakeable ring of determination in the words. Nick felt his heart shift in his chest. He sat slowly down on one of the paint-stained stools, aware that she didn't want him sitting beside her on the window seat.

'One day at a time.' She looked down at her hands, resting flat on the tops of her tracksuited thighs. 'Back to that.' Now she sounded bitter. Sick and bitter. 'The golden rule of the recovering alcoholic.'

'I know,' Nick said.

'Yes, of course you do.' She paused. Her mouth trembled and she had to catch at her lower lip with her teeth to steady herself. 'I honestly believed I was past that, that I had made it, really made it, to the other side.'

'You did. You will again.'

'Yes, I will,' she said. Back to determination.

A faint glimmer of relief touched him.

'I woke up this morning,' she went on, 'and I lay there thinking: back where I belong – just like my mother. Just a stinking drunk after all.'

'Nina—'

'And then I remembered Zoë.' Her mouth worked again for a moment, but she controlled it. 'I wanted so much to go into the nursery and pick her up, but I couldn't, because I felt so *dirty*. And so I lay there for a while longer, feeling sorry for myself—' She shook her head, a kind of grim half-smile on her lips. 'Sorry doesn't really cover it, actually.'

'Sweetheart,' Nick said gently, wanting to find a way to ease her pain.

'No, please,' Nina said. 'Let me tell you.'

He nodded.

'And after I'd given in to that for what seemed enough time, and after you'd come in and brought me some coffee, I made myself remember Zoë again. Which was when I made up my mind about a few things.'

Nick's heart gave another sick lurch.

'So I got up and called Bill. And then I took a shower and pulled on some clothes. And now I'm here to tell you.'

He tried to steel himself.

'I need to be able to trust you,' Nina said.

'You can.' Nick slipped one hand down beneath the seat of his stool and dug his blunt fingernails into the wood. 'You *can*.'

'And do you trust me?' she asked him.

'Of course.'

'With a bottle?' She bit hard into the pause. 'No, of course you don't. How can you, after last night?'

'It was just one night.'

It was as if he hadn't spoken. 'So how can I trust you when it comes to Holly Bourne?'

He looked right into her eyes. 'I hate Holly Bourne.'

'And I hate alcohol,' Nina said, simply. 'And until yesterday, I thought there really was a big difference between our two addictions. Mostly because Holly was three thousand miles away, and in your past. But neither of those things are true any more, are they? Holly was in LA just the night before last. In your bed. Talking about having your child.'

Nick stood up, frustration rising. 'She broke into my hotel room. Like a *burglar*. You know that, Nina, and if you're trying to say it was any other way, then you're just inventing, and you're sure as hell doing what Holly wants you to do.'

'I told you yesterday, I don't give a damn what Holly wants,' Nina said, though today there seemed little anger. 'Right now – this morning – I only seem to care about one thing.'

She had not moved from the position she'd adopted when she'd sat down. She was still leaning against the window, was perhaps too weak to do otherwise, yet her voice had grown stronger and so, it seemed to Nick, had her resolve.

'Yes, I got drunk last night,' she said. 'Fell right off the wagon. *Slipped*. And there's not one single damned thing I can do to change that.' She took a deep breath and looked up at him. 'But what I am *not* going to allow myself to do is slide all the way back down again to where I used to be. I am *not* going to put myself through that again – the bingeing and sickness, and the awful, endless shame.'

Nick sat down again on the stool. He felt oddly diminished, marginalized, as if right now, in his own studio, he did not really matter to his own wife. It was a numbing sensation.

'I will *not* do that again to myself,' Nina went on, each word seeming to grow tougher. 'But much, much more important, I will not do it to Zoë.'

Nick waited for her to go on, but she did not.

'How can I help you?' he asked.

'Easily,' she answered.

'How?'

'Forget about Holly.'

'I have forgotten about Holly. I forgot about her years ago.'

'You misunderstand me,' Nina said. 'I mean, forget about trying to find her.'

Nick stared at his wife. 'How can I do that? Especially now, after what happened in LA?'

'You can leave it to the police,' Nina said. 'The way I asked you to when we were in Arizona.'

'The police aren't doing enough, Nina.'

She shut her eyes. 'Have you called Wilson or Capelli yet?'

'Not yet. I wanted to wait till you and I had resolved this.'

Nina opened her eyes, turned her head and looked at him.

'And when you have called them, then will you leave it alone?'

Nick shook his head. 'I don't see how I can.'

'Then I can't take this any more,' Nina said, simply.

'What do you want me to *say*, Nina?' Everything was plummeting out of control, but he didn't know what to do about it. 'Do you want me to tell you *lies* about how I feel? Tell you how sure I am that the cops are going to come through for us now – that they're going to forget about me and heroin and child abuse, and put all their resources into finding Holly before she finds a new way to hurt us?'

'You're obsessed, Nick.' It was a statement, without recrimination. 'You say that Holly's the obsessive one – and I know you're right about that – but you're almost as bad in your own way.'

'That isn't true,' Nick said, trying not to get angry.

'I don't want to fight with you,' Nina told him. 'That isn't what I want at all.'

'So what do you want?'

'I want this to stop.' She shook her head. 'I know you think you can't stop. But I can. I can make it stop, for me and Zoë.'

Nick stared at her. He didn't want to know what she meant.

'I have to start taking care of myself again without you,' she said.

'No, you don't.'

'Yes, I do,' Nina insisted. 'So that I don't become a drunk again. You have to understand that, Nick. If I let that happen, I'll be hurting Zoë – and Phoebe, too. She helped me so much when I needed her, and now she needs me, and I'm not going to let her down.'

'She needs us all,' Nick pointed out. 'You *know* how much I care about Phoebe – you know I want to do everything, *anything* I can, to see she gets better.' He felt he was fighting for his life. 'I'd have been there all the time I could, if your father hadn't been standing sentry duty over her.'

'I know that.' Nina gave a small, sad smile.

Nick got to his feet again. He looked at the botched canvas on his easel, wanted to pick it up and smash it, only that wouldn't help

298

anything – all it would do was make things worse, if they could *get* any worse.

'So what are you saying, Nina?' He was getting closer to desperation, could feel it coming, like a thunderstorm. 'Do you want me to make promises I might not be able to keep?'

'No, that's not what I want.'

Nick waited.

'For one thing,' she said, 'I'm going to be going to AA meetings every day for a while, but I'm going to go alone.'

Nick said nothing.

He couldn't bear to look at her face.

'I'm so sorry,' Nina went on. 'But I'm just so afraid of destroying myself. I have Zoë to think about now. And I am so terribly confused.'

'Then that's one big difference between us,' Nick said quietly, still not looking at her. 'Because that's the one thing I've never been confused about from the day I met you. My feelings.'

He came back to the stool, sat down again. He had the sudden, terrifying sensation that if he moved too far – physically – away from Nina now, he might never get close to her again.

'Everything changed when I found you, Nina,' he said. 'Meeting you put my whole life into perspective. The past. The present. My hopes for the future. With you. That was all that mattered then, and it's all that matters now.'

He did look at her then. Her eyes were swimming with tears.

'I still love you, Nick,' she said. 'As much as I ever did.' Her voice caught in her throat. Abruptly she stood up. 'But right now, the only way I know how to cope is the way I did it before, by putting that old wall back up around myself and going it alone.'

'But you're not alone. You have *me*.' His own voice cracked with despair.

'I don't have you.' Nina brought herself back under control, wiped away the tears with the back of her right hand. 'Not all of you. Not as long as part of you is out searching for Holly Bourne.'

'Then I won't.' He felt almost like a boy, pleading. 'I'll stay here with you and Zoë.'

'That won't make any difference.' Nina shook her head. 'Even if you're not running around, physically searching for her, I'll know you're still thinking about her, making sure the cops or her father or your private investigators are doing whatever has to be done —'

'How can I *not* want her found?' Nick asked her. 'How can *you* not want her stopped, after what she's done?'

'The difference is I can leave it to the police. Trust them to do their job. To find Holly Bourne and to prove what she's done, and then to make sure she's punished.' Nina paused. 'But you won't do that, Nick. And I can't cope with that anymore – not now that I know I'm still a drunk.'

Nick stared at her.

'So what are you saying?' he asked again. The fear was back, more swamping than ever. 'That you really want me to leave?'

The answer was a long time coming.

'I'm saying,' she said, and there was genuine misery in the words, 'that it may be easier on me if you do check into a hotel. At least for a little while.'

Nick tried to speak, but his mouth was very dry.

He swallowed.

'What about Zoë?' he asked.

Nina went to the door. He watched her put out a hand to steady herself against the frame.

'You can see her any time you want.' She did not turn around, did not look at him. 'I'm so sorry,' she said again.

And went.

64

Holly has returned to Antonia Street. She hung around in LA for a little over twenty-four hours after getting out of the Mistral Inn, before boarding 'The Coast Starlight' at Union Station at nine-thirty on Monday morning, arriving at Oakland a little after eight in the evening from where she was shuttled, with the other passengers, to the Ferry Building in San Francisco by eight-thirty. She was mindful that Nick might have the police or his investigators checking names at LAX, and she had no passport or ID for Barbara Rowe. No such problems with Amtrak. And in a way, slow as it was, she liked it. Time to stop and drift. Just for her and her baby.

It was dark when she arrived at Antonia Street. She saw no one in the Miller house and no one saw her. She was thirsting to know what had gone on since Nick had returned from LA. But there was time for that. She would find out all she needed to from Vasquez and Samuel Keitel soon enough.

Vasquez telephoned this afternoon, ten minutes after Holly, watching from the third floor, saw Nina going out. Vasquez wanted to know where Barbara Rowe had been, where she'd been when Vasquez had been trying to reach her on her evening off. Holly was tart with her, put her in her place but then, instantly regretful, began smoothing the nanny's ruffled feathers with a request for another cooking lesson.

'You promised to teach me to make *chorizo*,' she said, humbly.

'It's difficult now,' Teresa said, with a touch of huffiness. 'Now that Mr Miller has gone away, my free time is more hard to find.'

'He's gone away again?' Holly felt her heartbeat speed up. 'Where to this time?'

'I don't think Mrs Miller would wish me to talk about this,' Teresa said, primly.

'Then you must not.' Holly was peaceable. 'Though since you and I are friends, Teresa, and since Mrs Miller and I don't know one another, I don't think there'd be much harm if you did tell me.'

She could almost hear the other woman thinking.

'He is in San Francisco.' Teresa relented. 'But in a hotel.'

'Why?' Pleasure surged violently, but Holly kept tight control.

'I think they had a fight. Mrs Miller is unhappy.'

'More trouble for you,' Holly sympathized. 'Poor Teresa.'

'I am responsible for so much now,' Teresa agreed. 'Too much, I think.'

'Which hotel is he staying at?' Holly posed the question lightly.

'I don't remember the name,' Teresa said.

'Really?' Holly didn't want to push too hard.

'I will remember it later.'

'Ah, well,' Holly said.

Keitel would find out.

Keitel returns her call just after four o'clock.

'Miller's moved into a hotel,' Holly tells him sharply.

'Yes, I know, Mrs Rowe. That's what I'm calling to tell you.'

'Which hotel?'

'It's called the Art Center,' Keitel says. 'A little bed and breakfast place in the Marina district. On Filbert Street. Seems a nice enough place.'

'How long's he booked in for?'

'I don't know that yet.'

'Find out.'

'Yes, Mrs Rowe.'

Holly puts down the telephone and sits back in her seat.

And allows the pleasure to rise.

302

65

One of the crazy ironies of my new situation is that Nina wanted me out of the house because she was sure I would not give up the idea of searching for Holly. Now here I am – I've been staying in this nice, friendly little San Francisco B&B for almost fourteen days – and I don't have anyplace *to* look. Since I spoke to Norman Capelli about what happened at the Mistral Inn – and since he got confirmation of my complaint from the LAPD – I get the feeling that he and Wilson really may, at long last, be making an effort to find Holly. And of course Interstate Investigations are still on the retainer I parted with just a couple of weeks ago. But still, no one has *found* Holly, and by now she could be anywhere from Maine to New Mexico or even further away. The cops think it unlikely she could have left the country under either the name of Bourne or Taylor without them finding out, but I don't really believe that. They still don't understand what they're up against. They still don't realize that Holly is capable of almost anything.

Anything.

I called Richard Bourne again yesterday, fenced for a while with the redoubtable Eileen Ridge, but finally nailed her with a 'news apertaining to his daughter's health' manoeuvre. I'd thought about it long and hard before landing this one on the poor bastard, but at the end of the day I figured that Bourne ought to know that Holly now seems to be having delusions about expecting my baby. I don't know, I told him, maybe she *is* pregnant, but it sure as hell would beat the Bible and all-comers if it's *mine*.

Bourne listened to what I had to tell him, and I have to say that in the self-control stakes he's pretty incredible. A guy calls him up and tells him that his daughter has moved on from harassment, wasting police time and attempted murder, to illegally entering hotel rooms, damaging property, exposing herself and claiming immaculate conception. And yet Richard Bourne can still remain, at least superficially, composed – though I did hear – or maybe I just sensed – the heartsickness beneath the surface.

I did feel bad for the man. But I still think he had to know.

'Are you being careful?' I asked Nina this evening when we spoke on the phone after dinner. She keeps it much briefer than I would like, but at least we do talk for a few moments each day, mostly about her sister or Zoë.

'Very careful.'

'Because you know she could be anywhere, do anything.'

'You've told me, Nick.'

I heard her irritation, knew I was breaking her rule about not referring to Holly. 'I can't help being anxious for you and Zoë.'

'I know you can't,' Nina said, but there was little understanding in her voice.

I changed the subject swiftly. 'How's Phoebe?'

'Better, physically.'

'But not otherwise.'

'No.'

My heart aches for Phoebe. I miss her so much. If Phoebe were able to speak, this would not be happening to us. She would knock sense into Nina. Into us both.

'Dr Chen still says the aphonia could be resolved any time,' Nina told me.

'And how are you doing, Nina?'

'Not bad.' She paused. 'One day at a time. You know.'

'Anything I can do?'

'No. Thank you.'

I took a moment, needing to straighten out my voice.

'Can I come by and see Zoë tomorrow?'

'Of course. What time?'

'So you can arrange to be out?' I couldn't hide my bitterness.
'So I can tell Teresa to expect you.' Nina answered me steadily.
We already sound like an old divorced couple.
Oh Christ, that scares me.

NOVEMBER

66

'Sue him,' Eleanor Bourne told her husband in the midst of getting ready for sleep on the first Monday of the month.

'Not a good idea,' Richard Bourne answered her from their bed, to which he had retreated in hopes of reading that morning's *Washington Post*.

Eleanor was too angry to carry on cleansing her face. 'Of *course* it's a good idea. He's slandering our daughter! It's the only thing we *can* do, except trying to get him locked up.'

'We can't sue Nick Miller if we think there's a chance he might be telling the truth,' Richard pointed out.

'*We* don't think any such thing,' Eleanor said, furiously. 'You're the only one here who's guilty of that. How *can* you defend him?'

Eleanor's carefully constructed world had been sliding further off-track with every passing week since Holly had gone missing and Richard had no longer had any alternative but to tell his wife all he knew, yet she was still steadfastly refusing to accept the facts.

Holly had been gone for a month now, with no word from her and not a trace of evidence as to where she'd gone, apart from Nick Miller's alleged sighting of her in Los Angeles – which had, if nothing else, laid the worst of their fears for her safety to rest. Jack Taylor, wounded, angry and bewildered, was staying in regular contact with Richard. Two eminent lawyers, both accustomed to being in control, reduced to anxious father and deserted husband. The big difference being, Eleanor was unhappily aware, that while Richard (despite the appalling fact that he doubted his daughter) would continue to love her no matter what, Taylor was not likely – and who could blame him? – to stay the course for much more than another month or so.

That would leave Holly divorced, jobless, her brilliant career in tatters. Everything she'd worked for – everything Eleanor had wanted for her – ruined.

'If Holly does have some problems,' she told her husband now, 'Nick Miller's to blame for them.'

'We don't know that for sure,' Richard said.

Eleanor slammed down a jar of cold cream on her dressing table so hard that the mirror trembled. 'Of *course* we know it. Making outrageous accusations, trying to wreck her career and her reputation – telling a string of lies to the police and paying private detectives to track her down like some sort of criminal. The man's a *menace* – he always was.'

Richard put down his newspaper, still unread. 'Nick claims it's the other way around.'

'Well, he would, wouldn't he?' Eleanor tossed tissue into her pale cream waste paper basket. 'What I can't accept is that you appear to believe a man who's treated your own daughter so monstrously – who's defaming her to anyone who'll listen.'

'That's hardly true.' Richard sighed. 'Eleanor, we have to stop fooling ourselves.' He was still trying to be as gentle as possible. 'Holly has never been the happy success story we both wanted to believe she was.' Lord knew that was turning out to be the understatement of the decade.

'And if she isn't, whose fault is that?' Eleanor got up and stalked into the bathroom, the hem of her negligée lifting a few inches off the ground in her wake.

'You think it's Nick's.' Richard raised his voice a little.

'Of course it's Nick's fault.' She came out again, rubbing cream into her hands. 'Who else's could it be?'

'Maybe it's Holly's own fault,' Richard said, quiet again.

Eleanor, midway through untying the belt of her gown, stopped, her eyes appalled. 'You really are on that man's side.'

'I'm on our *daughter's* side. I'm just trying to be realistic, mostly because I believe that's the best way to help her in the long term.'

'But we can't help her, can we?' Eleanor sat down on her side of their bed. 'Because we don't know where she is.' She shook her head in bewilderment. 'I can't understand you, Richard. After all that's happened in the past. After all you've learned about his run-ins with the police in California *and* New York.' She stood up again and began pacing back and forth across the Aubusson rug. 'He has a *record*, Richard. Nick Miller is a criminal.'

'He seems quite convinced that he's been set up.'

'By our daughter,' Eleanor said, frigidly, and sat down on the bed again, kicking off her slippers.

'Yes.' Richard paused. 'And I'm very much afraid that the police are beginning to believe him.'

'Well, I never will.'

'That's your prerogative, Eleanor. You're her mother.'

'And you're her *father*.'

Richard sighed and put his glasses on his bedside table. 'You have to admit that Holly isn't exactly helping the situation by disappearing the way she has.'

'She's probably scared to death.'

'Then who better to come to than her husband or her parents?'

'She's left her husband,' Eleanor reminded him. 'And why *should* she come to us when her own father's already made it clear to her that he doesn't trust her?'

Though Richard had repeatedly cautioned his wife to say nothing about Holly's troubles to anyone – especially not to the Millers – every time Eleanor set eyes on either Kate or Ethan she could feel her outrage simmering inside her.

Late the following Thursday afternoon, it finally boiled over.

She was parking her BMW in the driveway after a particularly irritating day's work when she saw Kate carrying her attaché case into the Miller house.

'Hi there,' Kate said.

It was enough.

'How dare you?' Eleanor said, stomping in her navy calf Ferragamo shoes across the grass to her neighbour's front path.

'I beg your pardon?' Kate Miller's clear blue eyes were startled.

'How do you have the *nerve* to stand there and "Hi there" me after what your son has been doing to my daughter?'

'I'm not aware that Nick has been doing anything to Holly,' Kate said steadily. 'On the contrary.'

'Your son is a criminal,' Eleanor said, loudly, hoisting the strap of her handbag higher onto her shoulder.

'Nonsense,' Kate said.

Her front door opened and Ethan appeared.

'What's going on?' He had a smudge of draughtsman's ink on his right cheek close to his nose.

'Nothing much,' Kate answered. 'Just Eleanor sounding off.'

Eleanor turned her full wrath on Nick's father. 'A message for you, Ethan Miller,' she said. 'Tell your low-life son to stop slandering my daughter, or he'll be very sorry.'

'Would you like to come inside, Eleanor?' Ethan tried to stay composed.

'Why?' she demanded. 'Afraid the other neighbours will hear about your drug-pushing, child-molesting son?'

Ethan stood his ground. 'I just thought you might prefer to make a horse's ass of yourself behind closed doors.' He loathed scenes, always had, but he also believed in the old maxim about standing up to be counted. 'I thought that you and Richard, of all people,' he went on, 'would know that you can't slander a person by speaking the truth.'

Kate's cheeks had grown hot. 'And maybe you should start being careful what you say, Eleanor, or you could be the one being accused of slander.' She set her case down on the paved path, trying to calm herself. 'Eleanor, I can understand how upsetting all this must be for you.' She put out a hand to touch the other woman's left arm—

'Don't you *dare* touch me!' Eleanor slapped Kate's hand away.

'Hey—' Ethan stepped forward a pace so that he was almost between the two women. 'Let's not blow things out of proportion here.'

'Ethan's right,' Kate said. 'We still have to live next door to each other, after all.'

'If you had a shred of decency' – Eleanor was aware she was out of control, but she couldn't seem to stop herself – 'you'd have moved away years ago.'

'Why's that, Eleanor?' Kate asked.

'Because your son breaks the law. Because your son is *trash*.'

'Okay, Eleanor, that's more than enough,' Ethan intervened. 'I think you'd better go home.'

'I'll go where I damned well like,' Eleanor snapped.

'Not on our property,' Kate told her firmly. 'And certainly not in the mood you're in.'

Eleanor's hands burned to slap the other woman's face, but she wasn't so far out of control as to forget either Richard or the State Department.

'Just give your son my message,' she said.

Kate picked up her attaché case again. 'I'll certainly tell him to mention it to his lawyers.'

'Okay, honey.' Ethan backed up towards the front door.

'And to the San Francisco police,' Kate added.

'Don't start with us, Kate Miller,' Eleanor warned, 'or you'll regret it.'

'So you said,' Kate said.

'Come on, Kate,' Ethan urged his wife. 'Let's go inside.'

'As soon as Eleanor's off our path,' Kate said.

'What do you think I'm going to do?' Eleanor asked. 'Steal your roses? Just because your son has a criminal record, you don't have to imagine decent people can't tell right from wrong.'

She swung sharply around and headed back across the grass towards her own house. Two feet from her path, the heel of her right shoe caught in the turf and her ankle twisted. Eleanor bent down, snatched the shoe from her foot and limped the rest of the way, aware that, though Ethan Miller had already gone back inside his house, Kate was still watching.

Eleanor hung on until her front door had safely closed behind her, and then she burst into tears.

'Damn them,' she said. '*Damn* Nick Miller.'

She could not remember the last time she had wept.

313

67

If Eleanor and Richard are desperately afraid for Holly's future, Holly is not. All those vaulting law school aspirations that began dying inside her somewhere around the time she first heard that Nick had married Nina, are entirely gone now, yet Holly scarcely notices. All her energies, all her talents, all her skills and attributes, are being poured into the single crucible out of which she lifts her machinations against Nick, like splendid, intriguingly formed, precious nuggets, one after another.

Every aspect of her life, devoid now of the clutter of parents, husband, employers, employees or clients, is being devoted to the only prize that counts.

Nick the needy.

Needing her.

She has been working hard on her house over the past several weeks. Painting and papering. Another set of talents no one from the past would have guessed she possessed. Needs must. She might, safe in her identity as Barbara Rowe, have used professional decorators, but since she could never have allowed them to visit the only part of the house that really matters to her, she decided to do without their help. Do-it-yourself. Holly Bourne's new watchwords. Anything from auto theft to carpet laying. You name it, Holly Bourne can do it.

Holly Bourne can do anything she sets her mind to.

Anything.

* * *

Vasquez has seen some of the areas Holly has worked on in her house. The nanny is an inquisitive creature; Holly knows how much she loves to be confided in, to be included, and so long as Holly needs her for inside information on the Millers, she knows that she's going to have to keep her happy in return. If it weren't for Vasquez, Holly would probably not have bothered painting her living room, or the den, or the kitchen. They aren't important to Holly. Only two rooms of the house are important to Holly, and neither Vasquez nor anyone else has seen them.

One is her secret room.

The other is the nursery.

Vasquez has asked to see the nursery a number of times, but Holly has told her that for the time being she's keeping that room under wraps for superstitious reasons. The nanny has expressed disappointment, but she knows better than to argue with the mother-to-be's fear of something going wrong with her pregnancy.

Holly is increasingly burdened by that fear. It is what has stopped her from visiting an obstetrician or clinic. She will not not risk her baby being tainted, will not have her exposed to potentially dangerous tests or infections.

Her.

Holly knows that she's going to have a little girl, which is why she has made the nursery utterly, perfectly feminine.

There has been no ultrasound examination, no amniocentesis, yet still Holly knows.

She is going to have a little girl, just like Zoë.

68

'Are you okay, Nina?'

'That's the third time you've asked me that today, Betty.'

'I'm worried about you.'

'I'm fine.'

'You don't look fine.'

'I can't help how I look.' Snappy.

'If there's anything I can do to help . . .' Patient.

'There's nothing, Betty. I've told you, I'm fine. Now can we please concentrate on getting a little work done?'

Ford Realty was still sliding. Everything was sliding, and Nina was far from being fine. Betty and Harold were not the only ones to notice. William kept calling from Arizona to check on her, no matter how often she assured him she was okay, and Teresa, who understood at least part of the reason for her unhappiness (namely that her husband had moved out), knew that her employer wasn't coping well. Even Zoë, normally the sunniest of babies, was grizzling more than usual.

Four weeks had passed since Nina had asked Nick to go, and her anger had already dwindled to a dull, throbbing sadness. She had been seeing Bill Regan and going to daily meetings, and she had not taken another drink, and so her terror of slipping again was, thank God, also starting to recede just a little. She had, she kept telling herself, known too many good, sober years; she had relearned the value of experiencing pure, sharp emotions – for better or worse – unblunted by alcohol. Yet she was still desperately confused by her feelings. Ashamed of herself for appearing to misinterpret Nick's reaction to Holly's break-in to his room at the Mistral Inn, she nevertheless – if she was honest – still found it impossible to accept that the whole episode might not have been avoided.

If Nick had chosen a decent, secure hotel. If he hadn't gone back to LA at all, if he had just agreed to leave it to the police. If he had come home with her from Arizona when she had asked him to. If he had done any *one* of those things, they might all be at home together now, safe and sound and at least relatively happy.

One of the worst things about living without Nick was having no one she could talk to openly. She couldn't bring herself to tell Bill Regan what was really going on in her life – and loading her troubles onto Phoebe in her present condition would be monstrously unfair. She *certainly* couldn't talk to William, whose prejudices against Nick were by now so irrational that it was madness to imagine he might even consider giving his son-in-law the benefit of the doubt. Which left only some kind of a counsellor, and Nina had not the time, energy or the slightest desire to contemplate that.

The situation was so miserable and crazy. Each day, at an agreed time, Nick came to Antonia Street to spend time with Zoë. Sometimes Nina was home when he came; more often she was not. When she did see him, she thought that Nick looked tired, too thin, sad and afraid. Much as she did, she supposed.

On November 13th – the thirtieth day of their separation – giving way to a sudden and terrible wave of weakness and longing, Nina poured Nick a cup of coffee in their kitchen and, out of the blue – surprising even herself – asked him if he wanted to come back.

He took a few moments to answer.

'Are you sure that's what you really want?'

'I thought it was what *you* wanted.' Fresh hurt pounded her hard.

'You know it is.' His heart was in his voice. 'But it seems to me that with me out of the house, you're doing fine.'

'You mean I'm sober,' Nina said.

'That's part of it,' Nick agreed.

'Maybe with you back home again, I might do even better,' she said, stiffly.

Nick waited another second or two. 'And what if something

develops, and maybe I feel I have to go away again? Do you know how you'll cope with that?'

'I thought you said you've hardly been out of the Art Center since you left.'

'That's true,' he said, 'but that's mostly because there's been nothing to follow up.'

Nick could hardly believe what he was saying, what he was *doing*. He'd felt sure that if Nina gave him the smallest hint that she might want him home, he would jump at it. Yet here he was playing devil's advocate, realizing suddenly how vital it was for him to be honest, for Nina's sake, no matter how painful it was for them both.

'Not one single clue,' he went on, making his point. 'Holly hasn't used a credit card, hasn't visited her family, or seen her husband or taken a plane ride – and if she's practising law anywhere in California or New York State, then she's not doing it as Holly Bourne or Charlotte Taylor or any combination of the two. She really has disappeared.'

'Isn't that what we both want?' Nina asked the question quietly, coolly. 'For her to disappear off the face of the earth?'

'Of course it is,' Nick agreed, 'but only if we're sure it's for good.'

'So the truth is you don't want to come home?' Nina felt rejection ripping another wound in her self-esteem.

'I think you know I want to come home more than anything in the world,' Nick told her gently. 'I just think that maybe we should wait for something to happen one way or another.'

'For you to find Holly, you mean.'

'For *someone* to find Holly, so that we can have a real shot at some kind of peace and safety.' Nick paused. 'In one way, at least, maybe we're part-way there. Even if they haven't gotten anywhere yet, at least the police do seem to be really looking for her now. That's something, isn't it?'

Nina looked at him across the pine table.

'Oh, yes,' she said. 'That's something.'

The resentment she felt told her that Nick was probably right about not coming back yet. The trust was still absent, and without that, their marriage was never going to work, no matter how badly they missed one another.

* * *

318

That aside, she began to find pretexts on which to ask him to call at Antonia Street. On the thirty-first night of their separation, a pipe under the kitchen sink sprang a leak, and it was nothing that she couldn't have taped up herself until a plumber called, but she telephoned Nick instead and he came straight over and fixed it. Next day, a piece of stair carpet came loose, and once again, though it was something that she could easily have handled, she asked him to do it for her.

On November 18th, their thirty-fifth day apart, and the day before Nina was due to leave for Arizona for a visit with Phoebe, Nick dropped in to Ford Realty and they had lunch together in a café on Union Street. And afterwards, they went home and fetched Zoë and her buggy, and took her for a walk in Lafayette Park. They were both aware of the bittersweet quality of their new relationship, conscious that they were starting to feel more like thwarted lovers than estranged partners. And yet Nina still knew that Nick was right. Holly might be missing, but she was still there between them.

She had a dream that night, in which Norman Capelli phoned to tell her that Holly had thrown herself from the top of Coit Tower and that she was dead. In the dream, Nina was almost overwhelmed by release and joy, was vaguely aware that maybe she should be ashamed for feeling that way; but there was no shame at all. In the dream, it was she who had to break the news to Nick, but just as she was on the point of putting her arms around him and telling him how much she loved him, Nick's face turned ashen, and he ran out of the house, and Nina knew that it was because he couldn't face living without Holly Bourne, and she knew, too that he was on his way up to Telegraph Hill to end his own life the same way Holly had.

She woke from the dream crying out, her eyes wet, and lay still for a long while trying to decide why she didn't feel more grateful that it had only been a dream. And then she understood that it was because Holly was still alive.

She told herself that she did, at least, have the comfort of knowing that if such news of Holly's death were ever to come – though Nick might experience shock and perhaps even some small measure of sorrow for a lost childhood friend – he would also certainly share Nina's vast sense of relief.

She *thought* that he would.

But she wasn't entirely certain.

69

Holly is in her secret room.

She spends most of her time in there these days. It is the place in which she feels closest to Nick.

It's filled with him. Photographs. Memorabilia. His belongings. Some from their past, in Bethesda and New York. Some from his present, which Holly has been pilfering from his home during visits to Vasquez.

Two shirts. A sweater. A vest, taken from the laundry basket a while back, before he left Nina. His scent still on it. A book of rough charcoal sketches. One of his paintbrushes. A palette knife.

An off-white terry guest towel from the Mistral Inn with which he must have dried his face or hands.

She always showers before she goes into the room. She goes in naked, then puts on one of the shirts. Sometimes she just sits in a chair and looks at his face in the photographs. Young Nick. Teenage Nick. Adult Nick. Nick signing copies of *Firefly* – the other woman and her sister cut out of the picture. Nick with the man from Meganimity in the picture which appeared in *Variety* last January.

Nick by the paddling pool in Carmel with the naked children.

Other times, Holly lies down on the bed, his vest in her right hand, closes her eyes, and rubs it over her body. Over her breasts, over the hard nipples on which he used to love to suck. Over her swollen belly, over the womb in which their child is growing. Between her thighs. Not Nick himself, of course, but something at least that was close to him not too long ago, that clung to his body and absorbed his heat and sweat. She opens her eyes, focuses on his face in one of the pictures, and masturbates with his vest. It comes back to her then every time. The way it was with him. The way he felt inside her vagina and in her mouth.

Holly needs more than this today. She gets up swiftly, her breathing rapid, her breasts and cheeks flushed, finds his paintbrush, wraps the vest, already wet with her juices, tightly around it, lies down again, brings up her knees and forces her homemade Nick-dildo into herself. It's too big and rough and it hurts, but it's all she has, and it's all she needs; just a few thrusts and she's crying out with orgasm.

And then, for a few minutes after that, she's simply crying.

70

Eight days before Thanksgiving, Phoebe and Nina were in the rose garden at the Waterson Clinic. A little, make-believe slice of England in the Arizona desert, the illusion kept lush and fragrant by the constantly humming sprinklers.

Phoebe had spent the morning enduring more tests. Another brain scan. Another set of damnable instruments probing her throat, making her retch, examining her larynx for anything the physicians might have missed on previous occasions. Nina had been with her, holding her hand, watching as the tears squeezed from between her eyelids. Dr Chen, for her part, had already as good as said that it was a waste of time and an unnecessary added trauma for Phoebe, and sure enough, nothing had been found, no new solid, physical reason for her continuing silence.

'We're going to get you out of here soon,' Nina told her, as they made their way along the smooth, paved path to one of the handsome handcarved wood benches. 'Now that you're rid of the casts, and once they've got you properly started on the physiotherapy, we can get you home and do the physio by ourselves, okay?'

It was good having her sister to herself for once, without their father's constant vigilant presence. Even William, semi-retired from his air freight company in Scottsdale, was sometimes required to take care of business, and Nina's arrival (happily, from William's standpoint, without Nick) had convinced him that it might even be in order for him to catch a day's flying – still always his own best therapy.

They reached the bench and Phoebe sank down with relief.

'Okay?' Nina smiled at her.

Phoebe nodded.

'You'll be able to write again soon.'

Phoebe smiled. A more-like-Phoebe smile, shaky, uncertain, but much less remote than it had been for such a long time. Mary Chen had told Nina that soon after the plaster of Paris had been cut from her arms and hands two days ago, they had tried to help Phoebe to start communicating with the kind of letter board often used by head injury and stroke patients. Phoebe had tolerated it for a short time, using one fingertip to spell out brief, basic responses to questions, but it had been clear that she hated the method. They had tried, some weeks earlier, to persuade her to do the same thing using her toes, but both her depression and the dosage of her pain-relief drugs had been more intense back then, and Phoebe had refused point blank to cooperate at all.

'I expect she regards it as an idiot board,' Dr Chen had told Nina and William at that time. 'Many patients find it offensive at first, before they grasp it as a lifeline. Phoebe doesn't want to use letters right now, and she certainly doesn't want to push them around with her feet – she wants to use her hands, and she wants to talk.'

Now, sitting beside her sister in the rose garden, Nina put an arm around her shoulders. Phoebe felt so thin and fragile, no surprise given that she barely ate enough to maintain any kind of strength. Her red hair, uncut since she'd been in Arizona, was tied back off her pale, unmade-up face, and Nina had asked her several times if she wanted the Waterson's resident hairdresser to call on her, but Phoebe had shaken her head, as if she were too exhausted to be bothered.

'Now don't go upsetting her with your own problems,' William had cautioned Nina before he'd left the clinic. 'You don't want to risk making things worse for her. Stick to news about Zoë and how well the book's still selling, that sort of thing.'

This afternoon, however, Nina was suddenly assailed by the realization that things could hardly *get* worse for her sister. Maybe if she started treating Phoebe *like* Phoebe instead of an invalid stranger; maybe if she stopped excluding her from what was happening in the real world, *her* world, Phoebe's traumatized subconscious – or whatever it was still causing her aphonia – might even be jolted, shocked into allowing the real Phoebe to return to them fully.

She removed her arm from around her sister's shoulders.

'Phoebe?' she said.

Phoebe nodded slightly but went on looking at the rose beds.

'Phoebe, look at me.'

Her sister turned her head.

'Dad thinks it's wrong to burden you with things that have been going on at home.' Nina paused, then plunged on. 'But I don't think I agree with that any more. I think we've been keeping things from you for too long, and I think it's time you started hearing about them, even if you can't talk back.'

A nurse walked slowly past their bench, pushing an old man in a wheelchair. He looked very frail, but he and the nurse were chatting, and as they moved further away along the path, Nina could hear him laughing. She thought about the way her sister's laughter had always warmed her, even when she'd been in the depths of her own drink-related problems. She had not heard her sister laugh since the early summer.

She'd wasted enough time.

'We need you back, Phoebe,' Nina began. 'But none of us needs you as badly as Nick.'

The green eyes flickered, became wary, but questioning.

Nina took a deep breath.

'Nick's in trouble, Phoebe,' she said. 'Bad trouble.'

71

Seven days before Thanksgiving, Holly wakes up in her bedroom at 1317 Antonia Street feeling cramping in her abdomen and wetness between her thighs. She turns on the bedside light and throws back the covers.

And sees the blood.

'Help me,' she says to the emergency room receptionist at Pacific General Hospital. 'I think I'm losing my baby.'

She tells them her name is Barbara Miller and that she lives in Richmond and that the bleeding started while she was shopping for baby clothes on Fillmore Street. With her pregnancy at risk, no one troubles her with insurance questions; they're too busy getting her to lie down, taking vital signs, asking medical questions and getting a doctor to check her out. They're swift, efficient and kind, but Holly's terror at this point is beyond their comfort.

'Be *careful*,' she urges the young, fair-haired, bespectacled doctor examining her. 'Please be careful.'

This is exactly what she didn't want, what she's been so determined to avoid, but she no longer has a choice.

The memory of the paintbrush, wrapped in the vest, flashes through her mind. *Oh, Nick*, she flails silently, *what have you done to me now?*

The doctor's sterile glove emerges stained with blood.

'Please,' she begs him, 'Please do something!'

Oh, please, God, let her live.

'It's okay,' he soothes her. 'Try to relax.'

She sees the frown between his brows, and her heart races.

'Please help my baby,' she cries softly. 'Don't let her die.'

* * *

'Who told you you were pregnant, Ms Miller?' he asks a while later.

'What's wrong with my baby?' Holly sits up a little way on the hard emergency room bed. The curtains are drawn around them. 'I'm still cramping,' she says. 'I'm still bleeding.'

'Yes, you are,' the doctor says. 'But you're not pregnant.'

'Oh, God,' Holly whispers. 'I've lost her.'

She can feel her heart beginning to break.

'There's no baby to lose, Ms Miller.'

'Of course there's a baby.' Holly's hands fly to her stomach. Anguish gives way to outrage. 'Are you blind?' She stares at him for a moment, then lies back again, staring at him. 'I thought this was supposed to be a hospital. I thought you were supposed to be a doctor.'

His smile is an effort. 'I was when I last checked.'

'Get me a proper doctor,' Holly orders. 'An obstetrician.' Her voice is growing harsher. 'I need to see a real doctor, one who knows a pregnant woman when he sees one.'

The young man is unfazed.

'Who is your regular obstetrician, Ms Miller?'

'I don't have one.' Holly sees the look on his face. 'I just moved to California. Which is why I came to the nearest hospital.' She sits up again. Her heart is still racing. 'Because I thought they'd have real doctors.'

She reaches down between her legs with her right hand, pushes away the sanitary pad he's placed there, and then holds up her fingers.

'You see that? You do have eyes? I'm bleeding, damn you.'

'Yes, I see it.'

He leans towards the trolley to Holly's right, pulls two Kleenex out of a box and wipes her fingers, and then he replaces the sanitary pad.

'When did you last have a period, Ms Miller?'

'April,' Holly answers. Her hands fold protectively over her stomach. 'I started morning sickness in May. I'm getting bigger all the time.'

'You don't look seven months' pregnant,' he comments gently.

'I'm a small person,' Holly says, 'who's going to have a baby.' She pauses. 'Unless your negligence makes me lose it.'

The doctor regards her for a moment. 'I'm going to arrange an ultrasound for you, Ms Miller.'

'*Okay*,' Holly says. 'About time.' She reaches out and grabs hold of his arm. 'But no instruments – no probes. I don't want anything that's going to hurt my baby.'

Still gently but firmly, the doctor disengages her fingers from his sleeve. 'It'll be a straightforward abdominal ultrasound, nothing invasive,' he reassures her. 'But I have to say, Ms Miller, that I think it's just going to confirm that there is no pregnancy.'

She looks at him with contempt. 'And I know it's going to confirm that you're a jerk.'

The doctor steps away from the bed towards the curtain.

'I think you're just having a period, Ms Miller.'

'Go fuck yourself,' Holly says.

They give her five glasses of water to drink until she feels her bladder is going to burst. A woman in a white coat rubs cold jelly over her abdomen, speaks kindly to her, then performs the examination, watching the screen beside the bed as she moves the scanner back and forth across Holly's body.

Holly lies very still, her eyes closed, focusing on her desire to pee.

'Is my baby all right?' she asks when the equipment is turned off.

'The doctor will talk to you about that,' the woman says gently.

'Is my baby all *right*?'

'You'll have to ask the doctor.'

Holly opens her eyes. 'It's my baby we're talking about, not the goddamn doctor's.'

'I'm sorry,' the woman tells her. 'I'm not allowed to answer your questions.'

Holly stares up at her.

'The hell with you,' she says.

And lets her bladder go.

She waits a long time. She's still bleeding, still cramping, but no one seems to care. The doctor she told to go fuck himself does not return to see her. Holly doesn't miss him.

Finally, another doctor arrives. A woman in a suit. No white coat. A psychiatrist. They've sent her a shrink. Her baby is in danger, and they've sent her a goddamned *shrink*.

The woman is talking psycho-bullshit about false pregnancy. Saying how uncannily the condition can often mimic the real thing.

327

How there can be a number of reasons for it happening to a woman, physical and emotional, and suggesting that Ms Miller should ask her own doctor to arrange some further investigations and counselling.

Holly isn't listening. Her ears are hearing, but she's paying no attention. This person is talking to Barbara Miller, after all, who doesn't even exist. Not Holly Bourne, who is carrying Nick Miller's baby girl.

The main thing, the *important* thing, is that the cramps do seem at last to be lessening. And if that dunce-doctor creep didn't seem bothered by the bleeding, maybe she doesn't need to be too scared by it either. She's taken care of herself up until now without help from them, after all, and clearly she's been right to do so.

One thing is for sure. It's time to get the hell out of this place. If she stays here much longer, they're probably going to try to talk her into getting rid of her baby.

She'll kill them before she'll do that.

Needing to calm down, settle herself before going back to the house, she takes a cab to Dottie Doolittle on Sacramento Street and asks the driver to wait for her while she goes inside and spends a king's ransom on a cream silk christening gown. She pays cash, has just enough on her to manage that and the cab fare home. She's been so careful until now with her no-credit-card, steal or pay cash, no-trail policy, and distressed as she has been this morning, she has no intention of screwing up now.

Back in the cab, Holly leans back, drained, trembling a little, the little silk gown, beautifully packed, resting on her lap. Her womb is cramping again and she's certain that she's still bleeding, but the gown is there, all soft silk and lace, like a talisman, proof that her daughter will be safe, will stay with her.

'I'll go to bed,' she murmurs to herself. 'I'll rest for a while, and everything will be okay.'

The memory of the paintbrush comes back again, but she pushes it forcibly from her mind.

'No, you don't, Nick Miller,' she says out loud. 'No, you don't.'

In his rearview mirror, the cab driver checks out the woman in the back seat. She's a looker, even if she is talking to herself. All kinds of people talk to themselves in the back of his cab. This one seemed upset when he picked her up outside the hospital, but the visit to the kid's store has boosted her colour. He chuckles to himself, thinking of his wife. Women and shopping.

Holly knows she's taking a chance, coming back to Antonia Street in broad daylight, but she's too tired to tramp around the city all day and, so far as she knows, Nina is still in Arizona with her sister and Nick is still living at the Art Center, so the hell with it. She checks out the Miller place from inside the cab, sees no sign of life, pays the driver and gets out.

Just as the door of 1315 opens and Nina Ford Miller comes out of her house. For an instant, Holly freezes, and her purse and shopping bag fall to the ground.

'Need some help?'

Nina is coming towards her.

'I'm fine,' Holly says quickly.

Nina has already picked up her things and is glancing at the Dottie Doolittle bag. Automatically, Holly's right hand moves to her stomach.

'Don't they have gorgeous things?' Nina says, nice as pie, smiling at Holly. 'When's the baby due?'

Holly takes the bag and her purse.

'It's going to be a while yet,' she says.

'Are we neighbours?' Nina asks. 'I don't think we've ever met.' She puts out her hand. 'I'm Nina Miller.'

'Sorry,' Holly says. 'My hands are full.'

And without another word, she hurries up the steps into her own house and shuts the door.

She's trembling again and feeling nauseous.

'It's okay,' she says to herself and the baby.

She walks up the stairs, past the second floor, on up to the third.

She goes into the nursery, opens the shopping bag, takes out the christening gown, hangs it on its padded hanger in the wardrobe.

'There,' she says. 'Everything in its place.'

And then she goes into her secret room, lies down on the bed and smiles at Nick in his photographs.

'The baby's fine,' she tells him. 'Everything's fine.'

She knows that's the truth. Even if Nina mentions their little encounter to the nanny, and even if Vasquez forgets her promise of silence, there's nothing much she can tell her boss, except that their neighbour's name is Barbara Rowe and that she's pregnant and in hiding from her wife-beating husband. By evening, Nina will probably have forgotten all about her. All will be well. Still going to plan. Nick has already left Nina. Holly is going to have his child.

It's only a matter of time.

72

'I met our new neighbour when I went out,' Nina told Teresa in the kitchen on her return from buying fresh coffee beans from Spinelli's on Fillmore. 'Have you ever met her?'

Teresa turned away towards the sink to hide the warmth on her cheeks. 'You mean Mrs Rowe?'

'She didn't tell me her name,' Nina said, putting beans in the grinder. 'She seemed in a hurry.'

'She is always rushing,' Teresa said, washing up the same plate twice. 'She is expecting a baby.'

'Yes.' Nina turned on the grinder, and for several seconds the shriek of the gadget prevented further conversation. She switched it off, knocked it gently a couple of times, then turned it back on for another second or two.

'She is living alone,' Teresa said when the noise had stopped, and then, swiftly, aware that she had already said more than Barbara Rowe wanted her to, she added: 'I met her once, when we were both going to the market at the same time.'

'I wonder if she'd like to come in for a cup of coffee some time.' Nina tipped the fresh ground coffee into a paper filter. 'She might like getting to know Zoë, if she's going to have a baby of her own.'

'I don't think so,' Teresa said, a little too abruptly.

Nina glanced up, surprised. 'Why not?'

'I think perhaps she's a very private lady,' Teresa tried to explain. 'She's not friendly like you, Mrs Miller.'

Nina nodded. 'She did seem rather edgy when I ran into her.' She shrugged. 'Ah, well, she probably has problems of her own.'

She went on making coffee.

331

73

Phoebe lay awake in bed in her room in the Waterson Clinic, staring out of the windows at the dustings of stars in the night sky. It was the second night in a row she had been unable to sleep.

Not that insomnia had been much of a stranger this past two-and-a-half months, in this place, in these circumstances that had seemed – until Nina's last visit – so surreal, so wholly unconnected with her real life. Phoebe had felt, at times – many times – like a kind of machine: a soft-fleshed robot, broken down and out of synch, waiting for some mysterious missing component to be reinstalled.

The broken and smashed bones in her arms and hands had caused her great pain and even greater frustration, yet that had not seemed to her to be the source of her strange detachment from the rest of the world. It was what had *accompanied* those injuries, the condition – the *thing* – Phoebe felt she had brought up with her out of her initial unconsciousness like a bizarre, unfamiliar item of baggage. The thing that had stolen away, stifled her ability to speak. To communicate. The thing that had cut her off from her loved ones, from normality.

Aphonia.

Aphonia.

Phoebe longed to say the word. She had lain in this bed sometimes for hours at a time striving to say it, to produce its soft consonants and flowing vowels. It had become almost symbolic to her, the trophy she would lift one morning when a nurse came to check on her first thing, and she would sit up in her bed and just say it out loud:

'Aphonia.'

But it had never happened. She had acted it out in her mind, she had strained towards it; she'd gone the opposite route and tried to forget that the damned word even *existed*, to forget that her muteness mattered. She had decided that perhaps this condition was something like a desperately sought-after pregnancy, where a couple strove so valiantly for so long that their bodies somehow went on strike, and it was only when they gave up, only when they acquiesced to the fact that it was never going to happen for them, that they were suddenly rewarded. But that hadn't worked for her either.

Phoebe realized now that she had, in fact, truly acquiesced to her new, dumb state, that she had, perhaps, grown almost to *enjoy* her silence. There was a strange peace about being voiceless, about not being expected to participate in conversation and, therefore, in any of the decision making – important or trivial – of everyday life. She could not opt out altogether, of course; she was still able to nod or shake her head about what she was going to eat for breakfast, or whether she wanted to go for a walk before or after lunch. But there were no real problems. Everything of consequence had been suspended. The outside world had ceased almost to exist: even when visitors came from beyond, they seemed to enter wholly into her new world, her mute bubble. No one told her their troubles; ergo, no one *had* any troubles.

Until the day before yesterday, when Nina had strolled with her into the rose garden, and had brought the real world – still *her* world, after all – crashing alarmingly back into her life.

Her fall from those steps on Catherine Street had been no accident, Nina had told her.

It ought, it seemed, to have happened to Nina, not to her.

Because someone had wanted Nina to suffer this way, perhaps even to die, as she might have died, had she not survived brain surgery.

The same someone who had done all they could to make the San Francisco police believe that Nick – *Nick*, of all people – had done this to her. The same someone who had told the police that Nick was hiding heroin in his house – *heroin*, for God's sake. The same someone who had sent the police photographs incriminating him in a child abuse case.

Nina had blown a hole ten miles wide in her peaceful, voiceless, aphonic world, and since that last visit, Phoebe had been transformed. Until then, it had seemed to her that there was perhaps nothing much that she desperately wanted, or needed, to say. Her family knew she loved them; she hadn't needed a voice to tell them that. And what else was there?

'We need you to tell the police that Nick had no motive to want to harm you,' Nina had told her, out there in that beautiful desert oasis of *Boule de Neige* and Maiden's Blush roses. 'They have it in their heads that you might have found out something about his being connected with drugs or child abuse.'

Child abuse! Phoebe hadn't just wanted to talk then – she had wanted to *scream* – and not just at the police. She had looked into her sister's eyes, seen the deep unhappiness in them, and although Nina hadn't told her any more – Lord knew that was probably enough, after all, for a first sitting – Phoebe had known that there was much more to tell.

Suddenly, there were a hundred questions she was burning to ask. Surely Nina didn't – couldn't – believe that there was anything – *anything* – to those crazy, monstrous accusations? And what about their father? What about William, and the way she'd noticed – Phoebe supposed now that maybe she *had* noticed more than she'd let herself admit – the change in his expression whenever Nick had been around?

Oh, God, she had to start talking now.

Whatever it took, however much effort or pain, she didn't care. It was time to get back, to her family, to the real world.

It was time to *speak*.

74

On the Friday morning before Thanksgiving, sitting in his room in the old New Orleans-style Art Center, surrounded by trial sketches he'd been struggling with for a *Good Housekeeping* commission, Nick made a call to the Personal Crimes Division of the San Francisco Police Department, and found Helen Wilson at her desk.

'How are you, Mr Miller?' Affable, for her.

'I've been better.'

'Who hasn't?' Wilson commented.

'Have you found her?'

'Her?'

'Holly Bourne. We haven't talked for weeks. I need to know what's going on.'

'I'd have thought you'd have been glad of that,' Wilson said, in her dry way. 'Not talking to us, I mean.'

Nick wasn't going to let Wilson sidetrack him. He had almost managed to convince himself that he had ceased being the cops' prime suspect when he'd brought them the LAPD-confirmed news about Holly at the Mistral Inn. He was damned if he was going let Wilson sour-talk him into reverting to that role.

'You haven't found her then?' he said.

'We haven't yet had a conversation with Ms Bourne, no.'

'But you are still looking for her?' Nick gave her no more than a second. 'She's *dangerous*, Inspector,' he reminded her urgently. 'You have to find her.'

'And we hope to,' Wilson said, calmly, 'since we clearly can't eliminate her from our enquiries until we've spoken to her.' She paused. 'Though it might be worth remembering we still don't

335

have a shred of evidence that she is – as you claim – actually dangerous.'

'You didn't have any evidence against me either when you pulled me in for questioning.'

'We had just cause to question you, Mr Miller.'

'Because Holly Bourne called you and lied about seeing me on Catherine Street.' Nick hadn't intended getting angry, but Helen Wilson always made it impossible not to. 'She didn't even give you her *name*, and you call that 'just cause', but when I come to you and tell you that Holly broke into my hotel room, that doesn't count as evidence.'

'Unfortunately,' Wilson pointed out, 'there's no one else to confirm that she was in your room.'

'There was no one else to confirm that I was on Catherine Street.'

'But you were close to Phoebe Ford,' Wilson said, 'which made it our duty to talk to you.'

Nick made himself count to five.

'Are you looking for Holly Bourne as a suspect or not, Inspector?'

'You know I'm not going to answer that, Mr Miller.' Wilson paused again. 'But if you or your private investigators come up with anything new on the lady, I'm sure you won't hesitate to pass it on to us.'

'I'm sure I won't,' Nick said.

75

You could just never tell when things were going to turn around.

'Will you do something for me?' Nina asked Nick on the phone that evening, just a few hours after his comfortless talk with Wilson.

'Of course.'

'Spend Thanksgiving with us.'

'Us?'

'Your wife and daughter.' Nina paused. 'Dad's staying in Arizona. Even Teresa's going to be out at a cousin's, so it'll be just the three of us.'

Nick took a moment.

'Are you sure?' he asked.

'I wouldn't be asking if I wasn't.'

'I'd love to,' he said, softly. 'Thank you.'

'Want to see Zoë tomorrow?'

'Does San Francisco have hills?'

'I may not be around – I have some errands to run. But I'll tell Teresa to expect you. Morning or afternoon?'

'Afternoon, if that's okay.' Nick paused. 'And I could use a little time in the studio, if that isn't a problem.'

'No problem,' Nina said.

76

I put down the phone and lie back on my hotel bed.

Thanksgiving.

Just the three of us. Alone all day.

She sounded so happy when I said yes.

Did she honestly think there was the slightest chance I was going to refuse?

It's dark in my room, and quiet. Until now, each night when I've gone to sleep in this perfectly pleasant place, I've felt my loneliness more keenly than I can easily describe. Even on those nights after Nina and I have spent a few hours together, drawing closer. *Especially* on those nights, when I'm so intensely aware of how crazy it is that we're both going to our respective beds alone.

Nina, at least, has Zoë to turn to on those nights. I've had nothing but the knowledge of my own folly.

I feel differently tonight.

I have a strong sense that Thanksgiving may be the day we end this madness. *My* madness.

Nothing has really changed, of course.

Nothing has gotten any better on the Holly front.

But I am beginning to accept that there's nothing I can do about that. I'm beginning to see that Nina is probably – almost certainly – right. That returning to my family and using our united strength to shut Holly out, is the only real defence we truly have.

How much longer can I possibly allow myself to go on letting one insane person destroy my happiness with my own family?

There must be a limit, even to my foolishness.

77

Working for the Millers was really not the kind of job Teresa had hoped it would be. Too much tension all the time. Too much responsibility. The husband and wife, seemingly in love but living apart, their baby daughter coming last instead of first.

It could not happen in the Vasquez family. Not in any good Catholic family. It was not right. She knew that Barbara Rowe – whom she had not seen since Mrs Miller had returned from her last trip to Arizona – felt the same way, even though she, too, was separated from her own husband, the father of her unborn child. Still, the Rowes were a different case, with the husband such a cruel man. A woman was entitled to protect herself and her baby from that kind of man.

She was walking into a drugstore on Van Ness Avenue on Saturday morning to buy deodorant and shampoo when she thought she saw Barbara Rowe at the check-out counter. She was wearing a raincoat with its collar turned up, and a smart hat, its brim low over her forehead, so that Teresa had to look closely before she was certain it was her.

Barbara Rowe was paying for tampons.

She sensed Teresa's stare, and glanced up.

The expression on her face was cold enough to freeze blood.

'How are you?' Teresa asked her, a little shaken by the look.

'Fine, thank you. And you?'

'I'm well.' Teresa hesitated. 'Is everything all right with you?'

'Perfectly.'

The frost was unmistakable.

Barbara Rowe turned her back and walked away.

* * *

Holly rang the Millers' doorbell on Monday morning, fifteen minutes after watching Nina leave the house carrying an attaché case, presumably to go to Ford Realty.

Vasquez answered, the baby in her left arm.

'Mrs Rowe.'

Holly stood on the doormat, a small package in her hands.

'Peace offering,' she said, with her warmest smile.

'Come in.' Vasquez stepped back. She looked uncertain.

'No one else home, I take it?' Holly asked, going inside.

'No one.'

Holly handed Vasquez the gold-wrapped package of Godiva chocolates. No expense spared in the interests of diplomacy.

'You liked these last time you came to my house.' She smiled at Zoë. 'And how is this little beauty?'

'She is well.' Vasquez looked at the chocolates. 'You should not give me so many gifts.' She didn't invite Holly any further than the entrance hall. Saturday's snub had been too conspicuous.

'This one's an apology.' Holly put out her hand and stroked the baby's hair. Its softness sent a tiny shiver through her. 'For being awful to you the other morning at the drugstore.'

'It was nothing.' The nanny's tone belied her words.

'You see,' Holly said, lowering her voice though they were alone in the house, 'I had just had a small scare with my pregnancy.' She paused. 'A little bleeding.'

Vasquez's right hand flew to her mouth. '*Válgame Dios!*'

'It's fine now,' Holly reassured her.

'You're sure? The doctors have told you the baby is okay?'

'Perfectly.'

'I am so glad for you,' Vasquez said from the heart.

'So you understand now why I might have seemed a little strained when you saw me?'

'Of course I understand.' Vasquez paused. 'Do you have time now, for some tea? Mr Miller is not coming until the afternoon.'

Holly felt a pulse beating in her left temple. 'To see Zoë?'

'Same as every day.' Vasquez shrugged. 'He loves her very much, and if you ask me, he still loves his wife, too. It's all crazy, I think.'

Holly had an intense urge to slap Vasquez's face.

Instead, she smiled at her.

'You're very romantic, Teresa,' she said.

And went back next door.

78

Thanksgiving Day was all they had hoped and prayed it would be.

Just the three of them.

They worked together in the kitchen. Nina had intended to do all the preparations and cooking by herself, but then she had seen that that would only be perpetuating Nick as a 'visitor', so she changed her mind and told him to come early enough to lend a hand.

Clare Hawkins, who knew about the separation and the fact that they were sharing the festivities, telephoned at around ten in the morning to wish them the happiest day imaginable; and then Nina called William, who was spending a communal Thanksgiving with Phoebe and other patients and relatives at the Waterson, and William passed the phone to Phoebe so that Nina could tell her sister how much she loved her.

'Tell Phoebe I love her too,' Nick said, as William came back on the line.

'Did you hear that, Dad?' Nina said, with great firmness and clarity. 'Nick wants you to tell Phoebe that he loves her.'

'I heard,' William said.

'Tell her, Dad.'

'I will,' William said.

'Tell her now,' Nina persisted, 'so I can hear you.'

She heard him.

'Thank you, Dad,' she said. 'I love you.'

'Be careful, my darling,' William said, and hung up.

* * *

They used the dining room, laid a handsome table, lit candles, ate off their best porcelain from Gump's, used the silver cutlery, and placed Zoë's little infant seat where they could all watch each other. They ate pumpkin soup, turkey, mashed potatoes, yams, red cabbage and Brussels sprouts, and for dessert they abandoned tradition and ate warm pecan pie with Nina's home-made vanilla ice cream; and they both drank Calistoga water (every last drop of social liquor in the house having been thrown out, guests notwithstanding) right through to coffee, and they both felt as warmed as if they'd had the finest claret.

'So what happens now?' Nina asked at around five o'clock, after they'd washed up and cleared away and played with the baby for a while in the living room.

'Zoë's going to need feeding,' Nick said, softly.

'Yes, she is,' Nina agreed. 'Then what?'

'Then she'll need bathing.'

'Agreed. Then what?'

'Then she'll get real sleepy and need putting to bed.'

'That takes care of our daughter's needs,' Nina said. 'What about ours?'

Nick looked at her. 'You'll probably need a back rub.'

'Yes, I will.'

'I could take care of that,' he said, 'if you'll let me.'

She looked back at him, right into his eyes.

'I'll let you,' she said.

They were both silent for several moments.

'This is crazy,' Nina said. 'We both know this is crazy.'

Nick nodded, not trusting himself to speak.

'I know that no one's found Holly yet, and I know you said you think you shouldn't come home until she's been found,' Nina went on, steadily, though tears were pricking. 'But I think we've both come to realize that we're probably never going to need each other more than we do right now.'

Still Nick said nothing.

'Help me out here, Nick,' Nina said. 'Please.'

'I don't know what to say.'

'You love me, don't you?'

'You know I do.'

'You still want to come home, don't you?'

'More than life.'

'So do it,' she said, simply, and went straight on. 'And don't ask me what happens if someone calls you tomorrow to say they've found Holly. Or what happens if she comes to San Francisco and walks the Tenderloin all night until someone rapes her and then she calls up Inspector Wilson and claims it was you?' She took a breath. 'What if the next big quake hits tomorrow, Nick? What if—'

'All right,' Nick said. 'I get the picture.'

'What I want to know is, what happens tonight after we put Zoë to bed and there are no more chores to be done?'

'We go to bed,' Nick said.

'And in the morning?'

'I'll go to the Art Center and pay my bill and get my stuff.'

'And come home,' Nina said.

'Oh, yes,' Nick said.

79

We made love tonight. I won't say it felt like a first time, or even that it was remarkable lovemaking. It's always been wonderful with Nina, from the first. What made it perfect – for me at least – tonight, was simply that it felt so *normal*. Our bodies, fusing together in our bed, warmth into warmth, breathing life and joy into each other. I think we have both been very cold since we parted.

Nina's sleeping now. We always start out snuggled up, her head on my chest or my shoulder, or like spoons, my arms wrapping her to me, but sleep itself often separates us a little, one or other rolling away to a more private space, only a stray hand or entwined foot maintaining the link, keeping us joined. Nina usually sleeps on her side, her face often obscured from me by her hair. Tonight she's on her back, her right arm thrown back at an angle above her head on the pillow, her left arm resting on my chest.

I don't dare move in case I wake her.

I don't want to move.

Her skin is pale and smooth, her lips slightly parted. A few long honey hairs have escaped from those brushed back from her face, and they stroke her left eyelid and cheek. As she exhales, softly, regularly, the hairs ruffle then settle again, ruffle and settle . . .

I lie still and watch my wife.

The mother of my child. Our child.

Her breasts are hidden beneath the covers. They were so warm and so responsive when I touched them before, when I kissed them. My wife is a passionate woman.

I am the luckiest man alive tonight.

Holly Bourne slips into my mind for a moment, skulking in by some back door, and in my mind I take both hands and push her out again.

She has no place here tonight.

Nor any other time.

80

In the house next door, Holly, wearing one of Nick's stolen shirts, has eaten a solitary Thanksgiving dinner of left-over spaghetti and salad, washed down with most of a bottle of red wine. Now, after midnight, she is sitting in the dark in her secret room.

She is sitting at the window, watching the Millers' house.

Vasquez told her two days ago that Nick would be coming home for Thanksgiving dinner. But dinner has been over now for many hours, and Holly has been watching for every minute of each of those hours, waiting for Nick to leave. But he has not left.

Which means, of course, that he is staying.

Staying the night with Nina, snuggling up with Zoë, sleeping with Nina.

Making love to Nina.

The images pour through Holly's brain. Nick with Nina. Naked with *her*. His hands on her. His mouth on her.

His cock in her.

The other woman.

Holly cannot bear this. This is unbearable.

She stands up from the chair by the window and covers her eyes to try to stop the pictures, but they do not go away.

She can hear them now, too, in her mind. Through the solid walls and the space between. Their moaning and thrashing and the sound of their skin, hot and sweaty, the little smacking sounds their bellies make as they touch and part, over and over again, as he thrusts into her, back and forth, back and forth.

346

Holly cannot endure the sounds. She presses her hands over her ears and sinks to her knees on the floor, but they go on and on, the images and the sounds of it, and she cannot bear it any longer.

So she covers it with something else.

Pain.

Until she passes out.

When she comes to, she is lying curled on the floor in her secret room, her Nick room.

The shirt she was wearing – his shirt – is in shreds.

There is blood on it.

She lifts her hands and looks at them. Her fingernails are caked with blood, and with fragments of something else. Torn skin.

Holly feels the pain again, and looks down at her own body.

Her abdomen looks almost flat in this position.

It, too, is bloody.

Bloody from the long, gouging scratches she has raked into her empty, pathetic, useless belly.

81

The telephone rang just as Nick was dressing, getting ready to go back to the Art Center to pack his belongings and check out.

Nina, sitting on the bed, picked up the phone on the bedside table. 'Yes, Dad.'

She listened. Her eyes grew brilliant and her cheeks flushed.

'Oh, Dad, that's *wonderful*. I can't believe it. Yes, of course. Yes, of *course*. I can't wait.' She put out her right hand, gesturing to Nick to come to her, her excitement palpable.

She put down the phone.

'Phoebe's talking,' she told Nick. 'I can hardly believe it, but Dad says she's really *talking*.'

More warmth coursed through Nick. He hadn't thought there was room for more.

'What did he say exactly?' He laughed. 'What did *she* say?'

'She wants us to come.' Nina grasped his hand, and tears flooded suddenly into her eyes. 'Can you believe this? I'm crying – more good news than I can take in, and I sit here and *cry*!'

Nick sat down and put both his arms around her. 'You said she wants us to come. Does that mean *us*?'

'Of *course* it means us,' Nina said, pulling away from him and drying her eyes.

'How did your father sound about that?'

'He didn't sound anything except excited,' Nina said. 'And happy.' She looked at Nick's face. 'I gather Phoebe was very clear on what she wanted. Even Dad wouldn't argue with Phoebe right now – I think if she asked for Son of Sam to visit, it would be okay with Dad.'

'Thanks for the comparison.'

* * *

While Nina made airline reservations, Nick went to the hotel, checked out and came straight back.

'I've packed for you,' she told him. 'Hot weather clothes. Is that okay with you?'

'Sure it's okay.' Nick threw the suitcase he'd brought back with him from the Art Center onto the bed, ripped open the zipper and dug around in it for his shaving kit and washbag. 'What about Zoë?'

'I think she has a little cold,' Nina said.

Nick frowned. 'Does she have a fever?'

'Hardly at all.'

'But we shouldn't take her with us.'

Nina shook her head. 'I hate leaving her again, but Teresa's happy to hold the fort. I told her about Phoebe – she seemed really pleased for us.'

'What time's our flight?'

'Noon.'

Nick checked his watch. 'We'd better go.'

'I've called a cab,' Nina said. 'There's time to give Zoë a cuddle.'

He looked at her. 'You're so calm.'

'Yes, I am,' she said. 'I have reason to be. My husband's come home, and my sister's going to be well again and clear his name.'

'You think?' Nick asked.

'I know,' Nina said.

82

At ten minutes past three that afternoon, Teresa, sweeping leaves off the Miller's front path, noticed a brown paper-wrapped package lying on the porch of the house next door. Barbara Rowe had told Teresa three days ago that she was going out of state to her parents' home for Thanksgiving and didn't know when she'd be back.

Teresa's first intention was to walk over to 1317, pick up the package and bring it into the Millers' house until their neighbour returned from her trip. But then she thought about the other woman's almost paranoid concerns with anonymity. Probably it would be a greater kindness, Teresa decided, to take the parcel around to Mrs Rowe's back door, where it would, at least, be safe from prying eyes.

Teresa put down the yard brush and went inside to check on the baby. Zoë, less sniffly and more content now than she had been that morning, was lying on her back in her playpen, clutching a small, pink, baby-proof rabbit.

'I'm just going next door for one moment, *querida*.'

The nanny leaned over, felt the baby's nappy to make sure she was dry and took a swift look around the playpen to be completely certain there was nothing in there that could present the slightest danger.

'You want to come with me, or stay here?'

Zoë gurgled and blew some bubbles.

'Okay, *bonita* – you stay here in the warm. I won't be long.'

Teresa blew the baby a kiss and went upstairs to find her house keys.

83

Holly is taking a shower in the bathroom on the third floor between the nursery and her special room. Her body aches and stings with the hot water and soap, yet the fresh discomfort is doing its job, driving out the thoughts and images that so demented her last night.

Her hopes soared this morning when she saw Nick leaving the house, but then he came back with a heap of belongings, and within a half-hour he and the other woman were on the move again, carrying suitcases, and she imagined they were going to Arizona to see the sister, though she couldn't be sure.

Holly isn't sure of anything any more.

Except that her plan needs refining.

Nick back with Nina was never part of the deal.

She reaches up and adjusts the dial on the shower, making the water run hotter and faster.

She needs the pain.

Pain helps her now.

84

Teresa was at the back of Barbara Rowe's house.

The kitchen door was closed, as she had expected it to be. She tried the handle, expecting it to be locked, but to her surprise, the door opened, and suddenly she was uncertain what to do next.

It startled her that an efficient businesswoman like Mrs Rowe should be so careless. But then again, she *was* expecting a baby, and Teresa remembered that each time her own sister had been pregnant, she, too, had made many mistakes she would not normally have made.

But what to do now? Teresa felt a little guilty about going inside. And yet she and Barbara Rowe had, after all, become friends of a kind, had they not? And Mrs Rowe would probably, Teresa imagined, be grateful to her for making her house safe in her absence.

All she really *meant* to do was lock the back door, walk through into the entrance hall, place the package on the little table by the wall, and leave again through the front of the house. But Teresa had to confess to herself that she had recently been wondering more and more about Barbara Rowe. Even before that disquieting incident at the drugstore, the other woman's erratic behaviour and air of mystery had piqued Teresa's curiosity.

Teresa Vasquez had always been an inquisitive person.

'Your nose will get you into trouble some day, Teresa Maria,' her mother had warned her more than once, even as a child.

But surely a little peek into the mysterious third-floor rooms she'd never been shown could not hurt?

Mrs Rowe was away, after all. And the back door *had* been left unlocked. And surely it was only proper that Teresa should check throughout the house to make certain that no intruder had been inside.

As Holly was turning off the shower and stepping out of the cubicle to dry herself, curiosity was drawing Teresa up the staircase.

The nursery, a pink teddy bear hand-painted on its door, was easy to find. Teresa placed her hand on the knob, turned it and went inside.

'*Esto es hermoso,*' she exclaimed softly, gazing around.

It was a touchingly beautiful room, lovingly prepared for a new life. The white crib in the centre, draped with palest rose-coloured cotton, its mattress already covered in white linen embroidered with tiny pink flowers with a little matching satin quilt. Teresa had always admired the way the Millers had decorated Zoë's nursery: its purity and simplicity, and the sense of old-fashioned tranquillity which pervaded it. But this was a *movie star* nursery; this was the kind of room she had seen in glossy magazines, a room in which no expense or effort had been spared, from the beautifully stencilled fairies and *criaturas* on the walls, to the clothes that hung on silk-quilted hangers in the wardrobes.

Teresa wandered around, opening and closing drawers and doors, running her hands over the surfaces. Guilt had totally left her. She was entirely absorbed by the lavishness and charm of Barbara Rowe's maternal preparations.

She came to the dresser last, a wondrously carved piece, every corner and edge made smooth and rounded and safe.

And then she noticed the photograph standing on the dresser in a silver frame.

Teresa looked at it for a long time.

It was a photograph that could never have been taken.

Of Barbara Rowe, with Nick and Zoë.

Holly, her hair still wet, came out of the bathroom and walked, naked, into her secret room. The wounds on her stomach were fiery from the roughness with which she had dried herself.

She picked up Nick's sweater, held it to her face. It was blue lamb-
swool. It felt soft, and it smelled of him.

Her eyes burned.

She took the sweater and lay down on the bed.

Teresa stared at the photograph for a long moment. She felt suddenly
confused. Troubled.

Something here was not right. If Teresa Maria Vasquez was any
judge at all, something here in this house was very wrong.

She picked up the photograph in its frame. It was impossible. Mr
Miller had never, to the best of Teresa's knowledge, even *met* Mrs
Rowe, much less posed for a photograph with her and the *nena*. It
was, she supposed, possible that one of them might have seen the
other coming in or out of the house, or that they might have run into
one another on the street the way Mrs Miller and Mrs Rowe had –
but even so, the photograph still made no sense.

My husband is a very violent man.

Barbara Rowe's explanation for her need for privacy.

It still seemed reasonable enough. A woman hiding from the husband who beat her, a woman expecting a child, hoping to keep her
new home safe.

Yet something was wrong about the photograph.

Teresa considered, for a second or two, removing the actual picture from its frame, afraid of maybe being accused of stealing it
for the silver. But she could not be certain who would come home
to Antonia Street first, the Millers or Mrs Rowe, and an empty
frame might be noticed much more quickly than a missing photograph.

Teresa wavered. Perhaps she should, after all, put the whole thing
back, leave it alone? Not her business. Not her place. So what if Mrs
Rowe had a picture of Mr Miller and Zoë in her nursery?

'No,' she said aloud, making up her mind. She would take it next
door, hide it in a drawer, tell the Millers all about it and their neighbour as soon as they came home from Arizona. And if Mrs Rowe
returned first and asked about the picture, Teresa would simply deny
that she had ever seen it, deny that she had been in the nursery or
even inside the house.

The package. She would take the package back outside, unlock the kitchen door again, just as she had found it, and Mrs Rowe would have no reason to suspect she had ever been here.

She heard the sounds as she came out of the nursery.

Strange sounds, coming from one of the other rooms on that floor.

Teresa's heart began to beat uncomfortably fast.

Someone else was in the house.

Two rooms to her left, a door was open.

The sounds were coming from inside that room.

Teresa's left hand flew to her mouth. Her right hand, clutching the photograph, began to perspire. Breathing too fast, too hard, she started to move, then stopped again. All she wanted now – all she wanted in the whole *world* – was to get out of the house, but in order to get back to the staircase she was going to have to pass that open door.

'*Ay, Madre de Dios*,' she mouthed silently, transferring the photograph carefully to her left hand and crossing herself with her right. 'Holy Mary, Mother of God—'

The sounds were continuing. Awful, ugly sounds.

Teresa started to move, thanked the Blessed Virgin that the floor did not creak beneath her feet, crept closer to the open door.

She did not mean to look. *Don't look, just go*.

She could not help herself.

It was only one second, but it was an eternity.

Barbara Rowe was lying on a bed in the middle of the room, naked.

A large photograph of Nick Miller hung facing her on the wall.

The sounds were of her masturbation.

She was rubbing herself, with something blue.

Teresa didn't mean to gasp, any more than she had meant to look, but she couldn't help it.

Barbara Rowe turned her head.

If Teresa had thought that the look she had given her in the drugstore had been chilling, it had been *nothing* compared to the nightmare she saw in the naked woman's eyes now.

She dropped the photograph and ran.

'Teresa, stop!'

Holly was already off the bed, grabbing something from the top of the dresser – a canvas cutting knife stolen from Nick's studio next door.

'*Ay, Dios mio!*' Teresa sobbed as she started down the staircase. 'I didn't *see* anything – I will not tell anyone!'

'*Stop*, you stupid bitch!'

Holly caught Vasquez on the first landing and swung the knife at her. Vasquez ducked Holly's lunge, screamed piercingly and continued down the stairs, her breath rasping, her arms flailing, desperate to keep her balance.

'*Socorro!*' Teresa shrieked. 'Help me!'

She looked back over her shoulder, tripped on the bottom step and fell headlong, sprawling – Holly was on her, pinning her down, lifting her knife arm—

'*No!*' Teresa pushed back with every ounce of her strength, dislodging her and kicking out with her right shoe, catching the naked woman on her left hip. Holly shrieked in pain. Teresa kicked out again wildly, indiscriminately, caught her right breast, and Holly screamed and fell back.

Teresa scrambled to her feet, struggling for sobbing breaths.

She did not know that pain was a spur to Holly.

Holly grabbed her ankle, yanked at her, and Vasquez fell again, hard, onto her back.

It was all the advantage Holly needed.

With one last cry, she was on her again, raising the knife in her hand.

And then she brought it down and stabbed Teresa Vasquez right through her large, staring, terrified, brown right eye.

85

Minutes pass.

Holly sits naked on the floor at the foot of the staircase beside Vasquez's body.

She knows that Vasquez is dead. She saw and heard her die. Just after she pulled the knife out.

Not pretty.

Holly feels way beyond sick. She began to heave when she saw the colours on the blade, but then she closed her own eyes and breathed deeply and brought the nausea under control.

Still, she doesn't feel good.

This isn't right. This was not supposed to happen.

This was not part of the plan.

She feels many things, sitting here on the wood-block floor that will need cleaning and polishing if it's ever to match the rest again.

Mostly she feels rage. At Vasquez for placing her in this position, for coming uninvited into her house, for snooping and meddling. For betraying her. After all she's done for her.

Holly's right breast hurts. She looks down at it, sees the mark of Vasquez's shoe where she kicked her, sees the bruise already beginning to bloom. Her hip hurts less. And the pain from the scratches on her stomach is starting to fade.

She puts a hand to the breast and squeezes.

It takes her breath away.

And sharpens her mind again.

'Of course,' she says aloud in sudden realization.

This killing clarifies everything. *Everything*.

The death of Teresa Vasquez might not have been part of her original plan. But if Holly concentrates, focuses really hard on every tiny detail as well as on the bigger picture, it may yet become the nub of her new strategy to bring Nick to his knees.

After all, suspicion of child molestation and even grievous bodily harm both pale into insignificance beside the real thing.

Murder.

Holly digs her fingers into her bruised breast again.

A prosecutor could cite jealousy as a motive for Nick killing the nanny. Jealousy of the outsider who had constant, loving access to his daughter, his wife, his home, when he did not. Even if the timing is out, even if Nick has gone with Nina to Arizona, it could have happened before they went . . .

Except that Nina must have seen Vasquez alive before they left.

Damn Nina.

Another dig into her inflamed flesh to keep her brain working, keep the thoughts clear and flowing.

She thinks back to all the comings and goings that morning. To their final departure in the cab. Who was the last to leave the house?

Nick.

Holly shuts her eyes and goes back, making sure. Sees it all again. The two of them coming out of the house together, Nick handing their bags to the driver, helping Nina into the back of the cab.

And going back inside.

Okay.

Anything could have happened in those few minutes, couldn't it? Vasquez complaining about being left alone again – Vasquez was always bitching about that, wasn't she? Nick might have grown angry, telling her how lucky she was to be there with *his* baby, in his house, while he had been in exile. Or maybe Teresa might have been careless with Zoë, and Nick might have seen that, might have exploded, *lost* it . . .

Anything could have happened.

Holly's mind is fogging up again, but some things seem very clear. She's going to have to work this out carefully, methodically, take her time – be a lawyer again – think about precedents, calculate every shred of evidence. If Vasquez's murder is the one that's going to bring Nick crawling to her, it's going to have to be perfectly manufactured to achieve a solid case, as near cast iron as she can make it.

And in the meantime, she is going to have to get the body out, together with every sign that Vasquez was ever inside her house – Barbara Rowe's house.

If Nick killed her in his own home, he would probably have found somewhere to dump her temporarily until he could move her at a later time.

But what about the blood?

If Nick had stabbed Vasquez, there'd be a lot of blood, just as there is here. On the floor, maybe on the walls. Holly looks down at herself, at her naked, red-splattered breasts and arms and thighs, at her bloody hands. Nick would have had blood on his clothes. There would have been no time for him to clean up, hide the body and get back out to the other woman waiting for him in a cab outside.

Oh, God. Oh, God. It's not working out.

Something is wrong with Holly's thought processes – they're not razor-sharp, not logical, the way they used to be, the way she needs them to be now, of all times.

Okay, okay. Calm down. It's all right.

Nick would have worked it out. He would have known he barely had time at most to quick-change his clothes and dump the body someplace safe for the short-term, and then he would have had to find a reason to come back alone from Arizona, so that he could clean up and lose Vasquez for good.

All Holly has to do now, therefore, is move the nanny from Barbara Rowe's house to the Millers'.

She thinks about her neighbours' home. It is, in many ways, almost identically constructed to this one. She thinks about places where Nick might hide Teresa. There's an area beneath her own house – more of a crawlspace than a true basement. More than big enough to be useful for storage. She'd wager on the underside of 1315 being built the same way.

She stands up.

Her legs are half numb, and she has to support herself for a moment against the bottom of the banisters.

She's cold, too.

Time to get moving.

She's thinking of this as a kind of military operation. There are procedures to be followed now. *The Murderer's Practical Guide to Body Disposal*, by Holly Bourne aka Charlotte Taylor aka Barbara Rowe.

Check and lock all exits and windows. (This would not be a good time to be burglarized.) Go upstairs to third floor. Pick up framed photograph from where Vasquez dropped it, return it to nursery, wipe with cloth. Wipe every item, every surface Vasquez might have touched. (Better to do these thing now, while she remembers.) Leave nothing to chance. Don't forget the banister rails – or the door handles.

Take another shower, hard and hot, another brisk, painful rubdown with a rough towel. Go down to the next floor, into the bedroom, get dressed. Practical, tough clothes. Denims, sneakers and a sweater.

Now for the body.

Holly bends her knees, grasps Vasquez under her armpits and lifts her tentatively, experimentally, then quickly lowers her back down to the floor. She is – was – a small, light-boned woman, but it's still the hardest physical work Holly has ever attempted. And even if she is able to manoeuvre her out of her house and next door, there's a real risk that someone may see her doing so.

The effort of lifting sends fresh, sick agony through her. Holly wonders for a moment what damage the bitch may have done to her breast, but right now the pain is still serving its purpose, still helping to hone her mental processes.

She unlocks the back door, goes out into her backyard, to the shed at the side, drags the rusty wheelbarrow out, pushes it to the kitchen door, cleans off the centre wheel with a couple of cloths and pushes it through the door into Barbara Rowe's house.

Into the hall.

Vasquez looks as if she might just about fit into the barrow, but she's going to need covering. Holly remembers an old dustsheet in the shed. She goes back out again to fetch it, drops it on the floor beside the body.

360

'Okay,' she says. 'Let's do it.'

A sudden, irrelevant thought puts a small smile on her lips. If Eleanor could see her now. Or Jack, for that matter.

Then Richard comes into her mind, and the smile is gone.

She would not want her father to know about this.

The body is in the barrow, limbs dangling, head hanging back grossly, when it strikes her.

What is she *doing*?

What is the matter with her *brain*?

Nick didn't kill Vasquez or anyone else, dumb-ass.

So he won't be leaving the blonde in Arizona to come and clean up after stabbing his daughter's nanny through the eye. He won't be leaving his damned wife for *any* fucking reason. Which means he'll have an *alibi* – which means every single thing she's been doing, all the thinking and straining to heft this grotesque creature into the barrow, has all been a total waste of *time*.

What is wrong with her *mind*?

It used to function so crisply, so smoothly.

Oh, God. Oh, God.

Holly sinks down on the floor next to the barrow. Vasquez's left arm, still scented with the Yardley cologne she's always liked, is hanging close to her right cheek.

'Sharpen up,' Holly says out loud. 'Think.'

A solution to every problem. Always.

Okay. *Okay.*

Nick will have to be gotten away from Arizona. Some kind of a phone call, something bringing him back – preferably without the blonde – please *God*, without her. Something that the prosecutors can say, later in court, was his own invention, just an excuse to get back home and clean up the evidence against him.

All right. All *right*.

Holly stands up again. She's decided against the Millers' crawl-space. If she dumps Vasquez there now, she'll start stinking before long, and what Holly does *not* want is for Nick to come home and find the body, because then he'll just call the cops, and the whole thing will be wrecked. This latest plan, being unpremeditated, is clearly going to take a lot more working out, a lot of fine detailing and careful, meticulous planting of evidence.

What she needs most right now is time. To suspend time.

There's one simple way.

The chest freezer in the utility room adjoining her kitchen – Barbara Rowe's kitchen – is a big son-of-a-bitch and almost empty. Holly likes her produce fresh, not frozen, always has.

And Vasquez is a small woman.

It takes much longer than she expected it to. Three separate attempts until the body fits well enough to allow the lid to shut firmly. It drains Holly of strength, sends shafts of pain through her back, arms and legs, so intense that they dwarf the soreness in her breast.

But finally, it is done. Vasquez and Nick's knife are in the freezer. The Miller's house keys, retrieved by Holly from Vasquez's pocket, are now in the back pocket of her own Levis. The freezer lid, perfectly sealed, has been secured with a padlock. The time she needs has been bought.

A new thought.

She can't be certain that the Millers have gone to Arizona – she doesn't know *where* they've gone, or for how long.

What if they come back tonight, or even tomorrow morning? Before she's had a chance to work everything out? Before she's had a chance to move Vasquez again to a better place?

If either one of the Millers does get back, they're going to be looking for the nanny, and when she fails to show, they're going to get concerned, maybe even call in the cops.

Which means that now Holly is going to have to go next door, let herself in with Vasquez's keys, pack up all her belongings and get rid of them. Make it look as if the woman just upped and left while they were out of town. After all, however great the Mexican may have seemed to them, she wouldn't be the first nanny to run off without notice.

The planning starts flowing easily again, smooth as butter.

She'll pack up Vasquez's things, drive to Emeryville Station, stash them in a locker and toss the keys in a trashcan. Though perhaps it might be an idea to hold onto the locker keys for the purposes of incriminating Nick when the time comes.

And that time *has* to come, Holly thinks (her blood is humming again, almost singing now, the way it does when things are going well, really well) as she walks next door to Nick's house and lets herself in. Because then the original master strategy that Holly first began to plan back in July, on Catherine Street, will finally start unfolding far more effectively, and with greater poetic justice than it could have at that time. Now the DA's office really *will* have more than enough just cause to accuse and indict Nick Miller of a major-league crime.

Of murder, Holly thinks, standing in Nick's entrance hall.

And because Holly Bourne will have been the one to create the prosecutorial evidence, she will also be the only one capable of finding its loopholes.

The only lawyer – she rejoices, opening Nick's living room door – able to get him acquitted.

And then she finds Zoë in her playpen. And seeing her blows all Holly's thoughts and plans – like suddenly inconsequential wisps of smoke – clean out of what is left of her mind.

Gone.

Gone.

Picking her up, holding this child – *Nick's child* – in her arms, alters everything. She has held her before, as Barbara Rowe. But never as Holly Bourne.

'You change everything,' she says to the baby.

Everything.

Vasquez's belongings no longer matter. It's too late for that. Later than she realized. Earlier than she realized.

The baby is crying.

Holly holds her close.

'It's okay, sweetheart,' she hushes her. 'Everything's okay now.'

She brushes the top of her head with her lips.

'Mommy's got you now,' she says.

86

At a little after five that afternoon, Nina, William and I are in Phoebe's room at the Waterson Clinic, listening to Phoebe talking. Her voice, newly restored by some kind of a miracle, sounds a little husky and slurred, but otherwise it's just Phoebe's voice, almost normal, the way Mary Chen predicted it might be.

However much effort it may be costing her, she's busy giving William a hard time.

Music to my ears.

'Dad, I still don't understand how you could even have *dreamt* that Nick could do any of those terrible things.'

'Phoebe, darling, you don't understand.'

'Damn *right*, I don't understand. Nick's always been like a real brother to me – almost from the day he met Nina. You know that, Dad – you *must* have known that.'

'The police seemed to think otherwise.'

Despite the joy of having his younger daughter fully restored to him, William is looking gaunt and drained. Phoebe, on the other hand – sitting on top of her bed, both arms still in slings but her green eyes brighter than I've seen them since July – seems suddenly packed with the energy of a warrior.

'The police don't know Nick,' she says. 'We do.'

I don't say a word. I keep my mouth shut and sit quietly beside my

364

wife, enjoying letting Phoebe fight my battle for me.

'*You* might know him,' William points out, 'but how often had I really met him properly, spent significant time with him, until your fall? A handful of special occasions – you don't really get to know a man on *occasions*.'

'But I did get to know him,' Phoebe insists. 'I got to know him very well indeed.'

'But you couldn't speak, my darling.'

'Nina could speak,' Phoebe says.

'Dad thought I was biased,' Nina says, gently.

'And so you were,' William says.

I go on watching and listening, still saying nothing. My time will come. I'm in no hurry.

'I can speak now,' Phoebe says.

'Thank God,' Nina says.

Amen.

'Which means I can tell you, and the cops – though, from what Nina said, they're going to need more than just *me* telling them anything – that all the accusations are bullshit – outrageous, insane *bullshit*.' She stops, a little out of breath.

'Take it easy, sweetheart.' At last, I intervene.

'No chance.' Phoebe throws me one of her sweet smiles. 'And you shouldn't try shutting up a person when they're saying good things about you.' She turns back to her father. 'So,' she demands, 'don't you think you owe Nick an apology, at the very least?'

William looks at me. 'It appears I might.'

'That's not good enough, Dad, not nearly good enough.' Phoebe has no intention of letting him off the hook. 'Nina told me the reason Nick was never alone with me was because you wouldn't let him visit me unless you or a dozen armed guards were around.'

'Don't exaggerate, Phoebe.' Nina smiles.

'But it's true – I realize that now.' She's still outraged.

'Your father was only trying to protect you,' I say, feeling happy enough right now to be generous even to Ford. 'If it were Zoë, I guess I'd probably do the same.'

'No, you wouldn't,' Phoebe disagrees.

I give a small shrug. 'Don't count on it. Fatherhood does strange things to a man.'

* * *

365

William has rounded off his apology with a firm handshake. For Nina's and Phoebe's sake, I hope I've been gracious enough about it – though it's not the easiest thing in the world to give absolution to a man who thinks you could try to murder his daughter. Mind, everyone in the room still knows – as Phoebe said – that there's no guarantee her affirmation of my almost blameless character is going to be enough to satisfy either the SFPD or the insurance investigators.

Still, one blessing at a time is enough for me.

'You two should go home now,' Phoebe says to us shortly before six.

'We've only just come,' Nina says.

'To hear me talk, and I have, and Dad's told you he's sorry, and now you guys need to go home to my niece and start over.' Phoebe grins at William. 'It's not as if I'm going to be on my own.' She pauses. 'And as soon as Zoë's over her cold, I want you to bring her on a visit.'

'You may be home first,' I tell her.

'The minute I can do at least a few damn things for myself,' Phoebe says, looking down at her twin slings.

'Won't be long now,' William says, softly.

'Touch wood.' Nina smiles and gets to her feet. 'I'll call home then, tell Teresa we may fly back tomorrow.'

'What's wrong with today?' Phoebe asks.

'It's already evening,' Nina reminds her, making the call.

'You trying to get rid of us?' I lean towards Phoebe and ruffle her red hair. It feels good to be able to touch my sister-in-law without William thinking I'm about to strangle her.

'No answer,' Nina says, still waiting for Teresa to pick up.

'Maybe they've gone for a walk,' William suggests.

'It's too late for a walk,' I say.

Nina puts down the receiver. 'Teresa's probably bathing Zoë. She knows better than to leave her to come to the phone.'

'Isn't it a little late for bath time too?' I ask.

'I do it earlier,' Nina agrees with me.

'Are you worried?' Phoebe asks.

'I'd rather there was an answer,' Nina says.

* * *

An hour later, there's still no reply from our house, and we've already called Clare Hawkins to ask her to go over to Antonia Street, and she's reported back that no one's answering the door either. And Nina and I are alternating between being mad at Teresa and afraid that Zoë's cold has turned into something much worse. Except that if that were the case, William pointed out a few minutes ago, surely Teresa would have called us here. Maybe not, Nina said, if things are happening too fast and Teresa's sitting with our little girl in the emergency room.

One thing is certain. We need to get home.

'Something really is wrong, isn't it?' Nina says to me when we're in the cab on the road to Phoenix.

'I don't know,' I answer softly, staring out of the window.

Don't think it.

I'm doing my best not to let Nina know where my mind is heading or how fast my blood is chilling. Doing my best to slap those nasty (*way beyond nasty*) thoughts down, down where they belong, with worms and slime and ghouls (*and Holly Bourne*). Doing my best to keep some slender line open to the Almighty (*please, God, let me be wrong about this*), but the struggle is getting harder the closer we get to the airport, to the flight and whatever awaits us at home.

Nothing, please God, nothing. Nothing but a little baby girl safely asleep in her crib, a phone not working, and a less-perfect-than-we-thought, too-heavily-sleeping nanny in her own bed.

But the struggle's still getting harder.

'Nick?'

I feel Nina's hand clutching my own.

'Nick, tell me what you're thinking,' she says.

'I don't know what I'm thinking,' I lie, not looking at her.

'You think it's Holly, don't you?'

Don't even think it.

Nina reaches up, tilts my head to face her and looks into my eyes. And I see that her own blood is turning to ice.

87

The house was silent and dark when they arrived soon after eleven-thirty.

Not right. Not normal.

They flicked switches, flooding the halls and staircase with light.

'Teresa!' Fear turned Nick's voice hoarse.

Nothing.

Nina ran up the stairs, and Nick heard her banging doors and calling, her voice growing more afraid with every yell of Teresa's and Zoë's name. Nick took the living room – no one there, nothing out of place – then headed for the kitchen.

The note was stuck to the refrigerator door with a yellow smiley face magnet. He walked towards it very slowly and pulled it away.

'Nick? Anything?' Nina was on her way back down.

'In the kitchen.'

She came in, saw him reading, her face distorted by alarm. 'What is it? Is it from Teresa? Is Zoë sick?'

Nick opened his mouth, tried to say the words, but they seemed to stick in his throat.

'It's from her, isn't it?' Nina said.

He nodded and held the note out to her.

She took it from him and sat down on the pine chair closest to them.

* * *

Dearest Nick,

I have taken the baby. Come and meet me, and come alone. You can get a little rest and be in Napa at the Visitors Centre in the middle of town by seven AM.

Come alone, Nick. It's been a long time since we really talked, and I have a lot to say to you.

I don't want to harm her. It's the very last thing I want. But if you call the police, or if Nina or anyone else comes with you, I swear you will never see your daughter again.

I mean that, Nick.

No cops. Not Norman Capelli or Helen Wilson – not even a Napa patrolman. I know cops – I can smell them. I've learned a lot since you and I first pinched copies of Cosmo *from our local drugstore back in Bethesda.*

I say it one more time, just so you believe it.

If you want to see our baby again, no police.

> *Love,*
> *Holly.*

PS Tell Nina I'll be calling your house now and again towards dawn, and she'd better be there, waiting. Tell her I want her to experience what waiting for you feels like. God knows I've been doing it for long enough.

'*Our* baby,' Nina said, and her voice was full of anguish and hate. 'She thinks Zoë is her baby. Hers and yours.'

'She's crazy,' Nick said, beyond helpless.

'She's evil,' Nina said.

The second piece of paper was in the playpen in the living room, tucked beneath the small pink toy rabbit that Zoë had lately favoured. Nina's grim and barely holding-it-together face was already white, but, upon realizing what this was, it turned a sick, parchment colour.

'New York,' she said, faintly.

Nick took it from her, saw what looked like lines of poetry hand-written on one of the prelim pages from *Firefly*.

'Your writing,' he said, confused. 'Isn't it?'

369

'It's a quote from a Wordsworth poem,' Nina told him. 'A woman at a signing at Doubleday in New York City asked me to write it for her.'

Nick stared at it.

> A simple child,
> That lightly draws its breath,
> And feels its life in every limb,
> What should it know of death?

'It's horrible,' he said.
'It was Holly,' Nina said. 'Even then.'

88

If there were alcohol in our house, Nina would be on her way back down. As it is, she's having to suffer this night stone-cold sober.

When William and Phoebe called, we told them everything was okay, that there had simply been a fault on our phone line, now fixed, that Teresa had been here all along (*where the hell* is *poor Teresa? we hardly dare wonder*) and that Zoë was tucked up safe and sound for the night.

No need for them to suffer too. Not yet.

Besides, neither of us is certain that William could be trusted not to call the cops or even to fly himself to Napa.

No risks. We agree on that.

We have not slept. Of course we have not slept. Nina, when she spoke at all, told me I should try to rest before my journey, and I pointed out that the drive to Napa before dawn in late November would take an hour at most, which meant I needed no more rest than she did. Apart from these and a few other brief, tight exchanges, we have spent most of this night drinking too much coffee and wandering around our house like a pair of disconnected ghosts, of little or no help to one another, isolated with our own thoughts and terrors.

'I can't wait much longer,' I said, abruptly, a little after four.

'But she said—'

'She won't expect me to wait,' I said.

Nina gave me an awful look. 'Won't she?'

We were sitting in the living room, Zoë's empty playpen in front of us. We were both cold, so I had made a fire. Earlier on, we seemed to take turns pacing, sometimes in this room, moving restlessly back and forth across the hearth and over the rugs, sometimes all around the house. Once, for a few minutes, while Nina was the one stalking around upstairs, I heard the sound of her weeping. Ugly, cracked, deep sobs. I sat forward on the edge of my chair, longing to go to her, to console her, but I knew there was no point. I would not have been a consolation to Nina. How could I be?

I am the cause of her child being taken away and endangered. She blames me. How can she not?

If Holly hurts Zoë, I will be to blame for that, too.

There is no avoiding that simple, stark truth.

The pacing stopped some time back, when we both slumped, suddenly, into armchairs. Becalmed on our bottomless sea of fear.

Our silence is oppressive.

It comes to me at four thirty-three that if I don't make some kind of sound again soon, whether it's to speak or to cry or even to scream, I may find myself, like Phoebe did, unable to talk at all.

I keep it up for another five minutes.

'So we're both quite agreed,' I say, 'about not calling the cops?'

My voice sounds too normal, too conversational. It ought to mirror the way I feel. Flayed. Bleeding.

'We're agreed,' Nina says.

Her voice sounds dead.

Still, at least I have her sanction on this one thing.

The rest, for the time being, is on my own shoulders.

God help me.

372

89

He left just after five, planning to head out north on US 101 in the Land Cruiser, to cross the Golden Gate Bridge, turn east onto Highway 37, skirt around San Pablo Bay as far as Vallejo and then to continue onto Highway 29, the road that ran right through the Napa Valley as far as Calistoga. He remembered another time when he and Nina had made this journey (oh, Christ, poor Nina, having to stay home waiting while he, at least, was able to try and *do* something), remembered how, on that trip, he'd felt a compulsion to stop en route and make a swift pastel sketch of the gently undulating hills a little way out of San Francisco. Those hills had fascinated him, had not resembled any other hills he had ever seen, looking from a distance as if they were made of a kind of fur, or maybe moleskin.

This time, it was too dark to see either moleskin hills or the duller, flatter, marshy land on either side of much of 37. It was raining, too, but even if it had been daytime and sunny, the tail-end of November, with all the grapes long since harvested and pressed, was not the greatest time to visit the valley.

The murky darkness of the early morning suited Nick's mood.

Cold, flat fury.

Not the simmering rage of that long-ago time with Holly. The kind of rage that had pushed him until he'd had to explode, had to hit out at her.

This was very different. This was cold and calculating and all the more deadly for it.

Once he had Zoë back, safe and sound, he knew what he was going to do. Once he had Zoë back, Nick was going to make Holly pay. He was going to frighten her, and he was going to hurt her, and

373

he was going to go just as far as he figured the law, under the circumstances, would be likely to let him get away with.

He wasn't going to go to jail for Holly Bourne. Oh, no.

He was willing to go to jail for Zoë. He was willing to *die* for Zoë. But not for Holly.

Oh, no.

90

Nina was in the kitchen, trying to bake bread, when the phone rang for the first time after Nick had left for Napa.

She snatched up the receiver.

'Yes?'

Silence.

'Holly, is that you?'

The line went dead.

Nina put down the phone.

And went back to weighing ingredients.

Joanna Ford, Nina's mother, had taught her daughters to bake at times of emotional crisis, before they'd left England, while William Ford had still been in the RAF. Before Joanna had become a full-time drunk.

'It doesn't matter how it turns out,' she would tell them. 'What matters is the doing. Every part of it. The weighing and measuring, the mixing, the folding, the cleaning up.'

Nina remembered Joanna telling them there was no point cheating about things like cleaning up. The more tedious the chore, the more point there was in doing it when you felt really lousy or afraid.

Afraid.

Nina finished weighing the flour and began sieving it.

She finished sieving it, and then started again.

And again.

The phone rang.

Same as before. Holly listening for just a moment, then hanging up.

Nina put down the receiver, turned around, picked up the mixing bowl, and threw it, with every ounce of her strength, against the wall.

As the china shattered, Nina screamed.

And watched the cloud of flour rise and fly and fall.

91

Napa was much the way Nick had expected the small town at the gateway to the valley to be at six AM on a cool, no longer rainy but still damp Saturday morning on the last day of November. Dark. Dead.

He left the Toyota in an almost empty parking lot, and checked the tourist signs for directions to the Visitors Centre. It was in a modern mall on a corner plot, its broad glass doors locked (what else had he expected at that time?) and a notice informing Nick that it was not scheduled to open until nine o'clock.

'Great,' he said. 'Just great.'

He knocked on the front door, and then, getting no response, pounded harder, but it was patently obvious that the whole place, reception and rear, was deserted.

'Now what?' he said.

He wandered around the silent shopping mall until he found a payphone, looked up the number of the centre in the Napa directory, called it, listened to a message informing him that they were closed, and then phoned Nina instead.

'I'm here, but the Visitors Centre's closed till nine.'

'She's been calling,' Nina told him tersely. 'About every half hour. She just calls, listens to me for a second or two, then cuts off. It's driving me nuts.'

'I'm going to try and check around town until seven,' Nick said. 'Just in case she's hiding out in one of the local hotels or diners.'

'Even if she is, I'll bet she's made sure you won't find her.'

'No harm in looking. Better than standing outside the damned centre, waiting. Anything's better than waiting.'

'Tell me about it,' Nina said.

It was hopeless in the short time he had. Nick managed just three inns and one bed and breakfast, but if any of the enviably early-Saturday-calm innkeepers had seen a dark-haired, grey-eyed, pregnant woman in her late twenties with a little baby girl with red-gold hair, they weren't about to share that information with a desperate-looking stranger.

He was back at the Visitors Centre at ten before seven, because that was where Holly had directed him to be, and because he had no better alternative.

The morning was growing lighter and the weather improving, but other than that, there was no obvious change. The glass doors were still locked and there were no more signs of life than there had been an hour earlier. No Holly. No Zoë. Panic soared like a high-speed elevator. God, what a *fool* he was for believing the bitch.

And then he saw the envelope. On the ground about four feet away, one sharp white triangular corner protruding from the base of a trashcan. He had no way of knowing if it had been there at six o'clock. He only knew, with absolute conviction, that it was there for him.

Hands shaking, he bent and picked it up.

His name was on the envelope. Typewritten.

He tore it open.

Another note, much shorter, and also typed.

> *Be outside the Pieter Winery on the Silverado Trail at seven-thirty. Come alone. Then wait and see.*

He called Nina again on his way back to the parking lot, told her where he was heading, knew from her voice that she was holding up badly but knew, too, that short of bringing home their daughter, there was still nothing he could do for her.

They had driven the Silverado Trail – the elevated road above Highway 29 – together the previous spring, and though they had moved quite swiftly away from the Napa district to the Sonoma Valley, Nick remembered that the Trail had offered a string of wineries and fine views across the valley. If the Pieter Winery gave him back Zoë safe and sound this morning, Nick vowed that he would return next spring with Nina and buy every last damned bottle they wanted to sell him, but right now he didn't care about either wines or vistas. All he cared about on this increasingly bright, pleasant, late fall morning was finding his beautiful baby girl, and then – and only then – dealing with Holly Bourne once and for all.

He found the Pieter Winery without much difficulty, not far from the Yountville Cross Road. It was on the right hand side of the Trail, and appeared to be a small, private establishment, with an arched rough stone gateway and a neat, shrub-lined tarmac track leading up to a creamy house with a red tiled roof, surrounded by vineyards.

Nick pulled off the road just outside the gateway and got out of the car. He thought, for a moment, about heading up to the house and asking if anyone had seen Holly or Zoë, but the note had not instructed him to do that. The note had told him to wait and see, whatever the hell that meant.

He took a few moments, looking around. A Ford Explorer drove past but didn't slow down; then a small Volkswagen; then a Cherokee; then, after a longer pause, a Bonneville. He stopped checking cars. There was nothing else to see, unless you'd come for the scenery, nothing except trees and hills and early winter vines and a great view of the valley down below. Not as great, though, as the view from the two brightly-coloured hot air balloons just floating into his eye-line. Nina had wanted to take a ride in a balloon last spring, but they'd only had two days, and all the early-morning flights had been sold out, so Nick had promised her a rain check.

In another lifetime, maybe.

He turned around and looked back up towards the winery. A man had emerged from the house and was walking around the side. He was talking to someone. A woman. Nick narrowed his eyes, trying to see what she looked like. She was wearing coveralls and she was tall. Too tall. He looked away, back at the road. A car was coming closer, heading towards Napa, and it was slowing down.

Nick's heart rate increased. It was a blue Volvo, and there was a dark-haired woman at the wheel.

He stepped out a little way into the road.

The woman slowed right down, looked straight at him and drove on.

Not Holly.

Nick was sweating and his pulse racing. He wanted to pick up a stone and throw it at the goddamned car. What the hell had she been *looking* at?

Probably at the idiot man standing in the road, looking at her.

He shook his head to try and clear it, crossed the Trail, climbed over a low stone wall dividing the road from the slight wooded incline on the other side, and looked up. Where there had been two balloons just a short while ago, there were now four, three of them seeming, from this perspective, quite close together, the other gliding through the now almost perfectly blue sky in splendid isolation.

Nick stared at the balloons.

And understood.

Wait and see.

Holly was up there in one of those balloons. With Zoë. A small baby with a cold – his and Nina's small baby – Christ-only-knew how high in the sky with a crazy woman.

He heard a sound, something between a moan and a bellow, and realized that it was coming from him. He was standing there on the edge of the Silverado Trail and he wanted to stretch out his arms and snatch his daughter back – he wanted to fucking *fly* – and he couldn't do either of those things – he couldn't even tell which of the balloons she was *in*.

Jesus.

Jesus!

He turned around, vaulted over the wall, raced back across the road, and ran under the stone gateway and up the tarmac track to the cream-coloured house. Close up, through one of the open first-floor windows, he could smell bacon cooking, could hear Mozart playing and voices gently chatting.

The man and the tall woman in coveralls had disappeared.

Nick knocked on the front door. Then hammered.

The door opened. A young peach-skinned woman with golden

hair tied in a long, thick plait, and wearing blue jeans and a handsome white cable-knit sweater, looked at him enquiringly.

'What's up?'

'The balloons.' Nick was breathless and too abrupt. 'Where do they come from? Who operates them?'

'Balloons?' The young woman was unfazed, her blue eyes a little bemused but perfectly friendly.

'Up there.' Nick half turned, jabbed his right hand up at the sky and saw, to his horror, that there were now five balloons aloft over the valley. 'Oh, Jesus.'

'Is something wrong?'

Nick turned back to her. 'You could say that.' He couldn't afford the time to explain. 'Okay, forget where they came from – tell me where they're going to land.'

'I can't.'

'What do you mean, you *can't*?'

'Just that.' Her smile was easy. 'They land where they land, within reason. It depends on the breeze, I guess.'

Nick felt panic rising again, tearing at his heart and his guts, but he knew he couldn't afford to let it take him over. He had to force himself to think logically. *Okay. Back to square one*.

'Do you know the company that flies them?' he asked.

'A bunch of people.' She gave a little shrug. 'Quite a few companies in the valley operate balloons.' She shielded her eyes with her flattened left hand and took a good look. 'There may be two – maybe even three – from one outfit, but I can't be sure of that.'

'Need some help here?' A middle-aged man with silvering blond hair, casually dressed in slacks, yellow pullover and loafers, came up behind the young woman. 'I'm Pieter Van Lindt,' he introduced himself, 'and this is my daughter, Helen.' He had a slight accent that Nick thought was most probably Dutch.

'The balloons,' Helen Van Lindt told her father, pointing. 'Any way of telling which ones belong to whom?'

The man looked up briefly. 'The usual people.'

'Who are?' Nick pressed. 'Who *are*?'

Van Lindt looked back at him. 'You seem very agitated, sir.'

'I am. I have to know where they're going to land,' Nick said, 'but your daughter says there's no way of telling.'

'That's true.' Van Lindt smiled. 'Which is why they use chase vehicles to track the balloons. They pick up the passengers from the first balloon to land, and then they all go on chasing the second, and so on.'

'But they'll all be coming down soon,' his daughter told Nick.

'How do you know?'

'It's almost eight o'clock,' she explained. 'They have to go up early because of winds and air currents, and they're usually all down by about eight-thirty.'

Nick fought against a sudden urge to scream. He had to *do* something. He had to come up with at least a semblance of a workable strategy, but his mind was blank, too jammed with fear to have space for anything else.

'Do you have a friend in one of the balloons?' Van Lindt asked. His blue eyes were concerned, understanding. 'Someone you're anxious to meet when they land?'

'My daughter,' Nick said, numbly.

'I see,' Van Lindt said.

'She's just a baby.'

The other man looked puzzled. 'I don't think they allow babies, or even small children, on board. I believe there is some height restriction, but I'm not sure. Is she with her mother?'

No, she's not with her mother. She's with a psycho who's either trying to terrify me and her mother to death, or—

A vision struck him with all the dizzying impact of a baseball bat between the eyes. Holly standing near the edge of the basket with Zoë in her arms, lifting her, holding the baby out over the edge—

He shut his eyes and swayed.

'Are you all right? Sir, do you need to sit down?'

Van Lindt's voice brought him back. Nick opened his eyes. *I don't think they allow babies on board.*

He stared back up at the balloons.

Please, dear God, let him be right.

He thought, very briefly, of telling the Van Lindts the truth, but they were bound to want to call the cops, and he wasn't about to forget the warning in Holly's note. *If you want to see your baby again, no police.*

'You could try calling the local companies.' Helen Van Lindt was growing more concerned now, like her father. 'I'm sure I could find

382

you a list inside. They may have passenger lists, so then at least you'd know where to go.'

Nick thought for a moment. It was either that, or a wild, possibly fruitless zigzag across the valley chasing one balloon after another, without any proof of which one they were in. He looked at the young woman. Her suggestion made more sense than anything else he was likely to come up with, with his brain fast scrambling and Zoë's life at stake.

He managed a ghost of a smile at her.

'If you could try finding that list,' he said, 'I would like to use your phone.'

92

Holly is calculating again.

It's strange the way her mind is working now. Has been ever since she first found her baby. Things were getting a little fuzzy before that, she thinks – she *thinks*. She can't really remember everything about before – only some things. *Key* things. The rest aren't important anymore – if they were, she would remember.

It's now that counts.

Present and future.

And her brain is like quicksilver.

She can't see Nick, yet she knows – she really seems to *know* – what he's doing, what he's thinking, what he's planning.

Quicksilver.

Right around now, for instance, Holly knows that he's going half out of his mind – *three-quarters, at least, let's keep it accurate* – trying to work out which of the balloons over the Napa Valley she and the baby are in. And to comfort himself, to keep himself going, he's figuring out what he's going to do to punish her when he has it worked out.

She knows the way he thinks.

Ought to by now.

Oh, but it's so good to feel in control again, so re-energized, so *renewed*.

She looks at her watch.

Wondering if it's time yet to make her next move.

Not quite . . . Just a tad too soon . . .

Almost there.

93

It had taken Nick twenty minutes – twenty precious minutes – just to get to speak to a live human voice at one of the numerous hot air balloon flight companies in the valley. The voice mail recordings and answering machines had been courteous enough, even helpful, if what one wanted to learn had anything to do with weather-checking or reservations or gift certificates; it wasn't those companies' fault if a madwoman had kidnapped a baby and was maybe, that same morning, contemplating tossing that baby out of a basket in the sky.

Nick had recorded extreme urgency messages at every company on Helen Van Lindt's list. The first real human voice – even more courteous than her company's outgoing message – called him back almost as soon as he'd put down the receiver after his last attempt.

Babies were not, on the whole, she told Nick, permitted on board hot air balloons.

There might, on rare occasions, be exceptions.

Were passengers allowed to bring large bags or maybe picnic hampers along for the ride? (*She might have hidden Zoë. She might have done anything, even drugged her.*) No baggage of any kind was permitted in the basket, he was informed; ladies were asked to leave even their purses locked in their cars before departure.

It became more conclusive.

They had no reservation in either the name of Bourne or Taylor. Nor in the name of Miller. If Nick wanted to call back in a half-hour or so, by which time the passengers would all be enjoying their sparkling wine brunch, it ought to be possible to confirm absolutely whether or not the woman and child had been on one of their flights.

The woman and child. *Child.*

His child, his and Nina's. Not Holly Bourne's.

Nick sat in Helen Van Lindt's chair and wanted to weep. He couldn't remember a time when he'd done that in public, not, at least, since he was a young boy, but he felt he was getting perilously close to it now. Either to that or to a terrible, out of control rage. But neither of those things would do anything except release some of the banked-up steam that he felt was about to explode out of the top of his head. They wouldn't help him, and they wouldn't help Nina or Zoë.

They wouldn't even harm Holly.

He asked Helen Van Lindt if he might make one more call, this time to his wife in San Francisco. He'd been hoping to have something – *something* – to report to Nina when he called again, but it wasn't fair just leaving her sitting there waiting, going out of her mind.

'I'll leave you to it,' the young woman told him. 'Anything else you need, just call.'

'You've already given me coffee and let me take over your office,' Nick said gratefully. 'I don't know how to thank you.'

'I just hope you find your daughter soon,' she said, and left the room, closing the door quietly.

Nick picked up the receiver and slowly pressed their home number.

'Yes?'

He'd never heard Nina answer a phone that way, so cagey and hostile. (*Like a woman waiting for her child's kidnapper to call – or for her husband to give her bad news. How did you expect her to sound, jerk?*)

He told her fast.

'You are going to check the balloons, aren't you?' Nina sounded brittle, like a piece of dry wood ready to snap or splinter. 'She hasn't called since way before seven, so she could have gone up.'

'Of course I'm going to check,' Nick said, 'but it's beginning to look like the whole thing was a hoax.'

'Holly never mentioned balloons.'

'That's true, but there was nothing else on the Trail.'

'Are you sure?' Nina asked.

He was already starting to doubt himself. Yet there *had* been

386

nothing else to focus on except the balloons. *Wait and see*, Holly had instructed him in her second note. Outside the Pieter Winery at seven-thirty. It had been around eight when he'd begun making the calls, and all he'd seen apart from the hot air balloons had been cars and scenery.

'I'm as sure as I can be,' he told Nina.

She didn't say anything for a moment, and he knew she was fighting to hold it together.

'What then?' Her voice shook a little. 'When you've done all the checking. What's next?'

'I guess I come home,' Nick answered. *Alone.*

'Are *they* certain – the people at this vineyard – are they quite sure that Holly hasn't called or left another note somewhere?'

'They're certain, sweetheart,' he said. 'They're smart, nice people.'

'I'm glad you're dealing with nice people.' A touch of acid.

'Come on,' Nick said, gently.

'I'm sorry. It's just so hard, you know?'

'I know,' he said.

She was silent again for a moment.

'Honey, I'm going to have to get out of here,' he pressed her. 'They're checking the passengers at all the post-flight brunches.'

'I almost had a drink,' Nina said suddenly. 'I almost called the Mayflower and asked them to make a delivery.'

Nick heard the shame in her voice, and his heart ached for her.

'But you didn't.'

'No.' She paused. 'How could I, when our daughter's missing?'

'It would be understandable.' Nick found himself checking his wristwatch. He hated himself for having to cut her short now, just when she really needed to talk, but it was after nine o'clock.

'Blotting out my own pain at her expense?' Nina said. 'It would not be understandable. It would be unforgivable.' She took a deep, steadying breath. 'Go on,' she said. 'I'm okay. I just needed you to know how weak I am – what a lousy coward I still am.'

'You're not a coward.'

'I know what I am, Nick.' She paused again. 'You have to go.'

'Yes. I'm sorry.'

'Nick?'

'What?'

'If Zoë isn't in Napa, where is she?'

The shame and weakness had gone from Nina's voice, and only terror remained.

The same terror that was coursing, like an overspill from a bottomless source, through all his own veins, along all his nerves.

'I don't know,' Nick said.

94

By nine thirty-five, Holly almost knows the time without checking her wristwatch. She can feel her intuitiveness increasing with each passing hour. Like her detachment from outside, trival matters. Like her power.

The watch is an old one. She focuses on it for several seconds. Into the past. A more distant past. Blancpain. Given her by her mother and father years ago. She's always liked it better than other watches, even the platinum and diamond Rolex – Jack's gift – that she sold for cash before running out on him.

Interesting the way she seems, now, to remember some things clearly, while others seem covered by that thick blanketing of fog. Gifts have never loomed especially large for Holly – though some, of course, are carved forever in her mind. Like the silk and lace panties Nick gave her that long-ago Christmas birthday. The same day she gave him their first condom concealed in the finger of a sheepskin-lined glove. *A glove in a glove.* And they never even used it.

Holly glances at the baby.

So good and sweet.

And back at the watch.

Nine thirty-seven.

Time.

95

The phone rang.

Nina, in the bedroom, picked it up tentatively, saying nothing.

'Nina, this is Holly.'

Nina's right hand wrapped itself more tightly around the receiver, her fingers like claws. 'Where's my daughter?'

'The baby's with me,' Holly said. 'Safe and snug as a bug.'

The baby. Not 'your' *baby.*

'Where are you?' Nina asked, hate expanding in her throat like choking smoke.

'Nowhere near Napa,' Holly said, lightly.

Nina closed her eyes and thought of Nick, dementedly chasing balloons on the Silverado Trail.

'I'm next door,' Holly said.

Nina's eyes opened. 'What?'

'Right next door. Number 1317. I'm your next-door neighbour, Nina. Aren't you happy?'

In the centre of her chest, Nina's heart gave an odd, violent thump, and for a moment or two she thought she might pass out.

Barbara Rowe.

She remembered Teresa telling her that was their new neighbour's name. *A private person*, Teresa had said. *Not friendly*, *like you.*

She remembered the pregnant, edgy woman on the street, dropping her bags. She thought of the woman in the bookstore in New York City, dictating the poem. The woman Phoebe had recognized in court in Los Angeles. Charlotte Taylor. Barbara Rowe.

Holly Bourne.

'I want you to come over to my house, Nina. Right away.' Holly paused only briefly. 'If you love this little girl, and I imagine you do, you'd better do exactly as I say.'

'I will,' Nina said quickly. 'Anything.'

'Good.' Holly paused again. 'Don't think about telling anyone, Nina, because I know where you are, because I can see you right now through your bedroom window—'

Nina's eyes flew to the side window, narrower than those overlooking the street, and automatically she moved a little closer to see if she could see Holly next door.

'Yes, there you are,' Holly said. 'See me?'

Nina jerked away from the window again.

'Oh, don't be shy. Come on over right now. I'll know if you call anyone or waste any time, and then this little baby will be gone for good. Okay? Okay, Nina?'

This little baby.

'I don't think you'll hurt her,' Nina said.

'Are you sure?'

More choking, suffocating hate.

'I'm coming.'

Nina cut off the call and ran out of the bedroom and down the stairs. She was breathing too hard and sweating, fighting panic and faintness. She had to get word to Nick before she left – she *had* to – or he might never know what had happened, where she had gone.

For several seconds, standing in the doorway to the living room, she wavered, desperately trying to remember the name of the winery he'd called her from. She could call those people – '*smart, nice people*' – and leave a message for him in case he went back there or phoned them for news.

Her memory was blank. Completely blank.

She let out one short, frantic cry that echoed through the empty house, and the small release seemed to set the shock-clogged wheels in motion again.

If he makes another call, Nina, it'll be to you.

Conscious that Holly was probably counting minutes, she flew to the answering machine, pressed the rewind button on the outgoing message tape, then punched Record.

'Nick, listen to me.'

Her voice was too breathless and wild, but there was no time to think about that, no time to worry about what might happen if anyone else except Nick called and heard the message.

'Holly is not *in* Napa,' she went on, battling to sound coherent. 'She's here, in the house next door, right here on Antonia Street. Number 1317. She's been living next door to us, right next *door*.' She gulped air, steadied her voice, made it hard and clear. 'She has Zoë, Nick – Holly has Zoë – and I'm going to get her back.'

Nina stopped recording, wound the tape back and switched the machine to incoming message status.

And went next door.

96

At five past ten, Holly was waiting at the front door of 1317. She was wearing white. A simple fine wool shift dress with a scooped neckline that Jack had bought her a few months back on Rodeo Drive. Her skin was pale and smooth and taut. Her dark hair was loose and gleaming, as if she had just shampooed and blown it carefully dry for Nina's visit.

She had spent a long time preparing.

'Come in, Nina.'

Nina looked into the eyes of the woman who wanted to destroy her world. Grey eyes. Smug eyes.

She stepped over the threshold. The entrance hall was exactly the same shape and size as their own, but theirs was warm and welcoming, whereas this was clinical and stark.

'Can I make you some tea,' Holly offered. 'Or maybe you'd prefer something stronger? I know how you enjoy a drink.'

'I'd like to see Zoë, please.'

'All in good time.' Holly smiled at her. 'How about a nice cup of breakfast tea? While we get to know each other.'

She turned and walked towards the kitchen. Nina stood very still, debating whether or not to run straight up the staircase to try to find Zoë, but in a three-storey house she might be anywhere, and Holly was hardly going to let her simply go pick up her baby and walk out with her.

She looked around. There was a large patch of discoloured parquet on the floor near the foot of the staircase. A stain that someone had very recently tried to scrub out. Nina could smell bleach, could see brush marks scratched into the polish.

393

Teresa came, unbidden, into her mind, together with a terrible fear.

'Come along, Nina,' Holly said, from inside the kitchen.

Nina pushed the fear away and followed her.

'Have a seat.' Holly pointed to the white chairs around the small round table.

Nina sat down, watched Holly fill a steel kettle, light the gas stove, wait for the water to boil.

'Where's Teresa?' she asked.

'Around,' Holly answered, taking two ceramic mugs down from a wall cupboard and setting them on a counter near the stove.

Nina's foreboding magnified.

She had to moisten her lips with her tongue before she could speak again. 'We've met before,' she said, her voice a little hoarse.

'Twice,' Holly said, companionably. 'The tea won't be long.'

'At the bookstore in New York,' Nina said.

'Doubleday on Fifth.'

'And outside the house, two weeks ago. You were getting out of a cab. You dropped your shopping bag.'

'You picked it up for me.'

Nina said nothing for a moment, thinking.

'And you met my sister at that hearing in LA,' she added.

'Phoebe. Yes, I did.'

'And then you lured her to the house in Catherine Street.'

'Did I?'

Holly's eyes were calm.

Nina looked at her flat stomach.

'You're not pregnant,' she said.

The grey eyes blanked a little, but Holly said nothing. The kettle boiled. She picked it up.

Nina watched as she poured steaming water into the mugs and dunked teabags into them. Red Rose teabags. Nothing fancy.

Don't do that again, Nina. Don't put Zoë in greater danger.

'I'd like to see my baby soon,' she said, softly.

'You will.'

Holly set the mugs on the kitchen table and sat down.

Nina looked down at the table. White chipboard. Cheap, like the chairs. From the way Nick had described the Bourne family, she would have envisaged any home of Holly's very differently. More expensive. More tasteful.

But this isn't her home. This is just her trap.

'Drink your tea,' Holly said.

'I'm not thirsty,' Nina said.

'Okay.'

Holly stood up again.

'I do have something to show you.'

Nina got up quickly. Her whole body ached with her longing to see Zoë. Her whole being.

'Not the baby,' Holly said, reading her mind. 'Not yet.'

Nina said nothing. She could almost feel Holly's enjoyment, like a sick prickling under her skin. She thought, for a moment, about Nick. It was so strange – she understood more now about some of the things that he had allowed to happen, yet, conversely, at the same time, other things became even more impossible to understand.

He slept with this.

'This is something else,' Holly went on. 'Something Nick did. That I think you should see.'

She sat down again.

'It's sad about Teresa,' she said.

'What about Teresa?' Nina asked, thrown, still standing.

'Losing her this way.' Holly paused. 'I've come to know her quite well.' She ran her right index finger round the rim of her mug. 'Which is why I say it's sad.' She lifted her chin and looked up into Nina's face. 'But I'm sure you're going to be far more concerned with helping Nick than worrying too much about Teresa.'

Helping Nick.

Nina's heart was beating much too fast.

Holly stood up again. Moved slowly to her right, towards what, in 1315, was a utility room. 'That's why I'm going to show you this little problem first,' she said, 'before I outline my proposals for helping Nick. All right with you?'

'All right,' Nina said, bewildered.

'Come on then.' Holly beckoned to her, smiling, like a confidante. 'I can't explain how I'm going to help Nick until you know what we're up against, can I?'

Nina didn't move.

'But I am going to take care of him, Nina. You don't need to worry about that.' Holly slipped her right hand into the hip-level, right-hand pocket of her dress and took out a small key. 'How could I not help him, when he's been everything to me all my life?' Her eyes were suddenly tender. 'Brother. Best friend. Lover.'

Nina took one step towards Holly and stopped. Her legs were jelly. She felt nauseous and deeply afraid.

'Come on, Nina.' Holly held up the key. 'You have to come up close, or you won't be able to see.'

Nina followed her through the open door.

The room beyond was much the same as her own. Plain wall cupboards, a door that, presumably, opened onto a similar walk-in larder. Washing machine, drier. Chest freezer. A few cardboard boxes from supermarkets and grocery stores. Washing powder, softener, Chlorox bleach, rolls of paper towel. Vacuum cleaner.

Holly was about a foot away.

'I'm always going to be there for Nick,' she said, softly. 'You have to know that, Nina. Some things are just meant to be.'

She turned to the freezer and Nina saw that the lid was padlocked.

Her heart gave another of those odd, warning thuds in her chest, and her palms began to sweat.

Holly fitted the key into the padlock. Nina noticed, irrelevantly, that her nails were painted soft red, matching her lipstick, and that one of them was filed much shorter than the others, as if it had just been broken and repaired.

'And now that he's the father of our child,' Holly went on, still in that quiet, calm, almost gentle voice, 'what else can I possibly do but stand by him?' She looked up at Nina. 'You should be able to understand that, more than most.'

The padlock was open. Holly unhooked it, turned around and laid it on top of the drier, then turned back again and gripped the lid of the freezer with both hands.

'Ah,' she said. 'Just a minute.'

The father of our child. Our child.

Nina stood transfixed. She felt the way she thought small animals must feel at night when they halted in the middle of a highway, trapped in the beam of car headlights. Paralysed.

Holly was putting on gloves. The kind of fine plastic gloves people with skin allergies used around their kitchens. The kind that looked a little like the latex gloves surgeons and gynaecologists wore.

Oh, God.

Nina stared at the freezer, and a sudden madness shoved violently

396

into her mind, surged through her veins and arteries, through her limbs and up into her brain, pumped brutally by her out-of-control heart.

Zoë.

'Oh, dear God,' she said, out loud.

Holly glanced at her. She smiled again, reassuringly.

'Don't worry,' she said. 'It'll be fine.'

She gripped the freezer lid again and raised it until it rested against the concrete wall behind it.

'Come closer, Nina,' Holly said, still gentle, still soft. 'Don't be scared. There's nothing to be afraid of.'

If it's Zoë, I will kill her.

Nina stayed where she was, the madness still surging.

I will kill her every way there is to kill.

'Nina, come on.' Holly was a little firmer. 'Come see what Nick did.'

I will kill her, and then I will die.

Nina stepped up to the freezer and looked down.

Not Zoë.

It took a few seconds to comprehend. Frost had settled over Teresa. Over her black hair and her blue blouse and her unnaturally folded arm. The frost had coated Teresa's bloodied cheek and her nose and what had been her right eye in pink fuzz.

'Looks like fur, doesn't it?' Holly asked Nina.

She put her right hand into the freezer and pulled something out.

'This is the knife,' she said, and showed it to Nina. 'Recognize it?' She paused. 'It's Nick's. From his studio. It has his prints all over it.'

Nina tore her eyes away from the freezer and looked at the knife. She didn't remember it. She started to speak, but no words came. Her lips felt rubbery, her tongue felt thick. A strange, ugly moan emerged from her throat.

'Had a bit of a shock?' Holly asked, kindly.

Nina reached out her hand towards the wall to help her to stay upright, but it touched the freezer instead and she snatched it away as if it had burned her. A little of the numbness went away.

'I expect you'd like to see our daughter now?' Holly said.

Our daughter.

'Would you like that, Nina?'

Hold on. For Zoë.

Nina nodded.

'Yes, please,' she said.

She followed Holly out of the room, through the kitchen, through the hall and up the staircase. Past the second floor and on to the third.

To a white door with a pale pink teddy bear painted on it.

Holly opened the door.

'Come in,' she said.

There was a beautiful, draped crib in the centre of the room.

Zoë was lying on her back.

She was asleep. Her breathing was light and soft and even. Her little cheeks puffed out gently with her breaths as they often did when she was peacefully sleeping.

Thank you, God, thank you, God, thank you, God.

Nina ached to sweep Zoë up out of the crib, to hold her close.

'Isn't she perfect?'

Nina looked away from the crib up to Holly's face.

The proud mother.

Relief gave way to rage.

And then fresh terror.

Holly was still holding the knife. Still wearing gloves. She was not wielding it as she might have brandished a weapon. But she was still holding it. And she had already murdered with it once.

Hold on, Nina. You have to wait. For the right moment.

Nina looked back down at Zoë. At her child.

The madness had all gone now. Her mind was perfectly clear.

She stood very still.

And waited.

97

All the champagne brunches organized by the balloon companies are finished now. I got to two of the groups myself in time to check every woman and man; paranoia had me thinking Holly might even have pulled a swift sex change, and whatever the firms' representatives had told me, I couldn't help fearing that she might also have found a way to smuggle Zoë on board with her.

Seems I was wrong.

I've talked to just about everyone I could find who was connected to this morning's hot air balloon rides. I've driven them nuts, and I know they think I'm one brick shy of a load, but I don't care about that. All I care about is that neither Holly nor Zoë seems to have been anywhere near Napa today. Nina and I have been perfectly suckered in by that psychotic bitch.

So, at eleven-oh-three, I'm well on my way back home.

Listening to rock on KFOG to keep my own motor running.

They're playing the number from *Tommy* where the Acid Queen sings about what she could do with the child, given just one night.

Holly has already had our daughter for more than a night.

God help us all.

'If Zoë isn't in Napa, where is she?'

Nina asked me that question last time we spoke, and I still don't have any more of an answer than I did then.

But I do have another question, also unanswerable as yet, and all the more terrifying for it.

Aside from the pleasure she might have gotten out of torturing me and Nina, exactly why did Holly want to get me out of San Francisco this morning?

Fresh suspicion bursts through me as fast and menacingly as a newborn John Wyndham triffid.

I turn off the car radio and, for the first time in a while, take note of my whereabouts. I'm back on Highway 37, not too far from the Golden Gate Bridge. I could be home in twenty minutes or so, traffic permitting.

But all my instincts are bawling at me to call Nina *now*.

I might have been faster just staying on the road than looking for a phone.

But finally I'm standing here, slipping my quarters into the slot and listening to our line ringing.

The machine picks up.

And I listen to Nina's special message.

I put the receiver back on the cradle, and allow myself one more long, brain-bleeding moment to absorb what she has told me.

And then, for another too-long moment, I just go on standing there, vacillating like a big kid.

Someone help me.

Do I call the cops or don't I?

Holly's threat in her first note warned us not to.

But the acid queen has my baby *and* my wife now, and I can't talk this one over with Nina, so I have to guess all bets are off. Holly Bourne was always crazy, but what she's turned into now is a lying psychopath.

Not someone to make deals with.

Besides, I need all the help I can get.

And I need to *move*!

Why Norman Capelli is in his office on the Saturday morning of Thanksgiving weekend, I don't know, but it's one small piece of luck, and I thank God for it. I've been saying a lot of prayers over the last fifteen or so hours. I figured this was one time I might find out if anyone's listening, or cares. But Capelli *is* on the other end of this phone line, so maybe – just *maybe* – someone has been hearing me.

I tell him fast.

'You're sure that's exactly what she said?' Capelli says.

Anger erupts.

'If you don't believe me, Capelli, call our home number and listen to the message yourself – and if you don't believe me then about Holly Bourne, then *fuck* you, and if anything happens to my wife and daughter, it'll be on your head.'

'Take it easy, Miller,' Capelli tells me. 'I'll get a car over there right away.'

'*No!*' I yell at him, almost hysterical. 'She said in her note that if she saw so much as a uniform, we'd never see Zoë again. She said she can *smell* cops. Jesus Christ, Capelli, this is a *hostage* situation, don't you realize that yet?'

'Okay, okay,' Capelli soothes me. 'Then that's how we'll deal with it. But it's going to take a little time to set things up, so I'm going to need you to stay calm—'

'I'm not waiting,' I cut in, gripping the receiver so hard I'm surprised it doesn't crack, 'so don't even bother asking me to do that. I get back to Antonia Street, and I go straight next door—'

'Don't do that, Miller—'

'I'm doing it, Capelli. There's no way on earth I'm going to leave my wife and child alone with that murdering bitch one minute more than I have to.' I almost hang up, but I give him five more seconds. 'If your people can do something to help us – and I mean, *help*, not just make things more dangerous by going crazy with some SWAT team, then fine—'

'Don't go in alone, Miller,' Capelli warns me. 'You must *not*—'

'I'm on my way there now,' I override him. 'You call my house and you listen to my wife tell you what's going on, and then you decide if you'd do anything different if it was *your* wife.'

He's still talking to me as I slam the receiver back on the hook.

And get back in the Land Cruiser and put my foot down hard.

And think about what I'm going to do after I get Nina and Zoë safely back home – *dear God in heaven, if you are there, let me get them back home*.

I know what I'm going to do after that.

I'm going to kill Holly Bourne.

I am going to fucking *kill* her.

98

Holly was sitting in the rocker beside the white crib in which Zoë was still sleeping, telling Nina about her plans.

'I can't disclose to you the details of the way I intend to handle Nick's case. They're not complete yet – and anyway, it wouldn't be ethical for me to tell you. You understand that, Nina, don't you?'

Nina was standing between the crib and the nursery door. She heard what Holly was saying, but most of her brain was engaged in assessing her chances of escaping, safely, with her baby. She was aware that Holly was confident that she wasn't going to try to make a run for it, not without Zoë. And Holly was closer to the crib than she was.

And she still had the knife.

The knife she had used to kill Teresa.

It lay in her lap. Across the white wool dress, the nanny's defrosted blood staining the fabric a murky rust red.

'Are you sure you wouldn't like that drink now, Nina?'

'Quite sure, thank you,' Nina answered.

'You'll let me know if you change your mind, won't you?'

'I won't change my mind,' Nina said.

Holly looked up at her. 'You know, you're braver than I thought you would be. I mean, I thought that given your history, your alcoholism, you might be a weak sort of a woman. Most drunks are weak, aren't they? But you seem quite strong.'

'I have my moments,' Nina said.

Holly rocked a little, back and forth. The chair made a soft, creaking sound.

'For instance' – she returned to the subject of her plans for defending Nick – 'I haven't quite decided yet if the killing of Miss Vasquez is going to be enough' – she paused – 'or if perhaps it might be better for Nick in the long run if you die, too.'

Nina blinked.

'Just how would that be better for Nick?' she asked.

'Because if he had killed you as well as the nanny, I, as his lawyer, would have a far better chance of winning an insanity plea.'

'I see,' Nina said, numbly.

She wondered if Nick had called home yet, if he'd heard her message, if he was on the way back, how far away he still was.

Too far.

Or not far enough.

Depending on the extent of Holly's madness.

She was having difficulty judging just how insane Holly Bourne was. Some of the time, there was no doubt whatsoever that the other woman was dwelling in a separate, fantasy world of her own making, and she was certainly quite mad enough to have manufactured that world regardless of the cost to anyone else. Poor Teresa, for one. And Phoebe, whose 'accident' had, of course, been intended for herself – and surely that had been *evil*, not just madness? Yet it was also apparent to Nina that some areas of Holly's brain were functioning with more than a degree of precision. She *was* intending to try to use the law to extract Nick from his world and to place him inside her own, at her mercy – and that, of course, was an insane aim in itself, except that Nina was aware that this woman was well-versed in jurisprudence.

Which meant that she had to be fought with the greatest caution and as much respect as Nina could muster.

'Nina, I asked you to sit down,' she heard Holly say.

'I'm fine where I am, thank you.'

'Near the door,' Holly said.

Nina said nothing. Her eyes flicked back and forth from Holly's face to Zoë's peaceful, sleeping form in the crib.

'You know, you really don't have to worry about Nick at all,' Holly told her. 'I'll always be there for him. Whatever happens – whichever way the case goes – I'll visit him every day. I'll go on doing my best for him.'

Best. Nina suppressed the urge to snap back ironically. She had to try to get the crazy lady on side. She and Zoë were hostages now. That was the game hostages had to play, wasn't it?

'Nick knows that.' She knew she was floundering, knew that Holly would see through any limp attempts at siege-mentality psychology. 'He knows that that's all you've wanted – to go on being his friend.'

'Bullcrap,' Holly said, and stroked the knife in her lap.

Nina thought about sitting down after all, but that would mean going further into the room, away from the door, so she remained where she was.

Try another tack.

'He's hurt you badly, hasn't he?' she said, softly.

Holly smiled. 'Oh, yes.'

'I can see that,' Nina said. 'He's hurt me, too.'

'More bullcrap,' Holly said.

'No, it isn't. He's hurt me because he's never been able to forget you.' Nina waited a beat. 'He hurt me so badly I even started drinking again.'

Holly nodded slowly, and the small motion started the rocker creaking again. 'Was that when he left you?'

'Yes,' Nina said. 'Nick's a selfish man. Most men are, don't you think?'

'I wouldn't know,' Holly replied. 'I've only ever cared about one.'

'Nick,' Nina said.

'Nick,' Holly confirmed.

In the crib, Zoë made a small snuffling sound, but went on sleeping.

'He always let you down, didn't he?' Nina said. 'Even years ago.'

'Yes, he did.'

'And yet you were still there for him.'

'Always.'

Not good enough, Nina. Not nearly good enough to get you and Zoë out of here.

'It's not working, is it?' Holly said, reading her mind.

'What isn't?' Nina's heart gave another thump.

'This Stockholm syndrome shit.' Holly smiled again. 'You're a lousy actress, Nina. Your hate is much too visible. It shines out of you.'

'I don't hate you, Holly.'

'Of course you do.' Holly nodded towards the crib. 'You want to be her mother.'

404

'I am her mother,' Nina said, as gently as possible.

'I can understand your concerns,' Holly said. 'But this little girl can only have one mother.'

'I *am* her mother,' Nina said again, less gently.

Oh, God, Nick, where are you?

'Not any more,' Holly said.

Nina's legs were giving way again, the way they had when Holly had shown her the body in the freezer. She longed to sit down, but she knew she couldn't do that, knew she had to stay on her feet.

Try again.

'You know you could still visit Zoë, don't you?' she said. 'You're her father's oldest friend, Holly – you could be Zoë's friend, too.'

'I won't be visiting,' Holly said, peaceably. 'I won't need to visit my own child. The only visiting I'm likely to be doing will be after I get Nick into a secure unit, some place he'll be well cared for. And by that time, of course, no one else will want to know him any more.'

'No one except you,' Nina said, and the sickness was back.

'Exactly.' A small smile crossed Holly's face. 'I told you before. I'll always stand by Nick.'

She picked up the knife and stood up. Freed from her weight, the chair rocked back and forth.

In the crib, Zoë stirred.

Don't wake, my love. Not now.

The rocking ceased.

Holly looked down at the sleeping baby.

'I'll look after our daughter, too,' she said, softly. 'Until he gets out. If he gets out.'

Nina felt a sudden great heat, and recognized it as her rage starting to spiral up and out of control. The nursery was cool enough, but this heat was something strange and different, radiating in waves from somewhere deep inside her.

Holly was bending over the crib now. Leaning over Zoë with the bloody knife in her right hand.

'Hello, my darling,' she was saying.

The heat inside Nina swelled like a living thing, filling up all her internal cavities, a giant puffball ready to explode.

'Get *away* from her.' She hadn't meant to say that, it had just leapt from her mouth like saved up spit.

Nick, where are you? She wants our baby!

Holly was holding the knife in her right hand, and now she was stroking Zoë's red-gold hair with her left.

'Leave her alone,' Nina said, hoarsely, and took a step forward. 'Can't you see she's sleeping?'

'Oh, she's slept enough,' Holly said, still stroking the baby's hair, then tickling her left cheek with her index finger. 'I think I should know when it's time for my baby to wake up, don't you?'

Nina's need, her urge to get to Zoë, to shove Holly away, was almost overpowering, but awareness of the knife kept her still.

Get her away from the crib, Nina. Nothing else matters.

'Zoë isn't your baby, Holly,' she said, suddenly, harshly.

'Oh, yes, she is.' Holly, unperturbed, went on tickling.

Zoë stirred again. Her tiny fists clenched and released.

'Zoë's my baby, Holly.' Nina made her voice louder. '*My* baby.'

Holly looked up, away from the crib.

Yes, that's good. Go on.

'You don't have a baby, Holly.'

Holly straightened up. Her eyes were no longer calm.

That's right, Nina, get her angry. Away from Zoë.

'Zoë's *our* baby. Mine and Nick's.'

'Shut up,' Holly said, and took a step towards Nina.

Nina took two steps back, closer to the door, and Holly followed her. *That's right – get her as far from the crib as you can.*

'I gave birth to her, Holly. Nick made love to me, and I conceived. Zoë came out of my womb, not yours.'

'I told you to shut *up*,' Holly said.

She raised the knife in her hand.

Nina steeled herself to dodge left or right.

And saw Holly turn back to the crib.

And raise the knife over the baby.

'*No!*' Nina screamed, and flung herself at Holly.

'*My* baby,' Holly said, very clearly, just as the weight of Nina's body hit her, triggering the pain in her breast. 'From *my* womb.'

And she swung the hand that held the knife.

Straight into Nina's abdomen.

99

Antonia Street looked normal. Much as it always looked at around eleven-thirty on a Saturday morning.

No patrol cars. No obvious sign of the cops.

Nick took a long look around.

A couple unloading their weekend grocery provisions from the trunk of their Volvo. Nick didn't know them, but they looked familiar enough for him to be pretty confident they were just civilians. *Wait a minute*. There was another guy, middle-aged, wearing a dark tracksuit, walking his schnauzer, and Nick knew for sure he'd never seen him before, except that he and the dog were heading towards Lafayette Park, so surely he couldn't be a cop either?

Nick checked the dashboard clock. He'd made it from the Golden Gate in less than fifteen minutes, and there was surely no way that Norman Capelli could have mounted a major police operation in that kind of time. Which was good, because it meant no one was going to stop him going in to help Nina and Zoë. And even if he was scared – way *beyond* scared – of doing the wrong thing, all he knew for sure was that he couldn't – he could *not* – leave Nina to face Holly on her own for a second longer than he had to.

He took a slow drive past 1317 and their own house.

They, too, both looked normal. Edwardian serenity on a San Francisco hill. Nina's Lexus parked outside their locked garage. The exterior wood on their house, painted pale primrose and white, and in much better shape than its neighbour's. Holly's house. He'd hardly ever bothered looking at it properly since they'd bought 1315. It had looked back then, he could remember Nina saying, as if it needed work, but it hadn't been a falling-down dump, it wasn't going to be a threat to their own place or the value of the street.

Holly's house.

He continued up the hill, parking the Cruiser far enough away to be sure he was out of the eyeline of any of the windows in either house. Glancing in his side mirror, he saw a woman, pushing a stroller, coming his way. He waited until she was right beside the Toyota, then got out, pulled up the collar of his jacket, ducked his chin and walked – close enough for it to seem from a distance as if he was with them – back down towards 1315. Not too fast, not too slow, just a guy out with his wife and kid.

Until he got to his house, where he ducked around the side. And entered through the back door.

He raced through quickly and silently, knowing no one was there, but needing to confirm that the situation was as Nina had indicated on the answering machine.

Nothing. No one.

Everything looked as it had when he'd left early that morning, except for a mess of broken china and what looked like flour on the kitchen floor. Nick stared at it for a moment, wondering if there'd been a struggle in here, but everything else was in place; and it looked as if Nina had maybe been baking, and Nick knew that was what she did sometimes when she was on edge and needed to calm down, or wanted a drink badly and was trying to take her mind off it.

The phone rang.

Nick ran to the living room as the machine picked up.

'Mr Miller, this is Inspector Joseph Naguchi of the San Francisco Police Department. If you're there, please pick up the phone.'

Nick stood very still.

'Mr Miller, it's urgent that I speak with you now. Please pick up the phone.'

Nick made a move towards the phone, then froze again.

If you talk to them, they'll find a way to stop you going in.

'Okay, Mr Miller' – Naguchi's voice was steady – 'if you're there, or if you pick up this message, Inspector Capelli wants you to know that we've listened to the tape, and we're dealing with the situation. I *repeat*, we are dealing with this situation.'

Nick was staying absolutely still, his eyes trained on the machine, as if Naguchi might see or hear him if he moved a muscle.

'Mr Miller, you must not – I *repeat* – you *must not* – take any action by yourself.' The inspector paused. 'Mr Miller, if you are there, please pick up the phone and talk to me. It's in the best interests of your wife and daughter, believe me.'

Another longer pause.

'Okay, Mr Miller, then I'm going to assume you're listening to me. Sir, you have to leave this to us. We know exactly what we're doing – we have experts assessing the situation as we speak—'

Assessing.

Nick stopped listening, started moving, got out of the living room and went back upstairs. In their bedroom (while Naguchi's voice continued its admonitions downstairs via the machine) he moved cautiously to the side window that overlooked Holly's house. There was nothing to see from that angle; the facing windows on all floors were obscured by drapes. He forced himself to stand there for another moment, checking over the general shape of the house, running a mental comparison with 1315. It seemed largely of the same construction. Which meant that the entrances were likely to be in all the same places. Front and back door and garage.

In his and Nina's house, the garage, accessed from the street by a downward-sloping driveway, had another entrance at the side of the building and a third door leading by steps up to the utility room next to the kitchen. If 1317 was built the same way, and if he could get around to the side of that house without being seen, he could maybe break into the garage and make his way up into the house without alerting Holly.

Darkness might have helped, but there were far too many hours of light left to this stinking day. He was fully cognizant that he was probably half out of his mind not waiting for the cops, but Christ only knew what Naguchi's phrase about '*assessing the situation*' meant – and Christ also only knew what was happening – what might *already* have happened – to Nina and Zoë, and maybe Teresa, too, if they were inside 1317 with Holly.

What if you're wrong?

Phoebe and William sprang into his mind, but he pushed them out. No time for that.

He could not waste one more minute.

It was down to him.

All down to him.

He was going in now.

No need to change clothes; he was already wearing jeans, grey sweatshirt and sneakers. Perfect daylight burglarizing outfit courtesy of Levi Strauss, Calvin Klein and Nike. All he needed now was a crowbar from his own garage and the ancient baseball bat that lived in the hall closet.

And the first pure good fortune he'd had in a long while.

100

The side door to Holly's garage was where he had expected it to be, on the far side of her house. The passageway between 1317 and Holly's other next-door-neighbour was very narrow, no more than two feet wide, and having gotten into position by the door, Nick figured he had a fair chance of not being noticed by anyone who wasn't actually looking for him.

He put the bat down on the stone path and set to work with the crowbar, praying that his first ever attempt at breaking and entering would be quiet enough to at least get him past first base, and praying too that neither Holly nor the previous occupants of the house had installed an alarm system.

Apart from cutting the palm of his left hand while levering the door off its hinges, getting in was surprisingly easy. No bells rang, and though the sound of splintering and cracking wood seemed deafening to his own ears and jangling nerves, no one came running.

Nor did anyone see him picking up his baseball bat and slipping through the open doorway.

Into Holly's garage.

Lit dimly by daylight sliding in through a small rectangular window above the up-and-over door, it all looked perfectly ordinary. A workbench and a few tools. A bag of something that might have been cement. Not like his and Nina's garage, which had steadily become jammed (too jammed now for the Lexus) with stuff left over from picture framing and DIY and summer barbecuing.

Nick's hand was bleeding quite fast, but he hardly noticed.

411

The first and only thing he really did notice as he climbed slowly and tentatively up the steps towards what he guessed was Holly's utility room, was that up there in the main part of the house, Frank Sinatra was singing '*All the Way*'.

Holly's old obsessional favourite.

Nick had learned to hate that song over the years, but this time, in spite of the fresh warning prickles it was sending up and down his spine, he was grateful for it too. Because, as he neared the top of the steps, he realized that Holly had turned the volume of her hi-fi system (wherever in the house it was) up high – crazily high – and so maybe she wouldn't hear him coming. Though on the other hand, Nick had a feeling that she was probably just biding her time.

The acid queen, waiting for him to come.

The door at the top of the steps was unlocked. *Take it slow*. His heart pumping, he opened it with great care, ready to strike out with the bat if he had to.

No one. Just some cupboards, a walk-in larder and a bunch of things you'd expect to find in a utility room. A washing machine and a drier and a big chest freezer and an upright vacuum cleaner and a few cardboard boxes from local shops. Just a regular utility room.

Until he passed the open freezer.

And found out more – much more – than he wanted to know about what had become of Teresa Vasquez.

He allowed himself about five seconds to think about blacking out or puking or just plain old-fashioned losing it, and another three seconds to think about hightailing it straight back next door and leaving it to Naguchi and friends.

But then he took a few deep, shuddering breaths, clenched his shaking hands more tightly around the baseball bat, and got himself back under something approaching control, turning his head away from the awful pink frosted thing that had been the face of his daughter's nanny, and pushing himself out of Holly Bourne's utility room and on into her kitchen.

Again, there was no one around, the only signs of life two mugs of tea, looking untouched, on the round white table, and a pair of soaked tea bags in the sink. Nick checked around the room, opening cupboards with a new kind of dread.

Nothing. Thank Christ, nothing.

He opened the door to the hallway even more cautiously. It creaked a little, but Old Blue Eyes was covering it, sliding his long warm notes over every tiny sound Nick made as he crept around the cold, stark first floor of Holly's house, seeing nothing of note except a brown paper package addressed to Barbara Rowe in the entrance hall.

Still no sign of life.

He started up the staircase, the baseball bat clenched in his right fist.

Nothing on the second floor either.

But on the blue carpet in the hallway on the top floor, he saw a trail.

Of blood.

The music grew louder.

The trail led to a door.

His heart was right up in his throat, choking him.

He gripped the bat harder and opened the door.

The trail of blood led to Nina. She was lying hunched on the bare hardwood floor of a cold, empty, unfurnished room. Her eyes were open, staring at him.

Nick thought, for one endless, dying moment, that she was gone.

Her lips moved.

'Nina—' Nick fell on his knees beside her. 'Oh, God, Nina, sweetheart – what did she do to you?'

She gave a moan.

'It's okay – I'm here.'

He tried to take hold of her hands, but she resisted, and then he saw that they were bunched up in fists against her body because she was trying to plug the wound in her abdomen; and there was blood seeping through her knuckles, and he realized that if he took her hands away, the flow might increase.

'Okay, baby, don't move.' He felt like screaming, but his voice sounded almost calm. 'I'm going to get help.'

Sinatra stopped singing, then began again.

'Hold on, baby,' he said, starting to get up.

'No,' she said, very faintly, staring at him fixedly.

'It's all right,' he told her, fighting to keep hold, trying *not* to think about Zoë, knowing he had to focus on Nina first, on saving her life. 'Everything's going to be all right. I'm going to get you some help.'

'No. Wait.' It was hard for her to speak – hard to hear what she was saying.

Nick got closer, put his right ear up against her mouth, and stroked her hair. His hands were shaking violently again.

'What is it, sweetheart? Is it Zoë? Has she hurt Zoë too?' He could smell his wife's blood. He felt murder rising in him.

'Holly has her,' Nina whispered into his ear, weak but frantic.

'Where?' He could feel the veins in his neck standing out, hard as iron. 'Where are they?'

'I don't know. There's a nursery – a bear on the door . . .'

'Okay.' He kissed her hair. 'That's okay. I'll find her.'

'Be careful.' Nina's eyes were filled with pain and terror. 'She has a knife. She killed Teresa.' She swallowed hard. 'She thinks Zoë's her baby. Yours and hers.'

Nick bent his head to kiss her mouth. It was very cold.

'It's all right, Nina,' he whispered. 'It's going to be all right.'

'She's completely mad,' Nina said against his lips.

'I know,' Nick said.

And stood up.

He went into the room with the bear on the door swinging his bat.

The crib was empty.

He went next door.

The room was full of him.

Like a fucking shrine.

Holly was lying on a bed. With Zoë on her stomach.

Holly wore a white bloodstained dress. Zoë was naked.

Holly turned her head and smiled at him. The knife was in her right hand.

'I'm going to kill you,' Nick said. 'You're going to give me my baby, and then I'm going to beat your head in until I know you're dead and gone for ever and ever.'

'Remember the song?' Holly said. 'It was our song,' she said. 'Remember?'

Zoë started to cry.

'Give me my daughter,' Nick said.

Holly held up the knife.

'I don't think so,' she said. 'Not till you've heard me out.'

'I don't have time to hear you out,' Nick said. 'My wife is lying on the floor in the room next door, bleeding to death.'

'Is she still alive?' Mild interest, nothing more.

On her stomach, Zoë kicked her legs, and Holly held her still with her left hand. The baby cried harder.

'Give me the baby, Holly.' Nick still gripped the bat. 'The cops are on their way.'

'No, they're not,' Holly said. 'You wouldn't take the chance of calling them – not while I was alone with your wife and our baby.'

'You're wrong.'

Holly moved Zoë onto the bedspread and sat up.

Nick got ready to swing the bat.

'She's too close, Nick. That's another chance you won't take.'

His trembling was worse than ever. He stared at her.

'Ready to listen to me yet?' Holly asked.

Nick thought about Nina and all the blood in the cold, empty room. There were things of his all over this room. Not just the photographs. Clothes he'd missed, a palette he thought he'd lost. The room even smelled of the Armani cologne Nina had bought him a few months back. It was like a surrealist nightmare.

'Go ahead,' he said.

'Sure?'

'Go *ahead*.'

The song went on and on.

All the way.

'Go *ahead*, Holly.'

'In my own time,' she said.

Zoë was still crying. Her arms and legs were flailing, and she had wet the bedspread, and Nick's whole body ached to grab her, but the knife was less than two inches away from her.

'Why don't I just hold her while you talk?' Nick said.

'No one holds my baby but me,' Holly said, suddenly sharper.

'Okay,' he said. 'Okay.'

'Don't be in such a rush, Nick.'

'My wife is bleeding.' Hate bloomed in his voice.

'It's taken me a long time to get you to listen to me,' Holly said.

'And now you've got me. Captive audience. One night only.'

'Maybe. Maybe not.'

'What do you want, Holly?'

'Put the bat down.'

'No.'

Holly held the knife up, over Zoë's tiny, fragile face.

Nick put down the bat.

'Better,' she said.

He straightened up and waited.

'You're going to need me, Nick,' she said.

'I am?'

'Badly.'

'Enlighten me.'

'When they come for you. When they arrest you for the murders of Teresa Vasquez and your wife.' Holly paused. 'Did you enjoy your ride out to Napa, by the way?'

'Not much.'

'I thought it was fun. And so simple to organize. Just a few calls – I didn't even have to go out there myself – just paid someone to type the note and leave it in the right place – someplace you'd find it, but not *too* easily. Did you think we were up in a balloon?'

'Oh, yes.'

She smiled. 'You never were as clever as I was. My mother always used to ask me, when we were kids, why I liked spending so much time with someone who was so obviously beneath me.'

'Why did you?'

'You know why.' The smile was gone, and she was very serious. 'You were everything to me. You still are.' She paused again. 'Which is why I'm going to be the best lawyer in the world for you. Because I still love you. And because I know you so well. Better than anyone.'

Nick wasn't really listening to her any more. His eyes were on Zoë, who had stopped crying. The sash window in the room was wide open and it was raining again outside and there was a cold wind, and she was too exposed, and it frightened him that she wasn't crying any more – though maybe it was just because she was always

416

such a good, easy baby, and maybe that meant she was still okay now.

Her mother wasn't okay.

Her mother was alone in an empty room, dying.

Holly stood up.

'Here.'

She held out the knife.

'Take it.'

Nick stared at it, thrown.

'Take it, Nick.'

He put out his hand and took it.

'Use it, by all means,' Holly told him.

He eased it into his palm, settled it, got a grip.

'Except, of course,' Holly said, 'then there'll be no one to defend you. No one to believe in you, like I do. Your prints all over your own knife – it is yours, you do realize that, don't you?'

Nick looked down at it.

The Sinatra tape, or CD, or whatever the hell it was, paused between end and restart, and in the brief silence, Nick heard a sound.

An awful sound.

Nina.

Holly smiled.

'I think maybe your wife just died,' she said.

Something snapped.

He dropped the knife and threw himself at her. She fell backwards onto the floor beside the bed.

Memories swam through his mind like wild, black, ugly, dizzying fish. All the things she'd done to him, and to Nina, and to Phoebe, and to Zoë, and to poor, poor Teresa.

No more.

It ends today.

He was on his knees, straddling her, pinning her arms to her body with his legs, and Holly was staring up at him, silent and waiting. He put his hands on both sides of her face and banged her head against the floor – once, *twice* –

She made a strange, gasping sound, and he felt her body arch beneath him.

And realized that she was climaxing.

* * *

417

Shock poleaxed him.

He let go of her head and fell back, winded.

On the bed, Zoë was screaming.

Sinatra was still singing.

Nick was losing his mind.

He didn't hear the feet treading carefully up the staircase.

Didn't register the movement of the police officers in the doorway behind him, or the sound of their voices, or the static of their radios as they assessed the scene and broke silence.

Holly's voice, faint but clear, was the first thing Nick was conscious of hearing.

'Thank God,' she said.

Nick's eyes were fogged up. He blinked, trying to focus.

He saw Holly on the floor. Crawling away from him, clasping her head. 'He's *crazy*,' she was telling someone behind him, and her tone was terrified and convincing. 'He's already killed two other people and he was trying to murder me too—'

'Okay, ma'am, take it easy,' a man said, still from behind Nick.

Nick tried to sit up. The room was spinning.

'My name is Holly Bourne Taylor,' she said, still gasping. 'I'm an attorney.'

And Nick heard another voice.

Another woman.

'My name is Inspector Helen Wilson, SFPD.' Hard-voiced.

He blinked again. There were a bunch of people in the room, some in uniform, some in plainclothes. All cops.

More voices in the hall outside, raised now, and someone was yelling something about paramedics.

Nina.

Nick struggled, made it to his feet. 'My wife.'

'She's okay,' someone else said.

Capelli. Dark and lanky, his eyes concerned, positioned between Nick and the door.

'She's been stabbed,' Nick told him. 'The bitch *stabbed* her.'

Inspector Wilson was talking. Nick looked at her, saw her messy fair hair, saw the cuffs in her left hand, the gun in her right.

'Charlotte Bourne Taylor,' she was saying to Holly, 'I'm arresting you . . .'

Still dazed, Nick looked for Zoë on the bed, but the cover was obscuring her, maybe *suffocating* her—

'Zoë!' he shouted. 'My baby!'

Wilson's eyes – everyone's eyes – flicked away from Holly to Nick's face for a second.

Too long.

Holly was up, too, moving fast, and she had Zoë.

'*No!*'

Capelli grabbed Nick, pinioned him from behind.

'Let me *go*! She's got my *baby*!'

'Take it easy, Miller,' Capelli ordered.

'Someone turn that music off.' Wilson was pointing her gun, two-handed, straight at Holly. Sinatra went on singing. 'I said turn the fucking *music* off!' she snarled.

Capelli was still holding Nick in the doorway.

'For God's sake,' Nick cried out. 'She's got my *baby*!'

Holly was backing away from the cops, away from Nick, holding Zoë tightly in her arms. She'd lost a shoe and her bloodstained white dress had a rip down one side.

'Stay away from me.'

She was moving towards the window – the open window.

Everyone froze.

She got up, backwards, onto the sill. Sat on it.

'All right, Holly,' Wilson said. 'Let's not do anything foolish.'

A man in a blue suit, a balding guy with glasses and a thin, tight mouth, appeared out of nowhere. 'I'm Lieutenant Begdorf, ma'am,' he said, his tone gentle, conciliatory. 'How about we calm things down a little bit here? How about you let me just take the baby while we talk about things for a few minutes?'

'How about you fuck off?' Holly said.

Someone stopped the music.

'Let me talk to her,' Nick said, suddenly.

His own voice startled him. It sounded almost calm. Level.

'That's okay, sir,' Lieutenant Begdorf told him. Polite but firm.

'No, it's not okay,' Nick said.

He felt Capelli increase the pressure on his arms.

'Get Miller out of here,' Wilson told Capelli, no longer prepared to take her eyes off Holly for so much as a millisecond.

'I'm the only one she's going to listen to,' Nick said to Capelli, quietly, insistently. 'It has to be me.'

'Go on, Capelli,' the lieutenant said. 'Take Mr Miller outside.'

Nick wasn't going anywhere. He rooted his feet to the floor, watching Holly's face. 'That's right, isn't it, Holly?' he said, raising his voice. 'It's me you want to talk to, isn't it? It's me you want, period.'

'You can go fuck yourself, too,' Holly replied.

She shifted a little on the sill and kicked off her second shoe. There was a ladder in her left stocking. Zoë wailed more loudly, her cheeks scarlet, tears streaming down her cheeks.

'It's like you said to me,' Nick said, quieter but clear. 'You've always loved me. And you know I've always loved you back.'

'Crap,' Holly said.

'Why do you say that?'

He felt Capelli's grip ease a little. He waited for the lieutenant to intervene, but the balding man stayed silent.

'Because you love Nina.'

Nick glanced sideways, imploring Capelli, who looked at Begdorf for assent. The lieutenant nodded.

Nick moved a few feet back into the room.

'So what's happening here, lieutenant?' Wilson, not taking her eyes off Holly or the baby, asked Begdorf quietly.

'Let Mr Miller talk to her,' the lieutenant told her. 'Back off a little, inspector.'

Wilson backed off two feet.

Nick walked past her, closer to the window.

'Stay where you are, Nick,' Holly said.

'Or what?' Nick asked.

'You know what.' She gripped Zoë more tightly. The little girl, who'd quietened down for a moment, started wailing again and urine ran down her chubby, naked legs.

'You won't hurt the baby,' Nick said as if he meant it. 'Not our baby.'

'I don't want to,' Holly said.

'I know that, Holly.'

He moved another step closer, then stood still.

Zoë stopped wailing again. Her little nose was red and blocked.

Nick could hear her breath, rasping a little. It killed him to hear that and not be able to hold her.

'It's like you said, Holly,' he said, hanging on. 'Like you've always said. I'm here for you. I always will be.'

Suddenly his mind felt crystal clear – he couldn't *believe* how clear it was – every thought and word seeming to flash into place with pinpoint accuracy.

He knew what he was doing now – knew where he was going.

'The way I always was,' he went on, 'when we were kids.'

'Yes, you were, back then.' Reproach in Holly's voice.

'I was, wasn't I? I always took the rap for you, didn't I, Holly? Whatever we did, whenever we got caught. Didn't I always take care of you?'

'Not always, no.' Holly's right hand was squeezing the skin on Zoë's right arm too hard, and the baby was crying again. 'You let me down.' Holly raised her voice over the noise. 'You betrayed me.'

'You mean with Nina?'

'Yes, I mean with Nina,' Holly answered coldly.

'That was my mixed-up period,' Nick said, easily. 'And it lasted a long time, I know it did. But I'm not mixed up any more, Holly.'

'Oh, I think you are,' Holly said.

'No, I'm not.' Nick felt himself starting to lose it for a moment, felt his head swimming again, but then he made himself focus on Zoë again, and the sharpness returned. 'I can see now how much you've been willing to do for me, Holly. All this. All the things you've done, the risks you've taken, everything you've given up. Just for me.' He paused. 'It's made me realize that I married Nina on the rebound.'

'Rebound?' Holly was still cold, still suspicious.

There was the sound of fresh activity in the hall behind them, footsteps tramping up the stairs, new voices, quickly hushed by the people outside. Another set of footsteps. *The paramedics, maybe*, Nick thought, prayed, *taking care of Nina*.

'On the rebound from you, Holly.' He had to fight to regain the thread – he was fighting for Zoë's life now, he was ready to say anything. *Anything*. 'I was so miserable without you when I left Manhattan – all alone in LA, missing you, but not wanting to admit to it to anyone, not even myself – thinking of you back in New York.' He paused. 'You were so brilliant, Holly. I thought you were better

421

off without me. Like your mother was always saying. I always knew I was marrying second-best.' He paused again. 'The same way you probably felt when you married Jack.'

Holly stared at him for a long moment. Zoë quietened again.

Nick looked right back at her. He saw – thought he saw – something new in her eyes, something like hunger.

'It was the same for you, wasn't it?' he asked, softly. Christ, he felt so *sick*. He didn't know how much longer he could keep this up without vomiting.

'Maybe,' Holly said.

He took a breath.

'I love you, Holly. I know that now. I'm always going to love you.'

She looked at him.

'Swear it,' she said.

His bowels turned over.

'I swear it.'

The grey eyes were wide, unyielding. Devouring.

'Swear it on the life of your child,' she said, softly.

God forgive me.

'Our child, you mean,' he said.

Holly's lips smiled.

He felt his gut rising.

'Our child,' Holly repeated.

Nick stepped closer to her. The other people in the room behind him stirred and then became very still.

'Let me take her, Holly,' he said, very gently.

'Our baby,' Holly said, and suddenly her eyes were wet.

'I know she is,' Nick said. 'I know.'

He held out his arms.

Holly looked down at Zoë, then back up at Nick.

'I'm so tired,' she said.

'I know you are, Holly.' He kept his arms out.

'You be careful with her,' she said.

'You know I will be,' he said.

He stopped breathing.

Holly lifted Zoë up a little, and kissed her on her mouth.

Nick felt his blood roaring in his head.

And then Holly held Zoë out.

He took her.

He held his baby – his and Nina's baby – close for one long moment, and then he turned slightly to his left.

'Please,' he said to Helen Wilson, softly. 'Will you take her? I'm afraid I might drop her.'

The inspector glanced at Lieutenant Begdorf, who nodded. Capelli and a uniform raised their guns while Wilson holstered her own and stepped forward to take Zoë.

Nick felt the weight leave his arms.

A little of the tension went out of the air.

There was one more thing he had to do before he could stop.

He knew he had no more than two seconds, tops.

He turned back to Holly. Still sitting on the sill.

He heard and felt them moving behind him, coming closer.

Now he had about a half a second left.

Holly looked him square in the eye.

'That's right,' Nick said, and raised both his arms.

And with every remaining ounce of his strength, he shoved her backwards into the rain.

101

I knew what I was doing.

I told them that right away. Even while all hell was breaking loose.

I remember the shock on Capelli's face.

And on Wilson's.

She'd been the hard case of the duo, but I knew, right there and then, that the shock and compassion in her tough, weathered eyes were for me now. Not for Holly.

Capelli told me that they had gotten into 1317 through the side door that I had been obliging enough to break down for them. And that they had found Teresa's body.

Then Nina.

I don't think Capelli was supposed to be sharing this information with me, but he did it anyway. Nina, he said, had still been conscious and able to tell Wilson that Holly had killed Teresa and stabbed her. A day or so ago, Capelli admitted to me – crazy as it sounds – I might have had a tough time proving that I had not been the one who'd murdered the nanny.

If Nina had died, the way Holly meant her to – *wanted* her to – I guess it is just possible that she might have got her way. I might have been charged with double homicide.

As things stand now, it's just one count of attempted murder.

Holly isn't dead.

102

They cuffed him, Mirandized him, took him downtown, booked him, took away his belt and the laces of his sneakers and put him in a holding cell. Capelli and Wilson, for so long Nick's enemies and now his only friends in the system, talked whoever was in charge of such things into giving him his own cell.

They figured he'd been through enough.

They knew there was more to come.

It was a blur. Fingerprinting and mug shots and ritual humiliations and lousy food and the general stink of the place. Even the naming of his attorney. Chris Field. Young Cold Eyes. What difference?

None of it mattered.

Except that Nina was at People's Hospital – the same hospital that Holly had been taken to – and he wasn't with her. Because of him, Nina was alone again when it really counted. Capelli had got word to him that she was in pretty bad shape, mostly because of blood loss and shock, but that Holly's knife – my knife – had missed all her major vessels and organs, and so the doctors had told him that Nina was going to make it.

He ought to be *with* her.

Instead, he'd let Holly get the better of him again. The way he always had. From the beginning to the end.

Except that even now, she still wasn't gone.

And it still wasn't over.

DECEMBER

103

Holly doesn't know too much about anything.

She knows that Nick tried to kill her.

She knows she's in People's Hospital, wired up to all kinds of monitors in Ward 11B. The arrest ward.

And she knows that, from the waist down, she has no feeling.

So far, there is only one advantage. Some of the other patients are cuffed or chained to their beds. At least no one seems to regard her as an escape risk.

Still, she doesn't think that being paralysed was ever part of the plan.

She can't be entirely sure about that, of course, because she can't seem to remember exactly what the plan was. Oh, she knows about the fundamentals. Loving Nick. Wanting Nick to need her again.

But the specifics seem all wrapped up in a haze.

Quite a comfortable kind of a haze.

There's been no word from Jack, but her parents have been to visit her.

They were very quiet.

Both in shock.

Richard's eyes were red-rimmed, as if he had been crying. Eleanor didn't look as if she had wept, yet Holly sensed that her mother's pain was every bit as great as her father's.

That did surprise her somewhat.

* * *

They haven't spoken more than absolutely necessary about what has happened. They know that she has been charged with the murder of Teresa Vasquez, the attempted murder of Nina Miller, and the kidnapping of Zoë Miller. And that it was Nick Miller who pushed her out of a third-storey window of a house she has been living in, under an assumed name, since October.

They didn't know anything about the house. Or about Barbara Rowe. They didn't even know that she was in San Francisco.

It's been a lot for them to take in.

She feels pity for them both.

Holly doesn't think that Eleanor will ever accept that her daughter is a killer. There's only one person to blame for this whole tragedy in Eleanor's mind, and that is Nick Miller.

Finally, something she and her mother can agree on.

Richard is a different story.

Holly can understand his feelings. He is a lawyer, after all, and a fine one. And he has always loved her. Not in the tight, inexorable way that Eleanor has loved her. Eleanor Bourne's love for her only surviving child has always been a hard, strangely cold, unrealistic thing. Richard's love, much less blinkered than his wife's, has been warm and giving and vulnerable, and now his wounds, his bleeding father's soul, are more visible than Eleanor's. Yet Eleanor, too, is bleeding now, Holly realizes. It's just that when Eleanor's soul is wounded, she conceals the blood, keeps it, together with her older scars, somewhere deep inside.

She had her old dream again last night. More or less the same dream she always has – the one about Eric drowning. Only this time it was a little different.

It started out differently.

They're stealing flowers from a garden – she and Eric – or rather, Holly is stealing the flowers and Eric is telling her to stop. And then a park superintendent – an old man with eyeglasses and a uniform – comes to yell at them, and Eric grabs the flowers from Holly's hands and tells the old man that he's to blame.

Don't blame my little sister.

It wasn't her fault.

It was all my idea.

I'm her big brother.

And then he's back in the pond, drowning again, and Holly's scrambling out of the water onto the bank again, the way she always does.

And then she turns around to look at him.

And suddenly he isn't Eric any more.

He's Nick.

It's Nick who's coming up that one last time.

Looking at her with his own warm brown eyes.

So like Eric's.

Except that Eric's eyes were always kind and sad and patient, and Nick's eyes are angry and hurt.

I won't take the rap for you this time, Holly.

No more big brother, no more friend, no more lover.

You're on your own.

You're the one who's drowning now.

And suddenly Holly is leaning over from the bank, and she's stretching out both her hands, and she's laying them over his dark, wet head, like a priest making a kind of benediction, and then she's pushing him down.

And he goes under again. First his face, then the top of his head, disappearing beneath the surface.

And she hears the sounds again. The way she always does.

The bubbles coming out of his mouth while he's struggling to breathe. The sound the water makes when it closes over his head that final time.

The first clump of earth hitting his coffin.

Only this time she can't hear her father weeping or her mother screaming. There is no one else.

Only her.

Nick, please come back now.

Nick, please don't leave me.

Nick, I need you.

And then the silence.

And the darkness.

Which is when she realizes. There is no one else, because she is the one lying in the coffin.

And Nick is the one burying her.

104

Nick's arraignment had been swiftly over. Chris Field's attempt to win his release without bail had failed, as they had known it would, and bail had been set and met at one hundred thousand dollars bond.

That was the house gone if he skipped town.

Not that he was interested in going anywhere except to the hospital to see Nina and then home to see Zoë.

Nina was out of intensive care and in a private room. She was still weak and in some pain, but improving fast. Her room was filled with flowers, reminding them both a little too vividly of the traumatic days following Zoë's birth, but this time round Phoebe had sent a bunch of brightly coloured balloons, which made it very different.

William was there, too; and Kate and Ethan Miller had flown into San Francisco to take care of Zoë and the house and anything else they needed.

William was treating Nick with unprecedented warmth and courtesy, leaving him alone with Nina whenever they wanted.

'Take all the time you need,' he told Nick in the gentlest of tones.

Strange man. So long as his son-in-law had been more or less innocent of all the accusations being thrown at him, he had treated him like America's Most Wanted. Yet now that he had done his damnedest to actually *kill* a woman, William – not unlike Capelli and Wilson – seemed almost to be Nick's buddy.

'He's proud of you,' Nina explained to Nick. 'He says that you did exactly what he would have done, given the chance.'

'Maybe he's just glad I'm finally going to jail,' Nick said wryly.

'Dad doesn't think you will go to jail.'

'I wish I shared his confidence.'

They were silent for a while. Nina lay very still, watching Nick's face, waiting for him to be ready to talk.

'I went crazy, Nina,' he said, finally. 'I don't mean that I didn't know what I was doing – I knew exactly what I was doing.'

'I know you did,' Nina said softly.

'But I didn't stop to think.'

'You never do.' There was no real reproach in either Nina's voice or expression. Just a degree of sadness.

'I let you down again,' Nick said. 'You and Zoë.'

'No, you didn't.'

'Of course I did.' Nick looked at her pale face. 'I was so afraid when I called Capelli that I was doing the wrong thing – that Holly might stick to her threat, and—'

'You were right to call him,' Nina told him.

'The cops didn't want me to go in after you,' he went on, 'and a part of me knew they might be right – that I might make things even worse – but all I knew was that I couldn't leave you and Zoë alone with her for one minute longer.'

'I knew you'd come.'

'Did you?'

'I never doubted it for a single instant.'

The door opened and a nurse came in to take Nina's temperature and blood pressure and to check her IV line. She was young and pretty, and she regarded Nick with barely disguised fascination.

'Think she knows I'm fresh out of jail?' he said after she had left the room.

'Probably.'

They were silent again. Nina closed her eyes.

'You okay?' Nick asked her softly.

'Uh-huh.' She opened them.

'What's going to happen to us if I do go to jail?'

'Nothing will happen to us,' Nina answered.

'Zoë won't know me.'

'Yes, she will.' Nina shut her eyes again.

'Holly's paralysed,' Nick said.

'I know.' Nina kept her eyes closed.

'How does that make you feel?' he asked. 'About me?'

She opened her eyes, tilted her head a little and looked at him.

433

'How does it make *you* feel? About her?'

Nick took another moment.

'I wanted her to die,' he answered, simply. 'I wanted to kill her.'

'Do you feel pity for her now?' The question was loaded.

Nick held more tightly to his wife's hand.

'She stuck a knife in your stomach, Nina.' He knew he was gripping her a little too hard, but he couldn't seem to let go. 'She knifed a woman through the eye and put her in a freezer.' He was having trouble breathing. 'She kidnapped Zoë. She put our baby's life in danger.'

'Nick,' Nina said, gently.

'And then she *kissed* her' – he was shaking again – 'right on that innocent, tiny mouth. And I just couldn't take any more.'

'It's all right, Nick.' Nina lifted his hand, still clasped to her own, to her cheek and held it there. 'It's going to be all right.'

'No, it isn't,' he said.

'Yes, it is.'

'No, it *isn't*.'

His vehemence shocked her.

'Why not?'

'Because Holly's still alive,' he said.

105

'He's out on bail,' Eleanor tells Holly. 'It's unbelievable.'

'Not really,' Richard says, calmly.

Eleanor, outraged, would like to raise her voice – but just having to *be* in the same place as thieves and prostitutes and drug addicts and Lord knows what else is terrible enough, without having them all know her family's private business.

'How can you *say* that?' she hisses at her husband. 'After what he's done to your own daughter?'

'I'm only saying that I expected him to be released.'

Eleanor's eyes are gimlet-hard and full of hate. 'He pushed our child out of a window, Richard. Or have you forgotten that tiny detail?'

Holly has been regarding them, on either side of her hospital bed, fighting over her.

'I was going to defend him,' she says suddenly, quietly.

Dumbfounded, her parents stare at her.

'I was going to be his lawyer,' she goes on.

'What are you talking about, darling?' Eleanor asks her.

'It's quite simple, really,' Holly says. 'If they had charged him with killing his wife and the nanny, I was going to take his case.' She pauses. 'That was my plan.'

She started remembering that plan about thirty-six hours ago. Not everything about it, but enough.

She watches their faces now for several seconds.

'I'm not delirious,' she assures them. 'It might have worked out.'

'Oh, dear God,' Richard says softly, and covers his eyes.

Eleanor, her face frozen, is beyond words.

* * *

Holly began planning again at around four o'clock the previous morning.

She hardly sleeps in this place. There's too much going on. Too many sounds. Patients – prisoners – *like her* – coughing, vomiting, moaning. Nurses moving back and forth. Police guards running checks on the inmates. No privacy. Too much time for panic to slither into one's brain and get a grip.

Thinking helps. Planning.

That's another thing Holly has remembered, lying here.

She is nothing without a plan.

She has known for almost forty-eight hours now that her paralysis – the awful, terrifying, imprisoning deadness – was not going to be with her for much longer. The awakening began with some vague, prickling sensations in her toes; then later, over the course of several hours, she started feeling life – something like insects, at first, crawling, stinging a little, but growing warmer and more tangible as time passed – creeping slowly back into her legs and lower back.

She almost gave herself away when a doctor came and ran a pin test on the soles of her feet earlier today. Lord, it was so hard not to shout with triumph and almost *impossible* not to wriggle at the very least, but she did manage to control her reactions. Holly has always had magnificent self-control when required. The doctor watched her face as he tickled her feet, looked right into her eyes, almost as if he were challenging her, but she maintained the expression she thought she had probably displayed since they'd first brought her here. Terror, defiance and depression, all rolled into one. She knew she had him fooled. The same man had told her, before a previous examination, that with this kind of spinal contusion a full recovery was not too much to hope for, and it was quite possible that she would regain some, if not all, sensation and mobility in time.

'Nothing,' she told him, flatly, after the test.

And the doctor nodded, patted her hand and went away.

'No change?' Richard asked when he and Eleanor first arrived, soon after.

Holly saw the hope in their eyes, and considered, for just an instant, giving them some good news. But then she decided against. Time enough for good news later. In the meantime, while she's contemplating her new plan, she intends to go on acting. She's been a damned fine actress for most of her life, after all. Time now to give one of her very best performances.

Oscar time.

106

I brought Nina home two days ago.

William, the most all-round relieved father in the United States, has gone back to Arizona to start making arrangements to bring Phoebe back from the Waterson Clinic. Ethan and Kate wanted to stay, but I have to confess I want my wife and daughter to myself for a while.

Normality. At least until we find out if I'm going to be facing trial or not. Chris Field's opinion is that the DA's office will know they're likely to be hard-pressed to persuade a jury of my peers to send me to jail for shoving a monster: the monster who'd slain a harmless nanny, stabbed my wife, kidnapped and threatened my baby and gravely wounded my sister-in-law into the bargain. Even if I did shove her clean out of a third-floor window.

Personally, I think Field is a little disappointed.

Nina says I've never been fair on him.

I did a lot of shopping while Nina was still in the hospital and Kate and Ethan were still here to keep an eye on Zoë and the house. Ordinary stuff. Groceries packed full of goodies. An early Christmas tree. Gifts for everyone. Toys for the baby. We're planning a major family holiday at our place this year.

I bought fresh canvases and paints and brushes and charcoal and sketchpads and turpentine and linseed oil and palette knives, and I bought all kinds of cleaning stuff, too. I was having trouble forgetting that, if that room next door filled with my belongings was anything to judge by, Holly must have been roaming around inside our

438

house for the past month or two. That presumably (if we could presume anything much in these bizarre circumstances) Teresa had gotten to know Holly – or Barbara Rowe – rather better than she'd indicated to Nina; that maybe she had invited Holly in on more than one occasion. Poor Teresa. Anyway, I was determined to scrub the house – *our* house – from roof to crawlspace before Nina got home. To expunge Holly.

Richard Bourne came to visit Nina one afternoon last week. He didn't say much. There wasn't much he could say, poor man. Nina and I both feel for him.

Eleanor did not come.

Big surprise.

I've almost stopped wishing that Holly had died.

Capelli tells me that she's still in a locked ward at People's Hospital, still paralysed and facing enough charges to keep her locked up, either in jail or in some institution for the criminally insane, for the rest of her natural life.

It would probably have been better for her if she had died.

If I ever start feeling pity for her, remind me, please.

Just remind me.

107

Holly is going for another MRI scan. It was scheduled for this after-noon, but the department was backed up with too many patients waiting, and so the orderlies who brought her down were asked to take her back to the arrest ward until further notice.

They've come back for her now, at a little after nine PM – later than usual for tests or treatments. Two young men – one black, bespectacled and round-faced, the other white with a sallow, freckled complexion – with gurney and grins at the ready. Holly has observed other patients from her ward being taken out for tests or examina-tions; has noted, when the patient is considered dangerous, an almost tangible rise of tension, like a small vapour cloud hovering over the group as they go on their way. No one has been exactly mollycod-dling her here (she is, after all, a murderous, kidnapping psycho), but neither have they treated her with quite that level of distrust, partly perhaps because they think she's already paying a price for what she's done. Mostly, of course, because they consider her more or less harmless, being dead from the waist down.

Leaving Ward 11B for any reason has felt refreshing to Holly every time they've taken her for X-rays or CT scans or for her first MRI. They might be medical endurance tests to other people; to Holly they've been like trips to the beach, mini-escapes from jail.

As she and the two orderlies start out on this particular journey to the MRI department, Holly feels no differently about it than she has about any of the others. It has nothing to do with her new plan. Not when they leave the ward, not when they wheel her into the big ele-vator and start down. Not when they emerge into the corridor and trundle her gurney towards the unit.

Not when they push her through the doors into the MRI room itself. Not even when she sees how quiet it is.

Not until she sees the operator.

She is white, with dark hair and a slim build. Not unlike Holly's. She's wearing a white coat with ID tag – her name is Dr K.D. Vivian – and glasses and white hospital shoes. There is no one else around. No one at all. Earlier in the day, when they were sent away, the department was a mob scene.

Holly looks at K.D. Vivian, then turns her head and looks around the room. And knows what she is going to do.

If the orderlies leave them alone.

They transfer her, gently and carefully, to the table which will, in a while, slide her inside the MRI tube.

'Okay, guys,' the doctor says. 'We'll be about forty-five minutes.'

Silently, Holly blesses her.

'We're supposed to wait, Doc,' the black orderly says.

Fuck him.

'We can manage just fine without you, Lewis,' the doctor says.

Amen.

'I promise not to take a powder.' Holly speaks softly. Vulnerable.

The freckled orderly grins down at her.

K.D. Vivian is checking over some papers. 'Don't you like coffee breaks?' she asks lightly. 'Come on, guys, you know I hate people standing over me while I work.'

The black orderly shrugs. 'Okay, doc. Forty-five, you said?'

'Give or take,' the doctor answers.

The men leave the room.

'That's got rid of them,' Dr Vivian says crisply.

Hallelujah.

The other woman busies herself, asking Holly questions as she works. Her manner is pleasant but efficient. Impersonal. Holly answers each question appropriately, but she is only half listening. Her mind is already rising off the table, calculating her next move. She knows she's only going to get one chance. She has a tremendous urge to move her legs, to make quite certain they won't let her down when the moment comes,

441

but there's no way she can risk it. And she has been flexing her feet, toes, knees and muscles under the bedcovers for most of the past few nights. She knows they work.

They're going to have to.

'Now you've had one of these before, so you know the score.'

'Yes, ma'am.'

Holly has never said that in her life before, but it just seemed the right thing to say.

'Any problems? No claustrophobia?'

'Not really.'

'Good.'

'I think it might have bothered me in the past,' Holly says, 'but not now.' She pauses. 'Every minute of every day seems claustrophobic to me now.'

'You'll make it,' the doctor says.

A scrap of sympathy but not much. Holly thinks, in fairness to K.D. Vivian, that she probably treats all her patients the same way, even those *not* charged with homicide.

Everything is about set.

'Remember, Charlotte' –

(*Charlotte, not Taylor, which is what most people have called her since she became a prisoner*)

– 'the most important thing is for you to keep perfectly still. Okay?'

'Okay.'

'Other than that, there's nothing to it. All right?'

'Yes, ma'am.'

Holly's eyes are checking around the room, her ears listening for the slightest indication that anyone else is coming.

Nothing. No one.

'If you have any kind of a problem – if you feel like you want to move, try and focus on something else, something you enjoy doing.'

'Skiing,' Holly says.

'You like skiing?'

'I love it. Used to love it.'

Holly has never skied in her life.

'That's good,' the doctor says. 'You just picture yourself skiing on some snowy mountain and we'll be finished in no time.'

She moves away for several moments, checking equipment.

'We're all set,' she says, finally. 'Any questions?'

'No,' Holly says.

'Okay. I'm going to move you into the bore now.'

The doctor moves away out of the room, into the area from which she will view the images. Holly lies very still. Her blood feels as if it's rushing too fast through her veins. She feels immeasurably excited.

She waits another half second.

With a small jolt and a whirring sound, the table begins to move.

'Wait,' she says.

The movement stops.

'Problem, Charlotte?' Dr Vivian asks from the other side of the window.

'I'm not comfortable. Something's digging into me.'

'Really?' The doctor comes back into the room. 'Where?'

'Under my back.' Holly gestures with her right arm.

Dr Vivian frowns. 'Shouldn't be anything there.'

'I'm sorry to be a nuisance.' Apologetic.

'Don't worry about it.' She's on her way around the table to take a look. 'Might as well start out comfortable.'

'That's what I figured.'

Get ready.

The doctor bends over, runs a hand under Holly's back.

'Can't feel anything. Can you show me?'

I sure can.

'It's a bit higher,' Holly says. 'I'm really sorry.'

'That's okay. Let's take a better look.'

She moves up further along the table and bends over again.

With all the speed and force she can muster, Holly head-butts her, whacking hard into K.D. Vivian's forehead and nose. The doctor stumbles backwards, hits a trolley and falls, eyes rolling, nose bleeding profusely.

Holly gets off the table. Her legs feel weak, but they're working.

The woman is stunned, maybe unconscious, maybe not, but Holly only knows that she needs her dead to the world for the longest possible time. There isn't too much to choose from, but Holly selected her weapon several minutes ago, while poor bleeding doc there was still running her prelaunch checks: a heavy-looking sticky-tape dispenser on the desk against the far wall beneath a window.

Holly walks across, checks through the window, draws the blind so that no one will be able to see in if they enter the room on the other side of the glass, and picks up the black dispenser – it's heavy, weighted with sand by the sound of it as she turns it in her hand. She stands very still for another moment. Still nothing. No one. Her luck is holding. She comes back across, crouches down and turns the doctor over.

She groans and stirs a little.

Holly hits her on the soft part of the back of her head with the dispenser. K.D. Vivian stops moving. Holly checks the hard black plastic part of the tape dispenser, the part that struck the woman's head. There's no blood.

She hits her again.

Now there is blood.

Now she can be pretty sure that Doc Vivian isn't going to move for a good long while. If ever.

She glances over at the door and sees that there's a lock with a key. She goes across and turns the key. Her legs still feel damned weak, but they're holding up well enough.

Holly gets to work stripping the clothes off the woman on the floor. It isn't easy undressing a deeply unconscious, maybe dead person, but at least she isn't going to have to go as far as the bra and panties stage. All she wants is the skirt, sweater, white coat and hospital shoes, and her glasses – provided they aren't so strong a prescription that Holly can't see through them. She puts them on, experimentally. A little blurry, but good enough. She continues with her task.

The sweater is snug, the skirt loose and longer than Holly would have chosen, but the white coat covers pretty much everything, and the shoes, thank God, are almost exactly her size. Holly would suffer the pantyhose if she thought she had to, but there's no real need, so instead she rolls them up, opens the other woman's mouth and stuffs them in. Just in case K.D. turns Lazarus and starts yelling.

There's a mirror over the hand basin on the wall opposite the window. Holly takes a look. Her hair's a mess, and there are three spots of blood near the collar of the coat that she didn't notice before she put it on. She checks over the room again. An old-fashioned typewriter stands on the desk beside the computer, a small bottle of white-out to its right. Holly grabs the bottle, shakes it and paints over the blood.

Good enough.

All too aware that the clock is ticking, that the two orderlies are due back in twenty to thirty minutes and may (if Lewis-the-conscience has anything to do with it) arrive early, Holly finds the doctor's purse and inside it a small hairbrush. Less than ninety seconds later, she's ready to face the world as just one more white coat.

Now for her patient.

The toughest part is getting her up on the table, but at least she's had practice with Vasquez; and when you've found the right way to pack a fully-dressed woman into a chest freezer, hauling a body in a hospital gown up off the floor onto a flat surface is a mere bagatelle.

Not so much a bagatelle, more like a fucking full-size pinball machine.

Still, she does it.

And still no one comes.

The phone on the desk starts ringing as Holly is straightening the doctor's bare legs and checking to make sure there's nothing she's forgotten.

She freezes for a long moment. The ringing stops.

Okay.

MRI time.

She goes behind the window, finds the switch and watches the table glide into what the woman called the bore. Now there are only two ways to see who's lying inside the imager. Through the hole at the end (and though Holly has always been quite proud of her feet, she supposes that to the average eye, one set of a woman's soles and toes looks much the same as another) and via the scanning screen.

'*Remember, Charlotte,*' K.D. Vivian said to her, '*the most important thing is for you to keep perfectly still.*'

This is one patient who sure as hell isn't going to move.

Holly hasn't been woman-handling her for the last several minutes without knowing that, even if she did not manage to finish Nina Miller, she now has two homicides to her name.

Her father's face flies briefly into her mind, and she banishes it.

She considers, just as fleetingly, removing the tights from the doc's mouth, but knows that she can't spare the time.

'*The dead don't die,*' D.H. Lawrence once wrote in a letter. '*They look on and help.*'

This dead woman started out the evening trying to help her. At least she's carrying on in the same spirit.

A grim and tasteless parody of a commonly-used proverb slips past Holly's brain as she takes the doctor's purse, leaves the MRI room, locks the door behind her and drops the key into the pocket of her white coat.

In for a corpse, in for a fucking morgue.

A good enough epitaph for a fledgling serial killer.

108

When the call came, just after ten-forty that night, the Miller family were all in bed. Nina had been tiring earlier than usual since getting home from the hospital; and whereas in the past, if his wife had been ready to hit the hay before him, Nick might have considered putting in an hour's work in his studio, these days there was no place he'd rather be at almost any hour than snuggled up under the covers with Nina.

He was lying on his back in a semi-doze, thinking about the painting he'd begun work on yesterday (of Nina and Zoë playing on the living room floor), and Nina's head was resting, heavy but welcome, on the soft spot between his left shoulder and his chest, when the phone rang.

Shrill and ugly.

He reached out too fast and knocked the receiver off its cradle. Nina gave a soft groan while he fumbled in the dark.

'Sorry, baby.'

He got hold of the dangling cord and pulled the receiver to his ear.

And listened to the police officer telling him the unthinkable.

Nina heard only his side of the conversation, but it was more than enough. She flicked the switch on her bedside light exactly as he ended the call.

'What's happened to Holly?' she asked, quietly.

'They let her out,' he answered, getting out of bed.

It was cold in the room. Nick, almost too angry to speak, opened the bathroom door and took down his robe from the hook.

'What do you mean, they let her out?' Nina was staring at him from the bed. In the space of those few moments, all the peace that had softened her face during the past days was gone. Her mouth and jaw were taut again, her eyes wary.

447

Nick came back to sit on her side of the bed and took her hand.

'You're shaking,' Nina said.

'They let her escape.' He shook his head violently. 'And don't ask me how that could happen, because I don't *know*, because they wouldn't *tell* me.'

'But they said she was in a locked ward,' Nina said, bewildered. 'They said she was paralysed.'

'She must have been faking – she must have been goddamned *faking*!' He shook his head again. 'How could they fall for that? I can't believe they could fall for that!'

'Not necessarily,' Nina said. 'Someone might have helped her.'

'Jesus.' It was almost a yell. '*Jesus!*'

Nina gripped his hand. 'Take it easy, darling.'

'How can I take it easy?' He took away his hand and stood up.

'We don't want Zoë to wake up.'

He looked down, saw how pale she was. 'You're right. I'm sorry.' He fought to cool down and take stock. 'The officer on the phone said he didn't know what happened – for all they know, she may still be inside the hospital, or maybe Richard and Eleanor are trying to fly her out of the country.'

'Or maybe she's on her way back here.' Nina was still quiet.

'He said they've put out an APB.' Nick was starting to get his shock under control. 'And they're sending a car to check next door and keep a watch on the street.'

He started towards the door.

'Where are you going?'

'To check on Zoë.'

Nina pushed back the bedclothes. 'I can do that.'

'Uh-uh.' He grabbed the quilt and laid it back over her. 'You need your rest.'

'You think I could sleep now?' She pushed the covers back again. 'I think I might make some tea.'

'I can do that.' Nick headed to the door. 'You just stay put, and I'll bring us both up a cup.'

'I don't want to stay put,' Nina said.

Nick opened the door.

They both smelled the smoke at the same instant, as the detectors in the hallways began to shriek.

* * *

'Zoë!' Nina was up and flying across the room.

'I'll get her.' Nick's mind raced. 'You wet some towels in case we need them getting out.'

The smoke was drifting up from below. He ran next door into the nursery and grabbed the sleeping baby unceremoniously from her crib. She woke, clenched roughly to her father's chest, and began to cry.

'Sorry, angel, we have to get you out of here.'

Nina came out into the hallway wearing a terry robe and clutching towels. 'I wet a face cloth for Zoë – is she okay?'

'Fine. Come on.'

'We don't have shoes.' Nina stared at his bare feet. 'Shouldn't we have shoes?'

'No time. Come on.' He held Zoë even more tightly to his chest and started down the staircase. 'Stay close behind me.'

'Where is the fire?' Nina sounded as scared as she felt.

'I don't know.' They were halfway down. 'We're going to get out first and then worry about where it is, okay?'

'Fine by me.'

Smoke was sliding out into the hall from under the kitchen door. Nick took a towel for himself and carefully placed the small cloth over Zoë's nose and mouth, then handed the baby to Nina. 'The front door's clear,' he told her. 'You take her out.'

'What about you?' Nina took the baby and started coughing.

'Get her out – I'll be right behind you.'

Nina got to the front door and opened it. A breeze blew in and fanned the smoke around the hall. She stepped out into the cold night air, took a deep breath and removed the flannel from Zoë's nose. The baby sneezed, then went right on crying.

'Is she okay?' Nick had to shout over the piercing noise of the smoke alarms as he felt first the living room and then the dining room doors, checking for heat inside those rooms.

'What are you doing?' Nina called from outside. 'Get out here!'

'Nina, go get help – get Zoë to a neighbour's and call 911.'

'I'm not going anywhere without you,' Nina protested. 'Get out here with us!'

'I'm pretty sure it's in the kitchen,' Nick shouted back. 'If it's a small one, I'm going to try to put it out – now go call the fire department!'

'Nick, please, just leave it!' In her arms the baby began screaming.

'Will you get our daughter somewhere safe and warm,' he yelled, starting to cough as the smoke hit his throat. 'And for God's sake get some *help*!'

Across the street a front door opened and Joe Tanakawa – a man Nina and Nick had met just a handful of times – came running over. 'My wife's called 911.' He came up the front steps, panting. 'What's happening? Are you guys okay?'

'Nick thinks it's in the kitchen.' Clasping Zoë close, Nina stared back into the house, but Nick had disappeared from sight. 'He's trying to put it out.'

Tanakawa was wearing a heavy sweater, jeans and sneakers. He looked at Nina's robe and bare feet. 'You must bring the little one over to our place.'

'I can't see him.' Nina held the baby out. 'Will you take her, please? Get her safely inside.'

'You have to come over with her,' Tanakawa said.

'I have to go find Nick.'

She tried to push Zoë into his arms, but the man resisted and took a step back. 'No way,' he insisted. 'Your baby needs her mother, not a stranger. I'm sure your husband will be right out.'

'Oh, my God.' Nina turned back to the doorway as realization hit her. 'It's Holly!' she yelled into the house. 'Nick, it has to be Holly – you have to get *out* of there!'

'Nina, come away.' Tanakawa grabbed both her arms, careful of the baby. 'Come on, you can't go in there.' He pulled her back out onto the steps.

'But I can't see him!' Nina started crying. 'I can't *see* him!'

The kitchen was hot and filled with acrid smoke, but Nick couldn't seem to locate the source of the fire. He moved further in, fastening the wet towel over his face with his left hand, trying to stay low. If the blaze wasn't rooted in the kitchen, then the next most likely place had to be the utility room.

He went through the door carefully, but nothing appeared to be burning in there either.

And then he saw the glow coming from under the door leading down to the garage.

450

He knew, even before he had it open, that Holly was in there. Waiting for him.

He kicked the door open with his bare right foot, and moved carefully down the steps.

She was there, standing in a clear space in the centre of the floor, a small figure framed by fire and smoke.

'I've been waiting for you,' she said, raising her voice to be heard over the sound of the flames. She was wearing weird clothes: a skirt too big for her, a black sweater too small, and white hospital shoes.

The middle section of the garage was clear of the fire, which was snaking around the walls and through the hoard of left-over stuff, tongues of orange, yellow and pure white flames gobbling up wood and paper and plastic and cardboard, licking right up to the ceiling, snapping out cables, sending white flares across the closed up-and-over door.

Nick knew that the door was double locked.

He stared at Holly through the smoke.

'Let's get out of here,' he said, and put the damp towel to his face.

'I don't think so,' she said.

He moved the towel so he could speak. 'The fire department are on their way, and the cops.'

'I'm sure they are.'

She was holding something. A big can with a handle and spout. He recognized it. Barbecue lighter fuel. His mind flashed back to two summers before – Nina telling him to throw it out because it was dangerous. But for some reason (*too lazy, too busy doing other things*) the can had stayed here in their garage along with all the other useless junk.

And now Holly was holding it in her hands like a lethal weapon.

Nick could smell the fuel burning, and knew she had probably poured it around the garage and then dropped a match.

'Why don't you put that down, Holly,' he said, 'and come outside with me?'

'I don't think so,' she said again.

'They told us you were paralysed,' Nick said.

'I got over it.' Her voice was husky and thinner from smoke inhalation, but otherwise she showed no obvious signs of physical

451

distress. 'Go ahead,' she said, 'tell me how happy you are about that. How happy you are for me that I can still walk. That I didn't die. Go on.'

'Let's get out of here, Holly, then I'll tell you I'm glad.'

'Sure you're glad, Nick. That must be why you pushed me out of a third-floor window. Because you wanted me to get up and walk away.'

'I was mad at you.' Nick started coughing and tried to breathe through the towel, but it was already dried through and almost useless.

'Yes, you were,' Holly agreed.

Nick went on coughing. He felt pressure in his chest, felt the soles of his feet getting warm, and took a wild look around. The concrete floor was clear of junk for a yard or so around them, and no fuel appeared to have splashed on it, so he hoped – *prayed* – they were safe enough for at least a few more moments; but the cracked rectangular window pane above the main door that was probably allowing in enough oxygen for them to stay conscious, was also fanning the flames.

He twisted around, could feel the heat growing more intense behind him, knew the fire had to be spreading into the house, knew he wasn't going to be able to back out the way he'd come in.

The side door.

He stared at it through the smoke. Its frame was already burning, the handle probably too hot to touch, but it looked exactly like the one next door that he'd broken through a week or so – a *lifetime* – ago, and maybe he could kick it down, or maybe if he just ran hard enough at it—

He heard sirens and thanked God.

'They're here,' he said. 'They've come to help us, Holly. Let's get out of here and save them the trouble of coming in and getting us.'

'You never did love me,' she said, suddenly, bizarrely.

'Come on, Holly,' he urged, like a football coach, trying to ignore the crazy switch. 'Let's do this outside.'

'You remember I told you about Eric, my brother?' she said, switching again.

Nick heard more sirens and horns, and imagined the street filling with fire engines and police vehicles, imagined Nina going out of her mind, the way he had when she'd been next door with Holly.

'Come *on*, Holly,' he said, 'it's time to go.'

She didn't move.

'It was my fault he drowned, you know,' she said, her voice growing hoarser, and for the first time since Nick had found her, she began to cough. 'Remember how I told you he jumped in the pond and I tried to save him?' Her eyes were red and watering. 'That was what I told everyone, but it wasn't true.'

The smoke was thickening, the temperature rising. Nick took another frantic look at the door behind Holly. It came to him that he could probably rush her or push her out of his way and escape without her, but as swiftly as the thought had come, he knew he wouldn't do that – not to her, not to himself. However much he had wanted her dead when he'd shoved her out of that window, however passionately he had wished her gone since then, that rage – the sheer, blinding *madness* that had driven him that day – was gone now.

She's the mad one, the killer – not you – you're not like her.

'I still dream about it,' she was saying, calmly, absently, like someone talking to their analyst in the safety of an office, not like a woman standing in the middle of an inferno she'd created. 'In the dream, Eric always tells me to lie, says I should say it was his fault – that was what we always did, you see.'

'Holly, let's *go*.'

Nick's voice was cracking, his throat felt like sandpaper. He thought one more time about rushing her, maybe trying to drag her out, but the can looked heavy enough to have too much fuel left in it, and if the fire caught that, it would probably go off like a bomb.

'Holly, we have to get out of here *now*!'

'I was always getting in trouble' – still remote, still detached – 'and Eric always defended me, always took the blame for everything. Until he went away.' Suddenly she was focusing again, coming back. 'I thought you'd come to take over from him, Nick – that you were always going to be there for me, the way he was.' Harsh again now, accusing. 'You made me believe that, Nick. You *conned* me—'

More sirens and horns and voices yelling.

'All in the past, Holly,' Nick told her, as forcefully as his parched throat and struggling lungs would allow. 'This is here and now, and we're both going to get out of here before it's too late.'

He began coughing again, tried holding the towel over his nose and mouth again, but it only made it worse, made him choke, so he threw it away, over to his right, where he heard, rather than saw, it being swallowed up by flames.

'It's already too late,' Holly said, lifting the can of fuel in both hands.

Nick took a step back.

She smiled. 'Scared?' She jerked the can, smiled again as he flinched. And then she raised it higher in a long, slow, smooth movement. Even in the ill-fitting clothes and shoes, Holly looked very graceful, almost as if she were dancing.

Nick thought he knew what she was going to do.

'Holly,' he said, uncertainly, 'put it down.'

'Too late,' she said again, and, with the spout right over her head, she closed her eyes, tipped the can and poured.

'*Holly!*' Nick said again, hoarsely. 'Jesus, Holly!'

He took a step towards her, then stopped, remembering what would happen if he got fuel on himself, remembering that he had a wife and child outside, out in the real world, the *sane* world, and he wanted to see them again, he wanted to live—

'End-game, Nick,' Holly said, opening her mad, inflamed eyes again. She let the can fall to the ground, and a few last drops rolled out of the spout and lay near her feet, round, glistening, reflecting fire. 'End-game for us both.'

Nick smelled the fuel soaking her hair and clothes and skin, and now he knew *exactly* what she was going to do.

'Holly, please,' he said, 'this is crazy. You don't want to do this.'

'That's just it, though,' she said, challenging him. She coughed again, then controlled herself. 'Who's going to know it *was* me who did it? This is the game where you get to try and prove it wasn't you who set fire to me.' She took one step back, closer to the flames behind her.

'Holly, *stop* it!'

'The police saw you push me out of the window, Nick,' she went on, 'and you didn't *need* to come in here after me tonight, so why wouldn't they think you were glad of the chance to finish what you started?'

'Jesus, Holly, don't *do* this –' His voice was almost gone.

'I would have done anything for you, Nick. You know that, don't you?' She shook her dark head and coughed again, and her voice was beginning to rasp. 'But not any more. No more. Now you can go straight to hell for all I care – fast or slow, it makes no difference to me.'

A loud, booming sound made them both jump, and the big up-and-over door vibrated and shook violently as the firemen outside began breaking it down. The central lock on the door smashed and flew into the air and fell to the ground, its metallic clatter almost inaudible beneath the roar of the flames and the firemen's battering ram.

The door began to move. Up and over.

A gust of early December wind fanned the flames.

Holly just stood there, not moving.

'Get out of the way!' Nick yelled a warning.

Still she didn't move, but a strange look flew across her eyes, and Nick had the sense that suddenly she might be less sure about what she was doing – that maybe she was *not*, after all, entirely ready to die—

'Holly,' he yelled, one last time, 'get out of the *way*!'

The look went away.

She held out her right hand to Nick.

'Come with me,' she said, quite calmly.

It happened before the firemen's hoses could reach her, fast as a lightning strike on a stifling August night. The wind blew the flames straight on to her fuel-soaked body, and the fire enveloped her like a blazing, roaring cloak, hooding her head with a swirling white-hot aura, whipping through her dark, blowing hair, melting her clothes, torching her eyebrows and lashes into tiny lines of miniaturized, sparking flames, devouring her cheeks and invading her open, silently screaming mouth.

Nick did nothing.

There was nothing to *be* done.

It was too late. It was already over.

Holly had just finished telling him to go to hell.

But she was already there.

109

They buried Holly last week.

In three days' time it'll be Christmas. Her twenty-eighth birthday.

For us it will be more or less the way we planned it. A family holiday. Zoë's first Christmas.

Phoebe is staying with us. She's in great shape. We've all been eating a lot of junk food since she arrived. The kitchen's still being fixed up, but even if it was fit for use, no one but me feels like cooking, and however much I nag the women to eat more healthily, Nina's hunger pangs are currently pitching towards hot dogs, sandwiches and burritos, and Phoebe – for whom knives and forks still represent almost impossibly hard work – has always loved few things more than sitting on a clean floor eating pizza.

Chris Field was right about them dropping the charges against me. He heard a rumour that Richard Bourne may have had something to do with that.

I feel such pity for that man.

Eleanor wrote a letter to Nina right after the funeral.

She said that she deeply regretted everything that had happened to Nina and to Phoebe and Zoë, but that she felt nothing but contempt for me.

Eleanor blames me for Holly's death, just as she always blamed me for all the troubles in her daughter's life.

I ought to have understood – she said in the letter to Nina – how much Holly loved me. I ought to have been grateful to have been loved by someone so special. So unique.

I ought, according to Eleanor Bourne, to have loved Holly back.
Maybe I did love her once, for a little while.
But that was a very long time ago.